The Morning Gift

Also by Diana Norman
Fitzempress' Law

The Morning Gift

Diana Norman

St. Martin's Press
New York

Library of Congress Cataloging in Publication Data

Norman, Diana.
    The morning gift.

    1. Great Britain—History—Norman period,
1066–1154—Fiction.   I. Title.
PR6064.O73M6   1987   823'.914   86–24801
ISBN 0-312-00159-2

First published in Great Britain by Hodder and Stoughton Limited.

First U.S. Edition

10 9 8 7 6 5 4 3 2 1

*To Samantha Norman
with all my love*

Prologue

The jolly young nobles lining the sides of the *White Ship* as she prepared to leave Barfleur Harbour for England on the night of Thursday, November 25, 1120 AD, were drunk. They jeered at the priests who had come to the dockside to bless their voyage.

The *White Ship* was beautiful, the finest in the fleet of Henry the First of England, Duke of Normandy, who had given her to his heir, William the Atheling. In his conviviality the Atheling had pressed wine on the crew and even on the pilot who was to guide his ship through the rocks and sand-banks which made this stretch of Normandy coast dangerous.

The tall young Count Stephen of Blois, who had been about to board the *White Ship*, looked around at the general drunkenness and changed his mind. He would return to England on another vessel.

The priests watched the elegant sterncastle slide erratically out of harbour into the night.

The rocks on which the *White Ship* tore out her side lay not far out to sea and the screams of the drowning could be heard by those on land. But nothing could be done; the water was cold and the currents strong. Two hundred men and women, among them the heir to the throne of England and Normandy, lost their lives.

When they brought the news to King Henry in England he fainted. Like the great king he was, however, he forced himself to recover and, like the great despot he also was, began to ensure that it was his seed which inherited his realm after him. The trouble was that his only legitimate surviving heir was female, the Empress Matilda. And England had never yet been ruled by a woman.

So it goes. One man changes his mind, a pilot can neither refuse liquor nor hold it, and because of them both a war begins twenty years later.

The waters which closed over the head of William the Atheling that night in 1120 AD were to form a maelstrom which would suck into itself the lives of thousands – among them that of a girl who had only just been born . . .

1

1134–1135

The first night of the marriage between Sigward, Lord of Hatfelde, and Matilda de Risle of Normandy was more complex and less brutal than fourteen-year-old Matilda – whose ideas of human copulation were based on stockbreeding – had feared.

But her relief that things had gone comparatively well were as nothing to that of her lord's.

As he rose from their bed the next morning his bellows of joy silenced cockcrow, set the dogs barking, scattered the pigeons from the loft and roused the drink-sodden wedding guests in their niches round the hall.

Matilda lay where she was, listening to Sigward thump down the stairs and hearing the castle come to life, waiting for her ladies to come and dress her.

As she'd known she would be, Berte, her nurse, was first in, her mouth pursed in triumph as if her lamb had vanquished the Devil single-handed. Their eyes met. "That'll silence *her*," said Berte. Silence seemed to be the last thing Matilda had achieved – the bell on the chapel roof was now adding to the hullaballoo – but Berte was referring to Matilda's predecessor in the bed, a previous wife whom Sigward had repudiated after six years of marriage. She had not produced a child in that time and so had been tidied away into a convent but had managed to appeal to the bishops' consistory court to have her marriage reinstated, although she was also spreading the rumour that Sigward was impotent.

"Contradictory, *if* you like," Berte was saying, tidying away the mandrake root, corn dollies and other symbols of

9

fertility she had concealed around the bed, afraid the priest would see them. "And lies anyway, so it do seem." She was begging for revelations but Matilda gave her none.

"Nine months from now . . ." Berte crooned and opened the chest at the foot of the bed to take out Matilda's robes and give them a shake. "Anyway, Sigward's purchased the bishops' goodwill to prove consanguinity between them and that'll finish *her* for good."

Actually it was difficult for a man and woman of the nobility *not* to be related within the seven degrees which the Church now said prohibited marriage. Matilda, who knew her pedigree as well as she knew the hunting coverts around her Normandy homes, was aware that she and Sigward shared a great-great-grandmother. But the laws were generally disregarded when it was desirable that two great families should be allied and invoked only when a husband wanted to rid himself of an unsatisfactory wife.

Sigward was down in the bailey now, whooping awake the guests who had been quartered in the outbuildings. Berte opened the shutters to watch him, smiling as at the antics of a small boy and letting in the smell of forest, bluebells, woodsmoke, horse manure and a Hertfordshire breeze that fluttered the garlands round the bed.

"Poor fat Saxon," she said, leaning out and presenting her own ample backside to Matilda's view. "Only needed a Norman spark to light his tinder."

"He's not Saxon," said Matilda, stung. The fatness could not be disputed.

"Spindle-side, spindle-side," chanted Berte. "His lady mother was Saxon and lady mother ruled this roost, so they tell me. It was her, God rest her soul, chose *her*, blast her. Good thing the Lord called her when He did, God rest her soul."

"You show him respect or you'll go back to Normandy." Berte presumed too much on a relationship begun when she, Matilda, was one minute old.

"Don't I respect him?" asked Berte. She turned back from the window and began brushing Matilda's pelisse. "Didn't I show that pis-aller cook how to honey the duck and didn't

10

his lordship chomp it up? Don't the king think well of him? Isn't he powerful? I like fat men: they're cosy in bed."

Matilda hissed with irritation: Berte was vulgar; worse still, she was right. Sigward's girth had been embarrassing compared to the lean, Norman lords at her wedding. But in the darkness those broad expanses of flesh had been comforting, symbolising the richness of Sigward's English acres. And Matilda, who loved richness in all things, had burrowed into them, joining the domain of bodies and lands and practising the submissiveness which Berte had advised. Berte had said: "Now you be humble, like a little child. None of your pride with him, my lady. *She* was bossy, so they do say, like the lady mother, and *she* was put away. We don't want to be put away, do we? So be soft. Shy, but willing."

Matilda had pretended to ignore her but her careful mind had considered the advice and found it good. Had she been put into a convent she would have had to please God; being married she must please her husband and God in that order. Heiress to large estates she might be, but wealthier women than she had been repudiated and left impoverished, their lords not having found it necessary to repudiate also the lands they'd brought with them. Only a generation before, Philip, then King of France, had repudiated his queen, Fat Bertha, after twenty years of marriage. The poor lady had died of shame and been buried in a commoner's grave.

So Matilda had made a game of the night, play-acting the role society urged on wives, becoming compliant, tender, admiring, submissive, while the true Matilda watched and learned about men, the lords, in order to manipulate this one to her advantage. The effect had been an overwhelming response of joy from Sigward.

Now there was clatter on the stairs and other members of her personal household came in with most of the lady guests, some peeking quick glances, others frankly staring to see how the night had changed her. Adeliza regarded her with horrified curiosity as if she had been to the grave and come back, reeking, to tell the tale. Adeliza of Louvain was the twelve-year-old who was to be brought up in Matilda's care until she should be married herself. They had been playmates and now, thought Matilda, they belonged to different generations.

Father Alors – nobody could remember his real name – her confessor and secretary stood at the foot of the bed with a crucifix upraised against contamination. His face was gloomy and getting gloomier with every shout of Sigward's from the courtyard. "Search your conscience, my child, and tell me that you are yet in grace."

As he had circled the two of them in bed last night, censing them with holy water, he had given improving selections from the Church's current marital teaching: "If the spouses take pleasure in their marriage bed they sin," and, "If a man love his wife too passionately he be guilty of adultery." Sigward's priest had been much jollier and winked at them.

"Father Alors always says Judgment Day is tomorrow," Matilda had muttered to Sigward, who'd muttered back: "As long as it's not tonight."

Matilda searched her conscience, reducing the matter to essentials. What Father Alors was asking was had she enjoyed the night and she would be blameworthy if the answer was "yes".

What did they want of her? She had not chosen to be married. She had been just as prepared to take the veil at Fontevrault. But then her two older brothers had died, one from measles and one from a hunting accident, and at once Matilda was heir, tenant-in-chief to King Henry, the Duke of Normandy, and a valuable asset to him since her marriage was in his gift.

He had given her, for a price, to Sigward. Matilda's advisers had felt she could have done better, although Sigward was of good birth, but Henry had given neither them nor Matilda the choice. It had been strategically important that Matilda's lands should not fall into the hands of the greater Norman barons in case they became too powerful and that Sigward, who commanded English lands and loyalty, should be bound even closer to his king.

So Matilda was married whether she wanted to be or not and now the Church in the shape of Father Alors was disappointed in her. It was better to marry than to burn, but

12

only just. Had she enjoyed the night? Would the Virgin Mary, who had replaced Matilda's long-dead mother in Matilda's affection, still think her worthy?

Well, it had been a peculiar night, full of strange textures and experiences and not nearly as bad as she'd imagined, but if it never happened again she wouldn't mind. Perhaps that would do.

She said, "I am as much in grace as I can be, being married."

Father Alors sighed. "It is all we can hope for. God keep you in that state, my child." He wandered off, nearly inert with the world's coming death.

"C'est à en Paques Avril, que chantent oisillons gentils . . ." Jodi, her minstrel, had perched himself and his lute on a cupboard shelf and to the accompaniment of his singing Matilda was dragged out of bed, her head dunked in a bowl of water and the business of dressing her begun. Garment after garment was dragged down over her upraised arms until her thin body was layered like an onion. In itself the beautiful pelisse was three layers, the inner cloth and the outer silk sandwiching between them the ermine which was proof, or nearly, against the spring breeze outside the castle and the eternal draughts inside.

"Do we all wear the same tunic again today, Matilda?" asked Adeliza. In the wedding procession yesterday bridesmaids and bride had been covered in the same Virgin blue to confuse the evil spirits who were abroad to bedevil a marrying.

"We do not," said Matilda. She loathed looking the same as anyone.

"Matilda spent the night wrestling with demons," drawled Ghislaine.

"But did she win?" asked Flore.

Matilda aimed a barefoot kick at them both and within seconds the chamber was a mêlée of scuffling, giggling girls. Berte waded into it and grabbed Matilda's hair which had become entangled in somebody else's circlet. "This," she said, "goes up." It was a reminder of her dignified marital status.

13

The girdle they fastened around Matilda's hips was set with carbuncles of topaz, agate, sardonyx and rubies which had been brought back from the Holy Land by Matilda's father. Some protected against fever, some lighted up darkness. Matilda had compared it to those of the lady guests and had satisfied herself it was richer even than Matilda of Boulogne's whose husband, Count Stephen of Blois, was representing the absent King Henry.

They were putting the finishing touches, dabbing her nose with saffron powder and her ears with rosewater when the two stewards made their entrance, tapping their rods of office. Matilda's, Rollo, who had come over temporarily and would go back to supervise the Norman estates, was beaming. Alfwin, Sigward's man, was impassive as ever. "My lady," said Rollo, "your lord begs you to go down with your ladies and accompany him to church . . ."

Waleran of Meulan loomed up behind him: "You've been a clever girl, cousin, and are to be rewarded for it, apparently."

"My lady," continued Rollo, "to church and there receive your lord's morning gift."

The breeze flattened the squirrel cloaks and discs of hawthorn blossom stuck to flying veils. Tiny tides of yesterday's thrown wheat ran over the ground to pile up under lavender bushes. Now, as yesterday, Matilda and Sigward stood in the church porch and faced their guests. Yesterday each had said: "I receive you as mine," Sigward's cloak had covered the two of them and Matilda had knelt to her husband and given up her legal existence. Henceforward her property, land, even her dower and marriage portion, were under Sigward's control for as long as he lived.

Today he was handing something back. "Know all assembled here that, for the love I bear her, I grant to my wife, Matilda of Risle, my manor of Dungesey in the County of Cambridgeshire with all its appurtenances, rights of custom . . ." The enumeration of rights rolled out in thick deep notes, easily reaching the back of the crowd and was assisted by the breeze down the hill, over the elm tops, to the tiny wagons on the track and even to the villeins and cattle in the valley fields so that they turned their heads towards the cawing of this master rook.

The gift was as vulgar and generous as the man who performed it, and as Saxon. No full Norman could or would have instituted the tradition of the morning gift which was a reward for giving sexual pleasure, a sign that a husband found his wife congenial. The Church's dislike of sexual satisfaction even in marriage had still not caught on among the lax and more matriarchal Saxons.

But the Norman Waleran of Meulan, who was Matilda's cousin, had shown waspishness when he'd called her a clever girl as if she had gained advantage by unscrupulous means. Even Matilda herself, a true Norman, felt a moment of nausea at the thought that she had betrayed her breeding, that the tall, lean, confident men facing her, these arbiters of what was proper and what was not, should think less of her. She was embarrassed by the sweating emotion of the fat man she belonged to who was implicitly betraying her. "I'm not like that," she wanted to shout. And at the same time, she was wondering what sort of manor it was.

It was nearly a year before she saw it because first it was necessary for Sigward to be introduced to his (once Matilda's) lands in Normandy. They travelled from castle to manor to castle in a party sixty-odd strong, including some of Sigward's dependent relatives, Matilda's ladies and household, a chamberlain, a priest, grooms, servants, cooks, household knights and men-at-arms, staying at each estate for as long as its provisions held out or until the cesspit overflowed.

They hunted, paid visits and were visited, attended the local courts, gave judgments in their own, feasted, played, danced.

It was as administrative partners rather than as playfellows that the marriage prospered. Matilda found a revelling Sigward embarrassing; he drank too much and cried into his cups, he ate too much and belched like a Turk. He was too fat to dance without appearing ridiculous and out hunting he became puffed long before the quarry was killed. She found him most admirable when he was wielding power as a lord. Never was she so fond of him as when he was up on the dais surveying villeins, decreeing fines, settling disputes and receiving homage as her father once had. If he'd been a noticing man Sigward might have become aware that it was on the nights after official appearances that Matilda was most responsive to love-making.

So it was to quell her unworthy embarrassment and to heighten her admiration that she encouraged and took part in his governing.

It began at Guercy in the Suisse-Normande. At the Thursday court Matilda sat with Sigward on the dais and whispered into his ear as each villein came forward.

"Alcuin has encroached unlawfully on to West Field, which is yours."

"Alcuin will be fined 6d for unlawful encroachment on the demesne," said Sigward, promptly.

"Pierre has been pasturing his bull on the common and Rollo says he gave him no permission to do it."

Pierre was fined 6d.

"The hamlet of St. Dreux has not put its sheep on your fallow to manure it this year." St. Dreux, who wanted its own land manured, was fined 3s.

By the end of the day the returns from Guercy were up on what they had been when Matilda's father was alive and Sigward was pleased with his wife. The villeins complained that they would starve, but villeins never said anything else.

After that Sigward took to consulting Matilda on most matters so that, as well as overseeing the preparations for the guests, the almsgiving, the menus and the general household conduct, she spent time with bailiffs counting tallies. She found herself to be a capable manager and enjoyed herself.

Their only disagreement was at Mainscourt near Rouen where Simnel, a villein, was presented at court for poaching a stag in the lord's deerpark.

"Hang him," said Matilda.

Sigward looked down on the man who was slouched

almost unconscious with terror between two men-at-arms, and said nothing.

"My lord," said Matilda, "there is no need to send him to the seigneur's court. Here we have the right of infangthief. Hang him."

"Judgment on Simnel will be postponed until tomorrow," said Sigward.

Over the dinner table that afternoon Matilda pursued the matter. "He should hang."

"The bailiff says he is adept at hunting truffles with pigs," said Sigward. "I like truffles. It will be sufficient to cut off one of his hands – his left if he is right-handed; we must keep him useful."

"It is a kindness to villeins in the long run to show them what is permissible and what is not," said Matilda, quoting a tenet of her father's. "If Simnel gets away with it they will all think they can poach deer and then we shall have to hang more than one."

"Losing a hand isn't getting away with it."

The whole table joined in the argument. Sigward's face went purple and he stood up, slamming his fist into Matilda's plate of stew so that her second-best silk, six-thread gown was bespattered with gravy. "It is not for women to take life but to give it," his voice went down the table, stunning it into silence.

Matilda stood up to swing her fist at him. "You . . ." She was going to yell "damned Saxon", but Berte's great forearm was jammed across her mouth and the other had slipped inside Matilda's elbows to drag her backwards. She heard Berte say: "Get her keys," as they fought their way up the steps to the solar and while Adeliza pinioned her feet Ghislaine unclipped Mainscourt's keys from her belt. Seconds later she was in the solar, shouting all the dirty words she knew and clawing at the wrong side of a locked door.

When Sigward came up later it was to find she had ripped one of the bedcovers in half and was asleep on top of it.

Later that night Sigward had a nightmare. Matilda was woken to find his flesh moving involuntarily on his body like a scared horse's and the bed damp with his sweat. She

17

struggled through the bedcurtains and shouted at the servant who slept across the door to fetch water, a cloth and a lighted candle.

"Wake up, my lord."

It was some time before he recognised her and the trembling stopped. "Send him away."

Matilda waved the servant back to his palliasse. "Tell me."

He told her in whispers. "I was in the impotency court, and the women had come to try and sexually arouse me, but they were hideous and I remained flaccid, so then the bishop – but he had horns – condemned me as *'non vir homo'*."

Matilda howled with laughter. "Is there such a court?"

"There is," said Sigward, "oh there is. You don't know. It is a bishop's court and the ladies who come to prove your potency are respectable matrons approved by the bishop."

Matilda laughed so loud that the servant stirred and Sigward hushed her, although he was beginning to smile himself. "God save us," stuttered Matilda, "canonically approved matrons: what can they be like?"

"These were awful."

He had never discussed his first wife and her allegations with Matilda and she suspected he thought she didn't know about them. She poked her finger into his chest. "Well, you have no reason to fear that."

"I don't, do I?" But before he went to sleep he said: "We will prove it to the world when you conceive."

It was the second time that he had referred to the fact that nine months had gone by and her periods were still coming regularly; this time she was not angry and so was not protected from an involuntary sounding in her head. "Barren." She lay awake as linked words advanced on her: "Barren: Repudiation: Landlessness: Shame: Commoner's grave." She heard the watchman walk his rounds, badgers snuffling and grunting round the midden, the pigeons shifting in the loft, a foal neighing in the pasture. Before dawn she got up, took the candle and stubbed her toe on the guard. "Get out of the way."

The man yawned: "Shall I come too, mistress?"

"No."

The stones were painfully cold to her bare feet, but Normans were never diverted from a course by extremes of temperature. As she emerged into the chapel by the hole in its floor the candle transformed its moonlit calm into something risky, writhing a shadow on the cross, winking the eyes of the demons who were dragging sinners to Hell on the wall.

Matilda knelt on a hassock to contemplate the stone Virgin Mary on the altar's right. It was black and extremely old, almost featureless with a round ball of a head balanced on top of a bigger one with protuberances indicating breasts, belly and arms. Matilda was used to it and stared through it to the beautiful saint.

"If you please, blessed Mother, make me pregnant."

In her heart of hearts Matilda loved but was puzzled by St. Mary. Matilda was orderly, a conformist who believed in the rewards and punishments of heavenly and earthly justice. The Virgin Mary was quirky and drove the Devil to exasperation by her refusal to stick to the rules.

Matilda always pictured her with her diadem slightly awry, hair streaming out behind her, as she rushed through the mansions of Paradise to pester the Son with another request on behalf of her supplicants. Such supplicants – thieves, commoners, adulterers, debtors, whose only virtue was their worship of Mary. In what Matilda regarded as misguided enthusiasm for her admirers Mary had been known to support the feet of a thief so that he did not hang; once, when a nun had deserted her convent and run off with a clerk and many years later crawled back to her abbey, it was to find that her sisters hadn't noticed her absence because the Virgin had covered up for her by taking her form all that time.

"Why do God and Jesus always obey her?" Matilda had asked Father Alors. "These are sinners and should be punished."

Father Alors had sighed: "They do not obey her. They are greater than she and obey nobody. But God obeys His commandment: 'Honour thy Father and Mother.' She is Jesus' mother and can only request: He, as her son, must comply with the commandment to honour His mother."

She was so . . . earthy. She would squirt her milk on the sores of a sick man to cure him. But at least she had milk. She was fertile and gave fertility. Matilda's numb fingers laced. "Why don't you help *me*?"

But she knew. If Mary was everything feminine and life-giving, Matilda's soul was a man's. She had always suspected it; as a child she had longed to be a boy and shown more administrative capability than her brothers. The woman-liness which had won Sigward on their wedding night was a pose. She was not pregnant because she was the wrong spirit in the wrong body. If she mended her ways and became more womanly she would find favour and conceive a baby. But womanliness meant irrationality and Matilda didn't know how.

The stone and living women stared at each other with incomprehension. Matilda dragged off a ring from one of her fingers and dropped it into the dip formed by the swell of the figure's stomach, but the quiet of the chapel increased. Matilda began to shake. She made her last offer. "If I give you the poacher . . ." and the saint replied through the scream of a vixen in the fields.

Matilda took up the candle and strode off to her room on feet she could no longer feel. "Not a deer left, of course," she muttered crossly as she climbed into bed and jammed her feet against Sigward's warm buttocks.

"What? What?"

"I have spoken to the Blessed Virgin: the poacher can live for me."

"Just a hand?"

"Just an ear if you like," said Matilda, "but just this once."

By the time they arrived back in England Matilda was pregnant and as a reward Sigward took her to receive seisin of Dungesey.

The land went flat as if collapsed by the Devil sucking out its innards. The party going down the last hill went on to a tabletop of vast horizons, aware of the unseen sea to the east, afraid their weight might tip the table and make it rush at them. They dwindled from humans to beetles to ladybirds to

20

ants, specks in the eye of God under a skyscape which altered natural laws. Skimming clouds became slow-moving in contrast with the distance they had to travel. A skein of birds formed a circle and wheeled it so that the earth spun.

Anything of any height at all, an elm, the tower of a church, achieved significance against a skyline all its own.

Foreshortened, crushed into squatness, they transferred to boats on water that changed shape. First it was orderly but unnatural, running straight between towpaths, the King's Delph, a Roman road of water which led the eye to its distant, grey-green disappearing point.

"Is this Fens?" asked Matilda. Barges carrying building stone and wheat travelled it with them, pleasing her sense of efficiency.

"Part of it."

They had left their horses on the uplands; to Matilda it had seemed like dismemberment. Sigward said: "We have special horses for the Fens. On the whole one does not ride there."

"What does one do, then? How does one hunt?"

"Boat," shrugged Sigward, "on foot. You'll see."

Matilda tried to imagine chasing a stag by boat and failed.

"You won't be hunting anyway, my lady," chipped in Berte.

"I shall if I feel like it." But she didn't feel like it; she felt sick. They travelled for miles hearing nothing but the hail of bargees and the cloop of moorhens until gradually came another sound like demons screaming in different keys, which became thunderous. "God save us," shouted Father Alors. "What's that?"

They saw what it was as they emerged from the Delph on to the biggest lake in England, Whittlesey Mere, a vast, grey plane of water, eighteen thousand acres of it, from their view as shoreless as the sea. The noise was the call of birds which covered it. But even that clamour was as nothing to the volcano of sound which erupted at their arrival.

The surface lifted upwards in sheets of grey and white bodies, duck, gull, swan, pelican, geese, until the boats were imprisoned in layered walls and ceilings, splashing droppings and calling in alarm. The humans covered their heads, as much to protect themselves from the noise as from the droppings.

It was a phenomenon and at first they marvelled at it, but the oars dipped and lifted through minutes into monotonous hours and the passengers coped with boredom – they were used to boredom – by falling asleep. Matilda woke with her head on Sigward's pillowy shoulder, her clothes dampened by moisture and her second-best boots up to their insteps in bilge. Water still dominated the eye, but it had changed its character again, becoming shallower, diffuse and sinuous. Now for the first time she saw carr, alder and buckthorn which covered such land as there was in a low, brown mass, edging their stream so that they moved down its tunnel, soundless except for the slip of water on the oars and the sob of hidden curlew. They talked to each other, voices echoing from boat to boat, to hide their intimidation.

"Is *this* Fens?"

"Part of it. The home of the true English."

"How did they find it?" Or their way in it once they'd found it. Even Sigward was using a local man to guide them. Until this moment she had never understood how Hereward and his fenmen had stood out so long against William the Conqueror; she saw now an army could dive into this place and disappear like water-rats, bobbing up to shoot from hidden positions. Her sympathy was with the Conqueror and his frustration at a fluid enemy.

The tunnels spewed them out into washes like deltas where sedge emerged above brown water in spongy islands and the boats hissed on the roots of dead rushes, and again the sky took over and disturbed the Normans by its untrammelled freedom.

Father Alors muttered St. Guthlac's trials in this home of demons: "Save us from them, O Lord, with their great heads, long necks, lean, pale faces, stinking mouths and teeth like horses . . ."

Whatever human activity the Fens permitted was finished for the winter except for here and there rows of bobbing backs along a line where creatures cleared a drainage ditch.

The people in the boats were seen but not greeted, the bare elder boughs clacked secret signals, the water hid its fish. The whole landscape excluded them.

Sigward said: "The Fens take the water of thirteen counties. It is England's drain."

From Jodi's boat came a scatological echo. "England's pisspot."

A bank formed a dark bar against a sky that was losing light, and then gave way to a horizon of indeterminate greys against which a heron was walking. The heron was twice as tall as a man, and waded the water on scalene legs. Adeliza screamed. The heron had a man's head.

"No, no," Sigward was saying, "it is a man but on stilts. They use stilts here and walk on paths under the water which they follow because on those they do not sink, nobody knows why. They call them roddons."

Matilda leaned over the boat side and was sick. Heron men stalking hidden paths completed the horror of this place. Since the journey started her island, which had been picturesque and conical in her mind, like Mont St. Michel, had diminished into what she knew must be the reality, a barely discernible mound rising out of this primaeval soup.

And so it was. By the time their boats bumped against the wall of Dungesey's hythe they were lit by flares but it wasn't dark enough to hide Dungesey's flatness and ugliness.

Stupefied by fatigue and disappointment she was led to an open place surrounded by people at whom she did not look but who gave out an impression of lacking respect. From the corner of her eye she saw men whittling pieces of wood, others plaiting. Nearly all the women spun from handheld distaffs. One woman had a living, struggling duck under her arm and was plucking it. Matilda did not object to the cruelty but the creature's squawking got on her nerves.

Adeliza whimpered, Ghislaine sniffed, Sir Percy of Alleyn kept his hand to his sword hilt, as befitted Matilda's champion, Father Alors prayed and Jodi remembered St. Guthlac. "Rough ears, wrinkled foreheads, stinking mouths, teeth like horses – those weren't demons: those were the natives."

She had expected a noble-looking people. These English

23

of the Fens had put up the only serious resistance to the Normans. She had expected a lot of things. She spoke over her shoulder: "My compliments to Steward Peter and that woman is to stop plucking that duck." A proper steward would not have needed telling. Ghislaine spoke to the shadowy figure of the island's steward who spoke to the woman, though not with the sharpness he should have. The duck was released and cantered off with its head outstretched and its nether parts obscenely bare. The woman took a distaff from her belt and began spinning instead.

"Sparky little flower," shouted Badda to Thurchel on the other side of the circle, and he shouted back: "She'll verrylike give us a tidy amount of no good." The words went over Matilda's head in incomprehensible loops of sound, long-drawn-out vowels and guttural consonants which slid up and down the scale always ending higher than it began.

"Where *is* Sigward?"

He came down the yew avenue from the darkness, having put on his mail. He stepped forward into the circle to face her and raised his voice: "Can you all see, you English?" The magic of ritual began to work; the women's movements slowed down and the men's whittling quietened, but they would not willingly show interest. They grunted.

With elaborate pantomime Sigward took off his right gauntlet and held it up. "See the War Glove. I give it to this lady." Matilda felt the harsh weight slip on to her hand.

"The Vestita Manus," boomed Sigward. "Lady Matilda, do you swear to defend this land against all comers?"

Matilda's blood responded to ceremonial. "I do."

He took a small, bronze dagger from his belt and from one of the yew trees cut off a twig and brought it to Matilda who took it in her gauntleted hand. "The wood of Dungesey," said Sigward. He knelt and drove the knife into the grass, jagging it round four corners to cut a turf. "The soil of Dungesey."

Peter the steward came forward with an earthenware cup. Sigward took it and Matilda felt liquid trickle over her wrist and down into the gauntlet. "The water of Dungesey. Meadow, pasture, field, fen, marsh, turbary and sedge. All are yours." He stepped back, snapped the cup in two, took the blade of the bronze knife in his left mailed hand and the hasp in his right and twisted it so that the blade broke. The two halves of cup and knife, now like no two others in the world, were put into Matilda's hands.

"Lady, this is your manor and these your people. English of Dungesey, this is your lady."

He made passes with his arms and walked away through the encircling peasants, leaving Matilda in the middle of them with her symbolic wreckage. The English louts stared at her and then turned away to the vat of ale which had been provided to drink the lady's health.

There were half-hearted congratulations from her household. Sigward rejoined them: "And what do you think of your morning gift?"

"The flies are nice," said Jodi. Matilda said nothing. She had given Sigward estates which a king could be proud of, she was carrying his baby; in return he had given her this.

Sigward wheezed. "There are reasons. Reasons. Enter your hall, Lady of Dungesey, and you'll see some of them." They walked under shadowed archways up steps into an old-fashioned hall. Matilda was prepared to despise it, but that night her eye and everyone else's went to the long table in its centre and stayed there.

Rounded, gold-tan breasts shiny with basting, ribs of browned beef with the red juices welling out of them, bowls of stew the size of wheels with a herbal steam rising from dark gravy in which floated dumplings like snowballs, dishes of transparent jelly showing eels nestling inside, long silver fish sprinkled with parsley and roasted almonds, huge plaits of bread cut to show a milk-white interior – the table was a treasure chest of edible jewels.

Normans knew a thing or two about food and here, although there were none of the peacock-tailed, swan-headed trimmings, was the best. Percy of Alleyn, usually a silent man, enumerated the poultry in ecstatic chant: "Capon, greylag, wigeon, teal, oriole, by God . . ."

There was an unseemly dash to the benches. Sigward led Matilda to the top and gave the signal for grace which Father Alors said at speed. Conversation lapsed. Sigward speared a dumpling and popped it into Matilda's mouth. "This is a fen floater," he said, "elsewhere they're sinkers." The ugly but heavenly smelling shape on one of the dishes was lamprey, the favoured half-eel, half-fish. "Nowhere better than in the Fens," said Sigward. "You see . . ." but he decided to make a speech of it instead and thumped the table for attention.

"This Christmas," he said to chewing faces, "we shall attend the king's court and for the fourth, or even fifth time, I shall swear to uphold the cause of his daughter when he dies."

There was teeth-sucking round the tables. As a potential ruler Matilda, Henry's daughter, was three times disadvantaged. First, hardly anyone knew her; she had been sent away at the age of eight to marry a man of thirty-eight, the Holy Roman Emperor, and had spent the time lording it over Germans which had made her haughty and disagreeable. After the *White Ship* went down Henry had summoned her back and married her off again, this time to a fifteen-year-old – she was twenty-six – Geoffrey, Count of Anjou, who was her second disadvantage since Angevins were the Normans' traditional enemies and spent their time slaying priests and eating raw meat. It had not been an easy marriage but it had at least produced a son, named Henry after his grandfather.

Thirdly, she was a woman.

"A pig in a poke we'll be getting," said Father Alors.

"A sow in a poke," said Jodi.

Sigward waved a fat finger at them. "She has fourteen kings in her ancestry on her mother's side, from Egbert King of the West Saxons to the Confessor himself, besides being a granddaughter of the Conqueror. And I have sworn to uphold her." There was silence. "But it's true that not everyone is satisfied with the succession and, indeed, we may be in for a time of Unrest." He made it sound like an attack of indigestion. "And what do we desire for our dear ones in a time of Unrest?"

"Not Dungesey," thought Matilda.

"We need a Safe Haven. A constant Food Supply and out there" – Sigward swung an expansive arm around the walls – "is the richest source of wildfowl, fish and, when it's

26

not flooded, pasture in the world. The Abbot of Ely demands a rent of three thousand eels from Wisbech and gets it. The Abbot of Ramsey feeds his pigs on wheat."

He turned to Matilda and, as when they were alone, stopped being pompous. "I just wanted, my dear, for you to have a bolthole, somewhere to hide should trouble come, where you and our children will always be safe and hidden and have plenty to eat. I know it seems an odd little gift to you and it will take time to get used to its people – these are the true English and nobody is odder than they – but I shall feel happier that you have it."

She tried to think of some favourable comment. "Well, it is certain nobody would ever find me here."

His enormous face creased into delight. "Tomorrow we shall explore your island."

But that night Matilda woke up in pain. Keeping her trunk and legs rigid she dug Sigward with her elbow. "Fetch a light." When he came back she twitched off the covers. "Am I bleeding?"

"Yes."

"Fetch Berte."

As once before she lay in bed and heard him rushing down the stairs, shouting. She dare not move. She had always been healthy but now her body was out of control. "Sweet Mary, save me." She could hardly get the words out for panting. "Dear God, Son of God, save me. Mother of God, save the child and me."

Half the household came in but Matilda saw only her nurse. "Well?"

"It's certainly a show," said Berte, "but nothing else seems to be happening. One thing for sure, you don't move from this place till that baby's stuck firmer in its womb than it is now."

"The Christmas court?" asked Sigward.

Berte shook her head. "The journey would bounce the baby out."

Across the Channel in a hunting lodge at Lyon-le-Fôret somebody else had been feasting off lampreys, against

27

doctors' advice. "Always they made him sick and yet he loved them," said a chronicler later. For once the doctors were right and Henry of England had taken his last mouthful of anything.

An archbishop, a bishop, three earls and two counts leaned over his bedside as he died to try and hear what he was saying. What he said or whether he said anything at all was about to cause the most vicious war in Christendom. Quite likely he was trying to wrench in breath, but even that will could not command the impossible.

2

1135–1136
Matilda, the Empress, was as unprepared for her father's death as anyone. When the news broke she proved how politically unreliable she was by being (a) far down in Normandy and (b) pregnant again.

Stephen of Blois was ready though. In the only completely perfected manoeuvre of his life he was across the Channel, hailed as king by the Londoners, had taken the royal treasury at Winchester and been crowned by the Archbishop of Canterbury. All this before Henry's body had even reached England for burial.

After they'd got to know him people were to wonder how he'd been so efficient. Then they realised he had acted on the advice of his two supreme allies, his brother and his wife. Stephen's wife Matilda – it was confusing that there were so many important Matildas around then – was not only the best general in his army but Countess of Boulogne which gave Stephen access to the most useful Channel ports. His brother was Henry, Bishop of Winchester, who was responsible for the ease with which the treasury fell into Stephen's hands, and the cleverest plotter of the age.

Matilda of Boulogne had thrown, as it were, and Henry of Blois had caught.

And what of the oaths everybody – including the Archbishop of Canterbury – had taken to uphold the succession of Matilda Empress?

Stephen's supporters said they'd been forced on them and didn't count. Besides, they said, at his last moment Henry the First had changed his mind and nominated Stephen his heir. Here their pièce de résistance – literally their crowning

29

argument – was Hugh Bigod, Henry's seneschal, who swore on oath before the archbishop that Henry on his deathbed had disinherited the Empress and designated Stephen. (As the Bishop of Angers, one of the Empress' supporters, was to say later: "How did he know? He wasn't there.")

But it was good enough for the archbishop who allowed himself to believe Bigod and anointed and crowned Stephen at Westminster Abbey on Sunday, December 22, 1135, though he dropped dead before the end of the year, which may have been a judgment on him.

Henry was still not buried. His body was at Rouen where parts of it were interred, the rest being cut up and salted for the voyage. The man who cut him up worked with his head wrapped in napkins to avoid the smell. He'd demanded a large sum for the job but, the chronicler said, "he had poor reason for rejoicing at his bargain since he met his death therefore. He was the last of many slain by Henry."

There were three disgusting weeks before there was a favourable wind for England . . . "liquid matter oozed through the hides to be caught in vessels placed beneath the bier and carried away by servants fainting with disgust." He was finally buried in Reading Abbey on January 4, 1136.

By then his nephew, Stephen, was King of England whether Henry had wanted it or not, whoever liked it or didn't like it, because the mystical ceremony of anointment *made* him king, wrongfully perhaps but irrevocably.

Many didn't like it. The first to declare rebellion was Baldwin de Redvers who attacked and occupied the new king's castle at Exeter.

The latrines were filled in and re-sited every week. Every week the dung carts came for the manure from the stables and horse lines. Nevertheless after three months of continuous heat the siege around Exeter Castle had become so smelly that the stink of glue being brewed by the crossbowmen to laminate new bows was almost acceptable.

Now there was a new smell, a tiny whiff, that came and went on the dawn not unpleasantly but faintly, a timid maiden of an aroma lifting up from the castle on a thermal from the River Exe far below. It reached the nose of the man with a bad back lying under an oak tree in the arbalists' section.

Willem of Ghent was still half-asleep when the smell entered his dream, coming and going so subliminally fast that he was unable to grasp it, although he knew it was important. He sat up to sniff it again, cursed and lay back, forgetting everything in the pain that wrenched the left side of his lower back. This would have to be his last war.

"Bowman's back" scourged the archer's trade and none so much as the crossbowmen who lifted their own weight from a stoop every time they made ready to shoot. The priests said it was a curse on them for being crossbowmen in the first place.

Willem rolled sideways off his pile of bracken to ease on to all fours, the only way of getting off a bed without bending the spine. He looked round like a dog to see if he was being watched, but his company was asleep so, again without flexing his trunk, he walked his hands up the bark of the oak until he was upright. He spat. By the time the others were awake he had performed the morning's requirements and could kneel with them without seeming difficulty to pray to St. Sebastian under the oak tree.

All over the camp mercenary sections, which were not allowed to cathedral services and to which no priest would administer, nevertheless prayed in their scores of languages. They communicated with each other in a form of dog Latin: to God they spoke in their own tongue.

"*Et dimitte nobis debita nostris,*" begged the clergy in the cathedral, "as we forgive those who trespass against us."

"*E pardune a nus les noz detes,*" prayed the Normans.

"*And forgif us our gultes,*" said the English.

"*Ende vergheef on onse sculden,*" said Willem with his men to the image nailed on the tree. Jácopo had liberated it from some monks during the Sicilian campaign because they didn't appreciate it. Really it was a bit of driftwood warped into the shape of agony and someone had exploited its lines and knots with paint to represent features and limbs. The quarrels which pierced the wooden body would each have caused fatal haemorrhaging and yet, as Willem knew, St. Sebastian hadn't died of arrow wounds. He won a lot of money betting on how St. Sebastian died.

From the knoll where the trebuchet had been set up there came the first clatter and thud of the day as the business of lobbing boulders and decomposing animals into the castle bailey began.

Touching the knobbled feet of St. Sebastian for luck, Willem turned to face the castle which dominated his skyline and, at present, his life. The view still shocked him with its gaudiness. The red castle clashed with a forget-me-not sky; below, the Exe cut a winking, sapphire swathe through ochre sandbanks. Although he'd seen red earth before – iron in the soil around Ypres made it not dissimilar – he'd never seen it as it was here, splashed in squares between green and corn-yellow on the crazy Devon hills so steep that cattle grazed lopsided. Not that there were many cattle now.

As the camp woke up so did the flies, a more immediate enemy than the castle garrison, which within the hour would send every living thing into hand-slapping, ear-twitching, tail-swishing, skin-biting movement while only vegetation stood still. All day swallows flicked above the ground scooping them up, but their number remained limitless and unrelenting.

Willem's men slouched into a line carrying their crossbows and ranged behind a straw wall which protected them from the castle's fire. One or two slid their eyes, wondering why he didn't join them, but Willem outstared them. He was the captain.

"At the loopholes."

Each merlon on the castle's crenellated top had a loophole and each of his men had a specific loophole to aim at; if he was on target his bolt went right through, with luck hitting a defender in the eye. If he missed the bolt hit the outside of the merlon and threw off a puff of red dust.

"Load." Thirty backs stooped as thirty right feet went into the stirrup and sixty hands pulled back the hemp string until it could be slipped over the firing catch and thirty prods bent to breaking-point. Thirty crossbows lifted to an angle at the red-toothed pattern against the sky.

"Loose." With a sound which reminded Willem of a man hawking and spitting, chwwt-pt, the bolts released at two hundred miles an hour and twenty-nine simultaneously disappeared. Only one bolt flirted in the still air with a tremor that widened into an irregular arc until it vacillated and, by pure mischance, hit something that moved across a crenel. Willem saw a barrel helm drop – a barrel helm, not the pot helmet of a man–at–arms.

Willem went down the line to a boy who was sucking the fingers of his left hand, moaning with pain and guilt. "Yes?"

The boy rocked back and forth but had the sense not to drop his bow. "I didn't breathe properly, captain. I sucked in but I didn't let it half out again."

"And last night?"

"I was on the tiles last night, captain."

"*Was* he," muttered Jacopo on the boy's right. "He invented it."

"And?"

"And I was thinking of a woman, captain. You said the string always hits our fingers if we're thinking of a woman when we shoot."

"And?"

"And I'm sorry, captain."

"And?"

"And you're going to clout me, captain."

It hurt Willem as much as the boy, who said: "Shall I try again, captain?"

"Stir the glue." In this heat, with his hangover, the smell would be punishment. There was answering fire from the castle so Willem dismissed the men to cover. "But stay armed." He and Jacopo ran for the oak tree and were sweating by the time they reached it.

"That boy'll have to go back to being a page," said Jacopo.

Willem quoted the bowman's standby: "*L'arc qui ne faut.*" Death was the only archer who never missed.

"A good archer can go out whoring and still shoot next

morning," said Jacopo, who knew. "We have our reputation to consider."

Willem grunted. They had a reputation and a contract with the king's marshal to supply thirty crossbowmen for Stephen's army. When old Paolo of Genoa had died they had been left with twenty-nine and Willem had promoted Alain of Arras from page to arbalist rather than take in an outsider.

The threat of demotion would be enough. Nobody in their senses would choose to return to that combination of body-servant, groom, cook and bolt-maker.

"I wonder how old Paolo is getting on," said Jacopo. The old man had been a master-arbalist and loved by them all and they often wondered if he was still in Purgatory or now on his way to Paradise. They'd wanted him buried in the cathedral precincts, but the Exeter canons had refused to pollute their earth with a mercenary; eventually Henry of Blois had intervened and prevailed on his fellow-bishop to allow Paolo burial in the old cemetery against the Roman wall alongside the river.

"Will they be as reluctant to bury me? And where will it be?" Jacopo was suddenly overcome by Latin misery and fell down at the feet of St. Sebastian.

"Does it matter?"

"It didn't," said Jacopo, sitting up. "It's beginning to."

They heard the sound they'd been expecting. A horseman was cantering up the hill; as they'd also expected he was angry and his voice reached them before his horse. "Which of you filth shot that quarrel?"

Willem sat down beside Jacopo and the two arbalists leaned back in the scalloped camouflage of the oak's shade, seeming to close their eyes as if bored – as indeed they were – by well-born knights who couldn't tell the difference between a quarrel and a practice bolt. Their indifference was an aggressive gesture across the chasm of class. The knight hated the mercenaries because they fought for pay and not feudal duty. They hated him back because he was an amateur and when his forty days' customary service were up he could, and probably would, go back to his manor and forget the war.

So Willem and Jacopo watched the prancing horse and rider under their lids and prepared to keep him simmering while behind him crossbows levelled at his cloak.

"What were we doing?" Jacopo was his most Calabrian. "Were we shooting at the enemy? Yes, we were. *Mea culpa.*"

"Not knights," screamed the knight. "Men-at-arms only. You're not to shoot knights at this stage."

Jacopo nodded. "Men-at-arms only. We understand that now. Thank you for pointing it out."

"But you've killed a knight." He was young and they hadn't seen him before; a new arrival. But they knew his type and temper. He could attack at any moment.

Willem opened his eyes. "Your father-in-law, was it?" That was the matter with the lad, with all the knights. They were so interrelated with the enemy they didn't know which side they were on.

"What father-in-law? My father-in-law's not in the castle."

"Then what are you worrying about?"

But now Willem smelled again the trickle of smell from the castle and knew what it was. He stood up. "Piss off and play. We've got business."

As the knight reached for his sword Jacopo coughed politely and shifted his gaze. The knight looked round and saw the crossbows. Self-preservation struggled with the need to save face and won, just. He yelled the knight's eternal complaint against bowmen. "Cursed was the first archer; he was afraid and dared not approach." The mercenaries had heard it before. He spurred his horse and, as he galloped off, swerved it so that its right shoulder hit the tripod over the fire and sent the glue in a hissing, translucent mess into the flames.

"Shall I shoot, captain?" yelled Alain and for a moment Willem was tempted. The knight had taken a better revenge than he knew; to make that glue they'd had to buy an ox at prohibitive price, slaughter it, cut out its heel tendons and soak them in lime and water for days. Hours had then been spent beating the tendons and pulling them into silky shreds to add to boiling fish glue until they had a fixative strong enough to hold together the laminated wood of the prod under drawing stress. He drew in a deep breath. "No." Sooner or later there would be trouble between the barons' men and the mercenaries, but he wouldn't start it.

He told Jacopo: "Keep them on alert in case. I'm going to the cathedral. And tell the pages to get another ox."

On the other side of the city from the castle, the cathedral precincts were royal headquarters. Flustered canons tried to drive away the market stalls set up on their lawns but failed. Stephen was favourable to the townspeople – it was they who had warned him a rebellious garrison had taken over the castle – and was compensating them for their wrecked and burned houses by allowing them to grow rich on trade.

The young knight who'd knocked over the glue was complaining to a crowd of silk-cloaked barons. A figure detached itself from the group and came towards Willem. "You are a wicked Flemish mercenary, Willem," said William of Ypres, "a disgrace to chivalry. Come and have a drink."

Willem jerked his head towards the castle. "They're cooking with wine in there. I've smelled it. Twice now."

A knight of inexperience would have questioned his sanity but Ypres was a good practical mercenary, the commander of all Stephen's mercenaries. "Not just flavouring the gravy?"

Willem shook his head. "They're cooking beans in it."

"And you don't waste wine on beans."

"Only if you've run out of water."

Ypres shouted to his squire: "The marksman." He turned to Willem. "We'll test it out. I thought it was an everlasting spring they had there."

"Not in this drought."

"We'll have that drink while we're waiting."

The mercenary captains had chosen an evacuated stone house just out of castle range as their tavern and put in it one of their own veterans, Rotrou, to run it. Its most salubrious period was now, in the morning, when it had been swept and fresh rushes laid, when the grooves of the whitewood tables were still damp from scrubbing, when sunshine came through the open shutters on to empty stools and benches and it smelled, not unpleasantly, of stale wine and basting chickens.

Its only customer at the moment was Fenchel, the siege engineer, who sat at a table in the corner, drawing plans on a slate and crooning one of his interminable, and filthy, songs.

Ypres ordered wine and installed himself in the window seat to watch for his archer. Willem carefully dragged up a high stool on which he could sit with his back straight.

"Back bad?"

"It's all right." His commander didn't press the question, but neither did he believe the answer.

"It's my last war, Willem. And you?"

"You can afford it. I'll have to see."

Their lives formed a sort of St. Andrew's cross, now meeting in the peculiar democracy of their trade, but starting from opposite beginnings and continuing to different ends. William of Ypres had used mercenary life as a means to an end. Willem of Ghent had grabbed it for a lifeline. Neither belonged to the third category of mercenary made up of men who liked killing and being paid for it.

The morning light bleached the tan on the commander's face, emphasising the grey among the bluish stubble on his chin, which, like his body, was thickening. He looked ruthless, but respectably ruthless, like a merchant. He'd been born near enough to great wealth to smell it; he was a bastard by a former Count of Flanders and a wool-carder. He'd missed the title by a whisker after his father died and had tried to grab it by force, missing again and being forced into exile to avoid reprisals. Stephen had given him refuge – one of the reasons Ypres fought for him – the other reason being that Stephen had made him Earl of Kent in all but title. And Ypres wasn't a man to quibble over Kent's title when he was receiving Kent's revenues.

The man perched opposite him was thinner, taller, younger and poorer; his had been a lower birth than Ypres'. In fact, in Flanders there was no lower condition than that of itinerant weaver, which was what Willem's father had been, a "blue nail", one of the hundreds who starved at the gates of the rich wool merchants waiting for the chance to work a sixteen-hour day for subsistence.

Clogs scraped through the rushes and Rotrou loomed up with two mugs of wine slopping in his enormous and only hand – the other had been sliced off by a Saracen. They drank suspiciously.

"Why don't you keep this sheepwash in the cellar?" grumbled Willem.

"You think that's bad you should taste the ale," said Rotrou. He paid no concession to the fact that he owed his living to their charity and they didn't expect any; nobody could look after a mercenary except mercenaries, nobody but a mercenary understood mercenaries. They were only really comfortable in each other's company.

"I've had hot wars," said Willem. "A cool war Stephen promised me. Two estates in Normandy and a moist, green war with cold wine."

"Is that why you joined him? I heard the Angevins had offered for you."

"They did, but it seemed to me Stephen was the only ruler who understands towns."

Ypres was puzzled. "You like towns?"

"No." He hated them. His mother and sister had died of malnutrition in a garret of one. He and his father had chased rats away from their corpses all night before they could be taken to the communal grave and nobody at all had noticed their passing. But Willem, who fitted into no social structure, had recognised a new force. Successful trading was giving towns an economic power which had nothing to do with the power of the lords who owned the countryside. Their traders and craftsmen were becoming rich and forming themselves into guilds so rigidly and democratically organised they could ensure security for their members and their members' widows and orphans. They were demanding liberties and charters to conduct their own affairs. Stephen – and Willem had no other regard for the king – recognised this new liberty and fostered it, which was why the towns loved him.

Willem liked new things. He liked Fenchel over in the corner designing a better and more powerful trebuchet, who wanted to build a cathedral with flying buttresses to support the spans.

"I seen it, I seen it," crooned Fenchel, licking his chalk, "I been in betwe-e-en it."

"Towns are the coming thing," he said. "Stephen understands that."

Ypres did not; the only power he could envisage came from owning vassals and land and collecting rent and tithes. "You'd better tell me your side," he said. "Was it a knight you killed?"

"When this is over I shall invest in town trade," said Willem. If his back continued as bad as this he was finished. This war had got to pay. Ypres could pay for the next round. "This morning? It was a knight, a mistake and a practice bolt. Untipped. Whoever it hit has a headache. But if he was dead, so what?"

"Bad feeling. The garrison must sue for terms soon and certain quarters think at this stage there's no need to shed noble blood."

"Stuff their terms," said Willem of Ghent. He believed in unconditional surrender, especially from a castle low on water.

"Sir," said a voice through the window.

"Fenchel," called Ypres, "come and show this bowman of mine whereabouts in the castle we can start a fire."

Fenchel spat into the rushes and lumbered over. "Destruction," he said, "that's all I ever get, destruction. Giants built that castle and you bloody pygmies want to burn it down." If they'd asked him to shore it up, he'd have complained.

"We don't want to burn it down, Fenchel," said his commander, patiently. "We want to start a fire to see what they put it out with."

Fenchel spat on to his slate and wiped a section clean with his sleeve. In a few strokes he had drawn a plan of the castle; it was his business to form a clear picture of it from spies and guesswork. "We reckon we dropped a rock through their stable roof last Thursday," he said, "and we reckon they've put their horses under thatch *there*." He drew a cross in the south-east corner of a square.

Peering in through the window the marksman said: "Range?"

Fenchel pursed his lips. "Ninety-five paces, ninety-seven?"

"There you are, then. Put a fire arrow in that and we'll smell what we shall smell."

"Consider it done," said the archer, and they did; a bowman didn't earn the title "marksman" for missing what he aimed at even when he couldn't see his target and had to work out a trajectory which would take the arrow up over the castle wall and drop down to an exact point behind it. They didn't even go and watch him but stayed at Rotrou's and had another drink, only emerging when, from beyond the houses which hid the castle, came a mixture of neighing and of filling buckets. They sniffed and smelled burning with a fruity, alcoholic depth to it. They were putting out the fire with wine.

To celebrate they went back in and had another drink. Then they bought the marksman a drink and Fenchel another, after which they began to sing. They were still singing when one of Ypres' men put his head through the window and said: "The buggers are coming out to parley."

The parley took place in the cathedral. Though the emissaries from the rebel castle were so desiccated by thirst they had trouble in enunciating, their words had juice. They would surrender on condition that their men keep their arms and that there should be no sack, no looting and no reprisals by Stephen's army.

Briefed by Willem and Ypres that the castle was out of water, Stephen's brother, the fat, cultivated Henry, Bishop of Winchester, advised the king to hang them.

The emissaries were sent back to think again and come back with an unconditional surrender. They did not return; instead they sent out more persuasive emissaries, the golden-haired wife and sons of the rebel Baldwin de Redvers. They were in better condition than the original parleyers, but they drooped prettily and pleaded for their lives and property in sweet, cracking voices.

Watching the proceedings, Willem saw the king look towards the altar and wonder what God and His Son would think of him if he hanged the rebels as his advisers were telling him to do.

Stephen's father had been one of the rare cowards of the First Crusade. He had escaped from an Antioch besieged by Saracens – he slid down a rope forever earning himself the nickname of "funambulus", rope-trick man – and came home to the reproaches of his wife, Henry of England's sister, and everyone else in Europe. Eventually he was persuaded to return and get himself decently killed but the disgrace had stained his family. Perhaps it was then that Stephen became self-conscious and lost the all-of-a-oneness of other princelings and began to wonder, and care, what God and his fellow-men thought of him.

Somebody else in the cathedral was watching the king – Robert, Earl of Gloucester, the best of Henry the First's many bastards. He stepped forward. "My lord," he said, "can it justly be said that these people are traitors? They owed their fealty to their lord, Baldwin de Redvers, and should not be held responsible for his rebellion."

There was a silence. It was an argument which struck at the king's authority. A long time ago, in the stormy years of Henry's reign, two rebels had stood before him and his barons had put a similar argument on their behalf. Henry had said, "Rubbish." All English and Normans were his lawful men, he'd said. "Let their eyes be put out," he'd said. And their eyes had been put out and England had gained long years of peace through it.

Willem, who respected Earl Robert as a commander, began to wonder whose side he was on. The earl had absented himself from Stephen's coronation and people had wondered if he was going to stand out for the Empress, his half-sister, or even himself. When he'd finally turned up at the siege of Exeter to support Stephen, the king had received him with honour and relief. Maybe, thought Willem, the relief was premature.

However, Stephen's face cleared. He shrugged off Henry of Blois' restraining hand. "My lord, they shall have God's mercy and mine. Let them go free without punishment."

For the first time in their alliance, he had disregarded his brother's advice. More important, he had allowed rebels to get away with it.

It was his first mistake.

3

1136

For the first week of her immobilisation Matilda was so frightened of miscarriage that she kept her legs and muscles clenched to form a prison of rigor from which the baby should not escape.

In her sleep the muscles would relax and she would dream she was in a soft, black, porous cave through which water containing tiny fish seeped away, and she would wake to go rigid once more.

She insisted her household attend Dungesey Church daily to pray for her welfare. "If I lose my place with Sigward so do you," she pointed out.

She herself prayed unremittingly to the Virgin Mary, promising her that if she was good enough to see this baby safely born she, Matilda, would build her a church.

"Where?" asked Father Alors, always practical.

"Anywhere," snapped Matilda.

"This island could do with a new one. I've never seen such a ruin. And as for the cleric . . ." Father Alors was obsessed by the ignorance of the island's cleric, Stunta. At first it was because the man preached in English. But other atrocities presented themselves every day.

"He's army mad," screamed Father Alors. "He tells your people more about their military duty than their duty to God." Outside Matilda's window someone was bellowing commands followed by the whirr of arrows. "He's making them practise their archery. Women as well."

"It's his duty, isn't it?" If the fyrd, the army of the common people, were mobilised it would be clerks like Stunta who led the parish levies to war.

43

"It's not his duty to tell them God prefers the yew to the ash bow. It's not his job on the feast of St. Simon and St. Jude to instruct them to honour only the former since St. Jude was the one who betrayed Christ. Nor that in the Exodus the people of Israel were scattered because the tailboard of their cart broke and they all fell out." He regarded with disfavour the heaving bedclothes. "If you're laughing, my lady . . ."

But it was no laughing matter when Father Alors discovered that Stunta had a wife. He erupted into Matilda's chamber, raving in Latin and clutching what little hair he had.

"A what?"

"Focaria," screamed Father Alors. "A concubine. She washes his clothes, cooks his food and doesn't go home at nights. They have *children*."

The very next day Father Alors was despatched to the Abbey of Ramsey, under whose control Stunta was, to ask for his dismissal. He enjoyed his stay among the comforts of the abbey guest house but achieved no success. "There is no abbot," he told Matilda on his return. "They are in the process of electing one. We must wait and hope that in the meantime the dolt gets stuck with one of his own arrows. *Qui gladio percutet, gladio peribit.*"

Never in her fifteen years had Matilda kept still for so long and as the days progressed she became bored and petulant. When Adeliza or Ghislaine or Flore tried to sneak off, being as bored as she was, she would demand: "Where are you going?" Adeliza, easily dominated, and Flore, financially dependent, would sigh and return but Ghislaine, who had lands of her own, would proceed on and out. Eventually they devised a shift system where one remained with Matilda and the other two went off – "to keep an eye on your island, my dear."

It seemed to Matilda they weren't so much keeping an eye on it as enjoying it. "What on earth do you find to do?" They told her of punting silently through reeds, of shooting arrows into a canopy of ducks, of hawks with a plethora of prey.

A letter arrived from Sigward, and Father Alors, the only

44

literate member of her household, came in to read it. "'I pray daily for the health of my beloved wife and the safe delivery of our heir. I send her a cloak of marten against the cold since women have less heat in their bodies than men, and a medicine against abortion mixed by the new king's own physician from a remedy of Soranus who attended Queen Cleopatra.'" Father Alors, who loathed gynaecological details, read this with some asperity and Matilda listened with the embarrassment that Sigward's un-Normanlike concern for her always aroused.

Sigward went on to explain that he had overcome his scruples about his oath to support Matilda Empress and was supporting Stephen, "since all great men do the same". Father Alors and Percy of Alleyn, who'd also come in to hear the letter, got into a lengthy argument over the ethics of Stephen's coup. Matilda became impatient.

"Such rubbish," she said, "of course the Empress could not rule England and Normandy. It is for men to command, not women. Now go and tell Berte to hurry up with my dinner."

As the winter became wetter and colder messengers got through less and less frequently and Sigward, thinking it wise not to be absent from court just now, came not at all. Matilda, encoffined in her solar, felt herself neglected. She began to decline into a paralysis of torpor. Like a dog chained up too long she began to spend more and more time asleep. The only positive thing she did was put on weight.

Berte refused to share the ladies' alarm. "A baby's like pastry," she said, "it needs quiet to rise in a warm oven. When she's ready to perk up, she'll perk. She won't sink won't Matilda of Risle."

So with less guilt they began leaving her for longer and longer. Even her page and maid could sneak out of her room without reproof, as long as Berte didn't catch them. For the first time in her life she was left alone.

But Berte was right. Matilda's nature, like Nature itself, could not endure a vacuum and in it began a relationship which was to be of permanent value to her. It grew in the stages of Genesis: out of darkness air, then water, then creatures, then people.

At first it was exasperation at the wind that rattled the shutters. This sound kept bringing her back from accidie like a fish-hook. It kept on, sometimes with polite insistence, sometimes with the violence of a demon denied entry. After a particularly bad night Matilda sat up and shouted: "Will nobody take those shutters off?"

From across the solar in the dark Ghislaine said: "We'll freeze."

"Take the poxy things down."

They were taken down. There was little chance that the ladies in their nests of linen and fur would freeze, but it was a different matter for the servants on their thin straw mattresses. The maid's chattering teeth irritated Matilda so she threw a cup at the sound which stopped it.

Soon everyone was asleep again, except Matilda; her exasperation had forced adrenalin through her body and made it wakeful. She considered waking them all up again but came to the conclusion that there was nothing they could do to lift her boredom. Dice with Flore, cat's-cradle with Adeliza, chess with Ghislaine would be as wearing as doing nothing. Jodi, curled up in some niche out in the hall, had exhausted every joke, every antic, every story and song in his repertoire.

"Boredom is a sin against the Holy Ghost," Father Alors would tell her. "Reflect on your sins and turn your mind to the eternal beauty of God." Her sins were dreary now she had the chance to commit so few. She did not dare recite prayers for fear of finding God as boring as everything else.

The wind whipped from one window slit to another, slicing through the frowst built up by six bodies and chamberpots. It brought to Matilda's nose smells which evoked her race memory. This wind had filled square sails, flipped the plaits of bearded, terrible men, invoked sea-dragons and uncouth gods. The Norse invader not so many generations back in Matilda's ancestry was invigorated by it. It had screamed across fiords and grey, cold water but now

some of its harshness was ameliorated by bending but resis-
tant reeds, its salt diluted by fresh rivers, streams and a
landscape which, in the end, had defeated even the Vikings.

With dawn came birds. Previously birds had meant only
prey for her hawks, or stuffed and cooked. Now came the
calls of a hundred wintering tribes, the advance and the
retreat of the whooper swan's whistling wingbeat. She heard
a booming like someone blowing into a giant conch shell, the
hoot of a long-eared owl on its way home and the tic-toc of a
crake hiding in the rushes. She found herself curious about
these solos over the undertone of reeds and wind.

All at once she was curious about many things. When she
was alone later that day she hauled herself upright – and
nearly toppled from the unaccustomed weight of her body
since she'd last stood it up. She pulled up her nightrobe to
consider her belly. There was a not-unpleasant sensation of
popping inside it which made the skin of its swell move
involuntarily. She nodded. The baby was alive and the
danger of miscarriage past. She was pleased with her girth
which promised, like Berte's sex-divining portents, that it
was a boy.

She looked out of her east window. She was fifteen feet or
so up. Below her the ground sloped down to a wall in bad
repair and went on until it met carr which lapped Dungesey
on this side like a grey-green sea. Lakes, monsters, an army
could be out there and you wouldn't know.

"Godless," thought Matilda, who always associated the
Almighty with hills. Then she shifted her gaze and saw that
seven-eighths of view was a sky through which God could
see everything without hindrance. She felt exposed to His
sight.

Her eye was brought down by a movement. Something
parted the branches and a flat-bottomed boat emerged from
the trees to ground on the mud. A man clambered out and
unloaded some fishing creels and carried them up a path
through apple trees out of her sight to the kitchens. Her
island had a secret back door.

She lumbered off the bed and with some difficulty hauled
herself on to a chest under the west window. This, being

away from the prevailing wind, was larger than its opposite and had a single wooden mullion for her to hold on to.

Her hall was on the north-east point of the highest contour of the island and around the contour ran a ragged wall containing the hall itself, outbuildings, the church, barns, a well, stables and huts. Over the arched entrance of the main gate she could see the view beyond – something about it made her uneasy.

At first it looked normal enough, perhaps uglier than most village scenes because this was February in the Fens, a dirty tapestry of browns, greys, greens, leafless trees and black puddles under a pewter-coloured sky. Only an avenue of yew trees down the central green looked positive and smart.

There were sheep enfolded on the green, dunging it and firming it with their hooves for summer. Beyond them was the village. The English believed in togetherness; their huts were jumbled together and as plain as barns, except for little projections of thatch at each end of the roof-pole like animal ears. They gave the impression of a nest of fox-cubs. The only other patterning was functional; neat, stippled rounds which were the cut ends of reed bundles stacked in every garden alongside a honeycomb of peat bricks.

Dreary, normal . . . and something was wrong, disturbing her to the point of irritation. "Where," she asked herself, "are the goats?" The goat was a symbol of poverty. It could live on very little and still provide milk and cheese. Every tenement Matilda had ever seen had its goat. But the green and gardens of Dungesey were goatless.

She looked back at the sheep. There were too many. By this time of year most manors had eaten their animals – there was usually insufficient fodder to see them through the winter anyway – but the black-faced, long-legged, deer-like sheep in these wattle pens made up a sizeable flock.

Angrily she searched for other signs of riches. There were horses in the stalls where the plough teams were kept. Horses. Horses that needed oats, not oxen that could live on hedge-clippings. One of the teams was hers, she knew, but the village was maintaining horses for its own.

It was as if she'd seen a beggar and glimpsed velvet and

sable beneath his rags. "If the peasant lives rich," her father had always said, "the lord is cheated." None of his peasants had cheated him of his rightful rents and tithes. "And by God," swore Matilda, "neither will mine."

There was a flap of slippers on the boards and Matilda was scooped off the chest and put back to bed by an outraged Berte. "Never known the like . . . what about the baby . . . eat your comfrey."

"I hate comfrey. Get my robe. I'm going out."

"It's good and gluey. You're *not*."

"I *am*." Matilda's tone pushed Berte back through her arguments to a last ditch stand of, "Don't blame me when you miscarry, and eat your comfrey."

Burping gelatinous greens, swaddled in Sigward's marten cloak, Matilda was handed down the outside steps of her hall accompanied by a hastily gathered escort. Insulated by her newly acquired fat she found the air delightful. The buildings around her were dilapidated, though functional, and alien; the gargoyles beneath her roof, the stonework and wood-work had other traditions, other memories from any of hers. She ignored them for the moment and headed for the church which was a stone rectangle with a small, fat tower at its west end. The stripwork round its arched door was of interwoven vines, monsters and flat-faced heads. Matilda preferred smart Norman chevrons.

Inside it was dark. She crossed herself with water from a stone stoup at the door and went to the altar to pray: "If the child is a boy, dear Lord, I'll do better for You than this." She stood up. "Mind you," she added carefully, "the boy must be healthy." She made for the door and stopped again. "And so must I."

Stunta the clerk emerged from the tower, stamping his feet as he marched up to her, his fists swinging up and down as if he were banging a drum. He was a big, red-faced man with cropped hair that stood up in a shock round his tonsure. "Recovered from the wounds, commander?"

At first Matilda assumed he was addressing Percy of Alleyn; once she'd understood his atrocious French she realised it was herself. All life was a battlefield to Stunta.

49

She ignored him anyway; the man was a buffoon and a profligate.

"Must talk tactics, commander. Fortify the wall."

Matilda stopped in the doorway. "Have you any idea," she demanded of Percy of Alleyn, "what the man's talking about?"

"He thinks there's going to be a war, my lady, and that Dungesey should be fortified."

Stunta barged forward. "Smell it. Old soldiers can't be fooled. Got to protect the little folk at home. David against Golgotha."

Matilda took a deep breath. "Tell him to use his tactics on their souls: I shall care for their bodies."

She hurried out and across the green to the village huts. Some ill-designed animals she supposed to be dogs got up and barked at her. She cut them dead too, chose a hut at random and stooped through its doorway under a great reeded roof.

Inside it resembled nothing so much as a clearing in a dark forest, and smelled like one. Its floor was deep in rushes and its stools tussocks of bleached grass. The walls were like crazy trees covered with baskets, bottles, containers all woven from rushes. A child with a bandaged foot was stirring the cauldron.

Matilda swept over to the crocks and lifted their lids, discovering one to be half-full of butter and another milk – she dipped in a finger – cow's milk. There was more milk souring in a muslin bag slung from a beam to allow the whey to drip into a bowl. A shallow, circular tray contained two enormous wheels of white, wheaten bread. Matilda slammed back the lids. She had been right to be angry. If peasants could afford luxuries like these, especially in winter, they must be bilking their lord – in their case their lady.

She rounded on the child. "Where's your father?" It not only didn't answer, it didn't blink. Matilda prodded its backside with her boot: "Where's your father?" but concluded the child was deaf.

In fact, the child was trying to ignore her existence. Her skin was too white, her clothes too exotic and the sounds she

50

made too incomprehensible to put her in the same category as the human beings he was used to. He decided she wasn't there at all.

Outside, her entourage was about to complain of the cold, then saw her face, and didn't. She marched them down a trackway between strip fields of dark, harrowed earth declining until the track was a causeway over swamp in which waders stalked on high, articulated legs and bobbed beaks like upholstery needles into the mud.

The sky tried to intimidate her with its immensity and press her down so that, though a tall woman, she felt her legs had become squat and that she waded rather than walked. It did not improve her temper.

The track bellied out to become the boarded floor of a quayside fronting a pool known as the Waits, a turn-around for barges using the sluggish little River Swallen which was Dungesey's main connection to the fen waterways. Along its banks grew pollarded willows, like cloves stuck into rolls of bread. Birds were everywhere, dotting the grey sky, floating on the Swallen, scampering over it in take-offs and landings.

There were warehouses on the right of the landing stage, but the only human life apparent was a woman on the left bank dunking fleeces into a vat. Matilda filled her lungs with fenland air and expelled it: "Steward."

A figure appeared in the sack hoist of a warehouse. "I'll come down, my lady."

"I'll come up." ("Trust your steward," her father had said, "but know everything he knows.") On the threshold she teetered against a smell of dried fish, salt, leather and an unknown stink which increased as she climbed the stairs to emerge into the loft. "God help us, what's that?"

"Eh? Oh, it's woad, my lady." Steward Peter helped her to the sack hoist and fresh air, then lifted a cask lid to show her unwholesome weed jammed into it. "We send it to dyers in the uplands, my lady, in return for cloth. May I offer refreshment? Shall we descend?"

"You stay," said Matilda. "You shall tell me many things. First, what does Dungesey mean?"

51

The question surprised them both; Matilda hadn't realised how the ugliness of the name had bothered her.

"I don't know, my lady. They won't tell me."

"They'll tell me, by God."

"The 'ey' means island," said Steward Peter, helpfully.

"Illuminating." The man was weak and would have to go. "Now then . . ."

There followed an inquisition so detailed that, when eventually he was released, Steward Peter felt disembowelled. First he had to prove she was not being cheated. He gave her details of the annual profit derived from the estate: it was considerably bigger than from many a larger one.

After that it was who paid her what. She made him give the name of every tenant, every villein, every rent, every customary right. "Half?" She got up and Steward Peter fell back. "You stand there, you liar, and tell me half these people are free tenants?"

Steward Peter picked himself up and wiped his neck. "It's like that in East Anglia. They've managed to retain their freedom. A difficult people to understand . . ."

"I'll understand them till their bones squeak. Get on with the rents."

Downstairs her attendants shifted, coughed and became cold. Finally they sent back to the hall for soup; some was taken up to Matilda who ate it absent-mindedly, offering the steward none.

English names were ugly and anarchic. Kakkr, Pampi, Toki, Badda, Sulse, Shudda, Ulf, Impa, Wifil, Wyrm . . .

"Wyrm?"

"It means serpent. He pays you fifty sticks of eels a year . . ."

"How many eels to a stick?"

"Twenty-five."

She did some calculation. "Do I need that many eels?"

"Usually not, so we commute it and make him pay eel-silver . . ."

"How much?"

"Four shillings, just as Kakkr – it means Humpnose – pays the same in fishsilver."

52

As she absorbed the new phraseology she looked out of the sack hoist. The laundress had taken the fleeces out of the vat and was attaching them to a clothes-line lying on the grass where they formed yellow puddles. The fleeces had been dipped in urine to kill their grease. Probably the whole village had contributed the contents of its chamberpots to fill that vat. Now she clambered down the bank into a coracle, dragging the fleeces after her. Using her linen prop as a pole she punted herself across the river so that the fleeces followed her through the water to rinse them. She began to string them up between the willows to dry.

Matilda turned back to Steward Peter who was drawing her a map of Dungesey in the dust of a barrel top. He was drawing two maps. "Either it's one shape or it isn't." But it wasn't. In summer it was like a hat with a wide, ragged brim of cultivated land: in winter only the crown rose above water and swamp.

"Can't we hold back the water? Then we could have a winter crop."

They had tried. The Swallen's two banks were kept in good repair, Crease Bank and the Driftway. But Driftway continued north-west to become Monks' Bank, the property of the Abbey of Ramsey and the abbot left it in disrepair so that the waters of the Nene could seep through and find their way to form the Washes, the unusable winter swamp Matilda had seen from the Causeway.

It appeared there was little co-operation over dyking and embanking in the Fens. Each landowner cared only for where the water came from and not at all where it went. Drainage was designed to pour water on to the next parish. "I fear that Sutton, which is to our east and south, complains grievously of our drainage."

"I shall speak to the Abbot of Ramsey," promised Matilda, ignoring Sutton.

Like noxious vapours solidifying into form, shapes appeared at the ends of the two Swallen banks against an amethyst sky. The English of the Fens were coming home from their work of scouring the lodes, drains and streams of the weed and rush which choked them.

Children, women and men muttered to each other across the river like a thundercloud turned human, and just about as black. Their faces and clothes were lumpy with mud, weed streamed from their shoulders as if resurrected from burial, and with them came the smell of freshly dug graves, wet earth and rotting vegetation.

From the sack hoist Matilda could hear Adeliza whimpering and because even she felt intimidated she went down to confront them.

As they skirted the Waits and came closer their appearance lost no horror. Eyes stared at her through lumps of clay. Beneath the mud on their boots gleamed some flaky substance as if their legs were swollen and silver with leprosy. Even the children on the mothers' backs had weed sprouting from their fingers.

One man had a string over his shoulder which led to the neck of a dead heron dragging through the mud. The dirtying of its feathers offended Matilda's soul. "Why is that man dragging that heron?"

"It's magic, my lady," Steward Peter hovered behind her, "they rub heron fat on their fishing tackle so it will catch more fish."

"I dare say, but it's getting dirty."

Steward Peter turned to the horrors and addressed them in grunting, sliding sounds.

"Don't they understand French? Why not?"

"I tried to make them, lady, but they never got the hang of it."

"They will. What's that man saying?"

Worriedly Steward Peter turned back to the English where a man was answering. An almost imperceptible tremor ran through the English but their faces remained blank.

"Well, what?"

"I asked why he was dragging the heron, my lady." Steward Peter looked defeated. "He said he'd tried pushing it but it didn't go."

Matilda's eyes narrowed. "Dismiss them."

Furiously she watched them slouch off and caught sight of the steward's haggard face as he watched them too. "He's fond of them. That's why they've broken him. He *cares* for them."

When she went to bed that night Matilda was a new woman. So this was fenland. Out there in that foul and flabby quagmire were hidden meadows where Dungesey cattle grazed with cattle from other villages "horn under horn". She took a last look from her window. The sun was setting suddenly fierce as if to make up for its previous weakness. The sky became momentous, giving clouds an oriental grandeur, blushing ducks' backs and turning the Swallen to amber.

"Riches," she said. "There are riches here."

Although she was now fit to travel she delayed by a week her departure for Hatfelde where Sigward wanted his son to be born. When the week was up she delayed again.

Dungesey intrigued her. She wanted to exploit this one piece of land she truly owned. She wanted to impose her will on these shiftless independent English.

That was what she told Berte, her household and even herself. There was another truth. At Hatfelde waited the birth stool with its seat in the shape of a horseshoe on which contraption Sigward's female ancestors had delivered his predecessors. Above it were the straps to pull on and the leather to bite on in the pains.

At Hatfelde they would burn squashed bedbugs and goat's hair under her nose and tie spikenard and artemisia around her thighs so that, the mouth and nose being connected to the digestive tract which was connected to the womb, the baby would be attracted away from the foul smells to the sweet. At Hatfelde they would make her sniff pepper and milkwort so that her sneezes assisted the downward force of her contractions. A priest would be waiting outside the chamber door to give the last rites if she or her baby should die, and waiting with him would be Sigward's relatives and nobles listening for the child's first cry and attesting that Sigward's heir had been properly born within his walls. She dreaded Hatfelde.

Berte denounced and fumed that they didn't leave at once

55

and the rest of the household was now bored with Dungesey, but Matilda said: "There's time enough," and began her exploration.

To the south was an oak wood where the island's pigs were taken daily by Tulsi, the swineherd.

Between that and her manor, screened off by a grove of pear trees called Perecourt, was an odd little settlement called Wealyham.

"The Wealas," said Steward Peter, "are a separate people. Celts. Your ladyship's bondsmen and women. Unfree. Quarrelsome when drunk, lazy when sober, immoral women and shiftless men – but usually the men leave when old enough, or kill each other."

Matilda saw from the state of their settlement how worthless the Wealas were. The lanes between the houses were filthy, roofs and walls had lumps falling off them, though they were complex with patterning. The only sign of life came from a hut where a tenor voice sang to a harp. "Minnesinging," said Jodi, entranced.

"Why are they tolerated?"

"Lady, they are expert wildfowlers and trappers and provide most of your table and they are fine animal doctors, especially with horses. Also they make good willow honey. But," Steward Peter sounded reluctant, "they are kept mainly because they know the secret of St. Gregory's cordial. A wonderful specific which can cure or alleviate the symptoms of the mal air of the Fens." It took away pain, inducing sleep and strange dreams. A Wealy woman had seduced the seeds and the secret of the poppy from which it was made out of a returned Crusader. But when he saw Matilda's interest – a magic potion which took away pain was above rubies – Steward Peter warned: "It must not be used too often or you want more until you cannot live without it. Luckily there is a limited supply."

They left Jodi behind them when they went, squatting outside the hut in the filth and following the notes of the harp on his lute. And for the rest of their time on Dungesey there he stayed.

Matilda held her first manor court on a day when rain

lashed the hall and turned the interior so dark that the English, gathered down one end, were still just shapes to her.

"Come closer." Her men-at-arms whacked a few behinds and the English shuffled forward. "That's enough." She could smell fish.

"Let the court of Dungesey commence and let every soul tell the truth as it stands in the fear of God. Debts first."

It was not a rent day and only outstanding debts had to be paid. Steward Peter ran his fingers down the notches of his debt tally. "Shudda owes a shilling sedgesilver." He added nervously to Matilda: "She is a widow and cut her hand so she could not mow and we postponed her rent." But an old woman came forward to the table and slammed a shilling on it.

"Shudda is quit," said Steward Peter with relief. The other outstanding debts were paid as promptly. "They've been borrowing from each other for it."

"Appeals," commanded Matilda. She enjoyed this part most; appeals enabled a lord to show power and wisdom over squabbles between tenants. But she was not to play Solomon today. A silence descended so they could hear the rain rattling on the shutters and the shuffle of the people's eelskin boots in the rushes. Sparrows whirred from beam to beam.

"Be quick." But nobody had offended anybody since last court, nobody's animals had broken a hedge or trampled his neighbour's crops. Nobody had taken anything without permission, nobody had cut peat out of season nor assaulted anyone. The English had closed ranks.

Matilda's foot tapped. "Steward, do you appeal nobody?"

Steward Peter produced some minor infringements which Matilda fined heavily since she suspected him of concealing greater wickednesses.

"Boons." There was more silence, more rain, more tapping from Matilda's foot.

"Kakkr," Steward Peter was getting desperate, "didn't you want permission for your daughter to marry Teoful?"

"I reckon she can wait," came a voice from the hall. They

would ask nothing of this new lord until they knew her better.

"The lady," announced Steward, "is to inspect her demesne and will need boat service. Stand forward Sulse, Toki and Pampi who owe her such customary rent."

Three men shuffled forward. They all looked alike to Matilda, though there was one whose shape was familiar. "Is that the one with the heron?"

"Pampi."

"I pick him." That would teach him. He'd suffer hardship through having to neglect work on his own land.

"The next command of our lady is this," said Steward Peter, "that in future any soul who asks a boon of her will do so in the French tongue, that being the proper language for her court." He added hastily: "You can come to me before-hand to learn the words."

Both he and Matilda had expected some cultural reaction, an outcry. The English surprised them by being mightily amused. The tension of the hall relaxed into tittering and nudging elbows. They bowed and curtsied to each other in what they imagined to be courtly salutes.

"You going to poyley-voy then, Up?"

"Up don't wholly speak English."

Matilda could have coped with an outburst: now she was at a loss. Angrily she dismissed the court.

"Funny ideas, that little ol' gal," said Kakkr to Shudda as they left, "but I reckon as us'll lick her into shape."

Matilda did some socialising and attended other courts, the shire's, the hundred's and that held by the intercommoning communities which shared grazing with Dungesey. She was surprised by the general efficiency.

But where the courts failed was in the most vital area of all; they could not enforce the drainage and embanking laws. The Nene was the main river of this part and the Nene was the Abbey of Ramsey's river, entering the Fens near Ramsey, and remaining so for most of its winding, north-easterly course. Ramsey barges used it. Nevertheless its banks were in shocking repair. There was a Saxon tradition that a man who allowed a bank to fall into disrepair should be walled up in it, but as the chief offender was the Abbot of Ramsey nobody, however bad the embanking, felt equal to buttressing it up with so influential and rich a body as his.

As this became apparent Matilda became unhappy. Water seeping into her Washes through Ramsey's rotten banks was costing her a winter crop. "I'll go to the abbot myself."

Father Alors was horrified: "In your condition?" and he was not worrying about Matilda's health but about polluting the abbot's sensibilities with a pregnant woman.

"Then you go." But Father Alors, though he was a well-born Norman and represented the combined might of Sigward and Matilda, had no more luck than anyone else in reaching the new abbot. A Brother Daniel, now prior, blocked the way. Everybody complained of him.

So did Father Alors: "Put off," he shouted on his return, "repulsed, *snubbed*, and by a jumped-up, low-born glass-blower."

"A what?"

"This Daniel is not only English but a glassblower before he took his vows. The cellarer told me all about him. He doesn't like him either. He's gained ascendancy over the new abbot. And makes a pretty penny out of it. Even built his own residence in the Fens, so they say."

"What about Monks' Bank?"

Father Alors' skull-shaped face adopted a mincing expression and enunciated with clarity: "His father-in-God the abbot must not be bothered with such matters. He was elected for his saintliness, not for his knowledge of draining."

"Damn his saintliness. And damn Brother Daniel."

It was Matilda who found the abbot.

She had been to ask the hermit who kept the bridge at Beale for a prophecy concerning her child. All hermits could tell the future. This one lived on an island in the middle of the Nene upriver towards Ramsey where a bridge spanned each stream to make a crossing point. The hermit kept the bridge and took the tolls.

He turned out to be a smelly old man with a hostile and

smellier dog living in a hovel in mud. Matilda didn't bother to disembark. Percy of Alleyn hailed the man and proffered a silver piece. "Matilda de Risle, lady of Dungesey, asks for your blessing and begs a prophecy."

The hermit stopped scratching his armpit, spat on the silver piece and waved a dirty hand in the shape of a cross. "It's going to rain," he said in English, and went back to scratching.

Percy of Alleyn translated. "I could have told *him* that," said Matilda, bad-temperedly. Pampi and his son began sullenly to pole them back the way they had come.

It did rain. Their boat, a peculiar combination of barge and punt with a rocker-bottom and sloped sides, had at the stern an upside down cradle of hoops over which canvas was rolled so that Matilda and Adeliza could sit in the dry. Pampi and his son had sacking round their shoulders which steamed as they poled. Percy of Alleyn and a man-at-arms held dripping cloaks over their heads.

Matilda brooded. Perhaps the hermit's words hadn't been a weather forecast only: perhaps they'd been symbolical.

Then Pampi gave a shout, an event so unusual that Matilda scrabbled at the calico to see what he had seen. They had reached the Stun, a stone on the starboard bank which marked the ending of Ramsey land and the beginning of Dungesey's. The river was wide here and swimming across it was a stag; its antlers, head and shoulders rose and dipped in the water. There was immediate pandemonium. "Kill, kill," yelled Matilda. Percy of Alleyn, hallooing and cursing his lack of a bow, grabbed the man-at-arms' spear and threw. Even Pampi and his son were ra-ra-ing and waving their poles.

The spear missed and the stag turned its head, frantically looking for a landing place. A slip in the deplorable bank gave it a chance and it heaved itself up and over the bank and disappeared down the other side. There was a long score across its flank where diluted blood patterned it.

They were diverted by another body crashing down the port bank from which the stag had come. A moment later a monk was swimming across the river in a careful breaststroke, his head with its tonsure rising and dipping as the stag's had done.

"A portent," said Adeliza getting hysterical. "It is a magic stag and an enchanted monk who pursues it."

The monk had gained the stag's landing place but when he tried to haul himself upright the weight of water in his habit dragged him down. He fell and lay in the mud, gesticulating at them. "See where it goes."

"What's he going to do? Strangle it?" But so urgent were the monk's pleas that Percy of Alleyn scrambled to the bank.

"Get me up there." Matilda gestured to the man-at-arms to carry her, using one hand while with the other she slapped Adeliza back to her senses. As she was carried up the bank she was reminded of its dilapidation. "Are you a Ramsey monk? Because if so . . ."

"What's it doing? What's it doing?" The monk slimed his way up. The land beyond Monks' Bank was a long stretch of bog, grey flat surface broken by tussocks of sedge. The stag moved across it in a series of jerky bounds. When it reached midway it looked back to see if it was pursued then did a peculiar thing; it rolled down and on to its wounded side and dragged itself along for some yards in that position. Then it got back up and disappeared into the distance.

"Ah ha." The monk crossed his arms over his dreadful habit in triumph. "I thought as much. I spotted him limping. Somebody's arrow had scored him, and I thought: 'I bet I know where you're going, my lad.' And I was right." He began squeezing water out of his habit, became aware of the silence and looked up. "I have this theory, you see. That's bog moss out there, sphagnum moss. The English say wounded animals roll in it. Well, animals are God's hints to us so I thought: 'Let's see. Is He trying to tell us sphagnum's good for wounds, cleanses and heals?' Tomorrow I'll get some of the brothers out here and gather tons of the stuff, dry it and try it out in the infirmary." The silence discomfited him. "I'm afraid I chatter a lot in company. Also when I'm not, actually."

"Are you the infirmarian, then?" He seemed young for

61

such a post. His habit, dragging downwards, revealed an unlined throat and his wet hair clung in leaves to his skull, like a boy's.

The monk looked shy. "Actually," he said, "they elected me abbot. It was nice of them, wasn't it?"

Percy of Alleyn pulled himself together and made hasty introductions. The abbot nodded gleefully at them all, even Pampi and son, to whom he was not introduced.

Matilda said with deference: "Will you come back to Dungesey with us, my lord, to feast and dry out?" She contrasted the ugliness of her island with what Father Alors had told her of the glories of Ramsey.

"Exceedingly kind, but I must be getting back if you don't mind. I've got a lot of praying to do, you see, and I need to be alone a lot. Brother Daniel understands that and sees I get a lot of time to be alone in."

"But you'll freeze."

"Actually I don't think so." Politely he held out his drooping skirts. "This is good English wool and wool is a material which retains warmth though wet. Did you know?"

They did, in the unspecified way they knew all their science.

"Well, goodbye." He nodded at all of them, Pampi and son included, tucked his habit into his belt revealing thin, white, muscular legs and jogged off along Monks' Bank, elbows and knees pumping in co-ordination. He looked ridiculous.

They were some way downstream before Matilda spoke. "Is he the abbot? Or is he mad?"

Percy of Alleyn considered. "Both I should think."

"Blast," said Matilda, "I forgot to complain about the bank." She had a happy thought. "I'll have to see him again."

She had never been a romantic but now she found herself hoping the abbot hadn't noticed her pregnancy: she wanted him to think her pure. Quite likely the man was a saint in the making; only saints cared for animals and the working-classes.

As time went on she wove a fantasy in which the abbot did

indeed become a saint and Matilda his friend in an intimate –
but chaste – tenderness, benefactress to his causes, his con-
fidante. There would be a touching scene in which the abbot
declared: "Matilda, you have been my inspiration but the
love I feel for you has become a passion against which I can
fight no longer. Yet I cannot turn from God. We must meet
no more." He would retire to an abbey and Matilda to a
comfortable, well-endowed nunnery but he would know and
she would know . . .

It was a nice fantasy and Matilda enjoyed it. She took it out
on the Fens with her, cutting down her escort so that if she
met him again they could have a tête-à-tête.

So with Pampi, one lady and a man-at-arms she explored
her land, sailing along rivers that were sometimes as grey as
the heron, sometimes as brown as the cattle, sometimes as
bright and jolly blue as the sky.

She was constantly surprised at the variety offered by so
flat a land. The mist above the water in the evening differed
in quality and colour from that lying above it at dawn. It was
never lonely because birds were everywhere and the main
rivers were full of traffic and English voices exchanging news
as their barges passed.

She looked for the conch-shell blower she had heard on the
night of her resurrection from boredom. Steward Peter said
it was a bittern. But it eluded her by its trick of standing in
the reeds with its neck, head and beak making a vertical line
in a clump of vertical lines.

A week after meeting the abbot she woke up feeling tired.
"I told you," Berte said. "Well, you're not going today."

She and the others had been due to attend the Fen version
of a duck hunt. A huge net funnel was to be spread over a
stream and thousands of duck driven into it. It was not to be
missed, apparently. The abbot might be there.

"The others may go and take young Pampi. Old Pampi
stands by here in case I want to join them later."

"You won't."

By midday she felt better, or well enough to defy Berte.
"It's not far and I won't be long."

It was a good clear day. As usual Pampi and Matilda did

not exchange a word. He was too sulky at the time she was taking up to talk to her, even if he could. Matilda suspected she already knew more English than he did French.

They floated up the Swallen, turned right into the Nene and then left into a small tributary called the Fleam, so narrow that branches brushed Pampi's face. They could hear the call of the decoys tempting the wild duck to perdition. Matilda realised the vague ache she had felt all day had localised in her back and was getting worse. It became shocking.

She held on to the side of the punt, her eyes wide, breathing hard. The duck calls were a distraction, like flies. There came a moment of such agony that the previous pain seemed nothing at all. It passed then another came. She was giving birth prematurely. The baby would be born in this boat and die. They would both die.

"Mary, Mother of God, help me." She screamed at Pampi. "Help me." He poled on as he had done for days. He did not understand what was happening to her because, as with the child in the hut, she was outside his scheme of things. Had she been a doe or a cow, a woman of his own kind, he would have known what to do. But she was not animal nor human, she was a lord. He would not be surprised if she spontaneously exploded.

She was exploding. Somewhere ducks were laughing. Pampi kept on watching and poling. Delicately the Devil took the bottom of Matilda's spine in his talons and tore it apart and up, like a wishbone. "Help me."

There were two Matildas now, a blind one that screamed and retched, and one inside the water's surface which had enfolded her in a tunnel of lights and reflections. Beyond and around the tunnel was mass threatening to crush her. It came inwards, contracting the tunnel and forcing her downwards. Out of the blind Matilda's lungs came an involuntary huff, a cross between a moan and a belch, universal to mammals in labour.

It brought movement in the boat and around the poor, suffering outside Matilda carryings, unfoldings, croonings in a strange language. But the inner Matilda had lost interest.

Lights in her tunnel flickered and she slipped down towards one that was constant. A contraction that rasped the outer Matilda pushed the inner one to the light's edge.

She was looking out on the Fens, but the Fens as she had never seen them and as no adult ever would see them because she was staring at them through unused eyes. It was spring and the river was laid into the turf like marquetry. A warm breeze twisted the willows so that the underside of their leaves showed white. She could smell catkins and small, pale daffodils.

She was to hold on to the memory of it as "my vision", though it contained none of the gaudy colours depicting the saints' revelations on church walls. This landscape was of varying greens and without figures.

Leaves uncrumpled from the bud in a raw freshness. Sunlight slipped down spiders' webs, but of the spiders, birds, butterflies and animals there was no sign, although they were there, hiding with God in the arcades of vegetation. The place piped with joy. Trees whispered to one another: "Any moment now"; among the water-lily roots fish and eel-gods opened their mouths to expel bubbles which formed the sounds: "Any moment now".

The outer Matilda's final contraction translated into the inner Matilda's grief that the landscape was not for her. She delivered her child into it and went away.

"She's where?" shrieked Berte.

"It was the nearest hut to the hythe." Steward Peter was apologetic. "He couldn't carry them far."

Not usually a lissom mover Berte crossed the green in unnoticed strides. She barged her way into Pampi's hut at the top of the slipway to the Washes. "Where is she? Where is it?" She teetered, unable to decide priorities. Her first love held and she homed to a pile of skins on which lay a flat, still Matilda.

Berte felt her forehead and stomach and lifted her skirts to make sure she wasn't haemorrhaging. She wasn't. Berte whirled round.

By the central fire lay a wicker tray on which a lump of

dough was rising. Implanted into it, like a big sultana, was a
naked baby boy curled up and asleep, still soapy and streaked
with mucus. Berte's thick finger rested on the white plastic
surface of the dough and then on the tinted flesh of the child.
Both were warm. The tiny, blunt nose breathed easily. The
cord had been cleanly cut and tied with fishing line.

Berte moaned, but mainly with frustration that none of the
rituals had been observed. Father Alors had gone to the duck
hunt. Berte tried to remember the emergency baptism and
dipped her fingers into the cauldron over the fire and crossed
the baby's forehead. *"Ego te baptizo,"* she said awkwardly,
"in nomine Patris, Filii et Spirituus Sancti."

When they were alone Pampi said to Wilberta: "Wonderful
to me they have babies like anyone else, gal. Make as big a
fuss and all."

"That was a hard birth, bor." In all the time it had been in
her hut Wilberta had not looked directly at the baby. Fenwomen tended their children for the first year but did not
name nor show them love. Affection for a child which was as
likely to die as to live was poor investment.

Pampi, however, having delivered the child himself felt he
was attached to it as surely as if the fishing line round its
navel was tied to his. "That'll be a lord and a half," he said.
"Proper little slodger. Proper little Fen slodger of a lord."

Wilberta grunted and picked up the dough on which the
baby had lain, wiped it with her sleeve and took it to the
communal bakery at Shudda's to bake for supper.

When Matilda woke up it was in her own chamber to hear
Berte rapping out commands. "You will live here and eat
what I tell you . . .." Underneath her staccato Steward Peter
was droning English translation.

At the end of Matilda's bed was a large and beautiful
woman with Matilda's baby suckling at one breast. Like an
Iceni queen she was tall with red-gold hair, her skin was
freckled and creamy. She threw out a calm so soporific she
seemed to exude oil on troubled airwaves. Her blue eyes
looked incuriously at Matilda and slowly lowered white
eyelids and lashes in the longest blink Matilda had ever seen.

"It's a boy." Berte dashed to the bedside. "Lusty and suckling like a piglet. That there's a wet nurse. It's a Wealy, the best I could do at short notice. But it's healthy and has plenty of milk. Just had one itself." She bustled away and dragged the Wealy woman's gown away from her other breast for Matilda's inspection. "See."

Now bare to the waist the Celtic woman lit up the chamber like a pollen-dusted lily. Steward Peter, being susceptible to Wealy beauty, banged his head against the wall. Berte squeezed an engorged coral-coloured nipple to produce a squirt of milk. "See."

It was the fashion among some high-born women to feed their own babies to avoid the pollution of low-bred milk, but Berte and Matilda had agreed this to be unnatural.

Matilda looked at her son, his skin and hair almost dark against the wet nurse's flesh. His chin rose and fell as he sucked and his tiny hand moved against the breast.

A terrifying emotion rampaged through Matilda. She did not want to touch the child and felt no jealousy; what she wanted was for him always to be protected, as safe and contented as he was now. She could kill for that. Along with that ferocity was something else, a weightiness as if she'd been threaded like a bead on to an infinite necklace.

"What happened to her baby?"

Steward Peter said: "It died."

"There was a child in one of the huts some weeks ago with a bandaged foot. What happened to it?"

"It was Ulsi's boy," said Steward Peter. "The wound turned putrid. It died."

Had the wet nurse's child or Ulsi's child stood in the way of her own son she would have mown them down, but they had been beads on the same necklace and she would rather, very much rather, that they had not been taken off. The chanciness of keeping a child breathing in and out brought menace into the room.

"Send for Sigward," she said.

The message for Sigward arrived while he feasted at the king's table at Winchester. He was already merry and sweating with the food and drink he'd had. As he hauled himself

67

on to the tabletop to shout the news of his son's birth to the company his face became purple.

"Lord, Lord," he screamed and whether he meant the king or God they never knew because as he said it his hands clutched at his upper arms and he fell down to die among the debris of food he'd loved too much.

4

Reckoning that he had a claim of some substance on it, Count Geoffrey of Anjou now invaded Normandy. He had, after all, married the Empress Matilda who was the true heir to it.

And this was where Stephen made his second mistake. Bedevilled by proliferating rebellion in England, he left the Normans to oppose the Angevin invasion by themselves. The Normans were in disarray and in Count Geoffrey they were facing a brilliant strategist.

They fought him – all good Normans loathed an Angevin – but gradually they were forced further and further back.

Which left the Anglo-Norman barons owning vast estates on both sides of the Channel in a difficult position. If they fought Geoffrey and were beaten by him they lost their Normandy estates. If they treated with Geoffrey, Stephen would hear of it and they would lose their English estates. It was not a situation that appealed to them.

Of course, if the Empress left her husband to win Normandy and invaded England on her own behalf there might be possibilities in treating with both of them . . .

Roger, Bishop of Salisbury, was a venal old man, an immensely rich and powerful old man, once Henry's viceroy of England and now Stephen's, but at the moment he was an old man with the wheezes. He sat in his beautiful apartment at his castle of Devizes wrapped in ermine and with his green-veined feet in a silver bowl of mustard-water. A high, musical fluting came from his lungs every time he took breath and mingled with the hiss of apple logs in the wall fireplace and the snoring of the hounds stretched before it.

Matilda of Risle irrupted into the room bringing with her noise, a dog, two ladies-in-waiting, a child and its wet nurse and a draught.

"My lord uncle," she shouted, "I am to be married again."

The bishop put one hand over his eye as if she'd shot him in it, the other extended so that she could kiss it. "Daughter in God," he said, "you are welcobe." It was a courteous, catarrhal lie. She wasn't in the least welcome. He had kept her waiting to see him all day in the hope that she'd go away.

The richness of the chamber reminded Matilda of the old man's power and she moderated her voice. "My lord uncle" – she stressed the relationship although it was distant – "I am to be married again."

"I congratulate you."

"No, you don't." She brought herself again under control. "My lord, I purchased your goodwill to persuade the king to let me remain in my widowed state. I understood through Osmund" – she nodded virulently to a clerk who was writing away at a desk in the corner – "that the gift of my manor of Tatton would not be displeasing to your lordship and that in exchange you would make the king agree that I marry only when and whom I pleased."

"And didn't I?"

"It doesn't look like it, does it?" howled Matilda. "I'm to be married at Lammas, to some novice monk. His father's a protégé of the Beaumonts."

"Ah." In the whistled exhalation of breath was Bishop Roger's defeat and Matilda's, but she didn't hear it.

Waleran of Meulan, her own second cousin, had betrayed her. When the king had summoned her to Westminster and told her that she, who was in his wardship as one of his tenants-in-chief, must marry again she had tracked Waleran down and demanded an explanation.

Untouchable and handsome Waleran had said: "Cousin, allow me to know your best interest." Her best interest, it appeared, lay with Vincent, son of Serlo de Luard, who had deserved advancement at Waleran's hands. Matilda and her lands were that advancement.

"But the land belongs to my lord." Now that Sigward

was dead her lord was a small, sucking baby nestling in the freckled arms of Epona, the Wealy woman.

"All the more reason why it should be protected by a stepfather during its minority." He had smiled kindly and in that smile she had seen herself as the Beaumonts saw her, something with no more significance than a skittle in the path of the golden, unstoppable globe that was the will of Waleran of Meulan and his twin.

She had fought and threatened, but she had been frightened. Her last words: "I shall go to Bishop Roger," had sounded in her own ears like a child's: "I'll tell my father of you." Waleran had laughed.

But she had been comforted on her arrival at Devizes by the solidity, newness and grandeur of the bishop's castle. Roger was still viceroy of England as he had been for as long as anyone could remember. The country was enmeshed in the network of his spies.

Beyond the castle it was spring, but in the bishop's chamber it was autumn. It smelled of ink, old men, dogs and wintergreen. Light came in through thin, red linen covering the windows and turned the gilding on the beams and the candlelight to red-gold. The corbels on the ceiling were carved likenesses of the bishop's fellow-administrators and their distorted, careworn features reproduced the living face of the man underneath. Henry of England had driven his servants hard.

Bishop Roger wiped his dribbling nose on his ermine sleeve. "Why do you oppose this marriage?"

She was amazed. She thought the reasons would be self-evident. This particular marriage would enhance neither her lands nor her prestige. She had achieved that rare period in a noblewoman's life of holding power and she didn't want to relinquish it. Women were perpetual minors, subject first to their fathers, then their husbands and, if they survived so long, to their sons. But she, as a widow with a small son, could look forward to a dozen or more years in which she could rule their estates herself.

Besides, she had not found sex so wonderful that she wanted any more of it.

71

She plucked a reason at random: "I don't want another baby."

The bishop said mechanically: "It was given only to the Virgin to give birth without pain since she alone conceived without pleasure."

"Well, she conceived through her ear." She'd always thought that vulgar of Mary: weasels conceived through their ears. It was irritating, too, the way men always assumed women found pleasure in copulation. "Anyway, this Vincent person has no lands to speak of."

"He is of good birth," said the bishop calmly, "and if his father is a protégé of Waleran's he is patronised by a powerful man. Anyone who can steal the Primacy of Canterbury from under Henry of Blois' nose and give it to his own creature must be powerful indeed." The bishop's lips twitched slightly.

It was still a cause célèbre. Everyone had assumed that when the archbishop died, Canterbury would go to Bishop Henry who had played so large a part in obtaining the throne for his brother. Certainly Henry of Blois had thought so. But one day when he was away from Westminster there had been a rushed but legal election in the king's presence and Henry of Blois had returned to find that the new archbishop was an unknown, Theobald of Bec – a friend of Waleran of Meulan.

It had been an amazing and dirty trick but those who did not like Henry of Blois had seen its comic side.

"He's not more powerful than you, my lord." Matilda was becoming frightened again. "My lord, you can do anything."

"After all" – the bishop raised his shoulders to get some air into his concave chest – "it is no disgrace to rise from humble beginnings." He himself had been a humble priest at Avranches who had first impressed King Henry by his ability to say mass quicker than anyone else.

"Do you stop this marriage?" Matilda rose and her dog, Fen, rose beside her and snarled. "Do I take back Tatton or not?"

The door of the chamber flung open and another angry woman, Maud of Ramsbury, came in followed by the king's messenger. "I can tell you this much," said Maud, "he's not bloody going."

Stephen's messenger was elegant and well-born. He looked round the beautiful room as if he had one like it at home. Matilda had not considered the bishop's bare feet in their bowl to be ridiculous until this young man looked at them. Maud of Ramsbury also followed his eyes and shifted the bowl so that it slopped, jerking the bishop's feet into her lap and towelling them on her gown.

The message had as little respect as its bearer. "Stephen the King to his Bishop of Salisbury, greetings. We command that you, with Nigel, Bishop of Ely, Alexander, Bishop of Lincoln, and Roger the Chancellor attend us in council in three days at Oxford." The messenger went out. That was it.

Only Roger's breathing could be heard going faster. "Did we have intelligence of this council?"

Osmund came from behind his desk. "No, my lord. And I don't like it. Perhaps the king is beginning to listen to the Beaumonts' accusations that you and your family are planning to support the Empress' claim."

"How can he say that?" Maud was rubbing the bishop's feet until they were pink and shouting at Osmund as if he and not the Beaumonts had spread the rumour. "Didn't the bishop do more to help Stephen to the throne than that bloody Waleran did?"

The bishop looked up at the anxious wooden faces on his ceiling. "Henry won't forgive, even from the grave, that I betrayed his daughter. But how could we have a woman on the throne? Worse still, a woman under the influence of Anjou?"

Maud sulked. "He's not bloody going."

Everything about Maud of Ramsbury was coarse, from her big feet to her waist to her thick, grey hair worn loose like a maiden which, though she was unmarried, she assuredly was not. Matilda had always been surprised the bishop tolerated her. The mistresses of most great churchmen were beautiful, retiring and discreet. Maud was none of these things. Nobody had dislodged her from her position in

73

Roger's household partly because the old king had liked her, as he'd liked all unpretentious people, and partly because the bishop never gainsaid her. When she interrupted his councils and swore in his company he would stare into the middle distance, humming slightly. Now, in any case, she had outlived social disapproval and become an institution. "Old Maud." The present chancellor, Roger the Poor, was her son by the bishop and there was a strong suspicion that Nigel and Alexander, the Bishops of Ely and Lincoln, known as "nephews", were also their bastards.

It was a peculiarity of their relationship that the bishop and Maud never directly spoke to each other in company, addressing their remarks to one another through a third party. Roger's hand went to rest on Maud's shoulder but his words were to Osmund. "I am disinclined for this journey, though I shall have to make it. I shall be about as fit at court as a colt in battle."

Maud's hands closed about the old man's ankles and her head dropped to his knees. Then she stood up and snarled at Osmund: "He goes with an armed escort and his woolly underclothes or he doesn't go at all."

In all this time Matilda had been standing, comprehending events only as they affected her. As the bishop with Maud supporting him went past she stepped forward: "Since you are to see the king, my lord, you can raise the subject of my marriage. *Then* you can have Tatton."

His rheumy eyes regarded her with amazement that she could still believe in his power. He nodded.

The castle was fully garrisoned so Matilda and her ladies, baby and dog had to sleep in a guest room which was no more than a wedge in an upper floor of the tower, while the men of her household squeezed into barracks and hall bays. The overcrowding was offset for the ladies by the two-seater garderobe in the outer wall. A warm, polished, wooden seat with two holes overlaid a drop to a gutter thirty feet below. There were exclamations of delight at the convenience but Matilda, though she filed away the idea for future reference, could not be diverted from her anxiety.

She lay awake while the others slept, nursing it. She did

not want to marry again. She did *not* want to marry again. Only now when she was faced with another wedding did she realise how nerve-wracking had been the first in a new country with strange people and experiences. She had been lucky with Sigward – now he was dead she invested him with all the virtues – but she didn't want to go through it all again. Having one baby had nearly killed her; another might finish the job. Alice of Vendôme had been given five husbands and died giving birth to her sixth child.

"They want to kill me," she said out loud. "If one husband doesn't do it they'll give me another who will."

The sound of her voice brought a pattering on the floor and the bitch Fen jumped up on the bed with her. She was not a demonstrative dog but she was always there when she was needed. Ghislaine, next to Matilda, shifted and complained but Matilda allowed the dog to stay.

Just before she'd left Dungesey Pampi had asked for an audience. He'd been ushered into the hall muttering sentences in a voice so truculent that Matilda, still tired from the birth and shocked by Sigward's death, had snapped: "What's he complaining of now?"

Steward Peter had explained. "He's not complaining. He's trying to say, if you'll forgive the impertinence, that he's pleased with you and offers you the gift of this dog."

"*He's* pleased with *me*?" But she had been gracious and accepted the unedifying animal. Her lymerer had been appalled and refused to accept it into the kennels. Adeliza had been afraid of it and Ghislaine had drawled: "Not something to enhance the prestige, my dear."

Fen's face with the frill of her inner lip hanging out of her grinning mouth was indeed a shock, as were her large ears, her long body and almost hairless legs and tail. But Matilda's confidence in her own prestige could not be altered by a dog. Besides, Fen had a ridiculous idea of her own prestige. She hated the lymerer back, she ignored the ladies and extended only to Matilda a respect which Matilda found disarming. When it came to hunting the bitch was mustard. Even the lymerer said he'd never encountered her equal over wet ground for speed and nerve, let alone ferocity.

75

She was also prepared to kill in Matilda's defence. On their first day back in Hatfelde a page, who was being chased by another in fun, had not looked where he was going and crashed into Matilda. Fen, misinterpreting the accident as assault, had leaped straight for his throat. That she had missed the jugular had only been because the page was looking behind him. As it was she took a large chunk from the area where neck meets shoulder.

After that Matilda took her everywhere. At nights she lay across the bedchamber door, despite Ghislaine's objection to her farts and fleas.

Comforted by her dog, Matilda now fell asleep and woke to find that the bishop and his entourage had just left for Oxford. Annoyed that she'd missed him, she went up to the keep roof where Maud of Ramsbury was watching the long procession of men, horses and wagons taking the road north. Matilda joined her in the crenel. "Will he remember to stop my marriage?"

Maud ignored her.

Up here it was impossible not to feel in command of the Salisbury Plain, the giants that strode it, even life itself. From up here one could see the order of things. Foreshortened humans below made patterns of efficiency as they scurried about their work. The penned sheep waiting to be sheared were neat, white squares against the green. The wind brought their bleating in pleasant tenor and baritone.

"See that crow following them?" Maud pointed at a speck flapping northwards. "Saints preserve the poor little devil. I don't like it."

"He'll remember to stop my marriage, won't he?"

"Look, my lady." Maud turned wearily towards her. "He's held England together for over thirty years and now he's going to face stoats who are jealous of him because they can't. He has bad dreams, he's poorly and bad luck is following him. Your marriage is the least of his problems."

"It's not the least of mine," said Matilda, sulking. "Do you mean he can't stop it?"

Maud hammered her fists on the crenel parapet. A man-at-arms who was doing sentry duty round the allure stopped

76

and asked if she was all right. "Piss off," she told him. She took Matilda's arm and sat her down so that they perched with their backs to the ninety-foot drop. "My duck, I don't know what's going to happen but it will be bad. We'll have to suffer it like women always do."

Matilda shifted. She could smell Maud's flesh and the pennyroyal on her clothes. She did not care to be bracketed with what was, bishop or no bishop, a fallen woman. Maud pulled her closer. "A word to the wise," she hissed. "If I were you I'd put that lad of yours somewhere safe. Serlo of Luard's not a bad man but he wants what he wants, and if you marry his son he'll want an heir of his own blood. Your babby'll be in the way." She patted Matilda's clenched jaw and stood up. "I'm not saying anything, but I know men. If the times are good, they're good. If times are bad they're as trustworthy as the Devil's arse."

Having eased her own worry by adding to someone else's, she lumbered off.

The man-at-arms was alone on the roof with a tall, dark-haired young woman who seemed to observe his every move as if determined to report any sign of slackness to his constable. He wished she'd go away: he wanted a sitdown.

Matilda had no idea she was watching him, had no idea Maud had gone. She'd known really. The old trollop had only put into words the fear that had been over her like a miasma since she'd been told she must marry. Though she knew Edmund was asleep and well only a couple of floors beneath her feet she suddenly wanted him here, under her eye.

Serlo would not kill the child: he'd be too afraid of God and public opinion for that, but it was in his own son's interest that it did not prosper. He could stack the chances against its survival.

Matilda stared into a future in which young Edmund struggled to keep breathing in the charge of a careless nurse, against too-strict discipline and punishment, through over-enthusiastic military training, on a vicious horse, in a battle for which he was too young.

Impotent with terror, she called on the one person she knew who had suffered through a son. She cricked her neck back so she could see the clouds. "You've got to listen. Blessed Mother, everything else I've wanted is nothing. I'll never ask you for anything again. You shall have Dungesey Church, you shall have two churches. If you can't stop this marriage, accept it as a sacrifice. But show me how to keep my son safe."

A minute tangle of wings launched itself off a pot of marigolds in the roof's herbary and landed on Matilda's hand. She felt the fringe of its legs tickle her skin and watched it crawl off the back of her fingers on to the stone as fixedly as she'd watched the man-at-arms and with no more attention.

She stood up and gazed over the landscape, waiting for her answer. There was a raincloud slanting its way west, but there was no Marian significance in a shower, nor in the rooks which infested the elms along the road like fleas. Mary might answer her in a pigeon; pigeons were Mary's birds, so were doves, so were . . . the Mary beetle.

She jumped back and went on to her knees searching the face of the stone for the ladybird. It was typically humorous of Mary to send a portent in so minuscule a creature. Then she spotted it, like a dot of red wax paddling determinedly downwards. "What should I do? Escape? Fly to the Empress? But that will mean losing the English lands."

As the ladybird progressed down the wall so did Matilda's nose following it. The man-at-arms wondered if he ought to call Maud.

Growing from a crack between the stones and flags of the allure was a bunch of red valerian. Matilda's nose wrinkled at the smell of it. The ladybird crawled up a stem, on to one of the leaves and stopped.

"Well?" demanded Matilda. The ladybird opened and shut its wings and stayed where it was. Matilda slanted her head and gently pushed the leaf upwards until she could see underneath a cluster of tiny, yellow, skittle-shaped things.

Her memory evoked Berte's voice teaching herbal lore in the walled garden of Risle. "No, we'll let those be. They're Mary beetle eggs and the Mary beetle helps good gardeners."

78

She let the leaf fall back and the black circles on the lady-bird's back stared up at her like eyes. "I see," she said slowly. "Blast."

At Oxford Stephen laid a trap which was to become his speciality. He received his viceroy, his chancellor and the Bishops of Ely and Lincoln with honour, and then arrested them.

Bishop Nigel of Ely managed to escape. He hoisted up his robes, nipped through a window and got away on a horse.

But Bishop Roger of Salisbury and his other two sons were caught by surprise. Even as the chains were loaded on them they could not believe that this was happening, to them who had ruled England for the throne for so long. They *knew* England. Until now Bishop Roger's spy network had informed him who was plotting what even before the plotters themselves had known it.

The king's brother, Henry of Blois, fighting down his own resentment at having been passed over for the Primacy of Canterbury, intervened for them. "Stephen. My dear. You are breaking the vow you made at your coronation to us bishops to uphold the Church in all things. And you have broken the laws of hospitality. The old king, God knows, lost his temper, but he never lifted a finger against a guest in his palace. You've proved yourself untrustworthy."

It was a terrible charge. The laws of Christ had a certain variability, but the laws of hospitality were rigid.

But even as he spoke Waleran of Meulan, smiling, whispered in the king's ear, and Bishop Roger and his chancellor son saw who would be running England in their place and who, with the king, would benefit from the castles they had built and the treasure that was in them.

And Henry of Blois, Bishop of Winchester, saw that England was no longer safe in his brother's hands and left his brother's court for his own palace at Winchester and sent a messenger to the Empress Matilda in Normandy.

A week later Willem of Ghent and his arbalists arrived at Devizes Castle where their commander was still supervising the transfer of its gold and silver to the king's treasury.

"God Almighty," said Jacopo when he saw the dimensions of the walls. "A bishop built it? Some bishop. How did the king get it to surrender?"

"Maud of Ramsbury surrendered it," said Ypres shortly, "when we threatened to hang her son. Willem, I want a word with you."

They went to the great autumn chamber where, nine days before, Matilda de Risle had pleaded with Bishop Roger to save her from remarriage.

His commander poured Willem a cup of wine. "How's the West Country?"

Willem sat down straight on a stool; his back was no longer in spasm but had reverted to its everyday ache. "A dyke," he said, "with holes in it. Why did you recall us?"

Ypres was striding around the room, touching its hangings and its carvings to assure himself of their quality. "The whole country's springing leaks. Bigod in East Anglia. King David in Scotland. Lesser men everywhere. And they call us mercenaries."

Willem became uneasy at the evasion of his question. Ypres lifted the top off a porcelain pot and sniffed its contents. "There's been a Lateran Council edict. Innocent II has banned the crossbow."

"Eh?" For a moment he thought the Pope was criticising the crossbow's weakness in being able to let off only three quarrels a minute.

Ypres quoted: "'The deadly art of crossbowmen, hated of God, should not be used against Christians on pain of anathema.'"

Bloody amateur, thought Willem. "Why?"

"Because of the way it kills, I suppose . . ."

"Efficiently?"

". . . it reminds people of St. Sebastian."

"St. Sebastian didn't die by the crossbow. He didn't die by arrows at all. And if he did? Are they going to ban all archers? Who's to stop a cavalry charge?" Now he knew why he'd been recalled. "Good King Stephen's not renewing his contract with us, is that it? Well, that's all right by me." His arm sent a flagon on to its side. He didn't notice. "There's others

80

won't be so squeamish, I can tell you. My men can fetch their own price anywhere . . ."

Ypres closed his eyes. "Willem, Willem, I never suspected this naughty temper of you. Sit down. Sit *down*. Now then, the king is not renewing your contract. Sit down, will you? Look at it from his side. He daren't offend the Pope any more. He needs his good opinion and God's." He looked around and lowered his voice. "The trouble with righteousness in war as you and I know, Willem, is that it isn't effective. If he'd hanged those buggers at Exeter we shouldn't be knee-deep in rebels like we are. Now then, the king may not be renewing your contract, but I am."

He dipped a finger in the spilt wine and drew on the polished tabletop. "If insurrection continues we'll need castles to contain it. We'll need them in East Anglia around the Fens. I've consulted with Stephen and he agrees; we want you to build them."

"I'm not a builder."

"No, Willem, you're an arbalist and the Pope doesn't love you. Damn it, I'm not asking for this" – his arms indicated Devizes – "I want these." Little phalluses were drawn in the wine. "You've kept your men alive and together for two years. You're a good organiser."

Willem thought. "I can't see my band in the Fens."

"Neither can I. You go alone. With Fenchel. And the king's warrant."

"I'm not disbanding." His men were his only asset, his sons, a beautiful machine. The Pope could say they were abhorrent to God till he was black in the face but Willem knew God found acceptable a thing as perfect as his band of crossbowmen.

"I know," said Ypres gently. "I'll keep them together. I'll wipe their noses and tuck them up at nights. It won't be for long. Even the Pope can't uninvent you. Let Stephen make his gesture; in a year, maybe less, he'll need you again. Give him his righteous time."

On a July morning Matilda kissed her son goodbye and handed him over to Epona, the Wealy woman. The

81

procession of carts and horses set off down Hatfelde Hill and turned north. It was before dawn. Only Matilda saw them off and only Matilda knew where they were going. Percy of Alleyn was to see it to its destination and then return.

A small but complete household was going and would stay with Edmund with Berte and Father Alors in charge of it. Father Alors hadn't wanted to go. He had taken a dislike to the Fens. "Unhealthy for the child's body and soul," he'd said, "a godless place."

"How come there are so many abbeys there, then?" Matilda had snapped. "And anyway, the Blessed Mother told me to put him there." She could think of no more leafy, secret hiding-place which fitted the Virgin's portent than her morning gift of Dungesey. Father Alors had given in; he couldn't argue with the Virgin Mary.

"And anyway," thought Matilda miserably as she watched them go, "it's a damned sight healthier than the household of Serlo de Luard will be."

Robert, Earl of Gloucester, finally made up his mind. He sent a formal renunciation of his fealty to Stephen and joined his half-sister, the Empress, in Normandy. Now she could invade any day.

In a windowless chamber in the tower he had built for himself in the blackest of the Black Fens, Brother Daniel, former glassblower, former witch's son, and now the power behind the throne at Ramsey Abbey, was consulting demons on the question which exercised everybody else in England.

On a table in the chamber a circle of glass had been set in sand and a boy was looking into it. The smoke which curled about the boy's ragged head smelled of hemp. The cowled figure of the monk leaned forward to kiss the boy's neck and run his hand down the child's knobbly spine to his buttocks and up again. "Scry for me," he said softly.

Because the boy was stupid the monk had reduced his question to essentials and made two crude drawings in the sand. Both were human figures with crowns on their heads.

One had large breasts and a cleft between its legs, the other had male genitals.

"Who'll win? The lady? The lord? Empress? King? Scry."

The demons entered the boy. His rolling eyes became fixed and saliva bubbled down his chin. His hand trembled and the monk took it to his own breast and then held it over the shapes in the sand.

"Who'll win? Her? Him?"

Her-him, coughed back the walls bronchially.

The demons took the boy's soul down his arm into his hand so that its black-nailed fingers clenched and stretched and the vein to the wrist throbbed blue. It became a raptor's talon. It hovered then stopped and the forefinger stabbed a deep navel into the figure of the man. "Him."

5

1139–1140
For the second time in her life Matilda de Risle was married at Hatfelde. Everybody at the feast table was tipsy, except Matilda who was not a winebibber at the best of times. And this, in her opinion, was not even a good time.

With her wedding wreath jammed firmly on her head and a look of disapproval she kept herself aloof. Especially from her husband. She didn't like him much. From the loftiness of her nineteen years he seemed a child, undersized, pustulated and tremulous. He wasn't healthy. His shoulders were hunched, he gasped and had a blue look to his lips. There was nothing wrong with his appetite, however; he stuffed down a sample of everything with the gusto of one who has lived too long on convent meals.

"You don't talk to your bridegroom, my lady." Waleran nudged her. "Do you keep your sweetness for the honeyed moments to come?"

"Honeyed moments," muttered Matilda with venom. She jerked her head round to the boy and barked: "You didn't take your final vows then?"

Some chewed pork fell out of the boy's mouth and he blushed. "No, no." He leaned towards Matilda yet kept his face mercifully away, as if speaking to a woman was disobedience. "My lord abbot said God had preserved me for duty elsewhere. He said I could enhance the abbey more by marriage than by chastity."

"Not with my lands, you can't," thought Matilda.

Vincent's prominent Adam's apple bobbed. "Shall I read you the Song of Solomon tonight?"

"Eh?"

84

"You know . . . tonight . . . my lord abbot says it's preparation for . . . you know . . . the marriage bed."

"Yuck." She was nauseated by this youth and his steamy old abbot for whom the highest eroticism was dirty bits from the Bible.

A strong voice behind them said: "Vincent, it's time to pay your respects to the company."

"Yes, father." Vincent rose obediently and Serlo of Luard took his place. Under other circumstances Matilda might have liked Serlo, as she liked men of power as long as they didn't threaten her own. He was short, strong, dark-haired and had intelligent, acquisitive brown eyes. But he *did* threaten her because his control over his son, and therefore Matilda and Matilda's estates, was absolute. There was an uncomfortable sexual frisson to him as he insisted on using "we" when he referred to his son. It was as if she'd married them both.

"My only regret on this happy occasion, my lady," he was saying, "is that our little stepson cannot be here with us. Where is he?"

She'd always known she'd have to tell him where. She crossed her fingers and made her eyes anxious. "He is sickly, my lord, and the doctors advise against travel. He is at my manor in the Fens. Not much of a place, I fear, but there is a wise woman there in whom I have faith. She feeds him poppy juice when the pain gets too bad."

And she knew she was right about Serlo. He relaxed immediately, one of the cares on his busy mind eased. He would not hurt the child: neither would he protect it. If Matilda was fool enough to put her ailing son into what all right-thinking men knew to be a noxious quagmire in the care of some crone, Serlo of Luard wouldn't deliver him from it.

His face showed sympathy that was not all feigned. "God save him, madam. You and I know what it is to have ailing children." Two wives had given Serlo five sons of whom Vincent was the only survivor.

"But tonight," he said, "we'll make more and stronger. With you, my lady, we shall begin a line to shake the world."

85

"My line," retaliated Matilda with dignity, "has already shaken it."

She and Vincent were taken off separately, undressed with giggles and attired for the night before being popped into the bed of the bridal chamber and the covers pulled up to their necks so that their nightcapped heads stuck out like a pair of lollipops. The boy's cold, bony foot touched Matilda's leg and she jerked it away.

The men swayed, hiccuping the old, old jokes and staring at them with the jovial hostility of wedding guests everywhere. Serlo's eyes took away Matilda's personality, turning her into a mere receptacle for his son's semen. To him the bed was a forge on which to found a lineage.

"Smile, cousin," said Waleran of Meulan. "Or can't you wait for us to go?"

Matilda stretched her lips. Her rebellion, her symbols of revolt against the lot of them, were tucked into the pillows and under the mattress. Before Berte had gone to the Fens she'd made up sachets of vervain to guard against Matilda conceiving. "That'll take the stiffness out of that young man's old man," she'd said. "We don't want no babies taking the place of our Edmund."

By God, they didn't. And by God, if Matilda had anything to do with it, there wouldn't be any.

Serlo stayed till last, glaring, as if he could impregnate her with his eyes. "Wield your sword well, my son," he said as he went. From behind the door came Waleran's voice: "Don't be afraid to hit below the belt." The door closed.

Vincent muttered some prayers and sat up to find himself regarded by two pairs of cold eyes, Matilda's and the dog Fen's. "Does she have to be here?"

"Yes."

"Shall I begin then?"

"I suppose so."

Serlo stayed outside the door of the chamber for a long time, not because he was salacious, but because he couldn't bear to leave the field of this vital ploughing. From inside came the sound of his last remaining son apparently reciting

86

in a high, breathless voice. He was *talking*, Mother of God; what was he talking for? If it had been himself in there with that fine young woman he wouldn't have been talking, by all Christ's saints. He cursed himself for having miscalculated and grabbed his latest wife, a very minor heiress, before his friendship with Waleran had entitled him to something better. If he'd waited it would have been him in there. As it was he was stuck with this Number Three who showed no signs either of dying or delivering him anything but daughters. "Take her, boy, take her."

Inside the chamber Vincent's voice rose with his excitement. ". . . thy belly is like an heap of wheat set about with lilies. Thy two breasts are like two young roes . . ." He looked up. "Can't you make her lie down?"

"Lie down, Fen."

He returned to the Song of Solomon, unable to believe that it could not be bringing Matilda to the same fever pitch.

Outside the door Serlo clenched his fists: "Take her."

At last his son's voice trailed away. There was silence, then snuffling, then the sharp, clear voice of his daughter-in-law. "Not there, you stupid boy. *There.*"

Just as it had been necessary to introduce Sigward to her Normandy estates so now a similar tour had to be made with Vincent. Serlo went too. Matilda was disconcerted by the presence of her father-in-law but not surprised. Vincent was merely a nuisance at nights. Serlo was the real lord of the marriage.

From the first he made it clear that while he would not interfere with the state she kept – her magnificence reflected on the Luards – she kept it by his permission. On the second day of the honeymoon he went through the accounts with her and her household steward.

"Sixpence a week for a saucer. That's what a man-at-arms gets in war. What's a saucer?"

"Someone who makes sauces." Matilda was bored. "A man-at-arms can't make sauces."

At each new estate there was a similar inquisition. He had

to know every tithe, every custom, every rent. At Pardieu the swords came out. "My lady, we should render to God material thanks for your marriage with my son."

"How material?" asked Matilda, suspiciously.

"We should give the hamlet of Bois-Barbot to the Abbey of Fécamp whose lands it adjoins."

"Bois-Barbot?" shrieked Matilda. "It produces the finest calvilles in Normandy." Suddenly the little grey, fennel-scented apples which were part of her childhood were the most precious things in the world. They must be safeguarded for Edmund.

Fécamp. Of course. The abbey that had reared Vincent. The abbot was to be paid for his favour in releasing the boy. "I should be failing in my duty to the young lord of this land if I let any of it go without profit to him."

"Indeed you would." Serlo was hearty. "His soul shall be prayed for every day by the Fécamp monks."

They quarrelled. At least, Matilda quarrelled: Serlo remained calm, reasonable and obdurate. He won that and every following argument.

Matilda panicked as she realised the only counter she had against him was guile, which was against her nature. But she was learning.

Her triumphs became dirty little victories achieved in the dark. However many battles with Serlo she lost, if she did not conceive she'd won the war. So far there was no chance of that. The boy got so het up with his reading of the Song of Solomon – Matilda nearly knew the damn thing by heart – that his orgasm came before he could penetrate her. Matilda put it down to the vervain, though her own cheerlessness in bed might have had something to do with it.

Serlo was avid to know if she was pregnant yet but couldn't ask right out. "I hope my son pleases you?" he'd say and Matilda would reply, "Why shouldn't he?" which got him nowhere.

She would dearly have liked to confide in someone but Berte was not there, Ghislaine and Flore had gone home to be married themselves, the ladies who replaced them were as yet unknown and Adeliza was too innocent. Besides, she did not know polite phraseology for premature ejaculation and felt that to describe it was beneath her dignity.

So she waged her secret war alone. After a while it became obvious to both her and Serlo that there was a term to it. The battlefield, Vincent, would not live long.

At first she thought his gasping was post-Solomon exhaustion. But one night he clasped his chest and she saw in the moonlight that his face was blue. She raised the castle – they were at Port Motte – and the infirmarian of the local priory was called. Vincent was thoroughly bled and given powdered St. John's wort mixed with raw eggs. He endured it with passivity but was obviously afraid. "Is it punishment for marrying?"

Serlo was sternly comforting. "It was your duty to God and your house."

The infirmarian took Matilda and Serlo to the other side of the chamber, carrying a pot of Vincent's urine in his hand. "I will not trouble you with medical terms. Put simply, his blood is too thick. I recommend the three great doctors, Dr. Purge, Dr. Diet and Dr. Rest." He was a jolly man.

"Will he recover?"

"No reason why not, no reason." The infirmarian remained jolly. "But he should avoid strenuous activity . . . and his chaplain should stand by at all times."

This was bad. They looked at the bed where the boy's newly shaved head stuck out at one end and his skinny feet at the other. His chaplain stood beside him reciting St. Anselm's prayer for When the Mind is Anxious with Fear. Vincent's purple lips shaped the words after him. For the first time Matilda saw him not as a husband who'd been foisted on her but as a bewildered, bullied human being.

She looked round at her father-in-law and saw there such panic and aggression that her pity faded and self-preservation took its place. Serlo knew, he had seen too many sons die not to know, that Vincent would die. The period until that death would be a race to perpetuate the Luards. Matilda's job would be to see the race was lost.

Serlo took the infirmarian's arm and led him away, muttering. Matilda knew he was asking whether the boy could safely continue marital relations. She saw the infirmarian shrug.

Vincent recovered; or, to be more exact, he did not die that time.

One beautiful autumn morning when the air was clear and chill over still-warm grass so that the scent of deer was beckoning to the hounds like an animate creature, and the bucks in the forested hills behind Harfleur were begging Matilda to come and kill them, she swept back into the manor and confronted Serlo. "You ordered my horse unsaddled. Why?"

"Hunting is dangerous for a lady in your condition."

"Condition?" Matilda's voice quivered the antlers on the walls. "I am in no condition."

Serlo had been brooding over a mug of wine. She saw he'd gone vicious, like a dog. "Then you should be." He flung the mug at her. It missed, spattering her with wine as it passed over her shoulder. "Too much activity in a female stops conception," shouted Serlo. "And anyway, why should you hunt when your husband cannot?" He looked up and said clearly: "It is a matter for complaint."

She picked up the mug and flung it back at him, also missing, then stamped back to her chamber. "A matter of complaint" was a warning. If the Luards could justify a charge that she was neglecting her wifely duties they could repudiate her. Stash her away, control her lands until Edmund was of age – by which time the lands would be stripped of all profit.

She felt again the panic when she'd thought she was barren during her marriage to Sigward. But this time not only would she suffer, so would the little boy growing up in the Fens. She was the only soldier in his army.

"Mother of God," she moaned, "you didn't have to fight off St. Joseph's advances to stop yourself getting pregnant again."

Then, with her hand on the latch of her chamber, Matilda paused. What about James the brother of Jesus? Dear, dear, had the Virgin not remained virgin? They didn't mention

90

that, these churchmen. She'd have to find out about it. Meanwhile . . .

She crashed into her chamber and her face could have ripped the bandage off a wound. She shouted: "I've come to minister to you, my lord."

In the unceasing war Matilda and Serlo waged over Vincent there were moments of truce in which they discussed like partners such intelligence as each gleaned about the political situation. For the Normandy they had both known was changing. In the areas they travelled it was outwardly peaceful, but it was a sickly peace such as had settled over England six hundred years before, when Rome withdrew her legions. There was the same feeling of approaching doom.

Serlo's intelligence came from other men. Now that Earl Robert of Gloucester had abandoned Stephen and gone over to his stepsister, he had given her control of Caen and Ouistreham, providing her with an embarcation port from which to invade England. It also gave her husband, Count Geoffrey, a spearhead in the north. From his position in the south he could use it to divide Normandy in half.

While the nobles were telling Serlo all this in the hall, their ladies in the solar with Matilda were imparting much more. They talked of "Which way up the wind's blowing", of secret journeys by trusted envoys to the Empress' camp, of quiet alliances and promises not to oppose Count Geoffrey if he let them keep their lands. Matilda didn't blame them. She too would treat with the Devil if it kept Edmund's estates for him.

"If I was blasted in charge," she thought, "I'd be doing the same. But Serlo won't. He's too loyal to the king and Waleran."

Vincent was not only repulsive to her now, he was horrible. The panting from his heaving chest seemed to dominate all sound. His uncut fingernails clawed at her at night and the blue lips swelled to become rolls of liver in her dreams. Worse, the boy was beginning to smell. He'd taken to wearing a hair-shirt which caused a weeping rash but which he refused to take off, just as he refused to wash.

Matilda, who regarded personal hygiene as the prerogative

of her class, bathed every Friday and used the resources of her immense household to keep her clothes scrupulous. Her hints, then pleas, then demands that Vincent wash were ignored.

The truth was the boy was in torture. Had he been left in his monastery he would have passed his life as an unremarkable monk, moving to the command of bells and being promoted on death to Heaven to sing happily among the lower angels.

But they had popped him in bed with a woman and told him to fornicate with her. While the woman's body made his senses squeal with pleasure, her sharp face and even sharper tongue inhibited him.

He longed for the sealed fountain of the Song of Solomon, the honey and milk, the mountain of myrrh. But he had been taught that the wickedness of women was greater than any other wickedness, that their bodily beauty was only phlegm, blood, bile and the fluid of digested food. He was being crushed between the millwheels of desire and abhorrence and neither would stop their grinding.

On the morning that Serlo came to his decision Adeliza, Matilda and Vincent were in the solar of her manor at Haut-des-Puys. Although it was chilly Matilda had opened the windows because of Vincent's smell, which not even the cherry logs burning in the grate could dispel. She was sewing up the jesses of her favourite hawk and wondering if she would ever fly him again and Vincent was treddling Adeliza's spinning-wheel making it squeak.

Serlo sent a request to be received – he was scrupulous in such matters – but his arrival was ebullient. "I come to apologise, madam." He was almost shouting and he clapped Vincent on the shoulder. "My son, we have been selfish, unthinking men, monopolising our dear wife's company, keeping her from her intimates." Matilda's eyes widened: she had seen a lot of her intimates lately. But Serlo went on: "We have been talking war while she has wished to talk babies and fashion with her cousin."

"What cousin?"

"The Empress."

Matilda was puzzled. Her relationship with the Empress

was distant. Then she got it. He was going to use her, Matilda, as a line of communication with the enemy. He couldn't go himself; it would be treachery to Stephen, so he would use her to open a dialogue. Serlo didn't like the look of things in Normandy; he didn't want all his eggs in Stephen's basket, he was going to put a couple in the Empress', just in case. Jesus and Mary be thanked, she was going to get away from Vincent.

Her smile was pure pleasure. "How thoughtful you are, my lord. What do you want me to say?"

With relief, Serlo got down to brass tacks. She was not to treat with the Empress, that would be treachery and Serlo was still Stephen's man. As he put it: "Indicate that while we are loyal to King Stephen we are not . . . well . . . irreconcilable to her cause should it prevail."

"For by strength no man shall prevail," said Vincent, suddenly. "Book of Samuel." He squeaked the spinning-wheel and Serlo got up and moved it away from him. "Now then . . ." he said, and began the provisos.

She was not to speak with the Empress alone at any time. The Luards' own trusted chaplain, Felix of Coutances, would be present at the audience. She was to be away no more than a week and, in order that she should miss no chance of becoming pregnant, that week would be her next menstruation period.

Serlo was firm on this point but his agony in trying to put it politely was pitiful. He ordered Vincent out of the room as he made it.

"There will be some days, a week when . . . when, well, for instance, you cannot enter a church." The week when Eve's curse made her so disgusting that conjugal relations were discontinued and the church didn't want her under its roof.

"Can you give me any indication, my lady, when this, um, condition, this, er, time will be?"

"Day after tomorrow," said Matilda promptly. She'd need a day to pack. She smiled. "A happy coincidence, my lord."

A north-westerly breeze floated seagulls above them and created a swell. To Matilda's amusement Adeliza and five

93

of the men-at-arms began to be sick. She stepped over their limp legs to the prow. She was enlarged. She was a hawk. No more Song of Solomon for a bit. The only smell was of sea and the only breathing the wind. She turned to Percy of Alleyn: "I'm a sailor." He was pleased she was happy. "You'll be a mermaid if you don't look out."

She staggered back to the stern and thumped down next to the Luards' chaplain who showed signs of wishing himself elsewhere. Matilda dug him in the ribs. "This James the Lord's brother," she said, "was he the Virgin's son?"

Felix forgot his queasiness in his shock. "Of course not. The Holy Mother was *virgo intacta* all her earthly life."

Matilda took a deep breath of sea air, puffed out her cheeks with it and expelled it, noisily. "What about St. James?"

Felix warmed to the discussion. "Origen would inform you that our Lord's brothers and sisters were St. Joseph's children by a previous marriage but he, of course, was Greek."

"St. Joseph?"

"Origen. But Jerome maintains that he who was worthy to be called the father of Our Lord remained a virgin always. And that is the view the Church adopts and why we honour St. Joseph as saint and virgin to this day."

Matilda took in more sea air. "And St. James? The brother of Jesus?"

"We think it means 'brother' in the sense of kinship. He was a cousin. Or adopted."

"You don't know, then."

Felix of Coutances glared at her. "It is the authority of the Fathers of the Church and not to be questioned. Certainly not by a woman." He leaned over the boat's side and appeared to find the sea of interest.

Matilda regarded the sky. They didn't know. They didn't *know*. These Fathers who'd never been fathers were trying to take Mary away from her. They couldn't bear it that after Mary had given birth to Jesus virginally – as was right and proper – she had gone on to become an ordinary wife and mother. But why not? It was why Matilda loved her so much, that she understood the condition of women. Why make a freak out of her?

"They're silly." The thought frightened and liberated her. "They're *silly* men."

When she had reached puberty Father Alors had taught her an old Irish prayer which he wanted her to say every night: "I am Eve who brought sin into the world. There would be no ice in any place; there would be no windy weather; there would be no grief; there would be no terror, but for me."

Even then she'd thought it was stupid. "Does Jesus want me to say that?" Father Alors had been disconcerted. "I fear Our Lord was not particularly censorious of the carnal sins. But it is Genesis and the Word of God. You are sensuous Eve, the Devil's gateway."

Why did they hate her so much? If God thought sex was so disgusting, why had He invented it?

"I can tell you this much," she addressed the clouds, "I don't like it much either. You can keep it."

She turned with sudden anger on the chaplain. "You can keep it." But Felix in his misery didn't hear her. He wasn't keeping anything.

There was no doubt the Empress intended to invade England soon. Ouistreham Harbour was crowded with ships, so was the Orne. At Caen half the population seemed to be soldiers. Their request for an audience was met with a curt, "The Empress will attend to the Lady Matilda when she has time," which was rude and infuriated Matilda.

However, her enforced ten days of waiting were spent most pleasantly at the Abbaye des Femmes. Anywhere without Vincent in it would have pleased Matilda but the nuns were hospitable, played volleyball and hunted. And it was at the abbaye that Matilda met and formed a friendship with a namesake, Matilda of Wallingford, wife to Brien Fitz Count.

They had a lot in common, about the same age, both heiresses, both widows now on their second marriage. The difference was that Maud of Wallingford adored her present husband. Within hours of first meeting – "My Lady Matilda." "My Lady Matilda" – they had exchanged intimate histories.

Brien Fitz Count had been brought up at the court of

Henry I profiting, like everyone did, from its learning and liberality. Through his marriage he had become a great land-owner. "He owes everything to the Old King," said Maud, "including me, of course, for whom he is amazingly grateful. He would have supported the Empress from the first, but like everyone else he'd believed Hugh Bigod when he said Henry had changed his mind on his deathbed. Of course, now that Bigod's shown his true colours . . . When the Empress invades I am to hold Wallingford for my lord." Plump, jolly little Maud was proud of herself. "I am expected to be *sieged*."

"Why?"

"Don't ask me. Because it's on the Thames and guards the way to London from the Midlands, I suppose. I'm going to have a lovely winter sieged in the mud."

"All in a good cause."

"All in the Empress' cause." For the first time Maud of Wallingford's voice was tart. The Empress had become her beloved husband's holy cause, his crusade. "One is quite prepared to die for her. But the knowledge that one's hus-band would shake one like a mat and put one down for the Empress to walk over is *not* uplifting to live with."

The Empress became one of their main topics. "She's not at all grateful," Maud told Matilda. "She's got all these splendid men rallying to her standard, Earl Robert, Miles of Gloucester, my own dear lord, of course, and she just takes it as her due. She's even miffed they didn't rise for her at the very beginning. And her marriage doesn't seem much to write home about."

"Well, I'm sorry for her," Matilda said, "I know what it is to be married to a stripling."

Maud of Wallingford rolled her eyes. "He may have been a stripling when she married him, but he certainly isn't now. He's gorgeous. Funny, intelligent and gorgeous, Angevin or not. Young Henry's very like him, only without the looks."

The Empress was a satisfactory subject of gossip because mystery surrounded her past. She had disappeared into Germany at the age of eight to marry the Emperor and hadn't reappeared until fifteen years later when her childless marriage was ended by his death.

"Of course, the Germans ruined her," said Maud. "All that solemn worship turned her stiff as a wooden saint. I shouldn't think she and the Emperor ever did it, you know, couldn't unbend enough. Had a funny end too . . ."

The story of how the Emperor had retired to bed and just disappeared never to be seen again was undoubtedly apocryphal, but the two Matildas preferred to believe it.

"What do you think happened?"

"I think she ate him."

The Empress' throne was on a block on the dais so that she sat higher than her advisers and had a hawk's eye view over the hall. This was full of men but so intimidating was the Empress' presence that they were talking in a subdued mutter which ceased altogether when she spoke.

Felix and Matilda were asked their names and business by a chamberlain and were conducted to a group waiting at the foot of the dais. The chamberlain refused their bribe for a private audience.

Felix was disconcerted; it would be impossible to conduct negotiations as delicate as his in full view. Word would get back to Stephen in days. However, all they could do was wait – for a full hour – before the Empress noticed them.

Matilda's dignity was affronted, but what was going on around her was so interesting that the hour was a quick one.

Every major landowner in the West Country of England, Earl Robert of Gloucester, Miles of Gloucester, Brien Fitz Count, Baldwin de Redvers, Richard Fitz Turold, the Earl of Cornwall, was in the hall. So were the nobles who had been disinherited by Stephen, their lands given to his favourites. More tantalisingly difficult to place were the secretaries, stewards, knights and chamberlains. Presumably they were representing lords who did not want to commit themselves yet, but were on the same errand as herself and Felix.

Her eyes kept going back to the woman on the dais. In this welter of multi-coloured cloaks and jewels the Empress was in grey, not a fluffy grey, but silk with the shine of steel; the

97

circlet above her veil was of diamonds. The monochrome
wrong-footed her companions into gaudiness and empha-
sised her dark hair and the white skin.

She was beautiful but it was a static beauty; at first one was
astonished by it, then got used to it and forgot it as it was
overridden by the bitterness of the personality beneath it.
The Empress was a bitter woman.

Matilda noticed with satisfaction that Felix was beginning
to sweat. Other emissaries like himself were presenting their
masters' respects to the Empress in speeches of uncommitted
goodwill, but each one was interrupted by the same question:
"Is your lord for us or against us?" which left them floundering. They were then dismissed without ceremony.

However, Matilda noticed that as each disappointed emissary turned away either the Earl of Gloucester or Brien Fitz
Count would quietly lead him off for a talk. Their Empress
might scorn compromise but her lieutenants were not prepared to alienate possible allies. "I must have a talk of my
own with those gentlemen," thought Matilda.

The chamberlain ushered her and Felix before the dais.
Felix dropped to his trembling knees but Matilda, having
curtsied, remained upright. She was, after all, a relative.

"Most glorious lady," quavered Felix, "my Lady of Risle
and her lord, Vincent of Luard, present humble greetings
and . . ."

"Master Felix." The cold, sharp voice quelled the murmur
of the hall. "Do your lord and lady acknowledge me as Lady
of England?"

Felix began to blubber: "You are the lady of our hearts,
madam . . ."

"Do they or do they not?"

Felix slumped to the floor in a faint. Matilda caught the eye
of Brien Fitz Count and jerked her head. He nodded.

As two men dragged Felix away, Matilda said triumphantly, "I'm ashamed of you." That'd teach him to make
St. Joseph a virgin.

Next morning a page fetched her to a room high in a tower
where Earl Robert of Gloucester and Brien Fitz Count

were waiting for her: "You had something to say to us, my lady?"

She'd been working it out all night. "My lords, I am prepared to instruct the steward of every estate under my control to give all assistance to your armies. Food, fodder, stabling, accommodation." With her estates so extensive it was a good offer.

Earl Robert was cold: "Your lord is loyal to Stephen."

"My lord is dying." She saw it accorded with information they already had. But they didn't like her any better for being truthful. Wives, even the wives of enemies, should obey their lords.

However, they were pragmatists. "Show us." They moved away from the square table in the centre of the room to disclose its top on which was a mass of moulded mud.

"Mud?"

"A map," said Brien Fitz Count, leaving Matilda no wiser. "We'd like you to mark on it all your estates in England." They sighed at her incomprehension . . . "try to imagine you are a hawk flying over England. This is what you would see." But to Matilda England was a castle surrounded by countryside, her house in London overlooking the Thames, travelling along a road, hunting in a forest. It was not a mud rectangle. They tried it another way. "But you know how far from, say, Arundel your manor of Holt is."

"Seven and a half miles north-west," said Matilda promptly. Fitz Count muttered a prayer of thanks and stuck a twig in the mud. They wanted to know everything, fortifications, fords, bridges, the state of roads, knights' fees, the names of constables, stewards, fyrd strength. Matilda liked their efficiency.

They were especially interested in Holt's relationship to Arundel, though they didn't say why. Matilda gave a good guess. The Empress would land at Arundel.

She was surprised that they showed no interest in the area round her morning gift.

"Seven miles from Ramsey, ten from Ely, twelve from Wisbech." In that section of the map Ramsey and Ely were shown side by side.

"Quagmire," said the earl, "and impassable."

"That's the Fens. They're navigable." But they were leaving. She realised she had given away more than they had.

"Just a minute, my lords. It must be understood that my co-operation depends upon your oath that my son, Edmund, inherits all this. Also that I am never married again against my will."

The Earl of Gloucester shrugged. "We shall discuss the matter with the Empress. If you would stay here until we come back . . ."

The room, now that she was left alone, seemed most peculiar. Its walls were lined with shelves stacked with manuscripts, leather books, astrolabes, an abacus, a stuffed owl, a toy horse on wheels, several spearheads and some jesses. There were bird droppings everywhere. Matilda became nervous. It might be the cell of an enchanter.

"What's fens?" asked a voice. She clutched the table edge. There was nobody in the room. It must be the enchanter. "I believe in the one God, the Lord, the giver of life," she said.

"What's fens?" asked the voice again.

She crouched down to peer under the table and found herself eye to eye with a small boy. He winked at her. "I'm a wonderful hider, aren't I?" He was a grubby child, dressed in well-worn leather and he was sitting crosslegged, like a tailor, stitching a red-suede falcon's hood which had split. But she recognised him from the description Maud of Wallingford had given her. There couldn't be two round-faced, grey-eyed, red-headed young devils loose in Caen Castle. This was the boy for whom Geoffrey of Anjou wanted Normandy and the Empress Matilda wanted England. If they won, the day would come when he ruled both.

Matilda never liked other people's children much, even princes. If they couldn't conduct an adult conversation she had no time for them. "Do you understand this map?"

"I made it." The boy scrambled out from under the table. "I've talked to everyone from England and improved on the one great-grandfather made." It was a shock to think of

William the Conqueror as something so domestic as some-body's great-grandfather. "I know everything about England. What's fens?"

"Not quite everything, then," said Matilda with satisfaction, but she told him, and his questions dragged out of her memory things she hadn't been aware of knowing.

He drew up a stool and knelt on it so that he could work on the map with what she told him, extending East Anglia with his freckled hands, flattening and enlarging the area below the Wash, scoring out the River Nene from Wisbech to Ramsey with a short, black thumbnail and embedding pebbles produced from his pocket for the Causeway from Ramsey to the uplands and Ermine Street. She told him of the unexpected richness of the Fens, of the terrifying flatness, of the enormity of its sky, how incomprehensible were its people. She was surprised to find that, though it contradicted every accepted standard of beauty, the thought of the place pleased her – and not just because it held her son. "It's a good place to hide," she said.

"If you were coming from, say Flanders, could you land here" – he arced a piece of the Wash – "and go through the waterways into the uplands and Ermine Street?"

He reminded her of someone; she couldn't think who. "If you wanted to. But why would you want to? It's easier to land at Dover."

"Vegetius the Roman says that in war you must keep open alternative lines of communication. Could you land an army there?"

Earl Robert and Brien Fitz Count had discounted her opinion of the Fens as if a woman's knowledge was worth-less: this boy treated her as an ally. "You'd need a lot of boats."

"But you could get a small party in or out without being spotted?"

"Certainly." She had it now; he reminded her of Ramsey's abbot; both were interested in everything, neither saw the differences made by age or rank or sex. In the presence of both she scented a mind that was not like any other she had ever encountered. "They are new," she thought.

It was in that moment, though she didn't realise it for some years, that Matilda made her commitment.

"There you are, then. Your Fens are a back door into the East, or the Midlands or the North. It's a sort of postern to England. I'm a wonderful thinker, aren't I?"

They discussed its uses. They made a plan. It was a game, but an exciting game. She no longer saw him as a child but as a credible future power. "My lord, will you have my son Edmund brought up in your court when he is seven?"

The grey eyes considered. "Does he cry a lot?"

"Hardly at all."

"All right, then. But he must learn Vegetius. All my officers will read Vegetius. It's going to be a wonderful court."

"And you must promise never to give me in marriage against my will."

He looked at the map, counting up her inheritance and dowry. "I'll see." Then she knew he would make a king. Another boy would have gained her support with an impulsive promise. Stephen would have made it – had made it, and broken it. To hold power over a petitioner by keeping him or her in suspense was the legacy from the Conqueror and Henry Beauclerk. Stephen still hadn't learned it: this child had it in his bones. She looked at him with respect and resentment. "Then why should I help you?"

"Because I'm going to win."

Boots were running up the passage, the door swung back until it hit the wall and a sergeant-at-arms came in with a soldier behind him. The sergeant was mopping his neck. "You haven't half caused me bother," he said, "and you won't be no favourite with the master-at-arms, neither. That's twice you've missed sword practice and you aren't good enough yet to miss any." He added as an afterthought: "My lord." He spoke with a thick Angevin accent, but he had the authority which all good military instructors have over their pupils, princes or not. The leopards of Geoffrey Plantagenet were embroidered across his surcoat.

He broke the spell. Like an enchanter the boy had made himself seem adult; now Matilda saw she had been discussing tactics with a child. He sucked in his breath and his face went a mulberry colour in ugly contrast to the carrot-red of his hair. "You humiliate me, you bugger . . ." He'd lost control. He charged the sergeant, arms whirling, shrieking language no boy of seven should have known. The sergeant side-stepped, picked the boy up by his belt and handed him to the soldier. "Get him down the tilt-yard."

They listened to the boy's incoherent howls diminish into the distance until the echoes came back as the mewing of a demented cat. The sergeant looked abashed. "Sorry for that, my lady. Wants a bit of handling, does Fitzempress."

"He wants a smacked bottom." She was disgusted at her-self for taking a little boy so seriously.

At that the sergeant looked concerned and stepped closer. "You mustn't think he's spoiled, lady. His temper's wicked, we know, but it's due to his brain working so fast – causes friction. We reckon that's singed his hair for it were black when he was born." He was still worried she'd got the wrong impression. "He's not a bad swordsman really and there's not a cowardly bone in his body. It's just he reckons you can beat an opponent by thinking. Gets it from that old Vegetary he's always reading. He reads, you know." If the boy did it while sitting on thin air the sergeant couldn't have worshipped him more.

When the earl and Brien Fitz Count returned they brought a sharp message from the Empress: "We accept your personal goodwill, but you must prove it. We will not tolerate those who sit safely on their demesne and leave us to fight. Those who support us in England must remain in England. If they do not hold their lands for us they will not later hold them for themselves."

It committed the Empress to nothing. But then, Matilda wasn't committed either: she could always withdraw her offer.

Nevertheless, as she sailed back, she felt she had perched herself nicely on the fence and done good work for Edmund. Now she must watch to see which side triumphed – and not become pregnant.

At the gates of Haut-des-Puys she was met by her steward in an agony of divided loyalty. As Vincent's health worsened

103

Serlo was stripping the manor of its assets and giving them to the Abbey of Fécamp in return for its prayers. "Our best bull has gone, my lady, the mill is to grind Fécamp's corn free of charge, the monks are pasturing their sheep on our land to the detriment of our flock." Like all good stewards, he couldn't bear the depredation of the estate in his care and out of which he lined his own pocket.

Matilda was haring up the steps to the hall before he'd finished. In the doorway she collided with Serlo, about to hare down. She began shouting at him, too furious to realise he was in a fury of his own. Anger clashed with anger. Servants gathered in the courtyard to listen. It was Matilda who stopped first, some sense of what Serlo was yelling having permeated her brain. Serlo's voice rang out alone. ". . . and I demand you dismiss that pale-haired trollop from your service."

"Adeliza?" There was only one blonde among Matilda's ladies.

"My son's essential fluids must not be dissipated. They must be directed towards begetting a legitimate heir."

"Adeliza and *Vincent*?" She pushed past him and went straight to the solar where Adeliza fell on the floor before her and sobbed on to Matilda's ankles. "Don't send me home in shame. It's so awful. I'll die. It wasn't my fault."

Matilda hoisted her up and sat her down rubbing her back. "Nobody shall send you away." Adeliza had always reminded her of a primrose, innocent, gently scented and quick to become limp. She wouldn't have her bullied by these men.

With frequent explosions of distress the story took time. In Matilda's absence Vincent had sought Adeliza's company. "We were never alone, 'Tildy, I promise . . . he seemed so unwell and so sweet."

Sweet? It was time Adeliza was married; a pity the husbands chosen for her by her family kept dying before the marriage. "Go on."

On the night before last the other women had left the solar to go down to the hall and see a pedlar selling embroidery silks, leaving Adeliza and Vincent alone. "I had enough silks and am on my tapestry anyway . . ."

"Get *on*."

She began to cry again and her account was so allusive Matilda had trouble piecing it together. Eventually Adeliza had heard Vincent's breathing close behind her, heavier than usual. "He was muttering to himself from the Holy Book."

"Song of Solomon?"

"How did you know?" She looked up. "It's not *funny*."

"Get on."

Suddenly Vincent's hand had plunged down the front of her dress. "The shock. I didn't know he was like that . . ." She'd jerked away from him, tearing her dress and run screaming out of the room to bump straight into Serlo. "And he – I couldn't believe it – he blamed me."

"He would." Serlo's usually practical mind had built an idealised picture of his son's marriage. If he were to retain it he had to find a scapegoat. "Essential fluids," thought Matilda angrily, "I could tell him what happens to his son's essential fluids."

"Make it all right again, 'Tildy."

"I shall."

There was anger and hard words from both sides before the matter was settled, but Matilda was aided by the fact that essentially Serlo was a fair man. He had to recognise that Vincent was not just interested in Adeliza but was equally prepared to fumble any other blonde as well.

There had been a dreadful change in Vincent since Matilda saw him last. As his health worsened his sexuality became rampant, as if the old Adam in him was looking for its last chance. He had no interest in society, ignoring Matilda and even his father. At table he sat in an invisible cubicle, muttering and praying as lust and fear of it warred in his head. Only the sight of a fair-haired woman, no matter of what age, size or beauty, evinced attention from him. It could be Adeliza, though she was now kept out of his way, or a servant or a villein's wife glimpsed down the end of the room. He had found his type; Matilda thanked God her own hair was dark.

"My lord, he is very ill," Matilda said to Serlo. "He should go somewhere where he won't be distracted like this. Fécamp perhaps."

Serlo refused to think of it. "He can still act the man."

Matilda doubted it. There was no more Song of Solomon. Quite often now Vincent didn't come to bed until the early hours; she suspected him of roaming the sleeping castle looking for blondes. When he did come there was no attempt at intimacy; he would pull her out of bed to kneel beside him in penitential prayers so long that Matilda often fell asleep with her head against the side of the bed. Even so she was grateful for this form of contraception.

Whether Serlo suspected what was going on in the nuptial chamber Matilda wasn't sure. She thought not. When they met each day his eyes would go to her waistline in case it should have swelled in the night. Time was running out, and he knew it.

Ten days after they had moved on to the castle at Échappe, they were celebrating the feast of the Blessed Virgin Mary when a page knelt by Matilda's place at the top table and proffered a chalice. "With the compliments of the Lord Serlo, my lady." In the chalice was a thick red liquid on the top of which swirled patterning of light pink. "What is it?"

"Drink it." Serlo was drunk. "It's the blood of a she-hare mixed with its curdled milk. It causes conception. Drink it."

"I will not."

He was on his feet and behind her so fast she didn't have time to knock the chalice out of the page's hand. His arm came round her throat and forced her head back. She felt the metal click against her teeth. "Drink it."

She drank it. When she opened her eyes Serlo was back in his place and the hall was quiet. One hundred pairs of eyes were looking at her. She left the hall. In the dark passage outside she began to heave. Nearby was a large earthenware pot of lavender put to sweeten the air; she vomited into it and went on vomiting until she was afraid she was retching up her own blood. There was a whimper and her dog Fen put her nose into Matilda's hand. Matilda slid down the wall to sit on the flags, put her arm round the bitch's neck and wiped her face and eyes in her fur. "We won again." She shook with the misery of the victory.

Much later that night she woke up to find that a giant harvest moon was lighting the chamber and throwing a long shadow from the mullion of the window across the floor. The three-hour candle was guttering which meant it was about two in the morning. The air was still warm from the heat of the day and carried the smell of scythed wheat and barley. It was a beautiful night. Matilda lay tense, waiting for the breathing and shuffling step of her husband to come up the passage outside. He was beginning to frighten her. But there was silence.

"Perhaps he's out in the courtyard." Perhaps some succubus had entered his body, perhaps he was sidling along the wall below or even climbing it like a fly. She didn't want to look: she couldn't bear not to.

She got up and went to the window. Fen joined her, putting her spindly paws on the sill so that woman and bitch looked out together.

Échappe was perched on the terrace of a hillside overlooking a tributary of the Seine; around and above it were irregular step fields flattened out of forest. The night was so replete with late summer that one more nightingale, one more scent of fruit and corn, one more pale flower, one more moth flying into the cresset down in the bailey, would have sent it into over-ripeness.

The roofscape of thatch and tiles below her was given the uniform quality of soft metal by the moon, like breathed-on lead. The octagon of the dovecote, the saddle of the church, the well-head's triangle and the beehives of the servant's huts sent a mingling of geometric shadows on to the cobbles.

The sound began deep in the register of the frogs by the river and climbed until it throbbed over the fields. The earth had cracked and was allowing Hell to seep out. Pain, triumph and guilt from one throat held Échappe and the moon taut as if the night might implode from the pressure of the noise. It cut off. But the air and those who'd heard it still quivered.

Fen bared her teeth. Matilda ran to the door, not to find

out what it was – she knew what it was – but to be among people.

There were already frightened servants in the passage. Percy of Alleyn came running – he was always there when she needed him – and looked beyond her into the empty chamber. He bundled her in his cloak and together they went down the turret stair to the bailey, others joining them as they went. The bailey rattled with questions and the swearing of men who'd been frightened.

Serlo was standing and glaring on the hall steps. Alleyn told him: "The Lord Vincent is not in his room."

The gates were unbarred and the watchman gave a torch to Serlo; almost the entire population of Échappe followed him into the fields, nobody wanted to be alone. The supernatural was loose.

Something large and white scuttled beneath the overhang of a hedge. First one person saw it, then another. Serlo ordered two men-at-arms to fetch it. Their eyes rolled, but they obeyed him.

Crickets stridulated in the stooks of corn which cast shadows over the dusty-white stubble; Matilda's bare ankles were scratched from the stalks. She was conscious that eyes glanced at her, but she felt nothing.

Between them the men-at-arms dragged a body with long hair which, like everything else that was yellow that night, was turned white. "Not Adeliza, I beg you," prayed Matilda. But when Serlo's hand jerked the head back by its hair the face was broad, with a snub nose, one of the hundreds of faces from this and other estates half-glimpsed from a window or as their owners curtsied to her passing. It might have been pretty but now terror had bared its teeth and dilated the nostrils. Serlo jerked his fist again. "Where is he?"

The girl was beyond speech but her eyes instinctively went to the top of the field and there, behind a stook, they found Vincent on the ground with his robe up around his waist. He was on his back where the girl had pushed his body off hers. Despite his lack of trousers, death had returned his dignity. He looked calm, as if he were listening to the nightingales.

Matilda watched Serlo take off his cloak and cover his son. She saw him take a dagger from his boot and advance on the girl.

He must not kill her, she thought. It would make too much noise, and she was so tired. Besides, the girl was her property and Serlo had no right over that any longer. She signalled to Percy of Alleyn to stop him and Alleyn, respectfully but firmly, took the dagger away.

"Who is she?" She was so deathly tired she could barely form the words.

"The farrier's daughter."

Matilda yawned. "She may have conceived," she told Serlo. "A bastard is better than no son at all."

They took Vincent to Fécamp for burial. Serlo cried from the *"Requiem aeternem dona eis,"* to the *"Requiescat in pace."* Matilda prayed hard for the young corruptible who had now put on incorruption, and for herself who could feel nothing but relief that he had done so.

Later she granted Serlo a final audience. Kindly, because he had no son to go back to and she had, she said: "The bull must be returned to Haut-des-Puys, and the abbey pay the rate for grinding its corn. However, in memory of my late lord, your son, Fécamp may pasture its sheep on the high slope in winter. And if the farrier's daughter turns out to be pregnant you may accept her as my gift."

One must, after all, be generous to a defeated enemy, and she was a magnanimous woman, thanks be to God.

6

1139–1140
The Empress invaded England at the end of September and landed, as Matilda had suspected, at Arundel.

Within days the Empress was surrounded. Her ally at Arundel, at whose invitation she had landed there, was her young stepmother, whom Henry the First had married in his dotage hoping still to breed a legitimate son. In a brilliantly fast move Stephen besieged Arundel, frightening the little stepmother who handed the Empress to him.

The war was over. Or it would have been if Stephen hadn't then let the Empress go and politely seen her escorted safely to Robert of Gloucester's castle at Bristol.

Why he did it nobody then or ever understood. Some say Henry of Blois persuaded him it would be better to have all his enemies isolated in the West Country – by this time nobody was sure whose side the Bishop of Winchester was on. Perhaps it was chivalry.

The war was on again and Stephen's chance of nipping it in the bud had gone for ever.

About the time that the Empress was crossing the Channel, Matilda of Risle and a small household were heading for England by the more dangerous route from Gravelines to the Wash. She had chosen her ship and shipmaster with care. Both had to be worthy to cope with the North Sea and the shipmaster had to be a man she could trust with a project she had in mind for the future.

She chose well. Turold was an Anglo-Saxon equally at home on the Continent. He was both a trader and a smuggler

110

and had allegiance to no one, especially not to those who put tolls on the cargoes of poor merchantmen. He respected nobody except Jesus, who had shown himself a super-sailor by treading the sea. But he warmed to Matilda when she indicated that she wished the authorities not to notice her arrival in England. "Don't we all, my duck," he said.

By the end of the voyage the two of them were having long and curious discussions over an arrangement which would, when the time was right, involve passwords, money, secret messages and a fishing hamlet on the Wash rejoicing in the name of Cradge.

It was there that he landed her and there, impatient as she was to see her son, Matilda spent time in other long and curious discussions with its people which again involved the exchange of monies and the arrangement of passwords, secret messages and cargo.

The view from the "cradge", the English for sea-wall, was of desolate stretches of silt and sea like ruled lines at the bottom of limitless parchment which folded at the horizon to sweep back in a way that made Matilda want to duck. The only windows in the Cradgers' huts looked landwards and they spoke of the sea as of a capricious ruler. It held monsters, they told her, which came ashore to carry off children, and green-headed, fish-tailed mermen. She noticed that several of their children had web-fingers and toes. They served her party with a delicacy they called samphire which grew beyond the sea-wall and smelled of sulphur and made Adeliza sick.

It was in a mood of self-congratulation that she finally stepped ashore on her morning gift of Dungesey to find that the king was building a castle on it.

"It's not a castle, my lady," said Willem of Ghent wearily for the fourth time, "it's a tower on a motte surrounded by a bailey."

"But it sticks up," screeched Matilda.

"That's towers all over," Fenchel muttered so that only Willem of Ghent could hear him. Matilda made him

111

nervous, not because she was in a rage – though indeed she was – but because he would have been as easy in the company of anthropophagi as he was in women of Matilda's class.

She hated these artisans who waved the king's warrant at her. She did not listen to their explanation that Dungesey's was to be just one of a series of keeps overlooking the Fens. They were hounding her, Matilda, personally. She felt frightened and ridiculous, like a hare which leaps and doubles to throw off pursuit and has frozen into her forme only to hear the hunter say: "Peep-bo."

The mercenary understood her panic; the Fen people had talked to him; he shared sufficient of its people's language to be understood and to understand. "If you wish to conceal your son here," he said gently, "the king won't hear of it from us. We are the king's builders, not his informers."

That they knew her secret infuriated Matilda more. She picked up the nearest object, a candlestick, and threw it. Willem caught it and put it on the floor.

"Elm," muttered Fenchel, "tell her about the elm, for Chrissake."

"Lady," Willem was placatory, "we're bringing elm from the uplands for the supports, so we'll only need to cut down half your pigwoods."

She caught the words "cut" and "pigwoods" and looked round for another missile. A stool came skidding at them. "I shall be ruined. Ruined."

Between the manor and Perecourt was now a huge and raw ditch from which the displaced earth was being rammed tight into a mound. The tower keep which would surmount this motte would rise above the height of the highest oaks providing a landmark for miles around. The secret island was being exposed.

Piles of stone and rubble were everywhere. Men carried buckets of nails. Scaffolding was being erected. The noise of shouts and rattles was dominated by the piercing squeal of the treadmill gin which was taking blocks of stone to the site. Steward Peter was having a nervous breakdown and her

112

English, pressed into service as labourers, were complaining they couldn't get on with their embanking or mole-catching or whatever foul activity they indulged in at this time of year. And she had to pay for it.

Percy of Alleyn had heard Matilda's screaming and came into the hall, followed by Edmund. Willem of Ghent turned to him. "Tell her," he said, "tell her I'm the king's officer, not his nark. If she wants to stay here incognito with the boy it's all right by me."

Edmund said: "Hello, Fenchel. Hello, Willem."

They grinned back at him. "Hello, my lord slodger."

Percy of Alleyn, as always, calmed Matilda down. In her distress at the invasion of her island she had barely noticed her son. He trotted over to her now and she hugged him. He looked extraordinarily healthy and was growing fast. He seemed on good terms with these brutes; one of the disadvantages in keeping him out of good society was that he would form unsuitable relationships with the lower orders.

Now that she was free again, she supposed she could take him away, to Hatfelde maybe. She could treat with the king to see that she wasn't married again, and this time ensure that he kept his word. But she was so tired.

She collapsed into the great chair. The terrible time with Vincent had drained her. She had no energy to make plans. Anyway, it was nearly winter and the roads would be bad for travel.

For the time being she would have to stay where she was.

Brien Fitz Count had been right. His castle at Wallingford was of strategic importance, straddling as it did the main lines of communication to southern England from the Midlands and holding the key to London. Having isolated the Empress in the West Country Stephen immediately marched on Wallingford and beseiged it, building towers outside to pin down the garrison inside. Then he marched on Bristol. But while he was on his way and taking the castles of South Cerney, Malmesbury and Trowbridge, Miles of Gloucester circled his flank to relieve Wallingford and make threatening noises at London. Stephen's army whipped round and started back. But before it could reach Wallingford Miles of Gloucester retreated and diverted Stephen by sacking Worcester and escaping again without fighting a battle.

It was bull-baiting with the Empress' smaller forces drawing the bull's attention away from each other and then darting in again. While such tactics weakened Stephen they weren't achieving anything definite for the Empress' cause. Of course, the countryside around each disputed castle was being devastated, soldiers were raping the local women and peasants were starving, but nobody was getting anywhere. Which left most of England's barons not knowing what to do and subsequently doing nothing at all.

Actually Matilda enjoyed that autumn and winter. The end of October was a St. Martin's summer and she spent most of it out on the fens with Edmund to avoid the noise surrounding her hall, lulled by drifting water and Jodi's lute. They picnicked under alders and watched sand-martins gather in the osier beds. Swallows flicked along the streams taking the gnats which danced above the surface. White cattle with black noses plodded along the skylines of the droves, some to be slaughtered, some heading for the higher pastures where, with luck, they would escape the winter flooding.

She and Edmund picked cranberries from red stems arched above the moss. She spent one afternoon with her back against a warm wall of peat bricks staring down into one of the pits from which they had been dug. Water had seeped into it and as the sun slanted it became a rectangle of amber in which a stray reed was preserved like a gold pin.

Fenchel was glad of her absence, but the mercenary from Ghent noted her departure each morning and made sure she was home safe each evening before he retired to his hut.

Ten days after her arrival at Dungesey she sought out the two men on the site of the motte. "You." She was addressing Fenchel. "Are you this monstrosity's mason?"

114

Fenchel's bowed shoulders humped. Willem answered for him. "He is."

"Then you can build a necessarium into it. In a cupboard, with a chute. A garderobe like they have at Devizes." She would turn some part of this cost to her advantage.

To the mercenary's surprise Fenchel did not protest. He was intrigued by the modernity of the idea. He produced a slate from under his apron and a piece of chalk from behind his ear. "It wouldn't take much, Willem. There'd be a runnel down the motte to a cesspit in the ditch and the chute itself could be corbelled out . . ."

"I do not wish for details." Matilda's voice cut through his calculations. "Do it."

Her youth and energy had come back; the sky and fens were full of game and the rivers full of fish. With Fen and a scratch pack of hounds she took her household hunting otter. On one glorious morning Fen ran down and tore the throat out of a young roe hind.

Through her son she was led into commoners' sport. At first she was distressed by the extent of Edmund's familiarity with the islanders and their ways, but Percy of Alleyn reassured her. "They love him and he's safe with them. Father Alors teaches him his table manners and catechism. I'm teaching him to master the sword and the horse. He'll not be the worst for knowing extra."

Nevertheless she lectured the child when he wanted her to go eel-glaiving with him. "Never forget you are a great lord, my son, and should follow noble pursuits."

He said stolidly: "I know I'm a lord. I like the chase. But eel-glaiving's fun."

And it was. There are many unpleasanter ways of spending a warm autumn afternoon than standing under the willows of Fleam Dyke watching the pools of a river for the smoke of disturbed mud and the wavering silver which is an eel. Epona, who had become part of the household, wielded her glaive with absent-minded expertise and awoke Matilda's competitiveness. It wasn't as easy as it looked. The twelve-foot ashpole with its flat leaves of serrated iron was heavy and the eel a slippery adversary. "If he gets his teeth in your finger he never lets go," said her son, "even if you cut his head off. And there's an eel king, isn't there, 'Pony? If you catch him you make him pay you a bushel of silver to let him go. Eels are magic." With the small glaive Pampi had made for him the boy was nearly as expert as Epona and only less successful because he wouldn't keep still. At one point he fell in the river. When it transpired that he could swim Matilda was immediately relieved and then disapproving. River-bathing was unhealthy. She forbade him to do it again.

On the whole she was pleased with her son. He had his father's appetite without his father's fatness, and his mother's ability to grasp estate management. Also, Matilda discovered, he had sense of his own worth. The camaraderie with islanders and commoners was, she now saw, proprietorial. "Shudda will do it for me." "I'll take Pampi with me." "I shan't allow Vag (Badda's son) to come: he's too stupid." They were *his* Fens and *his* people.

His approach was different from Matilda's who kept aloof from all commoners except Berte in the fear that serfs might "take advantage". What advantage they would take she didn't know but feared they would take it anyway. Edmund lessened the distance between the peasants and himself without decreasing his precedence. She supposed it was his Saxon blood. Although the islanders teased the child and called him "slodger", an attitude and title she found offensive, they also indulged him. "It's the English way," Steward Peter told her.

That afternoon Matilda managed to mangle one eel. She carried it home in triumph and made the cook put it in a pie.

But if eel-glaiving was fun there was a purity about wild-fowling which captivated Matilda for the rest of her life. They crouched in punts below the reeds between two voids of marsh and sky in a limbo from which it seemed they would never escape. It was a bit like grandmother's footsteps; the dawn crept up with stealth, apparently unchanging and yet, every time you looked, adding one more transparency to the horizon behind the spikes of the rushes.

A water-rail gave its cry which starts with a grunt and ends in a squeal like a pig's – and woke up the sky. They came in strata, whooper swans highest, then pink-footed geese, then mallards, smew, golden-eye and pochard, menacing in their numbers and even more in their noise; not so much the honking, shrieking, fluting of their calls, but in the whiffling sound which is also sensation as air is shifted by hundreds of thousands of wings.

The arrows whipping up were not shot in cruelty nor even, in Matilda's case, for food but carried an invisible line by which the wingless, finless humans on their punts could overpower the magic of the birds and bring down to themselves some of their beauty.

November was first warm and clear and then cold and clear. Fenchel and the mercenary took themselves off to prepare the site of another motte, this time at Burwell in the southern Fens. They gave careful instructions to the Dungesey labourers on the work to be done in their absence. The islanders listened, nodding. They realised the two men were carrying out their orders with as much humanity as possible – they had not used all the Dungesey men all the time, they had allowed the pigs to eat the acorns of Hogwood before felling half of it. Nevertheless as soon as Fenchel and Willem were out of sight the islanders downed tools and got on with their own neglected work. The tower on the motte stopped growing.

Matilda, who disliked Fenchel and had contempt for the mercenary, was glad to see them go for several reasons – one of which was Berte.

"You realise you are committing mortal sin," Matilda told her. Somewhere back in Anjou Berte had a husband and grown-up children. "And God won't only punish you for it but me as well; I'm responsible for you."

Berte was ashamed and furious. "That old fart of a priest's been poking his nose."

"Never mind who told me." Berte was right: Father Alors had discovered and informed on a liaison between Berte and Fenchel. "At your age."

"Just 'cause you don't like it. If God hadn't wanted us to

do it he shouldn't have given women a hole and men something to stick in it."

"You're disgusting. Get out."

At the door Berte turned: "And you could do with a proper man and all."

"Back to Anjou you go," hissed Matilda.

Their quarrels, which averaged one a year, always ended with Matilda sacking and Berte packing. Both resolutions failed at that point and for a week neither would talk to the other until some household emergency came up which necessitated a strained exchange after which they both relaxed and forgot. Father Alors insisted that Berte do a bread-and-water penance for a week for her sin in sleeping with the mason, a diet which did her no harm. She sulked through it. She told the cook: "She never said nothing to that Wealy woman" – Berte was jealous of Edmund's affection for Epona – "and she's been through them masons like measles."

As frost and ice came in with December Fenchel and the mercenary returned to Dungesey for Christmas. Matilda was dismayed. In obedience to the king's warrant she had to house and feed them, but although she knew the mason's reason for coming back – she forbade Berte to have anything to do with him – she could not guess at the mercenary's. She suspected he was a spy. "Discover his motives," she told Alleyn. "Simulate friendship for the swine."

Alleyn did not have to simulate it; he had already overcome his prejudice against mercenaries when he'd found Willem of Ghent's military expertise. The two of them had spent pleasant evenings in Fenchel's mason's lodge at the foot of the motte, swopping soldiers' stories. He went down there now for another: "What news?"

"The Bishop of Salisbury's dead. Raving mad at the end, they say."

Fenchel grunted. "Poor old bugger. I can't judge him as a bishop but he knew how to build."

"And we came through Ely on the way up. It looks as if Bishop Nigel's out for revenge and will declare for the Empress. From the amount of stuff going in through the gates I'd say he was stocking for a siege."

118

Percy of Alleyn was disturbed. The war was getting too close to his lady for comfort. He looked for reassurance. "I thought nobody could ever get close enough to Ely to siege it. It's never fallen through assault."

"It's fallen through treachery often enough."

Christmas passed pleasantly, though on a smaller scale than Matilda was used to. Epiphany brought weather so cold that the rivers froze and put all travel out of the question.

Somewhat against her will she was persuaded to attend the Festival of St. Wendreda at Ugg Mere. "To watch a lot of peasants skate?" she asked. Although St. Wendreda was not a saint with whom Matilda was personally acquainted she knew she was powerful in this area and celebrated in a peculiarly local way. Her bones had converted Canute to Christianity and were a cure for ague. Pampi had made Edmund a pair of ox-bone skates which the boy wanted to use in the races. Even Father Alors thought they ought to honour the saint and attend. But it was Adeliza, with uncharacteristic cunning, who clinched the matter. "The Abbot of Ramsey is bound to be there."

The darkness was so cold it was metallic and crackled. As they turned into the Nene a sheen came over the ice and one of the men drawing Matilda's sledge began to whistle. At the rear the Wealas started to sing. Ducks, hoping the water had become fluid, landed, skidded, and took off again.

The sun came up behind them and for a while the world turned delicious, the river acquiring the hue of crystallised pear; the bare trees were angelica and the sky was hung with plum and strips of apple peel.

Her nose freezing over the top of her furs, Matilda looked with disfavour at her English stumping along ahead of her. They did not seem to possess festal costume as Norman peasants did; they merely put on something marginally cleaner than usual. She had seen prettier hounds on a winter's day. She shouted, "Go faster," in English (of necessity she was picking up their barbarous tongue) but they muttered reassuringly and kept their pace. Edmund, sitting between

119

her and Fen, said: "We can't tire out the skaters before the races, mother."

Matilda expelled a breath which steamed exasperation, but said nothing more.

Though half the size of Whittlesey, Ugg Mere was enormous and across on its north shore the fishing hamlets showed up in untidy prickles of masts and trees. The south had no shore to speak of, just acres of marsh which disintegrated into the water of the mere and popped up here and there in tiny islands. Usually it was bleak, its edges trampled by cattle coming to drink. Today each island had a bonfire burning in its centre round which stood a ring of people and around them, on the frozen water, swirled skaters warming up. Matilda was amazed at the numbers. The Fen population averaged two or three people each square mile, but today it was here. Hermits had left their bridges, monks and nuns had emerged from their communities to cheer on their fancied skaters, pedlars, ale-wives, mead-makers had come to sell their goods, villages had turned out en masse. The air steamed with the smell of roasting chestnuts and with the oxen and sheep turning on their spits dropping their fat into glowing charcoal. It was all very bucolic. Matilda could see no sign of Abbot Walter. "This," she said to Adeliza, "will be a bore."

Three hours later the two of them, with Edmund holding their crossed hands, were skimming over ice screaming with joy, drunk on mead and exhilaration. Edmund had won the boys' race. A shape she had been avoiding for weeks splintered the ice as it stamped towards her.

"Request a war council, commander," boomed Stunta.

Matilda waved her free hand at him and zoomed off. "Later."

The race courses were winding and complex; it was difficult for the uninitiated to appreciate who was winning what, but it was apparent that the majority of winners were Ramsey men. Her son was upset about it. She felt vaguely that her Dungesey men could have done better.

She caught a glimpse of Pampi in a group of men and heard him say: "It may be scientific, abbot, but we say it's wholly cheating." Matilda's toes turned inwards and she

120

stopped. A familiar voice came out of the group: "Well, I did wonder, but there's nothing in the rules . . ." The peasants dispersed but the abbot, holding some skates in his hand, went on with his explanation to Matilda. ". . . antler horn is a harder substance than ox shin and makes a sharper edge."

"You remember me, my lord, Matilda of Risle?"

"The moss lady." He looked exactly the same except that he was drier and had bound Saxon trousers showing beneath his habit. "It worked, you know. Wonderful on putrid wounds. We're having great success in the hospital."

Chattering happily he followed her like Theseus led by Ariadne through the maze of skaters to the island on which her household was camped. She settled him on a rug with a leather cup of Berte's hot, spiced wine in his hands.

"My lord, do you happen to know a Roman called Vegetius or something? I should like my son to learn of him."

The abbot looked at her as if snakes had sprouted out of her head. "War," he said; in fact he almost shouted. "It turns up wherever you look. Their filthy war and their sieges and their blood. I'll have nothing to do with it." Wine tipped out of his cup and down his habit. He calmed himself down.

"I'm sorry. It's just that I'm sick of anything to do with war. They're trying to drag in the Church, my abbey, ordinary people, making them choose one side or another, when they're both the same." He smiled at Berte as she refilled his cup. "Yes, we have a copy of Vegetius in the library, but it is a manual for war, you know. Wouldn't it be nicer if your son learned the preservation of life, Galen perhaps?"

"There's a lot of war about," said Matilda. "He's going to be a knight, not a physician."

The abbot sighed. "Well, it's all learning . . . if you want to come over and copy it out, I'll arrange it. I'm afraid the librarian wouldn't let it beyond the walls."

She was charmed. She couldn't read or write; she knew of no woman who could. "I'll send my chaplain tomorrow, if I may."

Skating over the ice towards them came a monk and behind him limped a beggar who had neither skates nor

121

boots. They approached Matilda's island. The monk bowed to Abbot Walter, although to judge by his finer habit and the jewelled cross round his neck one might have mistaken him for the superior. Matilda, whose categorisations of class were unerring, recognised a commoner promoted above his station. The abbot introduced him with some pride, however: "This is my prior, Brother Daniel." She remembered the complaints of Father Alors and her fellow-landowners in the Fens. This was the obstructionist. She didn't like him.

"Forgive me, my lord." Brother Daniel was plump and moist and obsequious. "We have been doling out food and ale to the poor as you commanded" – he pointed to some braziers and a stall surrounded by a crowd a hundred yards away – "and this man complains of his foot. I thought perhaps . . ."

"Of course." The abbot drew the beggar up the rise and set him on Matilda's rug with an automatic: "Do you mind?" Matilda did mind; the man was filthy and covered in sores, doubtless self-induced; since he was one of the poor who would eventually inherit the Kingdom of Heaven she saw no reason why he should in the meantime pollute her rugs. However, in such exalted company she could hardly say so. "Please go ahead."

It was the abbot who unwrapped the rags from the foot. Matilda noticed that Brother Daniel didn't touch the beggar himself. He was looking at the abbot and she, looking at *him*, was shocked by the blankness of his face which had only a minute ago glistened with smiles and perspiration. It registered nothing. Some shutter had come down to hide something else. She thought: "I wouldn't turn my back on that little man."

A smell of dirt and corruption came from the beggar's foot, though the man himself was enthusiastic with drink. "You cure it, lord. Go ahead and cure it. I'm happy." He was prepared for one touch of the abbot's finger to drive out his foot's ailment. So was Matilda.

Three of his revealed toes were split and dark. "Snow got in it," explained the pauper cheerily, "but don't you

122

worry about that, lord, it don't hurt now. You go ahead and cure."

The abbot turned to Brother Daniel. "Get him drunk."

"He's drunk already."

"Get him drunker. It's frostbite." As Brother Daniel gestured to the monks in the distance, Abbot Walter turned to the beggar. "We've got to cut these toes off, my son. You shall come to my infirmary and we'll do it right away."

"Don't you bother, lord." The beggar was edging off the rug. "They don't hurt now. Don't you worry."

The abbot pinioned the man's ankles. "My son, they have an evil humour which, if it isn't stopped, will spread to your vital organs and you will die." He put his nose down to the foot and sniffed luxuriously. "See? You can smell the evil. I can't cut them off myself – I'm not allowed to shed blood – but I've trained the smith and I shall stop the bleeding with some wonderful moss . . ." Two monks came up to support the beggar, who was beginning to sway, and led him off.

Brother Daniel said sorrowfully: "I fear you can't be in the infirmary tonight, my lord."

"Why not?"

"If you remember, my lord, the Glanvilles are coming with other of our chief tenants." Brother Daniel was sweetly urging, as if talking to a child.

The spirit drained away from the abbot's face: Matilda saw he was older than she had once thought. "Can't you do it?"

"My lord, they wish to discuss the possibility of mounting a crusade against the Saracens at Lisbon."

"War again," shrieked the abbot; "don't they know we are on the point of great discovery? The schools in Paris, the Arab mathematics, the new medicine at Bologna . . . we are beginning to learn about this amazing plan God has made for us and all they can think about is killing. I tell you if they leave me alone to think and find out, away from all this bureaucracy and feasting, I could uncover the face of God."

Only Berte was equal to the embarrassment. She leaned forward and put another cup of wine into the abbot's hand. "You tell 'em."

The abbot stared into the cup. "I can't go on like this,

Daniel." The prior shrugged; obviously the solution, whatever it was, lay in the abbot's own hands.

When the two monks prepared to take their leave Matilda said: "Do you have to go so soon?" She did not understand Abbot Walter nor half what he said but when she was with him she felt in touch with new horizons; again she was conscious of the similarity between him and the boy Fitzempress. But hopelessly the abbot said he must.

"I must pray and make my confession before I meet these people."

He had completely won Berte's maternal heart. "What sins could you possibly have, lad?"

He looked straight at her. "I have this problem with lust."

The women watched him skate away. "Poor man," said Matilda, "perhaps we ought to invite him to Dungesey."

"Definitely," said Adeliza. "Poor man."

As they ate their lunch they were a sitting target for Stunta, the clerk. "Request a council, commander. King's sieging Bedford. Ely's in revolt. War's coming closer."

Matilda knew it and for this day at least had been trying to forget it. She looked at the man with loathing. Percy of Alleyn had used all his influence with her to persuade her to drop, temporarily, her attempts to get the clerk dismissed from his church. "He may not be much on the spiritual side, my lady, but these are military times, and if the parish is levied I'd rather see it led to war by someone like Stunta than, say, Father Alors."

The thought of Father Alors in battle had amused Matilda and she had given in – for the time being. Now she bit into a duck wing with a savagery which would have disconcerted a lesser man. "Well?"

"Muster the parish levies soon. Fight for the king for forty days. Dungesey unprotected. Women need defence. Teach them to shoot."

Why did the fool talk as if longer sentences would give away information to the enemy? "Shoot? They shoot already." More than once she had seen a Fen wife stop what she was doing, grab a bow and send an arrow at a duck or goose flying overhead. Usually they hit it.

"Crossbow. Deterrent. Nobody'd charge a woman with a crossbow. Too chancy. An expert in our midst." Stunta pointed to where a figure was pushing itself along one of the courses bent double, arms behind its back. It was the mercenary from Ghent, holder of the king's warrant. "Master-arbalist. Shame to waste him."

Matilda opened her mouth to send the idiot packing and then closed it to suck on the duck wing while she considered. She had every reason for not granting the clerk's request. She did not like him, she did not like the mercenary and certainly she did not like the crossbow, despicable weapon that it was. Further, no lord liked his peasants armed above the average; it gave them ideas and turned them into better poachers.

But the last few years had loosened the floorboards in Matilda's mind between what was conventional and suitable for women and what was not. The powerlessness she had experienced, especially during her marriage to Vincent, had deeply affected her. She had been frightened by her helplessness. Kings, men, commanded everything. They gave you a husband and told you he was your lord to be obeyed. He died and they gave you another and *he* was your lord to be obeyed. They frightened you if you were barren, they frightened you if you were fruitful. She wanted to defy and to spite. She wanted to control *something*. Waleran of Meulan moved across the shifting floorboards and a wicked Matilda rose up and pointed a crossbow at him; she wasn't going to use it, but Waleran didn't know that and was afraid. She took the duck wing out of her mouth. "All right. He can teach me at the same time."

The Dungesey men filed down to the Causeway to practise archery with the conventional bows they would use in the army, led by Stunta, and left the butts on Middle Green free for the women. Steward Peter had expected them to dislike their women being trained as home-front arbalists, but they had accepted the idea, though their jokes were unremitting.

"Try and miss the church bell," Kakkr called out, "that comes in handy."

"Try and miss the church," said Wyrm. "Same reason."

His wife, Milly, pretended fury and pointed her crossbow at him, which sent him off, miming terror. The mercenary strode down the line: "What have I told you?"

She sulked. "Only aim if we wants to kill. Only aimed at his head. Wouldn't hurt that. Nothing in it."

Willem waited for the cackling to stop. "You would kill him wherever you hit him. Why?"

" 'Cause they die from bleeding and shock."

Through the frosted morning air came the shouts from Stunta as he threw down the clout on the Causeway and paced out the distance so his archers could get the right trajectory. "Eight score. Loose." There was the rushing of arrows. Willem wiped the palms of his hands down his jerkin; anybody who'd been in battle sweated at the sound. But those arrows were only effective in the main if they hit exposed skin; they couldn't pierce mail nor, more often than not, the padded leather hauberk. The weapon he was putting in the hands of these women could pierce anything. He said: "If you, or any of you, do that again, you get out of this troop. Load."

They were using light bolts which needed a less powerful prod but which, with their superior speed, could penetrate as far. Six tassels vigorously polished six bolt grooves, and the bolts were inserted. "Cock." At least they'd stopped giggling at that.

Teaching women had brought more problems than he'd expected. Six pairs of feet were inserted in the stirrup – he'd made them with double stirrups so that they could put both feet in and get more leverage. He'd underestimated how strong they were; only Matilda, who'd never done the manual work which gave the others muscle, found it difficult to draw back the hemp string over the catch, but her determination made up for that.

"Aim." A child who'd been standing on a water-butt to watch gave a wail as it fell off. One of the bows wavered. "You dare," Willem shouted, "the enemy's advancing whether that kid cries or not. Don't think. Breathe. Let half of it out." Six chests took in the air and half-exhaled

126

it as six bows steadied on the butts sixty paces away. "Loose."

Chwwt-pt.

Tuna broke away from the line and ran towards her child. On finding it was all right she hit it which made it wail again. At least, thought Willem, she'd taken her bow with her. He'd broken them of putting the thing on the ground. Followed by the rest he walked to the butts.

Only a handful of the island women had been found suitable for training. Some were pregnant, the others were too old or crippled with rheumatism. The Wealas women had flatly refused, saying they had their own way of dealing with male enemies. ("Screw them to death, no doubt," Fenchel had said.) That left five and Matilda.

The yew trees had been lopped to within an inch of their lives to provide the heartwood for the prods and an elderly ox had sacrificed its existence and heels for the glue and his hide for the belts. The women had helped to make their own bows, all except Matilda who could not imagine a time when she would not have servants to do it for her. Willem had insisted, however, that she make and fletch her own bolts. "No arbalist worth his salt lets anyone else do his fletching." So with Berte holding a struggling goose Matilda, with distaste, had plucked likely pinions from its wings. "Right and left wings are flighted different. Use feathers from the same wing."

At first Matilda had been affronted by the mercenary's attitude, and had told Alleyn: "He must not talk to me like that. He must treat me with respect." But Percy of Alleyn had said: "He's a professional, my lady. He's teaching you as he would teach any man, lord or peasant. It's the only way he knows. Remember Jacques at Risle?" And into Matilda's memory had floated the long-quieted voice of the master-at-arms teaching her brothers. "Lunge, my lord, lunge. You're not a maiden afraid for her bloody honour. Lunge." She recalled the master-at-arms who had berated Fitzempress. Oh well, if princes could stand it, she could.

"At least he doesn't handle me," she thought, "and he'd better not." The mercenary would put his arms round the

127

other women, moulding them into the right stance, hitting their elbows down, but Matilda he never touched.

He was a mercenary and she despised him, but on the second lesson he had demonstrated how it should be done and casually shot six bolts, each one burying itself uniformly into the gold, and Matilda had seen she was learning from a master.

At the butts each of the six women had lodged a bolt in the target somewhere. They were getting better, though only two of them had the makings of fine archers. One of them was Matilda herself and one was Maggi, Stunta's woman. At first Matilda had been affronted that she must stand in the same line as the clerk's trollop, but when she had seen how good Maggi was at archery she had been overcome by the urge to be better.

Maggi, who had hit the outer gold, was a small, thin woman whose fuzzy red hair escaped from her cap to frame a small pointed face and blob of a nose, giving her the appearance of a russet hedgehog. "She's a natural," Willem had told Stunta, and the clerk had wept with pride. Matilda was less naturally gifted but she had a ferocity which the best arbalists possessed, launching something of their own will at the target ahead of the bolt. All the others just stood behind their crossbow and shot it.

"This is what you are aiming at." Willem stabbed his finger into the gold. "This. It's easy. Stop thinking about your bloody sex lives and shoot. We keep at it till we get it right. Tomorrow we'll try from the kneeling position. Retrieve."

As Milly went back to her place she winked at him. "Any position, any time," she said. Which was the other problem with teaching women.

Father Alors' sojourn at Ramsey Abbey while he wrote out the work of Vegetius in his careful script was extended. He found spiritual comfort in the beauty and lack of women of the abbey. He also enjoyed its cellar.

"You could have copied out the Bible in this time," Matilda told him crossly on his return, but soon she and the rest of her household were absorbed in the amazing tale Father Alors carried.

"Give up the abbacy?" Matilda was incredulous.

"Well may you disbelieve your ears, madam. I could scarcely credit it myself. But that is what Walter wishes to do, it seems." He drank off a beaker of wine. "Most of his monks say he's been manoeuvred into it by Brother Daniel and are afraid. They don't want him to go. But there are those who support Brother Daniel because of his big promises. Hysterical as women the lot of them. *Quem Deus vult perdere dementat prius.*" Father Alors, who had never approved of the monastic ideal, snorted, "St. Oswald must be groaning in Paradise to see his heir so effeminate."

"He's not effeminate," said Matilda, automatically defending the abbot, though she did not understand him. She couldn't see why deserting one's post should be accounted a female quality. She herself would never have abandoned such power.

King Stephen's army, which had come to put down Bishop Nigel's revolt, teetered on the edge of the uplands and looked out through fine spring rain across a puzzle of water and carr, to where the island of Ely lay, and wondered how the hell to get to it.

The local population was unhelpful. So was the terrain; rivers which promised at first to flow in the right direction turned back on themselves and went somewhere else. Two patrols which had been sent to locate the island had not come back.

The king's chamberlain entered the king's tent. "I have put the Abbot of Ramsey and his prior in the guest pavilion, my lord."

"Did you find out what they want?"

"My lord." The chamberlain tested his words as if he could not believe them. "The abbot wishes to give up his position at Ramsey and will request that you put his prior, Daniel, in his place."

"Relinquish his abbacy?" It was unheard of.

"That is my understanding. And, my lord, Prior Daniel

indicated secretly to me that he wished to see you first and alone." The chamberlain hesitated. "I think you should see him, my lord."

"I suppose you'd better show him in."

The monk was small and common but had triumphant eyes. He spoke in careful Latin. "My lord, as an earnest of my loyalty to yourself should you grant my abbot's request, I shall be happy to lead you to Ely."

The king perked up. "Do you know the way?"

"My lord, these are my fens. I was born in them. I know the hidden causeway leading to Ely which the Conqueror used." A traitor monk from Ely had shown it to the Conqueror, but Brother Daniel did not mention that. "I know many things which will be helpful to you."

"You will be rewarded." With his own hands the king poured wine and handed it to Brother Daniel, smiling.

"Do you mean to tell me," shouted Matilda, "that we've endured your invasion and mess to be left with an unfinished keep?"

As always she cowed Fenchel, but the mercenary stood his ground. "It appears that the king needs my friend here to work on more important keeps. I shall go with him and later rejoin the king's army and my men."

The message from Ypres had been terse: "Crossbow reinstated." The king's need had overcome the king's conscience.

"As far as I am concerned," said Matilda, "you can go to Hell where you belong. What about my garderobe?"

"Oh Jesus," muttered Fenchel. "Tell her she's got a first storey and an undercroft. Tell her she can keep her stores in it. Tell her the shit-pipe's corbelled up to the first storey. Tell her I'll be back. Tell her goodbye, for Chrissake."

"Ely will fall, my lady. Take care. Keep practising with the bow."

"Get out."

Outside Fenchel wiped his neck and the mercenary grinned: "That's my lady."

"Thank Christ she's not mine," said Fenchel. "I don't know what you see in her."

The mercenary didn't either. The fact that he loved her was a constant surprise to him. She possessed no quality he admired, except courage. He didn't love her because she was of the nobility or because she was beautiful, but because she was his completion. The way her hair grew out of her head, the way her mouth fitted over her teeth, the way she walked and talked and thought, made up a shape which fitted in every particular an empty space in his own soul. She was part of him if he never saw her again, which was likely, and if he never possessed her, which was likelier. He wasn't going celibate on her account, but she was his lady. The place had been filled for better or worse and there was nothing he could do about it.

He made just one provision before he left the island. "If you ever need me for anything . . ." he said to Percy Alleyn, and the knight nodded.

On Edmund's birthday Matilda despatched Father Alors and Percy of Alleyn to the Plantagenet court in Normandy. Alleyn was to size up the situation there and if, as her information went, Count Geoffrey was winning the duchy, Father Alors was to treat with him with a view to Edmund being brought up alongside Fitzempress in his household.

Edmund was young. Most young nobles didn't go to the household of the lord who would see to their knightly training until they were seven. But the situation in England was getting out of hand, the war was almost on her own doorstep. It could move quickly. England was not safe. But if Count Geoffrey were to become Duke of Normandy and accept Edmund, the child's Norman inheritance would at least be safeguarded. She would stay on in England and do her best to protect his lands over here. It was Edmund's due that he be brought up in a princely household.

Percy of Alleyn returned, as he had left, on Turold's ship, with a two-word recommendation: "Count Geoffrey." The leaderless, quarrelling Normans could be no match for the Plantaganet. Father Alors had already begun the negotiations.

"Very well." At least she could send with him the trusted

131

household with whom he had grown up: Berte, Father Alors, Jodi and the others. Epona was to resume her Wealy existence on Dungesey. Percy of Alleyn would stay with her, Matilda.

She went with them to the coast to see them off. The anaemic silt made a limbo of non-colour which stretched into sea on which Turold's ship looked insignificant, as if it would be sucked into nothingness. Edmund stood on Cradge's sea-wall and for the first time said: "I don't want to go."

His hair had been washed and cut, he was dressed in calfskin with a gold and ruby brooch on his shoulder, his sword was of the finest steel in a scabbard of gold brocade. He should have looked a miniaturised adult, but the shaven neck showed a baby's curve.

Matilda put her hand on his head. "Don't make a scene."

"I'm not going to cry." A tear rolled down his face. The muscles of Matilda's own face were so rigid she seemed stern. She might have disliked the boy. She took something from her belt and showed it to him.

"Look what Turold brought us." It was a battered sprig of broom, its spikes and leaves so young they were still feathery. "It's the *plante genesta*; Fitzempress' father takes his name from it. When you're safely arrived he'll send me another. It's a sign between us."

He brightened: "Like a secret message?"

"Yes, and I shall come and see you as soon as I can."

Turold shouted from the rowing boats in the creek: "The tide, lady."

She thought: "If I kiss him I'll be finished." She blessed him and watched him stumble down to join the boat party. He became smaller and more vulnerable with every step. Fen pressed her head against Matilda's knees and she gripped the dog's scruff. "I've done my best for him, I can't do more." But she wanted to pelt jewels after him so that he moved in a rain of treasure and his mother's love.

She couldn't stay on Dungesey; its supplies and cesspit needed time to recover from accommodating Edmund's

132

household for so long. She must start overseeing her estates again; she would return quietly to her main residence at Hatfelde and see what was what.

As Matilda and her diminished household rode under the archway of Hatfelde's gatehouse, a man was obstructing the other side of the arch with a scroll in his hand.

He stepped forward and a couple of men-at-arms, who were not her men-at-arms, ranged alongside him, and two more appeared behind her party so that it was trapped under the archway. The official began to read from the scroll in a high, thin voice: "'To Matilda of Risle, late the wife of our beloved Sigward of Hatfelde.'" She saw against the light that he had a chain of office round his neck and was a tall, bony, bald man with the heavy lids of a reptile and was of punctilious and uncomfortable cleanliness. "'Surrender to this, the king's special clerk, the heir of the said Sigward that he may bring the said heir to me at Westminster . . .'" His fingers turned the king's seal so that she could see it. "'. . . or surrender yourself to explain why not. Signed by me in the presence of . . .'" The names of the witnesses came unhurriedly, Waleran of Meulan's among them.

She thought: "Who betrayed me?"

"I am the said messenger, madam, Richard de Luci, and in the king's name I order you to produce Edmund of Hatfelde."

The tunnel echoed with the rasp of a sword leaving its scabbard and she clutched Alleyn's arm just in time to stop him using it. She felt Alleyn take her hand and wipe his eyes with it as if it were linen. He would blame himself for not protecting her. "It's not your fault," she said. The mercenary. The mercenary had betrayed her.

"Do you produce the said heir, madam?"

She was all at once exhausted, but the game had to be played. "I paid the king one hundred marks some years ago for the wardship of my son," she said.

"That agreement is no longer valid because of your treason. We have heard you have lately allied yourself to the enemies of the king. For the heir's soul he must now be delivered to the king."

She smiled with enjoyment. "The heir is out of the country and out of reach of the king."

Richard de Luci was unperturbed. "Then, madam, you will be hostage for his behaviour towards the king, and for that of your knights and tenants."

7

1140–1141

Stephen's hostages were part of his court, treated with as much honour as any other guest and almost as much freedom. They were seated at table in accordance with their rank, they took part in hunting and hawking, dancing and games, kept their own horses, dogs and servants.

Many of them were children who might well have been at court anyway since nearly all were noble and worthy to be brought up in the royal household. Certainly nobody was vulgar enough to mention that their presence kept their families loyal to Stephen.

The only suggestion they lived under threat came when one or other disappeared for a while. This happened when their family or a vassal opposed the king, at which the hostage was taken to the offending castle and paraded in chains with promises to hang him or her until the castle gave in – or didn't.

The hostages returned from this experience sullen with humiliation but not fear. Everybody knew Stephen wouldn't hang people of their station in life. As Peg of Grantley said to Matilda: "He hasn't got the balls."

Peg was a dreadful old woman, the bane of Matilda's and Adeliza's life with whom she shared a room. She had an unwashed, corpulent body, an even dirtier mind, chewed garlic for choice and suffered from flatulence. She was afraid of nobody, from the king downwards, and rejoiced in speaking her mind. Matilda seriously considered advising the king to hang her.

She and her grandson, William, were hostages for the good behaviour of Peg's son, John the Marshal, who was in revolt in Marlborough Castle against the king. At one point during Matilda's hostageship the little boy William actually was taken down to Marlborough, shown to his father standing on the castle walls, and a rope put about his neck. "We'll hang him, marshal," Baldwin Fitz Gilbert had shouted. John the Marshal had shouted back: "Then hang him. I've got the hammer and anvil to forge still better sons."

When the child was returned to his grandmother and the story told, Peg had approved of her son's sentiments. "Now he *has* got the balls."

Matilda did not take her capture quietly; she still had money and connections and she used both to plead her cause. Her spokesman denied her alleged treason. Yes, she had visited the Empress in Normandy; it had been a social call and, anyway, had been made at the instigation of her father-in-law, Serlo de Luard. No alliance had been entered into. This was Matilda's story in court and out. She told it so many times she indignantly believed it. Nobody else did.

It was sound economics for Stephen to dub Matilda a traitor; it meant he could take her lands into his own hands.

Although her estates were escheated, Matilda kept considerable personal wealth in a small chest of jewels. After her capture she had ordered Percy of Alleyn to lodge it with the Knights of St. John of Jerusalem, the most incorruptible order she could think of, at Clerkenwell, only to give up on presentation of her personal seal, which she kept hanging round her neck under her pelisse.

As the payments and bribes she had to make to further her case mounted it became obvious that some of the jewels must be sold. After a sleepless night, Matilda entrusted the transaction – and the seal – to her London tenant, Gervase of Holborn.

Her reservations were due to the fact that, as a merchant who was making a fortune out of the trading freedoms Stephen gave to his beloved Londoners, Gervase had admiration for the king. Nor did he owe the same feudal loyalty to Matilda which her landed tenants were oath-bound to give her.

But in his bourgeois way Gervase had a greater sentimental belief in the chivalry of the nobility than the nobility itself and was shocked by Matilda's predicament. "A great lady like you," he said, "accused of treason, practically put in chains. What can the king be thinking of?" Matilda was not practically in chains: she was being treated with liberality. However, she did not disabuse him.

Sympathetic and flattered by her need for his expertise, Gervase proved her greatest ally. He guarded her seal as fiercely as his own. He got a larger price for a smaller number of jewels than she would have believed possible and advised her on how to lay out the resulting monies. "Bribe the king's physician?" Matilda had not conducted business like this before. Gervase of Holborn had.

"He has great influence and, please lady, it's not a bribe. We are purchasing his goodwill." They purchased a lot of goodwill, including that of the judges who were to hear Matilda's case after Christmas. The more Gervase became involved, the harder he worked. He would even give up time to travel to wherever the court in its peripatetic progress round the country happened to be in order to report progress, or, more often, the lack of it. She in turn kept him up to date with wider events.

"The Earl of Chester has rebelled." In the negotiations between Stephen and the King of Scotland, the earl, known familiarly as Ranulf Moustaches, had lost out. To keep the Scottish king from invading England on behalf of his niece, the Empress, Stephen had given him Carlisle. But Carlisle was Ranulf's patrimony, his ancestral home, for which none of the king's compensation could make up.

Ranulf had taken revenge. He sent his wife and his sister-in-law on a social visit to the castellan of Lincoln. After a decent interval he went to fetch them home again. Since he turned up unarmed and with only three companions, the gate guard let him in.

They knocked out the gate guard. They knocked out the castellan. They seized swords and axes off the walls and fought their way down to the postern where Ranulf's half-brother, William de Roumare, was waiting with a force of armed men. In less than fifteen minutes they controlled the castle which controlled one of the most important towns in England.

Matilda's lips twitched as she passed on the news. She thought it was funny. But Gervase was as horrified by Ranulf's action against the king as he had been by the king's action against Matilda. "What are we coming to? Let's hope the king smashes the wicked man."

With Gervase of Holborn in charge of her case, Matilda relaxed in the knowledge that her future was in the hands of God. For the first time in years there were no decisions she was forced to take. She'd had word from Father Alors – Edmund was safe and well-regarded in Fitzempress' household. "And there's one thing," she told Adeliza, "with that damned Stephen gobbling up my revenues he's not likely to give them all up again by marrying me off. I'm free as far as that goes." And as the court moved to the Tower of London to prepare for Christmas she did feel surprisingly free, for a hostage.

Matilda had been touched by Adeliza's insistence on accompanying her after her capture at Hatfelde. "There's no need for you to suffer too. Go home to Normandy." But for once Adeliza had been stubborn. "I'm coming with you, 'Tildy."

They began to enjoy themselves. There was feasting every night while the cupboards in the hall and chambers were full of sweetmeats for those who couldn't wait until then. The guests were walking showcases of jewels and fine cloth and crowds lined the streets to watch their excursions as they went to Smithfield for the horse-racing. There were parades of the Tower's menagerie of cameleopards and elephants.

Stephen was at his best, giving expensive presents to guests and hostages, and bestowing largesse on the poor. Watching him showering silver pennies to the beggars on St. Lucy's Day, Matilda saw he was completely happy, not just as the centre of adulation but because he was pursuing kingship as he saw it. If Stephen could have spent his reign lavishing infinite monies on infinite deserving subjects, he would have died content.

138

It was on the night after that the new man came. He arrived late to the table and walked to the king's end to apologise. He stood out; in his own way he was beautiful. Though he was tall and well-built, his attraction lay not so much in his features, which were regular, as in his colouring; a fair skin tanned to apricot, blond hair, blue eyes and white, slightly backward-sloping teeth. It was the colouring of wholesomeness, of all honest and open things. Matilda would have believed anything he said as soon as he opened his mouth. He opened it: "My apologies, lord king. I was making sure my men are standing by in case you need them."

Stephen smiled with affectionate patronage. "You need not be so solicitous. There's unlikely to be trouble during the peace of our Lord's birth."

"I'm only a common soldier, lord," said the newcomer. "I'm concerned for your safety, peace or no."

There were grunts of approval in which Matilda nearly joined. The Normans liked to think of themselves as bluff, loyal subjects.

As the man walked back past Matilda their eyes met, and he smiled. "Who's he?" she asked of Peg, who was sitting next to her.

"Eyes off," said Peg. "He's a mercenary." Instantly Matilda's interest faded as the man joined Jews, heretics, Saracens and commoners in Matilda's category of untouchables. "A Fleming," went on Peg. "Name's Fitz Payn, though who Payn was, Christ knows. Commands a large force of brutes. Stephen finds him useful."

"And he's allowed to eat at the royal table?"

"Nowadays Stephen will eat with any scum who'll provide a force for him. Fitz Payn's not the only one at this table."

The man was still looking in her direction so Matilda jerked her head to show her displeasure; she'd had enough of mercenaries.

However, their one brief eye-contact seemed to have set him on her trail. When she was practising with her crossbow in the butts, she heard his pleasant voice with its slight foreign guttural behind her: "That's no weapon for a lady." Immediately she walked away.

"That brute's watching me," she told Adeliza, who answered loyally: "Well, you're a fascinating woman." Matilda, who had little personal vanity, did not believe it. Fitz Payn was harassing her. She found herself riding knee-to-knee with him on a hunt. His hand would be suddenly on hers in a round dance. There were nights when Fen would get up and mutter at the door with her hackles up. She confided in the other lady hostages who shrugged: "It's terrible. What can we do?"

Peg of Grantley put it more forcibly: "If beasts are brought to court, we're bound to step in shit."

On St. Stephen's Day morning Peg told Matilda: "The king had secret visitors in the early hours." She always knew what was going on.

"Who?"

"Three burghers from Lincoln. They want him to attack Lincoln and get rid of Ranulf Moustaches for them. Ranulf's men have dispersed for Christmas and he's unprotected."

"Will he do it?"

"There's an emergency council going on. Tell you later."

By tradition war stopped for the Twelve Days of Christmas. Knights wanted to eat up their Christmas tithes, serfs wanted the blow-out provided by their lords before winter starvation set in. Long before Christmas Eve trails of men calling seasonal greetings wound away from the battle zones to their green-decked homes, leaving the tracks churned up behind them. It would take weeks to ferret them out.

"We'll have to be in position before Twelfth Night." Stephen was jovial. "We'll need at least a thousand men. How many can we raise, eh, Waleran?"

The barons reckoned, oh, a thousand easily. But Richard de Luci's thin, clean fingers ran over his tallies and jotted figures on a slate. "Four hundred, my lord."

The barons guffawed.

"Don't listen to him."

"London's stuffed with them."

"We can send out riders for more."

De Luci was a new man who had risen through the ranks merely because he was clever. He dealt in statistics, not red-blooded men.

"We can send out riders for more," Stephen told him.

"My lord, you can't depend on more than another three hundred at most. The roads are boggy and many will be incapacitated by too much feasting." That was true. They made themselves ill; some, like Matilda de Risle's Sigward, died of it.

"Have you counted the hostages' men?" asked Waleran.

"We still have some Scots. Matilda de Risle's knights . . ."

"I have included them. In my view it would not be wise . . ."

"Wise?" Baldwin Fitz Gilbert's roar lifted the leaves of bay on the walls. "If we waited for your wisdom, turtle-head, we wouldn't move at all."

"You would not," said the turtle-head calmly. "I consider this enterprise foolhardy. We can treat with Ranulf more easily than fight him, but my place is to carry out the wishes of my anointed king."

"Your place is on the end of my boot."

"My lords, let us fight Ranulf and not each other." The king's voice was sweet. "It is St. Stephen's Day. My day. God's hand is in this request from Lincoln; I feel it. What must we do?"

"I'll tell you what we must do, King of the English." Fitz Payn stood in the full light of a window so that his complexion showed up like good, fresh bread. He moved to the dais and put one knee on it so that he half-knelt, half-stood, at once respectful and easy. "I'm an old campaigner and when other captains are letting their men slip away, I keep mine ready. My lord, I can offer you a force of two hundred and fifty . . ."

"He made them look like novices," Peg told Matilda.

"Scum," said Matilda. "There was a price, of course. These mercenaries only think of trade."

"Yes. It was you."

Matilda walked to the window and looked at the river.

141

A breeze wobbled its surface making shiny, black ovoids between the wavelets, constantly moving and going nowhere.

"You mean, he mentioned my name in full council?" There was no indignation in her voice. "God's teeth, I'm humiliated. I shall get my champion to challenge him. Or make the king banish him. Or . . ."

"The king needs those men. He showed shock for the look of the thing, but then went into private audience with Fitz Payn. He must have Lincoln. Giving you and your lands to that bastard might be worth it."

Matilda turned round and clawed at her. "Mary, Mother of God, save me. Forgive my sins and protect me. What shall I do?"

"Oh, go." Peg was almost distant, as if Matilda's problem was an infection she didn't want to catch. She took a gold ring off her fat finger. "Don't fetch anything or tell anyone. Go to Normandy."

"But I'll lose the English estates." Then Matilda panicked. She grabbed the ring and ran to the door. Fen looked up and galloped after her. Both skidded to a halt. De Luci and a page were standing outside.

"Madam, the king requires your presence." His lizard eyes blinked at Matilda's shout.

Shock stuffed her ears against the Tower's uproar as they went through it to the king's apartments. A royal army getting ready to move makes a lot of noise. Boots echoed on stairwells, courts rattled with mail, shields, spears and helmets being loaded into carts. Marshals shouted to men, barons to marshals. But to Matilda the air was sterile and silent. "You can stop it. Blessed Mother, just one twitch of your finger. Stop it."

The king was alone in a tiny wedge of a chapel in the wall of his turret. He took Matilda's hand and sat with her on one of the miniature choir stalls. "Dear daughter."

On the gaudy walls blood gushed in thick radials from St. Alban's neck. Hook-nosed men and women threw what looked like figs at a smiling St. Stephen. The king enquired of her health. He wiggled each of her fingers, as if he were

142

playing "Piggy-go-to-market" with a child. His voice played the same game. "Dear, dear daughter, we care so much for your welfare . . . in these troubled times in the loving protection of a strong man . . . our devoted and beloved servant, Ralph Fitz Payn . . . noble in soul if not yet in status."

Matilda barely heard him. She was praying too hard. "You can stop it. Just one twitch of your finger."

Sweetly she thanked the king. She dwelt on her ancestry and the kings and queens in it. She conjured up bishops and friends in high places all over Europe. A king who stood for her before God would not bring shame on himself and her by marrying her to an excommunicate mercenary. As Matilda reached her peroration, Fen squatted and piddled in the rushes. Matilda ended on her knees, one little hand touching the king's slipper, weeping as must, she knew, the angels who heard her.

The king beamed at her. "Above all, he is *handsome*."

All the time she'd been a fish, opening and shutting her mouth to an alien species. "I will not marry him. I will not consent."

"There will just be time for the ceremony before we ride to Lincoln, though none for the bedding, I fear. You must be patient."

Not just soundless, invisible. He had conjured up some different being to kneel in front of him. He was a magician who made the world as he wanted. "I will not marry the bastard." She pulled off his slipper as she stood up. If they wanted a fight they could have it; she had to say the words for the marriage to be legal and nothing they could do would make her say them.

The king's figure blocked her view of the altar as he knelt for a moment and rose. "Don't you hear me?" she shouted. "Are you deaf?" Fen got up on stiff legs and barked.

Stephen had gone and another man filled the doorway. The mercenary had been waiting outside. His blue eyes stared at her in wonder, as if the two of them had been carrying on an intimate correspondence and were meeting for the first time. "I am not worthy."

143

"That you're not." She inhaled deeply to stop herself from shaking. "I told the king and I tell you that I shall never consent to this marriage."

Not one jot of the wondering, silly love on Fitz Payn's face disappeared. He knelt to press the hem of her gown with his lips. "My honoured lady. Queen now and for ever." His tears were wetting her cloak and she jerked it away.

A snarling, brindled shape leaped from her side, punching Fitz Payn with its head, snapping at his hand. Fen had erupted through the surface of the sea they were drowning her in, speaking for her in yaps of hatred. Her only champion, her dog.

In one perfectly co-ordinated movement Fitz Payn stepped backwards, drew his sword from its scabbard and sliced through the bitch's throat.

Fen turned to Matilda as if expecting an order. Blood pumped out of her throat, her legs folded and she fell, with Matilda beside her. It takes forty-five seconds for a dog whose carotid artery has been cut, to die. All that long time Fen's eyes were on Matilda's face and her blood became a fenland river sliding shallowly over the chapel tiles, forming rivulets along the cracks and taking with it Edmund's childhood and the day they had gone eel-glaiving and the day they had skated on the ice.

The bitch's eyes blinked and grew tired but never left her. The disreputable head went down to rest in its own blood. A muscle twitched in the flank, and Matilda was alone with a mercenary and a furred carcase.

"Will you have a bridesmaid?" The man was smiling. She saw his backward-sloping teeth. "Shall we fetch the Lady Adeliza?" He would slit Adeliza's throat. He would kill everything she loved, but she could not hand down to Edmund's heirs an ancestress who had consented to a mercenary. She stood up and felt the weight of blood on the front of her gown drag it down. She said: "You are scum and your soul will turn on a spit in Hell."

He went to the door. "Get rid of the dog." He turned to Matilda to console her, as if they'd both suffered a loss. "Never mind." A thin, pock-marked man dragged Fen's body out into the corridor by its tail, making lines of blood to the door. He returned with a priest who swayed and giggled and smelled of wine and Hugh Bigod, stepping carefully: "What *has* been going on?"

"You, Bigod," screamed Matilda. "Witness I do not consent to this filth. He's killed my dog."

Hugh settled his cloak in becoming folds and leaned against St. Alban's execution. "Actually, lady, I am now the Earl of Norfolk. A minute ago, in fact. I'm here to witness your marriage, and only that." His word that the marriage was legal would give Stephen the excuse to believe it, as it had given him the excuse to assume the throne.

Matilda put her head down and charged for the gap between the men at the door. The mercenary's arm slammed against her chest.

He pinioned both her arms and his cloak muffled her as he brought over his right hand to clamp her mouth. She tasted blood on the palm where Fen's teeth had gone in. She forced her own teeth apart and bit into the wound. She would have kicked as well, but the pock-marked man had crouched behind her and held her ankles.

Despite the pain from his hand – she was grinding his flesh – the mercenary's voice was sober and proud. "I take you as mine." The falchion at his waist was nearly breaking her ribs.

The priest giggled again: "She must say the words as well."

Behind where the man was holding her feet came an exaggerated falsetto: "I take you as mine." They would say: "I heard her woman's voice accept him."

"Felicitations," said the Earl of Norfolk.

She slipped in her dog's blood as the mercenary pulled her out of the chapel, past Fen's body and down the corridors of the Tower, trailing her like a child, and all the way, like a child, she screamed: "I did not. I did not." Only God heard her; everybody else was in the bailey watching the king and his barons mount up. The noise of shouted goodbyes, orders, creaking wheels, stamping horses, the flap of standards and the cheers of the Londoners was such that Matilda's screams

145

joined the cacophony with no more effect than one more bird in the dawn chorus.

Fitz Payn picked her up and held her head against his shoulder, as one would hold a baby, scratching her face on his brooch. He went to the king's horse: "My lord. The Lady Matilda of Risle has accepted me as her husband. Father Oswald and the Earl of Norfolk were there and witnessed it." Matilda kicked.

The king nodded vaguely, his sight already on Lincoln. "Are your men ready?"

The mercenary galloped her over to where Richard de Luci was standing and set her down. He put her hand in de Luci's: "See you keep her safe. I want her here on my return with her seal and the charters to her lands. The king wishes it."

De Luci nodded. Hand in hand they watched the mercenary mount and kiss his hand to Matilda. Baldwin gave the order and the cavalcade moved out of the gates.

"I did not. I did not," whispered Matilda. "What shall I do?"

It was a rhetorical question because de Luci would have no answer for it; as the king's loyal servant he would obey the king's command and she would be closely guarded until the mercenary came back to rape her and her lands. Surprisingly she got an unclerkly reply.

"All you can do, my lady, is join me in praying that he dies in battle."

8

1141

The citizens of Lincoln opened their gates and applauded the entry of Stephen and his army, so relieved were they to be delivered from Ranulf Moustaches.

A day later, as Willem of Ghent rode up Steep Hill to his commander's HQ, the bells of each parish were still ringing their welcome, drowned by the Great Bell of the cathedral which tolled Bishop Alexander's forgiveness to his king.

Willem didn't share in the general thanksgiving; he had heard the news of the marriage between Matilda de Risle and the mercenary, Fitz Payn.

The soldiers gathered outside Ypres' headquarters weren't overjoyed either. "We didn't get here quick enough," one of them told Willem, pointing up at the castle. "Ranulf got away before we could surround it. Sure as eggs he's gone to his father-in-law, and sure as eggs he'll be back." Ranulf's father-in-law was Earl Robert of Gloucester.

Willem pushed his way through to his commander. Ypres' face showed strain. "We've advised the king to withdraw. We haven't enough men for a full-scale battle. We'll be caught here like rats in a trap. But you know what he is – he's loving all this." Ypres indicated the adoring bells. "Says it would be unchivalrous to leave when he's just arrived. Unchivalrous. Anyway, welcome back to the ranks of the godly, Willem. Your men are billeted in Thornbridge. Thirty arbalists in good working order."

Jacopo said the same. "Welcome back, captain. All present and correct."

Willem regarded his men sourly. "Present," he said, "but

147

not correct. Have trouble fighting the food in Kent, did you? They're fat."

Jacopo hitched in his stomach and admitted the food had been good. "Creamy and luscious, like the women. We only saw service once, with Stephen's queen at Dover. I have given my heart to that queen. Such a woman, such a consort. The spirit of a saint and the mind of a soldier. I tell you, Willem . . ."

"You can start earning your sixpence a day." Willem turned to his command. "We're in for a pitched battle any day now. You tub-bellies couldn't fight cold the state you're in. Tomorrow, let me tell you, we start training. I'll give you creamy and luscious."

His men grinned. Alain winked. "Good to be back, captain."

Ranulf Moustaches came back, quicker than anyone could have expected, and with him came an army with Robert and Miles of Gloucester and Brien Fitz Count at its head, its ranks swelled by barons and knights and men whose lands had been forfeited through their loyalty to the Empress, and others whose estates had arbitrarily been given to Stephen's favourites.

As a force it was very little bigger than Stephen's own, but it had the ferocity of the disinherited.

It didn't attempt to storm Lincoln but ranged itself on the plain outside and waited for Stephen to come out to do battle.

Inside there was argument. "Wait, my lord," Ypres advised the king. "Wait for reinforcements." The older barons supported him. But the younger barons, led by Hugh Bigod, Earl of Norfolk, set up a chant: "Battle-shy. Battle-shy."

Ypres turned on them. "Don't you battle-shy me, you buggers." His thick, hairy fingers grabbed Bigod's cloak. "Where are *your* men, eh?"

Bigod smiled. "Battle-shy. Battle-shy." It wasn't aimed at the mercenary. Its real target was the man whose childhood had been made painful by taunts against his father, the rope-trick man, the coward of the Crusade. Stephen was afraid

148

of being afraid. He said gently: "My lords, I am tired of skirmishing and sieges. Tomorrow we will go out and win this war once and for all."

Apart from Ranulf's men still sieged in the castle and the look-outs, almost the entire population of Lincoln that night attended the eve-of-battle service in the cathedral. It was also the eve of the Purification of the Virgin Mary, Lincoln's patron saint, which, insisted the king, was a lucky omen.

Willem looked round the packed, noisy congregation. "Which one is Fitz Payn?" Jacopo pointed to the ranks of the barons at the chancel steps. "The good-looking one." Willem nodded.

"But he's not as good as he looks, captain. And his men aren't nice at all. Hand-choppers, back-stabbers and stone-slingers." It might have surprised the feudal knights with their chivalry to know that mercenaries had their own ethics which, while not exactly a code of honour, were a basic trading standard. Fitz Payn's habit of cutting off his prisoners' hands did not accord with it. "Not nice, captain," went on Jacopo, "also short-sighted. One war's enemy may be another war's ally. And if the king was handing out great ladies in marriage to mercenaries, why not to you? Why Fitz Payn?"

"I'll kill that mouthy bloody Fenchel."

The cathedral fell silent. The moment had come for the king to make his offering for victory. They saw his figure from the back outlined against the light as he carried an offertory candle to the altar.

They saw him falter and flames appear at his feet as the rushes caught fire. The chanting stopped and for a moment nobody moved, then some choir monks stamped out the flames and drew back, leaving the king with half a broken candle in his hand.

"The candle broke," said a voice. The "Os" resonated up the pillars like sounding smoke-rings as the appalled congregation repeated it. "BrOke, brOke, brOke." The king went on, quelling the silliness of the candle stump by his grace. Bishop Alexander lumbered forward to meet him.

There was a crack and behind Alexander the golden pyx

which held the host crashed down on to the altar. The rings of the chain which had held it rattled to the floor. The echo seemed to last for minutes, before the smoke-rings sounded again. "Omen. OmenOmenOmen."

As the congregation filed out of the cathedral in complete silence, Percy of Alleyn came up alongside Willem. "A word with you, old fellow." They climbed the steps of East Gate and walked along the top of the wall to where the city's roofs fell steeply away. Smoke from chimneys and louvres was an unhealthy white against the grey February sky.

"I've had a message from her," Alleyn said. "As I thought, it was no marriage. She wouldn't consent, brave little lady. He gagged her and somebody else spoke for her."

He didn't look at the mercenary nor the mercenary at him. "As her champion, I've challenged him, of course, but the king won't allow it until the battle's over. But after what we've just seen, well, I'm not sanguine about tomorrow. God's no longer on our side."

Brought up to believe in the infallibility of kings, Alleyn's misery reached beyond grief for his lady. It weighted him so that standing beside that big, sad man was like being dwarfed by a monolith. He put his hand on Willem's shoulder. "Well, not to beat about the bush; if I should fall in battle tomorrow and you survive . . ."

"I'll kill him," promised Willem.

The champion nodded. "Thank you. That's what I wanted to know."

After the final battle plans were made that night, Ypres took his crossbow captain to one side. "Contract rules tomorrow, Willem," was all he said, but Willem understood. They were contracted to fight their best for the king – but not to lay down their lives in a lost cause.

As they walked down to their billet in Thornbridge, they pushed against a steady stream of citizens, their valuables piled on carts, making for the upper West Gate and the escape route to the north. Fenchel said: "Sometimes you fight a battle and win it and sometimes you fight a battle and lose it, but I'm buggered if we've ever lost a battle and *then* had to fight it."

The Battle of Lincoln was among the shortest on record.

Whether it was because God had demonstrated that He was no longer on the king's side, or whether they had made a secret alliance with the Empress, Stephen's earls such as Waleran and Hugh Bigod deserted the moment the enemy charged them, without striking a blow.

When he saw their cavalry wing galloping off the field, Ypres knew the day was lost and called on his own men to run. The only ones who fought were the king, the household knights who surrounded him and the citizens of Lincoln who loyally came out to help and were slaughtered.

Among the chaos, the panic and the noise, Willem received indelible images; the shocking and empty space where the earls' cavalry should have been protecting the king's right flank, Ypres' white face as he galloped past shouting: "It's lost. Another day." He saw Percy of Alleyn lurch off his horse, head downwards so that his helmet stuck in the mud and a passing horse stumble into his body, leaving him in a frozen somersault with a broken neck.

Not able to understand why Alleyn had toppled sideways rather than backwards, Willem looked back along the trajectory of the stone that had hit him to where one of Fitz Payn's stone-slingers was capering. Fitz Payn was clapping the man on the back.

Maybe the only completely fulfilled man on the royalist side that day was Stephen himself. As his enemies encircled him he fought like a berserker. His sword broke, so he threw it away and took instead a two-headed axe thrown to him by a Lincoln citizen, wielding it with a ferocious and satisfied intensity. He might have lost his kingdom, but, by God, he'd prove he wasn't a coward as his father had been.

When the news that the king had lost, that the Empress had won and the war was over, arrived at the Tower of London, there was joy for the hostages and panic among the king's servants. Most of the court staff deserted at once, fearful that

151

the Empress would be down on them any moment, red in tooth and claw.

Only Richard de Luci remained at his post. He was the new breed, a bureaucrat who served the throne, no matter who sat in it.

The ex-hostage Matilda de Risle stopped him as he crossed the Great Hall, preoccupied in reading a scroll.

"I wish your apology, de Luci, for having kept me here against my will."

For a moment he couldn't think who she was; there'd been a lot of hostages. Then he remembered. "My lady, I have here the list of the dead at Lincoln . . ."

Immediately she was transfigured. "Fitz Payn. I knew God would kill him. I prayed for it."

"There's no news of Fitz Payn. He's missing – deserted, perhaps." He proffered her the list and then remembered she was a woman and could not read. "Percy of Alleyn."

She didn't believe it. Alleyn had been her champion all her life. She didn't believe it then nor for some time later, not until they brought the coffin to Hatfelde when, to the scandal of the local priest, she had Fen's small coffin brought from the Tower and buried them side by side.

"You silly man, you've got the names mixed up. It's Fitz Payn who's dead."

Busy as he was he found time to feel sorry for her. "He may be. He may not be. But, lady, if it was no marriage, establish the fact with the new order, with the Bishop of Winchester, with the Empress. Get it beyond doubt."

He watched her walk back across the hall. He noticed that the other hostages withdrew from her as if she were contagious. Whether she had consented or not, she was tainted by alliance with a mercenary, especially a mercenary who had been on the losing side.

He shouted: "With the Pope if necessary," and hurried off about his business.

In the keep in the Black Fens Brother Daniel, the glass-blower, whipped the boy who was his connection with the Devil for being faulty. "You got it wrong."

The boy hiccuped from sobs and wiped his snotty nose. The smoke from the smouldering hemp weaved round his head and over the shine of the scrying glass. He breathed deeply to ease his way into the blessed, terrifying semi-consciousness. The pupils of his eyes dilated. His white little lips pursed as if in a kiss and through them came the voice of the demon.

"Wait."

9

It took time for Empress Matilda to get over her surprise at her victory. Not until she'd seen a calm and graceful Stephen actually in chains at Bristol did it become real.

Although Stephen's queen was holding out in the South-East the Empress was, in effect, Lady of England. To become Queen she had to gain the support of the Church, which meant winning over Stephen's brother, Henry of Blois. She must have access to the treasury at Winchester where the royal crown was. Last, she must persuade the Londoners to open their gates to her.

She found herself with new and surprising allies: Hugh Bigod, his manner suggesting that fighting for Stephen had been a minor hiatus in a career devoted to the Empress' cause, Waleran of Meulan and others.

The Empress swore on oath to Bishop Henry all the promises to the Church which his brother had made – and broken. That gave her Church and treasury.

It took until June to get London. The delay was not just due to the Londoners' reluctance but to garrisons still loyal to Stephen who opposed the Empress en route. The city gave way only because the Empress bought Geoffrey de Mandeville, castellan of the Tower of London, and it could hardly hold out with the Tower breathing down its neck.

De Mandeville's price was enormous; he was confirmed as Earl of Middlesex, Essex and Hertfordshire with the right to build castles where and when he wanted. The Empress gave away power on a scale that would have enraged her father, Henry the First. But the market was de Mandeville's and he squeezed it dry. The Empress entered London.

All that was necessary now was the coronation.

In the Great Hall of Westminster the Empress received petitioners. In the overlooking gallery her devoted supporter, Brien Fitz Count, banged his head against the balustrade with a violence likely to break one or the other. He turned to the Empress' devoted half-brother, Earl of Gloucester: "You've got to stop the bitch."

Earl Robert, whose calm was legendary, tore off his cap and stamped on it. "Didn't I try? You saw. She didn't even rise. I knelt before her and got bawled at like a butler who'd stolen the bloody spoons."

"We'll lose every ally we've got."

For two days now the Empress had received petitioners as if they were dirt. Lords spiritual and lords temporal were treated with the same disdain as commoners. To her poor, ignored advisers it seemed she only granted a petition when doing so would offend somebody else. She was rude to her uncle, King David of Scotland. She was rude to her new ally, Henry of Blois.

Matilda de Risle was only one of the petitioners turned away with a sharp: "Attend on me until I consider the matter."

The repelling calm which had distinguished the Empress when she'd fought for her throne was gone; she vibrated with a resentment that she'd had to fight for it at all.

"Is it a woman's thing . . . you know, the Change?"

Hoping to find the answer to a mystery in a mystery they peered down for symptoms of the menopause, looking for a hot flush in the pale, beautiful face.

"Should we send for the Plantagenet?" Fitz Count was reluctant but desperate. No Norman liked ceding to an Angevin, but her husband might be able to control her.

"He won't come. England's her problem. His is Normandy."

"It's an error Stephen wouldn't have made. He'd have been all things to all men by now."

"Regretting your choice?"

"There was no choice." In Fitz Count's book the hereditary principle had to be established. He was an orderly man. The killing, the seizing of goods, all the things he'd had to do to hold Wallingford for the Empress had been done with disgust and in this belief.

Below them a deputation of Londoners moved to the foot of the dais. They were genuinely worried men wearing torn cloaks to indicate poverty. "Your demand for tallage, my lady . . . it's not that we won't pay it, but at the moment we can't." They'd given their last penny to Stephen some time ago, not that they mentioned it now.

The anger which had vibrated the Empress all day almost oscillated her now. She swayed as she stood up. "You crawling swine. You filth."

The men in the gallery closed their eyes.

"You poured out your coffers to strengthen Stephen and weaken me. Do you think I'll show kindness to conspirators? I'll have justice from you traitors and I'll have every penny."

A voice from the crowd shouted: "You're not queen yet."

In Westminster Great Hall next day the servants prepared the tables for the Empress' coronation banquet. The chamberlain knotted his belt and his brow in the effort to memorise the precedence in which he must seat the guests. In the kitchens cooks were dripping sweat as freely as the hundreds of carcases on spits were dripping lard.

Cursing as only he knew how, John the Marshal had personally kicked every human backside in the stables until the horses for the Coronation procession were groomed to his satisfaction. The exercise made him grumpy and reminded him that he still hadn't been given all the estates the Empress had promised him. He stamped through the palace to her apartments, his boots dropping clumps of horse manure.

He found the Earl of Gloucester looking out at the river. "She's in the chapel preparing her soul. Leave her alone, marshal."

"She still owes me Newbury."

156

"You'll get it." He was watching the far bank of the river for the return of the army. Last night Stephen's queen had shown that she was still to be reckoned with by raiding Southwark. The earl had sent his main force to chase her back into Kent. He now wished he hadn't. He was picking up vibrations of bad luck.

John the Marshal, never sensitive to vibrations, never sensitive to anything, returned to his grievance. "Bloody female. Stephen wouldn't have made me wait for it. Say what you like about Stephen, he was a generous bastard."

"Stephen's in prison."

"And serve him right." The marshal was crude, vulgar and illogical, everything Brien Fitz Count and the earl were not. He believed a woman's place was in her man's bed. But in his belief that the rightful heir should inherit he was as unwavering as they were.

He nodded downriver. "They're starting the celebrations early."

"What?"

"The Londoners. Ringing the bells. Celebrating."

The sound had crept up on him, first one solitary bell and then another; he'd dismissed it as a fire alarm. The city was always burning somewhere.

But the ringing spread. Some three hundred churches were crammed into the square mile of London and now each one was ringing, as if an earthquake had shaken it.

The earl had been in Flanders when the towns erupted against their lords. He said: "Commoners ring bells as a muster to arms. Oh Jesus."

They pelted down to the palace yard and one of the earl's squires came riding in, shaking. "The Londoners are coming, my lord, thousands of them. They're armed."

Butchers had grabbed cleavers, slaughterers had fetched their knives and woodmen their axes. Women whose hands could snap a goose's neck picked up pokers, rolling pins and gridirons. After a night discussing its grievance, the corporate temper of the city had suddenly boiled. It was out for the Empress' blood.

The earl felt sick with, of all things, embarrassment. He

157

felt a fool not just because he had miscalculated in leaving the lady defenceless, but because, for an instant, he saw himself and all Normans as posturers who held their place only so long as the animal on which they pranced kept its eyes shut. Stephen was not his enemy: at root they were the same. The true enemy was at this moment streaming along the Strand.

"Well, for Christ's sake, say something. Evacuate. We can't hold them, but if they find this place empty they'll stop and loot. They're only cattle." Good and noble marshal. They were only cattle.

He gave orders.

John the Marshal half-carried the Empress, who had not adjusted to the emergency, to the western postern. As he urged her to mount the waiting horse, she made a stand for dignity. "I'll not ride like a man. Fetch a side-saddle."

The marshal picked her up and threw her so that her legs scissored open and she landed astride. "Get up there, you silly bitch."

An army headed by Ypres and Stephen's queen pursued the Empress west. Her retreat became a rout.

King David of Scotland had an epic flight in which he was captured three times and three times bought off his captors.

John the Marshal hid in a barn and his pursuers set fire to it. Even so he escaped, though a flaming spar fell across his face and burned out one of his eyes.

The Empress got away, but only because her half-brother turned to delay the pursuit. The earl fought like a lion, but in the end was captured.

With Stephen in prison on the Empress' side of the country and with the Earl of Gloucester in prison on Stephen's side, it was stalemate. Each held the other's ace.

So they exchanged. With elaborate safeguards, Stephen was returned to his throne at Westminster, and Earl Robert to his Empress at Oxford. The Battle of Lincoln might never have happened.

The reminder that anything had happened at all lay in

account rolls all over England which had once shown a profit. Now on the right-hand side where the figures should have been, there was written against estate after estate the one word: "Waste".

Because she didn't know what else to do, Matilda de Risle followed the Empress' court to Oxford. There could be no going back to Stephen who had betrayed her. She was committed to the Empress' cause now, win or lose.

She put such knights as she had left at the Empress' disposal.

With the money from the few estates remaining to her out of Stephen's clutches, she hired lawyers in every court she could think of to establish that she had never been legally married to Fitz Payn. She laid out a vast sum on an emissary to the Pope to do the same thing.

Gervase of Holborn advised her against it. "It's expensive and it could take years. Fitz Payn's probably dead, anyway."

"I know he's dead," said Matilda. "But everyone must realise I did not consent to him. I owe it to my son."

It had become an obsession. She bored everybody with the story, repeating again and again: "I did not consent."

Adeliza noticed that Matilda had begun to take a bath every day as if her skin had contracted some invisible infection from being enveloped in the mercenary's cloak.

It did her no good. Ladies of the court, previously her friends, avoided her where possible not just because she had become boring but because, whether she had consented or not, she had been disgraced. The Empress ignored her, but then the Empress ignored practically everybody.

Adeliza suggested: "Why don't we go to Wallingford and stay with Lady Maud? It's not far away. Gervase can send a messenger every day to say what's happening. You'd like to see Maud of Wallingford again."

Matilda was tempted but hesitated. She felt instinctively that she should stay at the hub of her contracting world, keeping an eye on the Empress and keeping in the Empress' eye. Sheer loneliness tipped the balance. It would be nice to see the jolly, friendly wife of Brien Fitz Count again. Gervase

159

of Holborn could be trusted to watch events at Oxford on her behalf. She went.

Matilda looked incredulously at the little woman who greeted her into Wallingford Castle. "Maud?" She recovered her manners. "My Lady Matilda." But Maud did not repeat the my-Lady-Matilda joke; there was no joking left in her. The unborn baby she carried might have been a succubus taking the goodness from her bones; her mouth had fallen into puckered lines and the eyes which had been lively boot-buttons stared wearily at nothing.

When they were settled in the keep solar, Matilda asked: "Was the siege as bad as all that?"

It had been as bad as all that. Wallingford had been sieged on and off almost since the war started and in all that time Maud had commanded it. Every time the siege was lifted Brien Fitz Count had come back, impregnated his wife and then gone off to rejoin the Empress. Maud of Wallingford said none of this. She said: "It was an honour to serve the Empress." She wasn't joking. The health of poking fun at the Empress had drained out with the rest. To avoid hating the woman who took her husband away from her, Maud had become her acolyte too.

"I bet it wasn't as bad as what I've been through, eh Adeliza?" and Matilda launched into her tale, ending with her usual: "But I did not consent."

"I am sure you did not." Maud was polite and vague. She hauled herself up. "If you'll excuse me I'll go and see to the sleeping arrangements."

She went out and Matilda cried. She wanted Percy of Alleyn. She wanted Berte and Jodi. She wanted her son. She wanted her old life back and all the people in it who had made it safe.

Adeliza cradled her. "You've still got me, 'Tildy. 'Tildy."

"Yes?"

"Let's go to Normandy. Count Geoffrey nearly owns it now. He'll welcome you. We can join all the others and everything will be like it used to."

Matilda wiped her eyes. "You go if you want to. It's time

160

you were married. I'm staying here. Somebody's got to protect Edmund's lands in this mess."

The solar, once a light-filled, fan-vaulted circle, a woman's place, was full of war. Its windows had been bricked in to become arrow slits, ladies' embroidery frames stood among clumps of spears. The cradle waiting for its occupant had rolls of rags in it for the bandaging of male wounds. Matilda sighed for the lost symmetry of things.

At Oxford, Gervase of Holborn was becoming uneasy. The court was disintegrating. Robert, Earl of Gloucester, had left it for Normandy to try and persuade Count Geoffrey Plantagenet to come to England and fight on his wife's behalf.

The moment he'd gone the Empress' supporters began to slip away. They weren't defecting to Stephen, but Stephen was attacking from the south and threatening their homes and they had to defend them.

If the gaps they left were dangerous, so were the men who came to fill them. Mercenaries of all kinds began to make an appearance – and were received. The Empress was desperate. For the first time she was forced to employ men on whom, a few weeks earlier, she would not have wiped her boots. She did it with disdain, but it was a seller's market; the mercenaries took her insults and upped their price.

Since the Empress was ashamed of these transactions, she conducted them in secret and Gervase had to bribe her chamberlain to keep tabs on what was going on. The chamberlain was eager to unburden himself: "I never thought I would see such things, never. She's sent this German brute, Fitz Hildebrand, to recover the treasury at Winchester for her. He's a known killer, you know. I never thought . . . and these scum don't just want money, you know. They want estates – and they're getting them. Her father would spin in his . . . and there's another one down in the hall this minute. She keeps them waiting for the look of the thing, but she'll employ him, don't you worry. Oh yes. She wants this one to recapture Ibber. God knows what his price will be."

"What's this one's name?"

"I don't know their names," said the chamberlain, pettishly. "They're all Fitz something. And they're all scoundrels."

Gervase of Holborn walked as inconspicuously as he could into the hall to cast his eye over the petitioners who filled it. Almost at once he saw the tall, sweet-complexioned man talking engagingly to one of the Empress' ladies and he knew what this particular mercenary's price would be. He backed out as quietly as he could, then ran for the stables.

Fitz Payn watched him go and beckoned to his lieutenant.

The riders caught up with Gervase on a deserted part of the track leading to Wallingford alongside the Thames. The moment he heard the hoofbeats he knew he'd miscalculated; he should have taken a faster horse than his usual palfrey.

Even then he tried to outride them. He was terrified for himself, terrified for his lady. She must be warned. Frantically, as he rode, he tried to remember his sins to confess them to God. "Absolve me from them, whatever they were."

They got him in the same way they'd got Percy of Alleyn. A stone hit his shoulder and toppled him off the horse. As he sprawled on the ground they put a spear through his heart, clean as a whistle, and threw his body into the river.

At Wallingford Maud's captain of the guard entered the solar. "A messenger from Oxford, my lady."

"Thanks be to God." Matilda had received no news from Gervase for two days and had been preparing to ride back to Oxford to see what was wrong.

"Not for you, madam. For my lady. A marshal of the Empress'. With a Praecipe." A command.

"Admit him."

"I shall," said the captain, "but not the crew with him." He hadn't guarded Wallingford all this time to let in any cut-throat who asked admittance.

But the marshal ushered into the chamber, though a stranger to them, was genuine enough and he carried a scroll bearing the Empress' own seal.

He had the brusequeness of a man doing an unpleasant job as quickly as possible. "'From Matilda the Empress to

162

our best beloved Maud of Wallingford. I command that she deliver without delay the person of Matilda of Risle to this my marshal to be safely delivered to her husband Ralph Fitz Payn. Sealed by my hand. Witnessed at Oxford by the Earl of Norfolk.' "

It took time, but as it sank in that Fitz Payn was alive and that she had been sold to him again, this time by a fellow-woman, the particles which made up the soul of Matilda of Risle unstructured themselves. Memories, myths, scoldings, landscapes, loves, everything which had formed the invisible Matilda and given volition to the physical Matilda splintered away from each other. She watched as her body acted on its own like a decapitated hen and threw itself at Maud of Wallingford's feet. "Don't give me up." A particle of her reason whizzed by and said: "Ridiculous. How futile."

Maud of Wallingford was white and holding her stomach. "Please, please."

Somebody else was sobbing. Matilda's face felt the wet, smooth face of Adeliza as the girl hugged her. Another particle said: "Protect Adeliza. Protect Edmund." To Adeliza she said: "Go to the Fens. Get a boat. Go to Edmund."

The marshal saw the hysteria could get out of hand. He told the captain: "Help me take her down."

The captain said reluctantly: "She'll need her things. It's getting bitter."

"Send a maid. Bring the boxes to the gate."

They pulled her up between them and took her to the door. Adeliza ran in front and tried to stop them but they pushed her down.

A passing particle of Matilda's past said cheerily: "I shall fear no evil," as they dragged her, screaming, down the stairs.

163

10

Ibber had been built and sited in the Conqueror's time and, although it was comparatively small, its importance lay in its ability to control Thames traffic from and to Wallingford upriver.

It stood on one of the few sites where the Thames narrowed to run through steep hills. In wartime it could put a boom across. In peacetime a ferry ran from a quay at the bottom of its keep to a quay with a tollhouse on the other bank, from which a track led up to the Icknield Way. Before sieging Wallingford, Stephen had taken it; now the Empress, through her new servant, Fitz Payn, had taken it back.

From the north, the river side, the keep rose up the escarpment so that, looking up from a boat, it seemed to swirl and topple. But to a visitor approaching from the south the hill hid most of the keep's height, so that Ibber looked a mere fortified manor surrounded by unsurprising walls.

For Matilda's arrival they were less unsurprising. Corpses of its former garrison hung from the crenels like untidy bunting. Matilda saw them as mere background in the atrocity of existence.

Fitz Payn met her in the doorway of the hall, asking tenderly after her health. His complexion shone with his own health; warmth gathered round his russet cloak and the jewels which had recently adorned Ibber's late castellan. "But where is your household, my dear? No ladies to attend you?" He was genuinely put out. As he swung her off her horse he called inside the hall and a blowsy, fair-haired woman came out. "This is Dyrika to look after you. A countrywoman of mine and good-hearted." To Dyrika in Flemish he said: "See you attend her well, you cow." Dyrika nodded amiably.

He kissed Matilda's hand and, holding it high as if they were about to dance, led her into the hall. Its fifty or so occupants, mostly men, had been feasting. The women were noisy and indiscriminately affectionate, which had caused a quarrel down the end of the table. It stopped the moment Fitz Payn appeared.

The pockmarked man who had held Matilda's ankles during the pseudo-wedding was Vladi, Fitz Payn's lieutenant. He bowed, taking his cue from his commander. "Captain, we your loyal lads congratulate you on your nuptials."

He pulled out chairs for them but when Fitz Payn saw that Matilda wouldn't eat he got up at once. "She can't wait." The company hooted.

Alcoholic breath on the cold air made a bower through which the couple walked to the keep. Men tapped their rutting forearms and the women wished Matilda luck in sudden, shrill goodwill.

They went up the narrow circling stairs almost to the top. They entered a room where the dirt on the floor showed lighter squares, having been once a storeroom. Now it contained a large, ornate bed, a table and a chair. Its one beautiful feature was a long, narrow window overlooking the fifty-foot drop to the river. It let in the cold; the stone ledge outside gleamed with frost.

Dyrika was sentimental and excited. "I'll show her the gong." She opened an aumbry door to reveal a garderobe; the wind moaned up through the hole in the seat. "Wonderful what they think of." Fitz Payn seemed as proud as if he'd installed it himself.

"And now, if you please, give me your seal. I shall relieve you of the management of your estates as a good husband should." The seal would give him even quicker access to their profits than the Empress' writ. But Matilda and Gervase had lodged it at Clerkenwell months before.

Fitz Payn's face became sad. "Go down and search her luggage." When Dyrika went he crossed to Matilda by the window and began to undress her. He unclasped her cloak and folded it neatly, then tackled the buttons of her pelisse, raising her stiff arms to pull her shift over her head. He loosened her hair, unhooked her shoes, rolled down her stockings. When she was naked he walked round her slowly. Her skin was almost green in the moonlight, goose-pimpled and puckered. Her eyes never left the river. "It's not there, is it?" he said.

He dressed her again as meticulously, adjusting the garters so they were exactly level and combing her hair with his fingers before folding it into its crespin.

He went and lay down on the bed with his arms behind his head.

"We'll get the Empress to send for Edmund," he said.

Some particules of the invisible Matilda re-formed, though her very dullness saved her because she knew, if she knew anything, that the man got his sustenance from fear. He created it around him, then sucked on it, like snakes absorbing mice. Just as his fingers had searched her body, his mind scrabbled at hers to tear an entrance. She shut him out and kept watching the river.

She knew two things. She must not be afraid and she must stay alive. If she died he would have access to Edmund as the boy's recognised stepfather. To stay alive she must not be afraid.

Outside it began to snow, flakes thickening into a hypnotic dance. Matilda watched the river and the mercenary watched Matilda.

About three o'clock in the morning her eyes grew small and her lids lowered. Then the obscenities began. Matilda's eyelashes flickered up. Expletives heard only from men in temper crept in caressing sibilants across the room. Atrocities to the human body were crooned in lullabies to dissipate in the cold air beyond her window. The fetor of sound seemed to come not so much from the bed but to escape from the walls.

Fatigue sent her unconscious but the whispering went on.

In the morning he had gone and she was still slumped against the window, but a woollen rug had been wrapped round her to keep her warm.

Stephen's generalship was surer now. His courage at Lincoln and his dignity in imprisonment had answered questions he'd wondered about all his life. Confident, he took his army through the Empress' territory, capturing Cirencester, luring her barons from her side by attacking their castles. That done, he turned and made a lightning march on Oxford and was in the city before its weakened defences could stop him. He besieged the Empress in Oxford Castle.

Seeing her predicament her allies acted typically. The newer, paid supporters deserted her. In this anarchy was their chance to carve out kingdoms of their own owing allegiance to no one. Fitz Hildebrand took Winchester (and its former castellan's wife) as his own. Fitz Payn refused to hand back Ibber, either to the Empress or Stephen.

Her old friends stayed loyal. The Earl of Gloucester came rushing back from Normandy and made a feint to draw Stephen away from Oxford. Brien Fitz Count with another army offered battle outside the city.

But Stephen didn't make the mistake of Lincoln again. He didn't budge. The snow was coming down and he was tucked up in a warm, well-provisioned city. As Ypres said: "Let the buggers freeze, my lord, while we starve the Empress out."

At first the citizens of Oxford were panic-stricken at being in enemy hands, but Stephen, always good to the towns, ordered strict discipline among his troops. One occupying army is rarely worse or better than another; Oxford learned to live with the king's as it had lived with the Empress'.

"What scared us," said the landlord of the inn which Willem of Ghent had requisitioned, "what scared us really was that you was mercenaries."

Jacopo was drinking with his eyes on the landlord's daughter: "Really, my friend? We're not so bad."

"*You're* not, I can see. But some we had were nasty. Murderers and such."

Jacopo winked at the girl while her father wasn't looking: "A lot of murders?"

"Couple of bad ones," said the innkeeper. "Poor girls beaten to death." He put his mouth to Jacopo's ear and gave details. Jacopo grimaced; he was against wasting women. "Who did it?"

"We had our suspicions." He told them to Jacopo who left his wine and the landlord's daughter to burst in on his captain. "Willem, he was here."

She must not be afraid; she must stay alive. She began to eat from the trays Dyrika brought to the room. The mercenary still hadn't touched her, but her body wasn't at all sure it wanted to stay healthy for the assaults his whisperings promised. She vomited. When she'd stopped she began eating again. She must not be afraid.

She had one resource. Years of kneeling and parrot recitation in church gave her now not the comfort of God – He had deserted her – but the comfort of words. " 'If I ascend up into Heaven, thou art there; if I make my bed in Hell, behold thou art there. If I take the wings of the morning and dwell in the uttermost parts of the sea . . .' "

The good-hearted Dyrika became worried and worked herself into sufficient indignation to brave Fitz Payn. "She's still at the window and she's still muttering. You want to bring her down here a bit." She lost her courage and cowered. "Only company, lord."

When she looked up he was crying: "She has been used to a queen's."

She was allowed down under the guard of Dyrika and a close-faced archer called Craik. The company took her impassivity for pride and reacted by showing off, mocking her if Fitz Payn wasn't around, even with occasional acts of kindness. She ignored them all.

She was tuned only to the awareness of Fitz Payn. Without looking at him she knew every move he made. She could sense his arrival and would tense seconds before he came into the room. There were nights when he didn't come to the chamber but the whispering went on just the same.

For fresh air they let her sit in the herb garden which some d'Oilli had made between the inner and outer bailey. It was overgrown but there were sage bushes, and rosemary had grown almost into a tree. Along the north wall ran a hedge of japonica still spiked with the yellow quinces. It was a white, green and brittle garden. But it had peacocks.

The hens were bad-tempered with the cold and stuck their heads into the bushes but one morning one of the cocks displayed for her. It was not just his tail that was beautiful; the fish-scale feathers on his back overlapped in fans which were edged with gold, never one out of place. His neck was shot blue, white outlines round his eyes and a fragile crown. " 'I stretch forth my hand unto thee; my soul thirsteth after thee as a thirsty land.' "

There was a crunch on the gravel behind her. "So you like peacocks?" Matilda's hand dropped. "We shall have them on all our manors."

He gave orders. His men hoisted the peacock which had displayed to Matilda to the roof of the hall and tied it to the weather-vane. Fitz Payn stood with his arm protectively round Matilda's shoulders while his men used it for target practice. The bird squawked and flapped, scrabbling with its pointed toes at an arrow in its wing. The stone-slingers ran round the bailey working their arms like birds and trying to imitate its mating cry. A bad shot finally went straight into the centre of the mess and killed it.

The other birds were served up at dinner. Fitz Payn had the cook beaten because they were tough. "But they never do eat as well as they look, do they, my dear?"

"A fine time to end a contract, Willem," said Ypres.

"It's not a bad time. The war's as good as over." He gestured in the direction of the castle. "The Empress can't hold out much longer in there. What'll the king do with her? Imprison her?"

"He can hang the bitch for me," said Ypres. "Sod all women. You, of all people."

Willem shrugged. "And you can have a new contract with Jacopo. I've told him our terms, by the way, so you can't undercut him." He shifted to be off. "Well . . ."

His commander surprised him by coming round the desk to hug him. "I'll tell the king you're putting down rats for him."

"I am."

Outside in the street it was black cold; the river had frozen over and snow lay on the ice. It would take some time to get there. At the inn his band waited for him.

"Have you got the boots?"

"Certainly, boots," said Jacopo. "I don't know the size but a lady of my acquaintance . . ."

"Clothes? Rope?"

"Oh, my God," said Jacopo, "are we taking an inventory? Everything. Except maybe somebody to go in with you."

"He'll be less suspicious of one."

"He can kill one easier as well."

"Let's go."

This night he'd brought her down to the hall so that he could play the part of the long-married man who valued conversation with his wife. He and Matilda sat at a table on the dais with a chessboard between them. Fitz Payn didn't know how to play chess, but he moved the pieces with the gravity of an expert then, when she didn't respond, moved her pieces in reply.

"You see, my dear, we must consider our position now that our benefactress is finished." It was the first she'd heard of the Empress' predicament, but who won and who lost no longer mattered to her. It mattered to Fitz Payn, who'd backed the wrong horse yet again. "This is a time of opportunity for men of courage. We must grasp it." He jumped a pawn over the queen and then the king, picked them up and dropped them on the floor.

He stood up and faced the noisy hall. He shouted: "We'll have our own kingdom." The company cheered. Vladi began dancing with Dyrika. Fitz Payn sat down again, peevish. "I need better men. These have no quality." He looked across at her quietly. "Give me the seal, please. Or I'll make one from Edmund's little spine. He's upstairs in the room below ours."

Her face remained blank and her hands clenched in her lap. She gripped one fact: it was snowing, blessedly and tenderly snowing, softening the outline of the keep and putting ridiculous caps on the heads of the corpses still hanging from the walls. And silting up the tracks. It was impossible to get to London and back, let alone to Normandy where Edmund was.

Nevertheless he'd sketched her son, small, chubby and frightened, still trusting her. A nerve twitched by the side of her eye. Fitz Payn saw it and his good humour returned. He didn't know chess, but in the game he was playing he was a master.

When he locked her in that night he didn't accompany her. She wrapped herself up and went to the window. "I mustn't be frightened." White, jagged panes of ice from upriver floated on the water; from here they looked like mutant fish. "He giveth snow like wool; He scattereth hoarfrost like ashes. He casteth forth His ice like morsels. Who can stand before His cold?"

The door unlocked and opened, but not enough to admit a human. A tabby cat came in. It was Fitz Payn; she could tell by the teeth. She broke. She ran for the highest point of the room which was the bed and the cat circled it below, rubbing itself against the hangings. Matilda whimpered.

The door opened to let in Fitz Payn. He smiled at her and saw she was ripe at last. He picked up the cat, walked to the window and dropped it down to the river. He turned and the moonlight outlined him in silver. "Now."

Matilda screamed. He began to punch her, crashing his fist into her face and breast. She fell off the bed, astonished even while she cried out by the violence. She tried to crawl under it but he dragged her out by her hair, stood her up and knocked her against the wall so he could hit her again. He was shouting but she couldn't hear what through her own noise.

He dragged her back to the bed and jerked her on to it. He crashed his fist into her mouth. He was wrenching her clothes off with one hand and punching her with the other, kneeling on her legs.

If he'd given her the chance she would have pleaded, abased herself, signed away her estates, anything to stop him. Time opened and closed, swelling to make every detail clear and then dwindling into a blur. The mercenary had multiplied so that there were a dozen men attacking her and howling. There were two female entities in the room: Matilda and Matilda's fear, a huge wobbling amoeba. He didn't enter the physical Matilda, though he pushed the hilt of his dagger into her vagina. It was Matilda's fear with whom he had sex, murmuring obscenities to it, fondling it, ejaculating into it, telling it how lovely it was.

Time closed and opened again. The mercenary had dwindled down into one gasping, pettish man. "Cover yourself up. You're disgusting. Why are you all so disgusting?"

Her split lips hurt but she moved them. "I'm sorry."

He'd gone. She was alone and disgusting. She was sticky and she smelled. She bled from the mouth and the vagina where the handle had ripped the membrane. She got off the bed and fell down, so she crawled to the window. The river would be clean.

She hauled herself up into the window. The view was beautiful, uncaring, sexless, inhuman. The snow was still falling. The river hadn't stopped. She took away her supporting hands to let herself go into it. She was pushed back. She leaned forward again — was held back again. She was between an unstoppable compulsion and an immovable prohibition. She was in a vortex formed by Hell past and Hell future. She became brittle.

There was a whirring, clicking sound as her feet began to revolve at the ankle and her arms to unscrew from their sockets. They unthreaded faster and faster so that any moment now they would fly out and drop out of the window and her trunk would fall on to the stumps of her legs and fracture into shards.

Just in time the Virgin Mary and Mary Magdalene stepped out of the garderobe. "Now stop that," said the Mother of God sharply. Matilda's feet screwed themselves into her legs again and her arms tightened into place. "And come down. You'll get your death of cold."

"It seemed the best thing." Matilda stepped back.

"Well, it isn't."

They led her back to the bed and snuggled her into it. They stroked her face and she could tell her lip and her eye stuck out to an unaccustomed distance. They smelled of holiness. She showed them where her lower incisor had been knocked out. "Shocking," said Mary Magdalene. She was a busty, pretty woman wearing the tall hat of a town prostitute balanced on her red-gold curls. "We used to get types like that at the whorehouse."

"Did you?" Matilda was interested. "As bad as that?"

"Worse," said the Magdalene, "the stories I could tell you . . ."

Matilda turned to the Virgin. "I couldn't help it."

"Nobody blames you," said the Mother, comfortingly. She too was on the plump side, something on the lines of Berte, but with bluer eyes. "Well, men will, of course, but they blame women for being women."

"And you did have babies normally after Jesus, didn't you?"

"Lord yes," said the Mother. "Joseph was a good, normal man, a bit like your Sigward."

"What shall I do?"

"The first thing" said the Mother, "is to go to sleep."

"You won't go away?"

The Magdalene kissed her. "We'll be here as long as you want us." She went off to sleep as they held her hands and gossiped quietly over her head.

Dyrika took one look at Matilda's face and ran for warm water and ointment. She washed her all over and salved her cuts and bruises. All the time Matilda chattered to her saints.

Dyrika went downstairs and told Vladi: "She's gone mad. She's talking to demons and she laughs. Shall I bring her down?"

Vladi looked towards his captain, slumped and unmoving in his chair. He'd seen Fitz Payn like this before. "She's lucky she's still alive." He called: "Shall the lady come down?" There was no answer. Vladi shrugged. "Get her down, then."

Dyrika stood outside the door of the chamber, reluctant to go in. "Lady, oh lady, come and eat."

"Shall I?"

"Got to keep your strength up," said the Magdalene. "What's the food like here?"

"Dreadful."

At the top of the stairs Matilda paused: "I'm mad, aren't I?"

"You are and you aren't," said the Mother. "You could stop if you wanted to, but in these circumstances I wouldn't want to."

They went ahead of her, arm in arm, while Dyrika supported her waist from the back in case she fell on her unsteady legs. Dyrika chattered kindly. "There is a new man come. To offer help he comes. To join us. A nice man I knew long, long time. He is goet."

"Sex mad, these Flemings," said the Magdalene.

If there was a new face among the company Matilda didn't see it, nor would she have recognised it. She was too busy talking to her friends. Her head turned from side to side and her poor mouth moved in light conversation. She saw Fitz Payn glance at her and look away. This time it was Matilda who smiled.

Vladi confided in Willem of Ghent. "We should be making a move before we're snowed up in this dump and besieged by one side or the other. Get the rest of our band and seize the woman's estates and form this kingdom, if that's what he wants. But he's had one of his fits and won't move. Talk to him, for God's sake."

Over dinner Fitz Payn regained awareness. He stood up and raised a beaker to Willem. "Welcome to our new colleague. Your reputation goes before you." He beckoned Willem to join him on the dais. "How many men can you bring with you?"

"Thirty. All master-arbalists."

"I've heard. Well, I need a new lieutenant. Vladi has no quality." His honest blue eyes looked straight into Willem's. "Why did you break your contract with the king?"

"He's weak and he's treacherous. And he treats mercenaries like scum."

Fitz Payn banged the table. "They all treat us like scum. They think because we're businessmen we have no honour."

174

He leaned back in his chair and became the generous host. "Bring your men tomorrow, but tonight share our hospitality. Rough, simple soldiers' fare, but you've had worse. We do our best. Sometimes I play chess with my wife. And that lady there" – he pointed at Dyrika – "sings for us."

"I remember. She's an old friend of mine."

Fitz Payn smiled. "She's an old friend of everybody's."

When the men went outside to urinate, Willem estimated the time by the moon. Ibber was badly guarded. There was only one sentry in the gatehouse and two more resentfully patrolling the walls. The tollhouse across the river was deserted because the keep was virtually invulnerable from that side.

He knew they didn't trust him. They sniffed him like a new dog in a pack. When he'd renewed his acquaintance with Dyrika he'd felt their resentment at his appropriation of one of their women. But Dyrika was his passport to get close to Matilda without suspicion.

It hadn't been hard. Dyrika threw herself át him at the first smile. Now as he went up to her she did it again. "Willem, do you remember?"

He smacked kisses on her cheek and they reminisced. As soon as he could he nodded at Matilda. "What's the matter with the lady's face?"

"*Wielden dieren.*" Wild beasts. "Gone mad, poor vrouw."

"Let's go and cheer her up."

Matilda stood alone in the shadow of one of the hall bays, cordoned off by her madness. The lids of one eye had puffed together, her jaw was swollen on one side and her lips and eyebrows were cut. She seemed amused at something.

His arm round Dyrika's waist, Willem spoke low: "You can hear me. In a little while I want you to go out into the bailey. Matilda, listen to me."

"What are you saying?" Dyrika's French was still basic. "Why do you look at her like that? She's no good now. I'm better."

"What's he saying?" asked the Virgin Mary. "Who is he?"

"Another mercenary."

"Ignore him."

175

Willem nuzzled Dyrika's neck. "Just go outside to the bailey." He had two contingency plans but they both depended on getting her out of the hall. "Take her out, D'ika, if you love me."

"You don't want her, Willem, she's not nice . . ." Willem kissed her. Fitz Payn was coming towards them.

"I allow nobody to speak to my wife."

"I was paying my respects. I thought it was the done thing."

Immediately Fitz Payn was the grand seigneur. "Living this rough soldiers' life we forget the courtesies. But we are not barbarians. We shall have music. Dyrika shall sing."

He led them away. Dyrika's voice was strong, a crowd-singer's voice. She was a kind woman but her reactions were self-indulgent and at the moment she was jealous. Willem was one of the few men who had been gentle in her life and she was convinced he was her great love. She didn't want to get him into trouble, but she couldn't resist teasing him. She chose to sing the song of Ghengolf and as the first line *"Nu hadde die Ghengolf ene vrouw,"* vibrated through the hall Willem winced. "Now had Ghengolf a wife and to him she was untrue . . ." The bloody woman was flirting her eyes back and forth between him and Matilda. She'd wink any moment: she had. He tapped his foot as if in enjoyment while Ghengolf's wife picked out a lover *"mitten te spelne in hermichede"*, with whom to play in secrecy.

He could feel Fitz Payn's antennae wave into the situation to smell and evaluate. Where the hell was Jacopo? The attack should have started by now.

Fitz Payn's attention never left Dyrika as she drew with every gesture a connection between Matilda and Willem. Ghengolf's wife made the acquaintance of the serpent and her lover's honeyed body. Vladi, responsive to the currents criss-crossing the hall, came to Fitz Payn's side. The man might not have quality but at that moment Willem would have swopped him for Jacopo.

The song ended throatily in Ghengolf's terrible revenge. In the silence before the applause began Fitz Payn spoke to Vladi. "Find out what she knows." He turned to Willem and became charming. "Advise me on my barony . . ." Willem had to listen to his plans to carve out a piece of England from the war, as Vladi led Dyrika outside. He came back alone after a few minutes, walking nonchalantly, avoiding Willem's eyes. Fitz Payn excused himself and went to meet him.

The knowledge that he would die painfully was overridden by humiliation. He would die looking a fool who'd made a plan that hadn't worked.

He got up and began walking down the hall, which had gone quiet. The company had immobilised into a frieze of rustic carving. He was level with Matilda now. Casually he took her hand and began running. It was worth the chance that Jacopo would attack at this one moment.

At a shout from Fitz Payn an arrow went into the ground in front of them from the guard on the wall. He pulled up. Matilda was muttering disgruntledly.

They were taken to the room known as the Malemit, below Matilda's in the keep. Fitz Payn was proper. Torture was for torture chambers.

The room was the same size and shape as the one above except that its window was an arrow slit and its bed was stone and not for sleeping on. Manacles stuck out of the walls at varying heights and chains hung on pulleys. Three feet away from the river window a grid was set in the floor covering a drain which ran down at a steep angle to join the corbelled vertical garderobe chute and ended thirty feet above the river. It was a combination of sewer and oubliette down which the ordure of prisoners could be sluiced away and down which their bodies were dropped when they were dead or, as Fitz Payn explained, "what is left of their bodies".

His hands were strapped to a hook and he was lifted up until his feet dangled above the floor. The band of mercenaries and women crowded excitedly into the room. Matilda was sat on the stone bed to watch.

Fitz Payn was almost fond. "Did you want her for yourself? Or does the Empress want her back?" He was shaking and exhilarated.

At that point, much too late, the attack began. They could

hear shouting and the boom of the gate being rammed. Somebody shouted: "Attack, captain. Captain."

Fitz Payn jabbed his dagger twice into Willem's shoulder, not so much in anger but in frustration at being interrupted. "Why do they always thwart me?" He moved to the door, giving orders.

"What about these two?" Vladi shouted.

Fitz Payn looked back over his shoulder. "Get rid of him. Keep her locked in. If they try and rescue her I'll kill her myself."

Vladi was left alone with the prisoners. He was a literal man. "Get rid of him," he said. "Lock her up." He twisted the catches of the grid and lifted it. Then he ran the pulley Willem was hooked on until it was over the oubliette. He lowered the chain. He had trouble getting Willem's kicking legs down the chute but eventually he managed it. He cut the straps which held Willem up. Willem dropped. Vladi replaced the grid, turned its catches and went to join the fight, locking the door carefully behind him.

Willem owed his life to the fact that the sides of the oubliette were thick with the faeces of years; instead of being slimy the cold had encrusted them. The friction against his tunic slowed him down just above the point where the oubliette curved steeply into the chute to become vertical.

He put out his feet and elbows to wedge himself. Luckily the oubliette was not wide – the bodies which went down it had been starved. He could hear the river and the crack of ice.

The pain in his left shoulder was paralysing. His back had been wrenched and the old shooting agony had returned, but he didn't have time to worry about it. He turned his feet outwards to get a grip on the sides and push himself up, but the crust broke away and he travelled down until his feet hung over the drop and only his fingernails held him to the oubliette. He squirmed his legs until his calves and not his boots were lodged against the sides; the material of his trews was a better grip than leather.

He managed to get his elbows into the oubliette and heaved. The movement tore his sleeve and left the bare skin against the plastered stone. He convulsed his body and the

178

pain huffed air out of his lungs, but he was back in the oubliette. He did it again, then again. The attrition on his elbow wore away the skin so that blood made it slippery. He had to manoeuvre the back of his arm against his jacket to wipe it away before he could move again. He lost track of time or why he was down here. He was absorbed in the terrain of the oubliette as if he were traversing mountains. There was no light coming from the grid above him. As he got higher he became aware of the distance he had to fall. "St. Sebastian give me grace and strength."

On the fortieth or millionth heave something tickled his hair. One more convulsion got his fingers round bars of the grid. He waited until his own panting subsided and he could hear something, the grizzling of an unhappy small girl.

"Willem, I'm sorry. I'm so sorry, Willem. He broke my arm, Willem. I had to tell him." Dyrika's voice came from far away.

"Where are you?"

"Outside the door, Willem. I thought you were dead." He visualised the door which had a squint for spying on the prisoners. Dyrika had her mouth to it.

"Can't you get in?"

"It's locked. There's fighting, Willem. My arm hurts."

He could hear the faint sounds of battle. "Listen, D'ika. I must have a light. If I have light I can live. Get a candle. Be very quick." He heard her grizzling die away.

"My lady? Lift the grid." He could hear her talking it over with someone. He couldn't hang on much longer. He heard Matilda say: "Well, if you think so," and the catches turn. It seemed the saddest thing in the world to dig his elbows back into the stone while the grid was lifted and he sobbed as he did it. One more heave and he was out. He lay with his head on Matilda's shoes until a wobbling yellow light approached the door squint and came through in the form of a candle.

"My arm does hurt, Willem."

He took the candle and kissed the hand that gave it. There was nothing he could do for her, the door was too secure.

179

He carried the candle to the slit and stood it upright, then jumped for Matilda and pulled her against the wall. The candle flame went out as an arrow with a cord attached whistled in and clattered on the floor. He hauled it in until the cord gave way to rope, which he tied round Matilda's waist. She was unresisting but looked at him with hauteur. "How dare you touch me."

"Lady, you're going down that hole if you like it and down it if you don't. Either."

"My dear," said the Magdalene, "don't worry about us. We can fly down."

Matilda was lowered down the oubliette. Her skirts rode up and exposed her legs to the cold but protected her from the substance she was passing over. She hung on to the rope as she passed out of the chute and saw the keep wall and her own breath slide upwards.

Willem paid out the rope until it went slack. Jacopo's voice called: "She's down." He went down himself, the contrast between the last time and this made it easy, though his shoulder and back were agony. At river-level Jacopo steadied his legs into the boat. Maulger rowed hard against the current while Jacopo used the rope now sagging from the slit window to pull them hand over hand to the quay and the tollhouse.

"Stopped to pick daisies, did you?" asked Willem. "You bloody near got me killed."

Jacopo indicated the keep they were drawing away from; faint shouts and clashes of steel rose up over it and the escarpment. "That's not us."

"Who the hell is it, then?"

His entire band, less sentries, was in the tollhouse warming items of clothing round a fire like ladies' maids. Willem grunted at them and they grunted back, overjoyed at having him safe.

"We don't know who it is." Jacopo took Matilda behind a screen made from a blanket; his voice came from behind it. "We think it must be Brien Fitz Count, trying to get the castle back." He broke off to talk to Matilda as he helped her undress and put on clean clothes. "Up with that little arm, there's a good girl. Upsy. It's a good little force, whoever it is, and it was in position when we got here. Now, I'm not going to hurt you, I'm a doctor. They were in the woods waiting to attack and I didn't like to say, 'Excuse me, my good men, but *we* want to attack instead.' For one thing – now the stockings, there's a good girl – there were more of them than us." They could hear Matilda muttering to her saints throughout.

He emerged. "Have you seen that woman's body?" For once there was no innuendo.

"Fitz Payn. Can she travel?"

"Only if she has to. What about you?"

"She has to. She's in danger from both sides now."

His men had been seeing to Willem, washing his wound and bandaging it. Maulger said: "Could be worse," which was his diagnosis of everything not actually fatal.

Willem's new clothes, like Matilda's, were of wool, layers of it, plus fur cap and double boots with suede inside and leather out. He put them on with finicky care; their lives would depend on keeping warm. He looked round at the component parts of his life, Calabrians, Genoese, English, Flemish, French, Normans, one Irish, a Scot, all meshing into his one perfect achievement. "I wouldn't be going now, not with that bastard still alive, if I didn't have to."

"If Fitz Count leaves anything of him, we'll finish him off," promised Jacopo.

"Contract rules, Jacko."

"Contract rules, captain."

His men filled the last minutes with instructions.

"The barn's six miles off. We left food there."

"There's a crossbow on your horse and another on hers."

"If you can't be good, be careful."

They'd chosen them both white horses and white cloaks, a camouflage touch he hadn't thought of. Matilda was almost collapsed by the time they got her on her horse: he didn't feel so good himself.

"Well . . ." The river was too loud and the presence of the enemy too near for grandiloquent goodbyes even if they could have made them. He just took the leading rein of

181

Matilda's horse and left, heading for the Icknield Way and being lost to sight quickly in the whites and blues of the hill.

At Oxford Castle another Matilda, also disguised in white, was lowered down part of its wall. Two men with white coats over their mail met her at the bottom and hurried her through gates, posterns and arches. When they came to the river they helped her over the ice, wading through its snow. Fifty yards away on either side two of Stephen's sentries stood stamping to keep warm, their heads steadfastly in the opposite direction. Nobody was sure afterwards whether they were bribed or sluggish with the cold.

The escapers were hoping to find outside Oxford some remnant of the army which had offered battle to Stephen, but the countryside was empty and quiet (Brien Fitz Count had gone off to quell Fitz Payn at Ibber). Therefore their nearest ally was at Abingdon, seven miles away across fields deep in snow. They couldn't use the roads.

It was a tall order for a short woman, but faint-heartedness was not one of the Empress' faults. Struggling, glaring at the snow which dared to impede her, she got there.

News of her escape spread all over England and then, despite the deep winter, to the rest of Christendom. Those who heard it, regardless of their allegiance, thought that by letting her slip through his fingers Stephen, though he might still win, no longer deserved to.

11

1142–1143

The Icknield Way was really the Icknield Ways; not just one, but two, sometimes three, and occasionally several tracks meandering at different levels along the sixty miles of the chalk Chiltern ridge from the Thames basin to the flat lands of East Anglia.

It had been an ancient route before the Romans came and even before the Iceni whose name it commemorates. Along its south-western section, which Willem and Matilda were entering, were valleys in which lived a small, dark, narrow-headed people who had been in England before the arrival of the Iceni, and even they weren't as old as the Icknield Way. They had been on William the Conqueror's route to subdue England and were now suspicious and fearful, more likely to hide than welcome. At the onset of winter they hibernated inside their earthworks leaving the landscape to deer, hares and foxes whose tracks decorated the snow in aimless stitching.

Willem rode like a drunk, only able to focus straight ahead. But his Eurydice looked behind to the darkness she was leaving and saw part of it detach and follow her.

When they reached the barn Willem got them inside, horses as well, put Matilda on some straw, covered her, unsaddled the horses, lay down, covered himself and slept. Matilda slept less well. She heard shadows scrabbling outside whispering to be let in, so she woke the saints and they chattered to cover the sound.

On the next day Willem headed for the high track on the ridge where snow had been thinned by the wind and where the beech hangars allowed them to see but not be seen.

Loss of blood was making him weak and irritable. Matilda's habit of looking constantly behind her as if someone was following them exasperated him.

He was not as concerned at Matilda's mental state as another man might have been; he'd seen similar condition in soldiers who'd suffered unbearable anguish in war. She'd get over it. Nevertheless the saints were wearing travelling companions, mainly because they occupied all her attention. It was the saints who heaved off her boots at night, lit the fires, dug her latrines, provided her food and it was the saints she thanked for it. It was an eerie, lonely time for Willem and hard work for a man with a bad back and an arm that wasn't healing well.

On the third night the only shelter they could find was a forester's hut, so small he had to leave the horses outside. In his sleep his pain formed shapes and sounds, a blunt thudding in his shoulder and a flat drone in his lower spine pierced by shrill squealing. In the morning just lifting the bar from the door was difficult.

The horses had gone. Behind the windbreak he'd built for them were jumbled marks in the snow made by eight hooves and two feet.

"Shut up, for Christ's sake." Behind him Matilda had relapsed into manic chattering.

The woods were beautiful, the trunks of the beeches might have been sketched in charcoal and a man could be standing behind every one. He listened. The place echoed with desertion.

He took Matilda's hand and backed with her to the hut where he'd stupidly left the door open. If someone had got inside and taken the crossbows . . . the crossbows were still there. He bolted the door while he got her ready for the walk ahead of them. She was shaking and talkative, though not to him. He had trouble fixing her cloak brooch – his left arm was almost useless. When she was ready he hung a crossbow and quiver over her head.

"Remember how to use this? Good girl. Of course you do."

He had to arm himself the wrong way round because of

his shoulder. He rolled up the thicker rugs and slung them round his neck and stuffed the flint and tinder fungus in his pocket. He looked with regret at the equipment they must leave.

After opening the door cautiously he listened for a long time, then ran, pulling Matilda after him. He ran to the edge of the trees and down the northern slope to the lower track. Matilda didn't like being out in the open and his back yelped as she pulled against him. "He'll see me," she told the saints. But he didn't dare stay in the woods where they could be jumped from any bush. He needed to see what was coming for them even if it meant being seen. Now they were on foot any travellers they encountered would consider them too poor to be worth noticing or robbing.

Nevertheless, as the ridge reared up to their right the exposure made him want to crouch, though at the same time they seemed to have become very small indeed, minute and impotent in an illimited expanse of white. If it was a peasant who'd stolen the horses he had no reason to kill them: if it was Fitz Payn, the bow was not his weapon.

Matilda walked with her face turned to the ridge and once she pointed, indicating some movement to her saints. Willem thought he saw something moving between the trees but his eyes were beginning to trick him. It could still have been a peasant who'd stolen the horses.

When they reached the flowers he knew it hadn't been a peasant.

They looked like flowers from far off, a concentrated relief of anemone colours, blue, purple and red, in a heap in the snow. Nearer, they saw the flowers were steaming.

Nearer still they turned into guts, the anemone-coloured, glistening, contorted ropes of intestines.

They were out of a horse; Willem had seen things like them emerging from the belly wounds of horses in battle.

A line of footprints led up to and then away from the pile, those coming heavier than those going away. He had carried them in his arms to place his bouquet in Matilda's path.

Matilda was quiet for once: she seemed puzzled. Willem

185

took her hand and followed the footprints to a depression in the snow further on where the horse she had ridden away from Ibber had been slaughtered and eviscerated. What was left of it lay in a pandemonium of pink snow, its legs frozen in an ungainly kick, its yellow teeth exposed in a last shriek.

Other than the thin track which connected the carcase to its intestines, there were no footprints. Instead a wide scar started off untidily in the depression as if something had scrabbled to expose the blades of grass underneath, and then ploughed upwards towards the ridge, gaining width as it disappeared into the trees. He was still puzzling out this phenomenon when Matilda said clearly: "That is absolutely disgusting."

He turned round to her. The sight of the animal had bypassed her madness to touch the horsewoman who had ridden more frequently than she had walked. For that moment she glanced up at Willem and she perceived him, not as some forked shape on the edge of a nightmare, but him, Willem. It was a moment of such contact that he said, "Hello."

They were still facing each other when they heard the hill sighing and glanced up to see a huge ball of snow capering down the scar towards them. It was a childhood memory turned murderous. Sparks of ice flew from its surface. Willem took the full force of it on his bad shoulder and was thrown on to the carcase. Matilda fell as she jumped back and was covered with snow as the ball exploded over them both.

She got up, fiddling at her neck to dislodge ice slivers. Anger had refreshed her mind. She saw clearly the outline of the beeches on the ridge and the figure that stepped out of them to follow the snowball and finish them off.

In her old, mad mind he had grown superhuman; now in this landscape he looked small, and he staggered as he ran. He had been wounded. He called to her like a lover.

With her new clarity she saw him as disordered; put together wrongly in the still, metallic perfection around him. Her brothers had once tortured a beetle by sticking a needle into

186

it, paralysing one side so that in moving it went in a circle. She looked from the running man to the man floundering in the snow. A right beetle and a wrong beetle.

"I'll have to kill him," she said.

The Mother sighed: "Poor beetle."

Willem was groping with his right hand for the crossbow, it was the wrong side and he got it tangled with the quiver. The man had a knife in his hand and was coming not for Willem but for Matilda. He tried to fit his feet into the stirrup and moaned as his back tore. Matilda watched him: "You stay still," she said kindly. "I'll do it."

Her arm brought the bow over her head and in the same movement down, cocking it as he'd taught her. Back over her shoulder two fingers gripped a goose-feather flight. She was part of the meshing mechanism of the world, a cog which interlocked with others to turn the wheel. The man was close now. She could see him smile and the blood on his jacket from the horse. She raised the bow and heard a voice repeating orders it had given in a sweet fenland a sweet time ago.

"Aim." She aimed at a patch of blood on the russet jacket.

"Breathe in." She breathed in and remembered to let it half-out.

"Don't think." She stopped thinking.

"Loose." The bolt hit Fitz Payn just below the throat and knocked him back out of Matilda's vision. The universe was tidy again.

"Good shot," said the Magdalene as she faded into transparency.

The Virgin's blue cloak became grey: "Goodbye, my dear girl."

"But I had to kill him. Don't leave me. I had to."

"Quite right," whispered the snow. "And quite wrong."

Two snowflakes touched her on each cheek. They had gone.

Five days later Matilda woke up in the nuns' priory at Markyate two-thirds along the stretch of Ermine Street which ran from Dunstable to St. Albans.

Her face was cold from an open window opposite her bed through which she could see rooks circling over tops of elms down a slope. Her body was warm and clean under quilted covers which smelled of lavender and a warm brick wrapped in wool exuded heat to her feet.

Besides lavender and beeswax there was the indefinable aroma that identified a Saxon dwelling and had something to do with vegetables.

The plank door opened and a nun came in with a tray.

"Time for supper." Her remorselessly bright voice had interspersed Matilda's dreams. She propped Matilda up with the air of one who enjoyed her own efficiency. "*One* for the Father, *two* for the Son, *three* for the Holy Ghost." The spoonfuls of soup had shreds of ham in them with leeks and pearl barley. Matilda opened and shut her mouth to oblige not only the Trinity but the twelve disciples as well.

"Do you know where you are?" Matilda shook her head. She didn't care much. "This is Markyate. You've heard of Christina of Markyate?"

Oddly enough, she had. She connected the name with East Anglia and Sigward. Sigward had talked with veneration of a Christina of Markyate as of a saint in the making. She was one of the rare Saxons who had obtruded themselves on Norman attention.

There was no need to rack her memory; the nun was a propagandist for her superior. Soon Matilda knew a lot about Christina and her wish for a virgin's crown in heaven, her fight against her parents who'd wanted to marry her off, her flight to save her virginity, her sojourn among the hermits who dotted this part of the country, her eventual recognition as a holy phenomenon by the bishops and her founding of Markyate Priory. She began to remember the things Sigward had said: "The Abbot of St. Albans won't make a move without consulting her. She could have been Abbess of Fontevrault, one of the most powerful women in Christendom, but her humility forbade her."

The name of the talking nun was Helison and she fatigued Matilda. She wiped Matilda's mouth. "There. You know

188

all about us. Do you want to tell me who you are?" Matilda shut her eyes and let herself drift into a warm and soupy sleep.

The next morning she was strong enough to face the fact that she had to give some explanation, if only to stifle enquiry. She, who had thought it the proudest thing in the world to be Matilda de Risle, would rather have no identity.

She asked Helison after breakfast: "How did I get here?"

"Poor soul" – the nun was eager – "you were left at our gate. On a sled pulled by a horse. There was a man but it was too dark for the porteress to make him out. He said you were a lady who needed our charity. He said he was hurt and couldn't protect you. He said he'd come back when you were better. And when he was."

Hurt? She couldn't remember him being hurt. Her mind made a brief foray backwards and recoiled as if scalded. Leading out of the scald was a bridge of days in which she and somebody had hauled each other along. She waved away her breakfast and went back to sleep.

After the evening feeding Matilda said: "I am a widow from . . . " Where was somewhere neutral? ". . . from Aquitaine. I am on a pilgrimage round the holy sites of Europe to pray for my husband's soul." Ridiculously, she couldn't think of a false name. "And under a vow not to reveal my identity." They could take it or leave it. She had disappointed the nun. "Who did you think I was?"

"Anyone. Somebody." The nun's eyes were wide. "You came so mysteriously. And it was near Christmas."

"I fell among thieves who robbed me. I was rescued by a strange man. He was kind and brought me here."

"Perhaps it was St. Christopher." The nun was determined to rescue something miraculous from a bleak situation. She did not question further; what happened in the outside world, unless it happened at the mother house of St. Albans, was of no interest. Matilda had trouble finding out what had occurred at Oxford. "The Empress got away," said Helison vaguely. "The war goes on."

In many ways Markyate was what Matilda needed. Its

petty, regulated life was soothing. She was tranquillised by female sounds, the sweep of brushes, hens, gossiping bondswomen, chanting. Her mind reassembled itself to canonical hours, not completely, not in the order it had been before, but enough.

All her life her happiness had depended on positive ambitions. Now, not to be cold, not to be in danger, not to be hungry or tired wrapped her in the negatives of peasant bliss.

Whiffs of her own childhood came back through the childlike convent where everything was kept in readiness for a miraculous visitor. They lived in constant expectation of the wondrous and, when it didn't happen, made mystery out of the commonplace. Inanimate had animate potential. Every bucket must be blessed before it was filled to rid it of evil. An ancient mule was being kept alive long after its usefulness because it had once brayed: "Christina."

During the summer they had got into a high old state over some bunches of marigolds left daily on their doorstep. Marigolds were the Virgin's own flowers, ergo they were a portent and their petals were pressed in linen – only to be thrown away when a villein's wife confessed to offering them for the safe delivery of her child.

The fire which kept this pot of nuns simmering was Christina herself in an unceasing series of petty miracles, visions and prophecies. The sisters recorded her every move to tell the monk who came regularly from St. Albans to write it all down. Matilda had stepped into hagiography in the making. Every local abbey and priory held its breath for this woman's sainthood to be confirmed by a sign, a transfiguration – perhaps martyrdom.

"It takes it out of her," said Helison. "She knows everything. She always foretells Abbot Geoffrey's visits to the day and hour. Always. She can tell what you're thinking. She knew when you were having sinful thoughts, didn't she, Godit?"

Godit, one of the bondswomen, grunted: "Who asked her?"

Matilda's own introduction to the wonder was delayed.

190

Eventually she was persuaded to leave her bed and join the community in its refectory for the main meal. It was surprisingly hard to face the gaze of other women, even Saxons.

Christina chose that meal to emerge from a period of fasting and prayer in her chapel, and was led, tottering, to the table where nuns ran to and from the kitchen to prepare mixtums for her.

Matilda ate steadily and watched. Christina was a ginger Saxon with freckled skin stretched over large bones. Her protuberant eyes were blue and the lids were lined above and below, like targets. She held her flat chest as she announced: "My beloved will visit me on St. Stephen's Day at noon." Her expression was exalted but she cast a sharp glance at one of her nuns: "Have you got that down, Lettice?" Lettice obediently made scratches on a slate.

"She means Abbot Geoffrey of St. Albans," Helison whispered to Matilda. "He likes to know her prophecies when he arrives."

Eventually the prioress permitted herself to eat and drink and her eyes to rest on Matilda. She made a space on the bench beside her.

"This is the lady we told you of, mother," said Helison. "She has been married."

It was an apology. It put Matilda over the boundary which divided the uncelibate from them, the virgins who would end up in a superior part of Heaven. But Christina remained interested.

"You were seen in one of my visions. You were fighting the Devil."

"I hope we all do that." Matilda, who had walked with the Mother of God and the Magdalene, felt disinterest bordering on contempt.

Christina nodded. "He was in russet," and gave permission for Helison to escort a fainting Matilda back to her cell.

From that moment Christina gained ascendancy over a humbled, admiring and frightened Matilda. The prioress was intrigued by this high-born Norman acolyte whom she had seen struggling in the arms of a russet Devil. The trouble was

191

Christina took the vision allegorically and assumed Matilda was fighting to extricate herself from lusts of the flesh – and Christina knew about that.

As Matilda discovered in the nightly sessions to save her from the burning, Christina was a sensual woman – hence her continual fasting, cold baths and prayer. The discipline had subdued her body, which was rheumatic, but had heightened her senses to a level of which Matilda had never dreamed.

"I know the toils of the flesh. Once I was tempted by a man, a cleric, who importuned me and for whom my lascivious body was torn with desire. I overcame it with God's help through fasting, nights without sleep, harsh scourgings. Believe me, I know what it is to be so inflamed with lust that the clothes clinging to my body might be on fire."

"Which is a bloody sight more than I do," thought Matilda. The marital state had never been like that. But if God and Jesus could love her . . . if she could make her besmirched body acceptable again. She became excited by the thought of new adventure in the unexplored country of the spirit.

The next day, while the nuns were at chapter, Godit popped her head round Matilda's door. "Got a message for you." She peeked back down the corridor; the message was secret. "He says he'll be in the neighbourhood three days. He'll come to the priory every night, starting tonight. Like he was a stranger." Godit screwed up her face to get the exact words. "So's he won't compromise you. He says if you want to leave to give him the nod through me." Willem had chosen his messenger well, Godit was delighting in the subterfuge. "Will you go?"

"I don't know."

"He wouldn't have to ask me twice." Godit was having sinful thoughts again.

Because of the war, travellers were rarer than they had been. Nevertheless, Markyate's gate was opened and a meal and a bed ready for who needed them. Men were allowed to enter, provided they left weapons outside, and such was the

192

veneration in which Markyate was held that the hospitality was never abused. Usually guests gave their name and provenance.

The man who asked admittance that night volunteered nothing beyond, yes, he would be grateful for a meal, no, he did not want a bed. Despite this, perhaps because of it, he caused a sensation. Matilda, now in tune with them, felt their expectation of a marvel rise. "Who is he?" was passed round with the salt.

She barely glanced at him. A fog had come in with him in which whirled obscene mutterings and drains and terror and, running like a handrail through them, the presence of this man.

"Who is he?" came from Helison on her left and passed on to Lettice on her right, but Matilda had remembered. "His name is Willem of Ghent," she said quietly to herself. "He is a mercenary. He has a bad back." He couldn't expect her to leave the authority of Christina, where it was safe and child-like and she could be sure of Heaven if she prayed hard enough.

Helison caught the last sentence. "He is certainly in pain. Look how stiffly he moves. But look at his well-shaped features, he is not a common man." She leaned across to Christina. "Mother, do you suppose . . . ?"

"We must suppose nothing." Christina was stern but her shrewd, hysterical eyes were fixed on the mercenary where he sat down the table among the low-caste visitors. "We must not surmise, Helison. But he does not look like a common man, nor does he eat like one." The mercenary was taking no more food than he needed, unlike his neighbours who were stuffing down meat, beans, ale and bread as fast as they could. "Helison, take this fish pie and offer it to him. Look at his hands."

Matilda's head went up to stare. Hands? God Almighty, they were looking for stigmata. She turned to look herself. Perhaps they were right. Perhaps he was the Christ. Christ as a mercenary? For the first time she saw him properly without the distortions of insanity or bigotry, prejudice or class, and she saw a man, not God and not a saint, but a man. A dull man for peacetime maybe, but a rock in war. A man to go boar-hunting with, who'd protect your back. An ordinary, kind man with the sins that men were heir to – and as attractive as all get-out. And he wanted her. Not as Christ wanted her, either. The cheek of it. The realisation made her gasp, then grin with unholy joy that she had attracted the man these nuns were in a flutter over, and still attracted him, else why was he here? It was shameful, it was presumption on his part, but it would be something to remember when she forsook the world.

Helison came twittering back. "He thanked you, mother. His voice is majestic, deep and lovely. He said with your permission he would return tomorrow." Her voice went into a squeak. "Mother, do you think . . . ?"

"Mother," said Matilda, "I am sure he is not the Christ." She could not identify him without identifying herself, but neither could she allow them to fool themselves.

"I have not said he was," said Christina, as if her word decided the matter. "St. Paul warns us against delusion by the Lawless One. But neither must we close our minds and hearts to the promised coming, like Jews."

"And it *is* near Christmas."

That night Matilda prayed: "Let me find peace, dear God. Let me find peace *here*," but she couldn't find it and eventually got out of bed and, for the first time since Christina had given it to her, flicked the little scourge across her shoulders.

The next day was Christmas Eve and given over to preparation for the festival of the mass and the promised visit of the Abbot of St. Albans. The nuns scrubbed and polished and decorated the church while bondswomen sweated in kitchens that pulsed with heat and emitted the smells of spice, reconstituting fruits, boiling giblets and onions. On her way back from the woods up the hill with a sled of holly and ivy, Matilda passed the kitchens and heard Christina's voice commanding something special to be cooked ". . . for the pilgrim".

It upset her that she knew better than Christina. She didn't want to know better; in Christina she had found authority and an all-seeing medium in touch with God. But the nunnery was whipping itself up into a state of near-hysteria. Christina looked ill and had to sit during Nones but at the versicle: "Today ye shall know that the Lord will come," she staggered to her feet and gazed on the altar, rapt. "Blast," thought Matilda.

By the time they opened the gates to the poor the nuns were almost frenzied. Christina was the only one who kept her head and ordered that the nuns stay in their places. She also ordered the bondswomen out. Christ was not to be drooled over by servants, if it was Christ.

But there was an audible breathing out when Willem came in with the beggars, and the door of the hatch between the refectory and the kitchen trembled from the prying heads behind it.

After grace, Christina rose and, with her sister Margaret, walked down the room, shifted a couple of beggars and sat opposite the mercenary in conversation. Helison skittered up and down the table, solicitously offering him food and ale and reporting back on what she overheard. The other nuns ate leaning towards the pilgrim as if bent by a strong breeze.

"Mother's impressed, I can tell," Helison said. "His answers are so wise . . . but there aren't any nail-marks on his hands."

Reluctantly Christina returned to her place; she was clutching her chest. "I have no doubt of it. As I listened to him my heart fluttered in my breast with spiritual joy."

The whisper went round the table. "He is."

Matilda sighed. She knew now she couldn't stay among these women. They were too young for her, even Christina who was twice her age. She was too old, she had been exposed to too much reality to submit herself to a life of delusion. Suddenly she was cross with them. What was wrong with them that they did not accept what God had put under their noses? Marigolds were beautiful whether they came from a virgin or a villein's wife. That man there was beautiful not because he was God Incarnate but because he was a man.

195

"Mother, it is time for me to leave. I thank you for your kindness and hospitality. I shall leave tomorrow."

Christina nodded: "Won't you stay for the procession?" but it was automatic courtesy. Matilda was no longer of interest.

"Is he coming for the procession, mother?" asked Lettice.

"I have invited him. Doubtless it is a matter of whether we are worthy."

The mercenary got awkwardly up from the table as if in pain. The nuns moaned with sympathy. That's what happened when you were crucified. As he turned to bow to Christina he looked for the first time at Matilda. She gave a brief nod. He turned and went out.

The trouble was, thought Matilda the next morning as she dressed herself carefully in her cleaned, outdoor clothes, they hadn't been able to arrange anything. Godit was being kept too busy to act as go-between. She presumed if she walked out of the convent and down to the road he would be waiting for her.

She must reward the convent for its hospitality before she went . . . she had no money. The jewelled belt her father had left to keep her safe and wealthy had been left behind at Ibber. She was penniless. Her estates were in the hands of others, both sides were her enemies. If she reappeared to claim the rents she would be liable to be sold to some other husband. She was a poverty-stricken refugee about to step into a hostile world with a man she barely knew and with nowhere to go.

She collapsed on to her bed and sobbed like a child.

It was Christmas Day. As dawn broke, the bells of Dunstable Priory chimed out the good news of the birth of a child in a stable to the rich Abbey of St. Albans whose own bells chimed it back. In between, along Ermine Street, tin bells in the roofs of tiny hermit cells swung in their frames, and villeins' wives stood at the doors of their huts and clanged the bells which usually called their men home from the fields. In Matilda's cell chimed a loving, fat voice from another Christmas. "I just wanted you, my dear, to have a bolthole; somewhere to hide should trouble come, where you and our children will always be safe and have plenty to eat."

Matilda, spreadeagled on the bed, stopped crying to listen. "An odd little gift," apologised the bells, "but I shall be happier that you have it."

She sat up and wiped wet hair from her face. "Sigward, you were my only true love."

Down the road Willem of Ghent, also concerned about the lack of a rendezvous, led his transport, a mule and a sled, into the woods and tethered it.

The horse remaining to him and Matilda, which he had found wandering near its dead companion, was dead itself, ridden to exhaustion through the snow to get Matilda to Markyate. He had sold its carcase for a few pennies and had worked for the past three days for Tosti, Markyate's neighbour, in order to earn a few more to buy this ancient, moth-eaten and bad-tempered mule. In his spare time he'd managed to construct the sled. Neither activity had improved the condition of his back. Stiffly he began to climb the hill to the convent gates, looking for Matilda.

Two nuns ran towards him and curtsied in the snow. "My lord, my lord, we are so blessed that you have come, that you have found us worthy."

Unacquainted with convent manners he supposed this enthusiastic courtesy was usual but it made him uncomfortable. With little pushes of their hands, as if they wanted to touch him but dared not, they urged him into the priory. "She is waiting for you."

At the door of the church the sisterhood was assembled, each carrying a candle decorated with holly. The prioress sank to her knees. "My lord, my joy is unbounded. Will you say mass with us? Will you lead the procession?"

It would be nice to take communion again, but he wasn't going to lead any procession. "Thank you, ma'am, but I'm just a common guest."

Christina's encircled eyes filled with understanding of his humility. "As it pleases my lord."

A priest who was there to administer the host acted as crucifer and led the way, the nuns followed, chanting at the tops of their joyful voices, and Willem found himself bringing up the rear with Matilda. "What's happening?"

She muttered back: "They think you're the Christ come again."

"Jesus!"

"Exactly."

Neither derived much spiritual sustenance from the eucharist; they were too aware of the veneration exuded by the rest. The priest was in on the good news that Christ was in his congregation and his hands shook as he proffered the wine. At the anthem "Christ is born" every nun turned to look at Willem, nearly pushing him backwards by the blast of their singing. He began to panic.

As the priest led the procession out of the church, followed by Christina and the convent, the gaze of each one seemed to eat him up. He joined Matilda in the nave. "I can't face this."

They would never get away. She looked around: "See that window?"

He nodded. "I'll meet you down by the road."

Matilda went out singing and carefully shutting the door of the chapel behind her. The convent was assembled outside, facing her.

"Where is he?"

"He's praying." That would hold them for a bit. She kissed Christina's hand. "Mother, I must leave now." Christina nodded, her eyes on the door. Matilda looked at the rapt faces which ignored her. She could have wept for them. "I'm so sorry," she said.

Outside the priory gates the world was its old, harsh, cold self. The snow enveloped her boots. She felt a revulsion of disgust which took in herself and the man waiting to meet her. She was only just recovering from the wounds received in a sexual assault from one mercenary and now she was about to go off with another. When he came up with her she looked at the transport. "Is that the best you could do?"

Willem wasn't in a charitable mood either. His back hurt. "There weren't any thoroughbreds going. Take it or leave it."

They had found their *modus vivendi*. Reviling each other they set off up the long, steep hill to Caddington and the route back to the Icknield Way.

Into the Life of Christina was written the story of the mysterious pilgrim and of how the Son of God manifested Himself at Markyate Priory and disappeared back to Heaven while praying in its church.

12

1143

The opposing armies were like mile-sized boots which advanced, circled, retreated and then went through the figure all over again. Their scuff-marks were left on the English landscape in flattened crops, burned houses and crushed people.

There was still one giant who had not yet joined the dance.

Geoffrey de Mandeville thought he had been clever. When the Empress had been on top he had won huge concessions from her. Now that Stephen was on top again he repeated the process and made himself one of the greatest barons in England.

He was powerful in East Anglia, where Stephen had few allies, and helped him contain Hugh Bigod, who was having another revolt all by himself, and where Bishop Nigel of Ely was holding out for the Empress after yet another revolt.

After Christmas Stephen held court at St. Albans and welcomed de Mandeville and other barons to it. When its business was over and everybody was leaving, de Mandeville was arrested by guards like a common criminal. He was accused of treachery and forced to surrender every castle he owned.

Stephen thought he had been clever by taking de Mandeville's power into his own hands. But those who saw the arrest saw a demon enter into Geoffrey de Mandeville. They advised the king to kill him because hatred like his would last until either he or the king were dead.

Stephen would not; he was pleased with his trick. He let de Mandeville go, a madman.

If conditions had been perfect it would have taken them only a week to reach the east where the safest ports lay and where Willem hoped to get Matilda abroad. But conditions were appalling. It snowed almost continuously, sometimes in flurries, sometimes in storms so thick they were nearly suffocated and had to crawl under the mule for shelter. The hills had changed to sweeping downs and in daytime they kept to the cleared tops but before evening had to make horrific descents into the valleys to find somewhere to stay the night. Usually they were lucky in finding a priory or monastic rest house. Sometimes, though, they had to pay for the use of a barn to a villein as poor as themselves, and Willem's money was running out.

They were struggling up a hill beyond Hitchin and the mule, who hated ascents, was holding back. Willem jerked its reins and hissed with pain. "For goodness sake," shouted Matilda and floundered through the snow to take the bridle from him. She gave a pull and the mule responded; it was more afraid of her than of Willem. "The next time you go rescuing ladies in distress you might see you're fit."

Willem gritted his teeth: "Don't flatter yourself there'd be a next time."

He watched her small thick boots as they stumped through the snow. He would have liked to tell her she was the most courageous thing he'd ever seen but their communication was through insult. It gave their relationship an equality which overrode her consciousness of his inferiority and her indebtedness.

If they had anything serious to say it was said in the mornings. As the day proceeded they jeered at each other like an old married couple, but by the time night came she was tense and barely spoke, as if in their frequently cramped shelter even the intimacy of exchanged words would be dangerous.

Willem was worried about finding a shelter at all tonight.

They had tried the lower road to Royston but had found it blocked and turned for clearer going on the upper way.

On their left the ground fell away into a seemingly endless vale of featureless white, ahead were more hills. Above and to their right was a hut among trees. Willem nodded at it: "We'll have to sleep there."

"No." It reminded her of the night Fitz Payn had pursued them.

"If you want to go back, go. But Wenceslas and me are sleeping there."

They would need a good fire. Willem put the sled in the hut for Matilda to sleep on and made up his own bed alongside it; the quarters were cramped. They saw to the mule, went off into the trees for their personal concerns, and came back to a dinner of goat-milk cheese and bread that Hitchin Priory had given them.

Willem said: "Do you ever wonder why I came looking for you?"

"I'm tired." He was breaking the house rules, but he had things to tell her, now that she was physically and mentally stronger, which she had the right to know.

"It wasn't for the sake of your bonny blue eyes. In the first place it was a promise to Alleyn." For the first time he told her about the champion's death at Lincoln. She had grieved for his death, now she wept for his murder.

"And in the second place I had a Christian duty to stop Fitz Payn killing you as well. He would have done, sooner or later, when he'd got as much out of you as he could. Wherever he went, women died. He was lunatic."

She stared upwards where a hole in the roof showed hard-edged stars, shaken by relief. Fitz Payn's assault had been a perversion of hatred, not sex; not inspired by the fault of her own body. His hatred had been wholesale; he would have done the same to any woman, had done. Stupidly she found herself thinking: "It was nothing personal," but it brought a blessed cleansing. In killing him she had avenged Alleyn and saved not only herself but an unknown sisterhood of victims.

In gratitude for her liberation she could have kissed the man beside her. She didn't dare even say "thank you". She could feel the flesh on her left arm which was nearest him stirring on the bone to touch his. Oh God, this was lust. This was what Christina had felt. "Disparagement has done this to me," she thought. She had been so disparaged that she longed to commit a sin which would cut her off from God for ever, just when she needed Him.

She put a forefinger knuckle in her mouth and bit it. She rolled away until she was pressed against the wall.

In the darkness the mercenary lay on his back and cursed under his breath so that his blasphemies curled up like smoke through the hole in the roof.

In the morning they were still alive. As she rubbed blood back into her feet Matilda said: "My eyes are brown, you fool."

"I know."

At Royston they received the news that de Mandeville had revolted in the Fens. They could see in the distance a large patch of flames where Cambridge was burning.

The frightened, homeless refugees from Cambridge spoke of yelling madmen who had looted and burned their town, with a silent, more terrible madman at their head.

Every inn was doing the business of a lifetime and asking a price for food and bed which would clean out the mercenary's purse. From the look of Matilda he decided it had to be paid. They had to wait for some time before they were served. The mercenary spent it asking questions. At last he said: "I thought we could cut across the Fens to the coast from here. But he's attacking indiscriminately. We'll skirt and keep to the uplands until we see what's what." He frowned. "We'll have to slaughter the mule if we're to eat."

"We need him."

"It's the mule or you."

A child was being sent up the communal stairs by its mother, who was drinking away her sorrows. As it climbed Matilda got a horrific glimpse not of naked little human legs, but a selection of pork chops. "Poor old Wenceslas."

The mule was despatched to its Heavenly pasture that night. In return for some of the carcase the landlord allowed

the mercenary to use the kitchen to turn it into stew. In
the early hours, while everyone else was asleep, Willem
worked. After a while there was a sound behind him. He
didn't turn. "Since you're here, make yourself useful. Stir
that pot."

Matilda splashed an inexpert ladle in the pot and tasted:
"It's vile."

The mercenary expired: "What do you want?"

"I'm not going to the coast. I'm going to Dungesey."

He lifted her up and set her on the chopping block. "Look,
I've got a manor outside Brabant. Nothing fancy. Two
ploughs. Sheep, pigs. You can stay there until the war ends."

"It's never going to end."

"I thought I saw the end of it once." It had been after
Lincoln. He hadn't been able to get news either of Matilda or
Fitz Payn and had gone to the Empress' stronghold at Bristol
in search of one or the other. (It was one advantage of being a
mercenary that you could cross lines with your wares.)

Gloucester's court had received him kindly and shown
interest in the arbalists he was apparently offering for sale.
"And this boy came up – I don't suppose he was more than
nine or ten – and questioned me about the crossbow. He was
the Empress' and Plantagenet's son. He was . . ." Willem
searched for a word to describe the effect Fitzempress had on
him: ". . . special. Then his tutor dragged him off to learn
Greek. And I thought: 'Maybe England won't accept his
mother, and I don't know as I blame it, but it might accept
him.' I thought: 'If you were a racehorse, my lad, I'd back
you.'"

"I've already backed him," said Matilda. "I sent him my
son. And I'm still going to Dungesey. I'm going to watch
the English estates for Edmund."

"A fat lot you'll see of them from Dungesey."

"I'll see. And I'll stay unmarried."

He was cooking the wrong mule. "Go to bed."

From then on they manhauled the sled, scouting villages
before they entered them, keeping to uplands and cover.
From the fires burning in the Fens they could tell de
Mandeville was keeping pace with them.

Always obsessional, de Mandeville had become obsessed with destruction. His disease infected others, rootless, futureless men who joined him or rampaged off on their own. But wherever stores were taken, barns burned and women raped, the generic term for it was "de Mandeville".

Taking a chance, Willem and Matilda slipped into a fenland which some base Midas had turned into metal, making the rushes brittle and the carr into intricate fretwork. They changed their pattern so that they travelled by night, lying up by day in what little warmth the sun gave. The only advantage of the cold was that quagmire iced over and they could set a straight course by the stars and ignore the twisting roddons and rivers.

Two nights later they reached the Nene five miles above the Swallen. Matilda was jubilant. Dungesey had grown in her mind as the ultimate haven. "Hurry up," she told the mercenary, "we're nearly at the Waits."

"We're not going in by the Waits. We're going to sneak in from the side."

"Why?"

"I don't know. But that's what we're going to do."

The sled went over the Swallen's ice with the sound of expelled breath. Matilda felt the air warmer with every step she took. She was back in a place where she'd been happy: she could be happy again.

A white owl launched off from a willow on the bank, dislodging snow and flapping heavily along before rising over Crease Bank and disappearing. The mercenary slewed the sled into shadow by the Driftway and jerked his head upwards to show they should climb the bank to get a view. His instinct was telling him to be quiet. Matilda clicked her tongue with irritation as she followed him up.

The bank was slippery with frost and from the top he leaned down to help her. But they had gone to ludicrous lengths these last days to avoid touching each other, so Matilda ignored his hand and rushed the last few feet. The top of her head clunked hard against the side of his face. "Blast you, woman." He hauled her and himself backwards.

Matilda's skull smarted and she wanted to rub it, but her

hands were clasped on his forearms as if they'd frozen there and through her mittens and his leather jacket she could feel muscle.

His cheekbone ached so that his eyes watered but he couldn't wipe them because his hands were tight on her shoulders and he could feel their bones. "Christ."

Wherever they were and for however long it was, it wasn't Dungesey but somewhere hot and sweet and smelling of each other's skin. But wherever it was it wasn't far enough away to stop a bony finger prodding each of them in the shoulder nor a querulous voice saying: "There's a sentry at the Waits. He's having a warm in the barn but he'll be out in a minute."

The finger prodded again: "You going to get under cover or stand there kissing till he sees you?"

She felt the mercenary's lips move against hers. "Sod it."

Kakkr was standing beside them, hopping from one ancient foot to the other. It was cold again.

"What sentry?"

"Oh." The old man's head shook with fear and impatience. "You want to chat about it so's he can shoot us? Or shall us get out of sight?"

They slid down the far side of the Driftway to the frozen Washes and crept along it to the back of the village while they got an explanation out of Kakkr. It took some time; what happened at Dungesey had been so overwhelming that he assumed they knew of it.

Four hours before, a rowing boat with six armed men in it had turned into the Swallen. Since de Mandeville came to the Fens the islanders had been keeping watch on the approaches, using the more reliable children as look-outs so that the adults could get on with their work. Wifil, Stunta and Maggi's son, had spotted the boat and had run as fast as his ten-year-old legs would carry him to give warning. Luckily, it had been evening and the islanders had been gathered in only three places: the few of them who served the hall were in it with Steward Peter, the Wealas were in Wealyham and the others were in their huts in the village. The stories of what atrocities had taken place at Cambridge and other settlements had demanded withdrawal until they could see what manner of men these were. There had been just enough time because the boat party had stopped to ransack the storehouses at the Waits.

Wealas and villagers had picked up their children and run to Hogwood, later retreating into Nightlairs Fen. The servants had left the hall, run round its back and crawled through the drain which led under the north-east wall into Snailstream, through the apple tun and into Wulfholes.

However, Steward Peter, with typical Norman belief in the safety of bricks and stone, had decided to find shelter in the keep. He had taken just too long to reach his decision. "They caught him and that poor lady of yours as they run up the green," said Kakkr.

"What lady of mine?" Matilda shook the old man. "What lady of mine?"

"That pale, weakly gal. They got her, anyways. And Steward Peter. They're in the keep with them now."

"Adeliza?" She began to tremble. "Adeliza's still here?"

"Nowheres else to go. There in't been no ships. Weather's been wholly bad." He turned to the mercenary. "They're bastard drunk. Shouting they wanted gold, I could hear them from Hogwood."

"But what about the village men? They could stop six."

"There in't no men, you duzzy fool. They're gone." He couldn't believe they didn't know about it.

"Gone where?"

"To the war. The king's men came before Christmas and rounded them up and took them off to fight and build things."

"All of them? Stunta? Pampi? Wyrm?"

"All," said Kakkr. Stephen's commitments were now so massive he was prepared to strip entire parishes of their workforce, especially in East Anglia which had shown so little loyalty to him. "There's only women and children and me."

Matilda had heard none of this. She was in terror. The thought of Adeliza suffering violence was not bearable. She had sent Adeliza to it. She had caused the whole thing by her wickedness. She had kissed the mercenary and immediately

God had brought this terrible thing on her in punishment. "We've got to get her out."

The mercenary looked down at her. "We can't. Look, it would take days to get the sheriff's men even if there are any now and even if we were in a position to call them in. Help from another village would take time. These men are marauders. When they've taken what they want they'll go on somewhere else." He hoped it was true.

"She'll be dead by then."

"She's probably dead already."

Matilda began to run between the huts towards the keep. The mercenary threw himself into a tackle to stop her and they struggled in the snow. He put his hand over her mouth to stop her shouting. "All right. All right."

She kicked, then lay still and he removed his hand.

"We've got to get her out."

"I said, all right."

He looked up to see that some of the women had come back from hiding and were staring at them.

"No time for them sort of games, bor," came Wilberta's voice disapprovingly. "We wants our island back."

They were the able-bodied women of the village, the ones he had taught to shoot, who had come back for their crossbows, Tuna, Maggi, Milly, Wilberta and Badda. The others had taken the children by a back route to the peat-workings on the Fleam to put them in the hut there before they died of cold. "And what were you going to do?" he asked them.

"Pick them off one by one." It was a good, if dangerous, idea. But he doubted if Matilda would wear it. She was prepared to make an assault on the keep all by herself to get Adeliza out.

Before anything they must get out of the cold themselves. He led them to Shudda's hut which overlooked the green and where the embers of a fire threw out some warmth. The women's figures were bulky and rustled with the straw-padded petticoats they wore in winter. He crossed to the window which faced the keep and shifted the reed blind over it. The keep's unfinished dimensions and jagged top storey made it ugly. There was light coming through the arrow slit he could see on the first storey: they had a fire in there and candles.

"One of the buggers is in the hall," Maggi told him. "We circled back through Wulfholes and we could hear him moving about and breaking things."

He told Kakkr to watch the keep and moved back to the door leading on to the green. Over the other side the hall looked unfamiliar in its desertion. The gates were in deep shadow but above and behind them he saw a pale light pass a window. They were right. So there was a sentry down at the Waits, one or more ransacking the hall and the rest in the keep with the steward and the girl.

"What you want us to do, bor?" asked Wilberta. "We could shoot that one down at the Waits, no trouble." They had put the responsibility for returning their island to them on him. He sighed. You set out to rescue one woman and you ended up with a gaggle of them.

Still, these were fenwomen – wildfowlers, anglers, rowers – for whom the demarcation between the distaff and spear side was not so sharply drawn as in other communities. And he himself had taught them to be arbalists.

"Have you kept in practice?"

They had, they told him. Since the men had been taken away they'd been using the crossbow regularly to bring down geese and duck.

"Maggi's wholly good," said Milly generously.

"We've got to get her out," said Matilda.

He went back to look at the keep entrance. Even unfinished, the place was formidable and the only way in was by the door. It was set high in the first storey with a movable, outside staircase leading up to it. At the top the staircase had a landing a foot below the sill of the door so that when it opened the admitter was standing higher than whoever sought admittance. And both would be outlined against the light from inside. The only cover within bowshot was Fenchel's lodge which still stood on site this side of the moat.

He did some hard thinking. The sentry down by the Waits

209

could go on living a bit longer, but the ransacker in the hall had to go because the hall overlooked the green and they would need to move along the green.

"All right, men, here's what we'll do . . ."

Kakkr was sent down to scout the sentry at the Waits. "Give a duck call if he moves." The job of retrieving her crossbow and his from the sled in the Swallen was given to Matilda and Maggi.

He couldn't dare spare the time to wait for them to come back, so, with Badda and Milly, the most agile, to show him the way, he left the others on guard and began the trek round the south side of the island to the back of the hall.

What worried him most was the men's identity. Had they been sent to Dungesey by de Mandeville who would come after them if they didn't return? Had they been sent by anybody else who would also come after them? On the whole he thought it unlikely. Dungesey was unlikely to be on a plunderer's map. To judge from their inefficiency they were a band of freelance robbers who'd happened to see the keep. That damned keep – he cursed his own part in locating it. It was like a lighthouse. And any time now Stephen could remember it and come back to finish it.

He'd have to kill them all. None of these men could be allowed to escape to bring others back in a revenge raid.

When they were behind the hall they stood in the shadow of Wulfholes' trees and heard muffled banging; the man was overturning barrels in the undercroft. It was going to be easy. "Give me your bow, Badda." They took him up through the apple tun to the drain in the wall; its grid was up and probably hadn't been down in years. "Stay here." He crawled through, sliding easily on the ice, and then ran as fast as he could round the hall and took up a position in the shadow of the gates facing the hall door.

His shoulder was better but he cursed himself for not having practised more; there would be no trouble killing the man at this range, the tricky bit would be killing him so that he didn't scream. He loaded and felt his back protest. He sighted slowly, moving the bow up so that it covered the steps and then the door at the top. Then he waited.

210

There was a faint but steady light behind one of the windows high up at the end of the hall. The man had a rushlight, not a candle; a candle flickered. What the hell did it matter what he was carrying? The glow moved along the windows. The door opened and a man came out on the steps, draped with stolen goods. Christ, he had a frying pan and some saucepans strung over his shoulder, with the frying pan covering his heart. Willem stopped thinking and changed the trajectory and shot him in the forehead instead. The man dropped without a sound but the pans clanged on the steps and one of them bounced down hitting every flight.

Willem ran and caught it at the bottom and raced up the stairs to stand at the top. He reloaded, his head twitching from the direction of the Waits to the keep. The noise would have alerted Ely, let alone the island. But nothing happened. After a while Willem bent down and relieved the body of its goods and dragged it into the hall. Five to go.

Matilda and Maggi crept along the Washes behind the Driftway until Matilda said, "About here." They climbed up the bank and slowly obtruded their heads above its top. Matilda had miscalculated; they were still within sight of the sentry, or would have been if he'd been looking in their direction. The sentry was in full mail and with the nasal on his helmet which made every soldier sinister. He was stamping to keep warm and every so often taking a swig from the bottle he held in his left hand: his right was on his sword hilt.

From the direction of the hall came a faint clanging, like different sized gongs being struck. The sentry swung round and drew his sword. Maggi took her bow over her head and she slid back down the bank to load it. Matilda shook her head at her; the night had gone silent again and the sentry relaxed.

Matilda joined Maggi and they began creeping again until Matilda recognised the spot where she had kissed the mercenary. One kiss and God had punished her like this. It wasn't fair.

She nodded and they climbed the bank again, this time they were round the bend from the Waits and the sled was underneath. Matilda went down to it and Maggi stood on the

211

top with the bow pointing towards the island. There was a professionalism about Maggi which reminded her of the mercenary. She picked up his crossbow and then hers and they went back the way they'd come. As they re-entered the village Maggi pointed back at the sentry: "He's young and he's scared."

"What difference does that make?" He was Fitz Payn and he had Adeliza.

"Makes a difference to him, I reckon."

At the hut they waited for Badda, Milly and the mercenary; when they came they left it and, keeping to the shadow of the huts, moved to the extreme south of the village, the point opposite Fenchel's lodge. The snow reflected back the brilliant moonlight so that the keep stared down on an arena lit for its benefit. Only the yew trees in the middle of the green made stiff, aggressive patterns of shadow. There might be a watcher in the keep or there might not. They'd soon know.

He kept his voice low. "Remember, don't panic if it takes a long time. Sooner or later they're going to open that door and somebody's going to stand on the threshold. Wait. Don't loose off too soon. All right, men."

He tapped Maggi on the shoulder and she began to run across the intervening space to the lodge. The rustling of her petticoat sounded like a waterfall. The mercenary kept his eyes on the keep. She struggled with the hut door which faced the keep; it had frozen into place and the snow piled up at its foot resisted it. She bent down to scrabble at it. "Mother, open the door to her," prayed Matilda. The mercenary looked across to see what was delaying Maggi and saw that her footprints had made a succession of clear, black dots across the snow. Christ, he'd forgotten they'd leave tracks. These were as explicit as signals. Well, it was too late now; if the men in the tower were drunk enough and incompetent enough they'd think the prints were old. "She's in."

He patted Wilberta on her stout back and she bustled off, carrying her crossbow like a basket. There was a clattering as the quiver on her shoulder bounced and jostled the quarrels. God Almighty, if the marauders let them get away with this they deserved to die. One by one the other three followed and still there was no sound or stir. The mercenary and Matilda were left. "Go with them," he pleaded. She shook her head. "It needs two of us." It needed a bloody sight more than that. What he should have done was knock her unconscious at the start and carry her off to the coast.

"And she's of my household," said Matilda de Risle.

The keep glared down at them as they ran to the shelter of Hogwood and then dashed to the moat, approaching the keep from the back. They slid across the ice and began the climb up the steep motte, slipping, grabbing frozen tufts of grass, panting. At last they stood pressed against the great stones of the keep's base. Wind had cleared the platform and they were able to circle to the steps without leaving prints.

As they got to the steps the screaming began.

Perhaps they had gagged her and not taken out the gag until then; perhaps they hadn't hurt her until then. At first it was a woman's terrified screams of disbelief at what was happening to her. As they continued they degenerated into animal howls that went skipping over the Fens like pebbles, alarming sleeping ducks, dislodging owls from branches and sending herons flapping to safer nests.

"A fire arrow." Matilda was clawing at his arm. "Get it. Burn the place down. Stop it."

He grabbed her and pulled her into the darkness under the staircase. "She'd burn to death."

"She'd rather. Listen. She'd rather be dead. I know."

"And I know." He shook her with fury. "You don't know you're better dead. You survived and you're glad. Aren't you? Aren't you?"

"Yes." He stopped shaking her. "But I can't bear it."

"You've got to and she's got to." It was a hell of a place and a hell of a time and a hell of a way, he thought, for her to tell him she loved him, for even if she didn't know it, that's what she'd done. "Now shut up."

The screaming had become automatic now, terrible regulated squawks as if it was a habit she would never break. Matilda covered her ears. He detached his mind from it except as it affected his plan. It would bring the man from the

213

Waits. He wouldn't want to miss the fun. The bleating of the goat attracted the wolf.

And so it did. Underneath the screams came the call of a mallard.

Crouched in the lowest angle of the steps they could see the figure emerge from the Causeway. It paused as it drew level with the hall and whistled for the fellow it presumed to be still in there. The mercenary bit his teeth together; he hadn't had time to do more than drag the body into the hall. But the man didn't go inside. He came on, unconsciously keeping step with the noises that pulsed out of the keep. He was level with Fenchel's lodge and the deep track running up to its door was at his feet, but his head was directed at the source of the screams and he stepped through it.

He passed out of the mercenary's sight, cut off by the gradient of the motte, but his retreating back was now in line with the door of Fenchel's lodge. It opened as he began his ascent of the steps cut in the incline and five bulky figures – Wilberta's the bulkiest – emerged and shut the door behind them. From here on the mercenary would only be able to tell what was happening by watching them.

They could hear the man puffing as he came up, and on the hygienic air came his smell and a whiff of wine from his breath. The steps shook and rattled above their heads as he clambered up them to the door. They heard pounding and his voice: "Open up. Don't leave me out of it." He sounded young and jolly as if wanting to join a party. The steps vibrated as he pounded again.

The five figures by the hut ranged themselves in front of it. If the boy turned he would see them. "Aim," breathed Willem. One by one the crossbows came up and the figures became a line of little statuettes.

There was fumbling at the door above them and bars were drawn out of sockets. "Breathe in," begged Willem. "Don't think."

The hinge grated as the door swung back. "Loose."

The statuettes didn't move. In Willem's unsynchronised time they seemed to have frozen. "Loose."

Raggedly they fired. Chwwt-pt. Chwwt-pt, chwwt

214

chwwt chwwt, pt pt pt. The triggers released Willem; he was up the steps while the man from the Waits was still falling with two bolts in his back. The man who had come to let him in stared at Willem as if affronted before he slid down the door which had swung back on him and held him up with the quarrel sticking in his sternum. Three to go.

Willem kicked him out of the way. Matilda was behind him. He stepped into the keep. The place smelled like an inn and was at blood heat. Willem saw that the three men in it were drunk; only one was on his feet and coming towards them. Willem shot him and leaped sideways to give Matilda a clear shot at the man slumped on a bench against the far wall but he felt his arm jog something: Matilda had been too close behind him and he'd hit the side of her crossbow. He registered the noise of a quarrel going into a wall.

There was no time to change direction. He had already aimed himself at the third man who was half-naked and still lying on top of Adeliza, soporific with orgasm and drink. Willem dropped his crossbow, drew his knife, lifted the man's head back by his hair and cut his throat.

The other man had reacted fast and had charged for the wall opposite the bed where his sheathed knife hung from a belt on a hook. Matilda was clinging on to his right arm in an effort to stop him and being dragged along the floor. "Drop," screamed Willem and threw his knife at the man. It was slippy with blood and hit the man's shoulder, but a quarrel aimed from the doorway did better, entering the back of his neck. Milly, still heaving from her rush up the motte, lowered her bow. "How's that, bor?"

Matilda scrambled for the bed. Adeliza kept on screaming even after they'd covered her up and taken her down to the hall. Willem found Steward Peter doubled up and stuffed down Matilda's garderobe chute. He had been tortured for the mythical gold – his fingers were burned at their ends – but it was the gag they had put into his mouth which had suffocated and killed him.

Early next morning Kakkr took a pickaxe and hacked out a grave for the steward in the frozen earth of the graveyard.

Matilda stood at its foot and spoke the words with the five other women arbalists bunched around her as if the experience of the night before had bonded the six of them together.

The other dead had no such ceremony. Willem and Kakkr dragged their bodies to a disused latrine near Hogwood and buried them. Maggi had been right: the sentry at the Waits had been very young.

Later the mercenary took a bath in the hall's smoke house next to the kitchen, using the vat in which old Shudda usually cleaned the grease from her fleeces. Little globules of grease floated on the steaming water but Willem didn't mind. He peeled material off skin which hadn't seen light for weeks, clambered in and stayed there the whole morning while the Dungesey women, preparing a celebratory feast, barged back and forth, making crude jokes, scrubbing his back and pouring in near-scalding buckets of water and dropping in soapwort, mint, sweet balm and thyme until he smelled like something between a stew and herbal tea. He didn't mind this much either; privacy was rare in his life and baths on active service were taken in public. He snarled to keep them happy, but most of the time he soaked in bliss and deep thought.

Whether he could persuade Matilda to leave the island or not, it needed defending. It had already suffered its fair share of death and atrocity, but with the war and de Mandeville God alone knew how much more was on its way. If he and Kakkr and some of the stronger women between them could dislodge the unfinished course of upper stones of the keep, leaving the undercroft and first storey only, and then plant quick-growing willow around its base it could be camouflaged a bit. The fact that there was such a tall rise would attract attention in this stretch of fenland, which was a curse, but it could also act as a watchtower, which was a blessing.

They must keep a constant look-out, there'd have to be signals and escape routes.

Upstairs in the solar Matilda was also taking a bath. She had commanded a tub and buckets of hot water be carried up so that she would not have to leave Adeliza who lay in her bed in a drugged sleep, periodically still shuddering with

216

rasps of whispered screams. The Wealy woman, Epona, had turned up that morning from wherever the Wealas had disappeared to, taken one look at Adeliza and produced a small bottle of St. Gregory's cordial, giving her some drops on a spoon and bringing peace after a night that had drained Matilda of all strength. The calm presence of the huge blonde was comforting.

There was a knock on the door. Epona opened it and Matilda heard the voice of Badda asking if she could have some of Sigward's clothes for the mercenary "so's we can wash hisn". Epona turned her head to the steam emerging from the washtub. "No," snapped Matilda out of it.

"That's mean," Badda said to Wilberta returning downstairs. "After all he's done for her."

But Wilberta said: "She's shamed. She can't put her husband's clothes on her fancy man."

So it was Maggi who turned out the best cloak and gown of Stunta the clerk. She sighed. "Wonder where the old fool is now."

In the circumstances the feast that night was wonderful; the women had worked hard to welcome Matilda and to celebrate their victory. They'd cooked goose, four types of duck, as well as carp, the ubiquitous eel, lamprey, bean and lentil stews, withered pears and apples, honey cakes and such ale and mead as the intruders had left them. Willem marvelled that they had coped so well all this time without any men between the age of Kakkr, who was at least sixty, and Wifil, who was ten, to help them.

Matilda left Epona with Adeliza to make a brief appearance and drink a toast with her fellow-liberators, but her anxiety was chilling and there was more relaxation when she'd gone. Then they drank to Willem and he to them. They drank in silence to Steward Peter, "Good old boy for all he was a Norman." Before they all got too drunk Willem made them a speech.

"Ladies and gentlemen." (Cheers.) "Last night five of you were the best troop I've ever had under my command. But what are you going to do if it happens again?" There was immediate silence; even the toddlers stopped playing.

He gave them with care, repeating the difficult bits, the accumulated wisdom from his bath that morning.

"What if they come at night?" shouted Maggi. He was beginning to respect Maggi: if they were really his troop he'd make her his lieutenant.

"That's good. Now you're thinking. It's not likely, but, well, what about dogs?" They shook their heads: dogs, needing red meat, were a luxury they could no longer afford.

"All right, better than dogs, you've got geese. And you intercommon with cattle, or you did; well, now intercommon for defence. Get the villages together. Make plans to protect each other.

"One last thing, when in doubt run away." Contract rules. "Hide your valuables and run, but run first. If anything like last night happens again – God preserve us all – and you have to kill, make sure you kill them *all*. Nobody gets away, nobody."

He sat down and stood up again. "But make sure they're the enemy. For Christ's sake, don't kill just anybody."

It was as well he added that; two days later when he, Kakkr, Milly and Badda were struggling with the upper stones of the keep, Maggi came panting up. "We've got one, captain." A man had skated up the Swallen. Maggi, Wilberta and Shudda who were on guard at the Waits had made sure he was alone, then emerged pointing crossbows at him and made him lie down. Wilberta had sat on his head while the others tied him up. "He's a Fleming."

In their tongue "Fleming" did not mean someone from Flanders, but was the generic term for "stranger". Nevertheless, the swearing coming from the prisoner in the hall was as Flemish as Willem's own. His nose was bleeding and he was angry. "These bloody women broke my nose," he yelled at Willem. "The fat one sat on my head."

"You were lucky. Who are you and what do you want?"

"If you're Willem of Ghent I've a message for you," said the man, sulkily, "but I won't give it now."

Willem was amazed. That a message should find him in the middle of a war when he was hiding in the most impenetrable part of England, which even he hadn't known he

218

would be hiding in, could only be delivered by some herald from God. Apologetically he sat the broken-nosed angel down, released his hands and called for refreshment.

"Ah hah," said the man triumphantly, "that had you. And I know the lady here, Matilda of Risle."

Matilda was sent for; she was abstracted and pale. "He's a sea captain. His name's Turold." She woke up. "Have you a message from my son?"

Turold thawed with the attention. He explored his nose and clicked it back into place. Young Edmund, it appeared, was thriving and sent his love. "But I'm here for Somebody Else." He delved into his tunic and produced a crumbling piece of vegetable matter. "That's a dirty old piece of plant," said Badda, leaning over his shoulder.

Matilda smiled for the first time in days. "The Plantagenet."

"Fitzempress." Turold smirked modestly. He turned to Willem. "I was to say that if you presented yourself at Caen as soon as maybe you might find yourself offered a position to your advantage."

Willem grinned: "He can't be above ten years old."

"Maybe he is," said Turold slowly, "only he seems older. His father's letting him have his own household, any road up. His choices wouldn't suit his mother, I dare say – too low-born some of 'em – but he met you at Bristol, seemingly, and liked the cut of your jib."

"When do you sail?" Willem looked at Matilda who looked away.

"Soon. From Cradge."

The mercenary nodded. "Looks like I'll be there."

"How did you know this man was here?" demanded Matilda. Was her name being linked with every mercenary in England?

Turold drew her over to a corner and spoke low: "That man" – a thumb bent at Willem – "was asking for you in Bristol. Fitzempress said he was a man who'd find what he was looking for. You'd mentioned this place to Fitzempress long ago as a good place to hide. And the prince heard you needed to hide." The ship captain leaned nearer. "I was to say he was sorry there'd been a . . . a tactical error in your case. He don't approve of what his mother done. And I was to ask: is the Postern still open?"

Matilda wiped her eyes. A tactical error; all that pain and horror reduced to a boy's idea of a mistaken manoeuvre.

"Does he treat my son well?"

Turold nodded. "He's one of the puppies always with him."

She had nothing left to lose. "Tell him it's open."

Once again in the solar she continued the fight for Adeliza's life. The periods between the drug were calmer and the dreadful shuddering had ceased. Her eyes followed Matilda, occasionally frowning in pain. New bruising kept coming out on her body and Epona was afraid something inside her had ruptured. "But she'll live?" Matilda was terrified. Epona shrugged.

During her consciousness Matilda talked to her, recalling happy times, promising happier times in the future. "You don't know you're better dead, Adeliza. Never. Are you listening to me?" Adeliza's big eyes watched her helplessly. "Promise me you'll try. Promise."

Adeliza's bruised mouth smiled. "Yes, Matilda."

Matilda blew out her breath in relief. Adeliza had always obeyed her. She changed into her nightrobe and lay down on the mattress on the floor beside the bed. Epona could watch tonight.

In the early hours a movement from Epona woke her up. There was high moonlight outside the window and the winter noises of the Fens, but there was a new silence in the room. She scrambled up and watched Epona crossing Adeliza's hands on her breast. "Oh nonsense, she promised me." But for the first and last time in both their lives, Adeliza had disobeyed her.

They knelt and prayed. After a while Matilda put her cloak over her shoulders and went out.

Epona watched her cross the courtyard and go out of the gates; the commander only had a thin nightshirt on under the cloak and flimsy slippers on her feet. She must go and bring her back to bed. Then Epona thought of somebody who'd do the job better. She went down to the hall bay where the mercenary slept: "You're needed."

By the time Willem was out of the gates Matilda had reached Fenchel's lodge and was standing in its doorway, facing the keep. She would pull the thing down and make the stones into a shrine for Adeliza so that no woman would ever be spitted on it again. "And how amazing I am," she thought, "that nothing will live around me and I feel nothing. I never will again. How amazing and dreary are the ways of God."

The mercenary paused where he could see her. She was talking to herself and her hands moved in little reasoning gestures. He had seen men like that when they'd been exposed to too much killing. She was in battle shock. He'd been like it himself once and the saving of him had been poor Dyrika, the camp follower, who'd said: "Willem, what you need is flesh," and taken him to bed and warmed him back to life. It didn't matter whether he wanted Matilda or should want her, she needed him. "My son, do as you have been done by."

He went up to the lodge and pulled her aside so that he could open its door and take her inside to Fenchel's bed.

The moment his arms went round her, Matilda gave in. "Mother of God, let me sin this once. Just this warm, one, lovely sin in this death-ridden world."

"Don't think."

As her body absorbed his semen and his sweat, she was amazed at how personal the making of love could be. Her husbands had committed the sexual act with the expected woman on the expected bed; they would have done the same whichever woman it was. This man made love to the person that was Matilda because it was Matilda. He lubricated her parched soul with it. When he wasn't making love to her physically he spoke it, holding her across his chest and crooning words as if he'd saved up every endearment from every language he knew to use on her now.

She tucked her head under his armpit and strolled her fingertips over him, exploring the varieties of textures which

221

had never concerned her before. "What nice backs men have."

"It's not their backs you should worry about."

Just before dawn he said: "Turold sails tonight. Do I still go to Fitzempress?"

"You know you do." She was sane – he had done that much for her. She had sinned against God and her class; only the Mother would understand, and only she just this once. This was still Sigward's island, there was still a war to be won and too many emotions and taboos to be coped with. "I want you to look after my son." Except for the English lands it was the only beautiful thing she had left to give Edmund.

"Who's going to look after you?"

"I can cope now."

She would be safe from remarriage, at least. As he dressed he lectured her, repeating the instructions he had given the islanders on defence, the constant look-outs, the geese, the escape routes. She barely heard what he said, she was watching every move he made.

"Will you promise me to remember all that?" he asked her.

"I'll remember."

He kissed her almost absent-mindedly. He had already gone back to war.

"Goodbye, commander."

"Goodbye, captain."

After he left she stayed on in bed for some time, her hands on the place where his body had been. Eventually she said: "Well, that's that," and got up. By the time she had got back to the hall, he had gone.

On the night after Brother Daniel received official, though completely illegal, confirmation from King Stephen that he was now Abbot of Ramsey, he had a boy brought to the cellar of the abbot's house. The other boy had died as they all did eventually, and this one was younger, but bigger, more intelligent, and he fought back. It took four days of starvation and drugs to get him compliant.

"Now then," said Abbot Daniel, "I want you to scry for

me. I want you, my darling, to ask Our Master how long I have got."

He murmured as he held the boy's head over the scrying glass until it was fixed like a hypnotised chicken's. The abbot's voice became smoke drifting across the glass and the sand bowl over which the boy's hand was poised. "How long, howlong, howlong, howlong, howlong."

The boy's finger drew a vertical line in the sand. "Howlonghowlong." By the side of the line, on its right, came a circle and then underneath it another circle.

"Eighteen," said Abbot Daniel. "Master, I thank you. A soul is well lost for eighteen years."

13

1144

When the castles were built they filled them with devils
and wicked men. By night and by day they seized those
whom they believed to have any wealth, whether they
were men or women; and in order to discover their gold
and silver, they put them into prison and tortured them
with unspeakable tortures, for never were martyrs tortured
as they were . . . If two or three men came riding towards
a village, all the villagers fled before them, believing that
they were robbers. The bishop and clergy were forever
cursing them, but that was nothing to them, for they were
all excommunicated and forsworn and lost. Wherever the
ground was tilled the earth bore no corn, for the land was
ruined by such doings and men said openly that Christ and
his saints slept.

So says the Anglo-Saxon Chronicle which was written at
Peterborough at this time.

Black Shuck, the Devil's dog, was everywhere, his huge
shape outlined against the sky as he ran along the droves and
banks to enter churches and drag out the worshippers in his
slavering jaws.

Realising the end of the world was at hand men and
women joined monasteries and nunneries or, in their terror,
founded new ones so that the number of convents doubled in
Stephen's reign and their voices rose to God pleading for
deliverance.

"*Exsurge, quare obdormis, Domine?*" Arise, why sleepest
thou, O Lord? Arise and cast us not off.

But not at Ramsey.

To Ramsey, at last, came de Mandeville and his army. They rode through the well-tended village, past the newly ploughed fields, through the orchards to the half-acre of lawn which rolled like a green carpet of welcome from the great gates of the abbey. He did not knock nor did he shout for admittance. He waited, staring down the carved eyes of the Saviour who presided over the writhings of the Last Judgment.

The Church had excommunicated him, cursing him within and without, sleeping or walking, going or sitting, standing or riding, lying above earth or under earth, speaking and crying and drinking, in wood, in water, in field, in town. It had cursed him by the Father, Son and Holy Ghost, by the angels and archangels and all the nine orders of Heaven, that he have no part in mass nor matins nor of none other good prayers that be done in Holy Church, but that the pains of Hell be his meed with Judas that betrayed our Lord Jesus Christ until he came to amendment and satisfaction made. *Fiat! Fiat!* Amen.

The gates opened and through them came the new abbot, confident in the Devil's love.

He walked up to the figure on the black horse. "Welcome, my lord," he said, "in the name of the Master we both serve." He smiled. De Mandeville raised his mailed fist and smashed it into Abbot Daniel's face. The horses stepped over him to go through the gates and be stabled in the holy cloister.

On the stone portico of the abbey something trickled down the carving of dragons and griffons and soaked into the ground. Another drop broke out on the Barnack stone further along, then another, until all the outer walls of Ramsey Abbey sweated red liquid. Many witnessed the portent and reputable men later wrote of it, that at this time the walls of Ramsey bled.

Later that night a shape that screamed and wore the muddied cope of an abbot squirmed back into the fen from which it had once emerged. "Eighteen," it was howling. "You promised me eighteen years."

But the voice of the Devil spoke back to him, amused and

echoing over the waterland. "Days, you bloody fool. I meant eighteen days."

July was the quietest month in the Fens because the birds which made them so busy the rest of the year hid their chicks in the long grasses so that there was an undertow of cheeps and rustlings to the silence.

The Fens became luscious, producing marsh marigolds instead of the buttercups of poorer lands. The colour and variety of the butterflies bewildered the eye as they bounced along the umbellifers lining the banks on invisible strings. They were nearly as numerous as the flies and Matilda batted crossly at both as she walked along the Driftway path in a tunnel of milk parsley and hemlock. The top earth had dried and powdered her boots in a black dust.

She stopped at an obstruction in her way, a contraption of sticks emerging out of the ground like a mad milking-stool, took the spade from its sling over her back and dug down round the buried trap until she could hear a movement from inside it. "Ah ha, you little sod." She lifted the trap out, opened its tail-gate and inserted her hand warily. "They bite like eels," Kakkr had said, "get 'em round the neck." Between her thumb and forefinger wriggled a small, black, velvet animal six inches long. She tapped its nose against the spade shaft, killing it instantly. Its seal-like flippers ended in perfect, tiny hands even down to the fingernails and the creases in the plump, pink palms.

She tied the mole on to a string which already held a couple of dozen others, carefully reburied the trap and walked on to the next where she repeated the procedure. Then she sat down to rest under an elder. She sat inelegantly with her coarse linen skirt up over her hocks for coolness and swigged from a bottle of water, then pressed the bottle against her sweating face; it was a miracle of function in its way, having three fitting skins of tightly woven rushes which allowed continual infinitesimal seepage of the oatmeal water inside it that, in evaporating, kept it cold. When she had time Badda was going to show her how to make one.

Matilda sighed and hauled herself to her feet. Before she

emerged again on to the track she stood on tiptoe to look at where the keep showed against the blue sky above newly planted trees. To Matilda it dominated the Fens. However, there was no flag hanging from it which meant that the look-out, Kakkr, had spotted no intruder in the miles under his gaze. "Unless he's fallen asleep." She'd left him plenty to do, turning out rushlights. It took skill to skin the rush of three-quarters of its outer green and leave the pith supported by a spine of the remaining quarter. They couldn't afford candles, but she'd grown fond of rushlight which burned with a strong, clear light.

She lived in a rush-patterned, rush-smelling world. Rushes provided Dungesey's light, beehives, eel-traps, sun hats like the one she was wearing, cradles, belts, sandals, spoons and chair seats, matting and trays. Not until now had Matilda appreciated the labour required by the business of staying alive.

At first she had sulked, insisting that Epona act as her serving woman. Then her natural meddlesomeness had taken over; she'd been unable to bear watching the ship go down for want of her own hap'orth of tar. She'd listen to the other women bemoaning a job left undone and snap: "I'll have to do it, then," and in doing it became absorbed in a new skill. Each job done was a gain enabling more crops to grow, making the coming winter safer and warmer, so that her sense of achievement was almost greed.

"I'll do this and this," she'd say, "so that you can do that and that." She became a miser with time, reluctant to let one minute go without squeezing it of usefulness. It gave her satisfaction that Kakkr was keeping watch *and* making rush-lights, that while their mothers dug peat bricks their children were keeping watch *and* spinning wool. She was the island's mole-catcher because Kakkr was too old to do the job as quickly as it might be done.

"Matilda the mole-catcher," she moaned. "If the court could see me . . ." But the moles, in their way, were as dangerous to the island as de Mandeville. The tunnels of their runs weakened the banks, filling them with water in a flood. "They'll hole across a bank," said Kakkr, who admired

227

them, "swim the dyke and hole the other bank like lightning buttered both sides." The Driftway had only just contained the spring thaw; it must not give way and allow water to flood the Washes which had been planted with legumes to provide winter food. Matilda gloated over those rows of beans and peas as if they were emerald bracelets striping the black velvet peat.

That the island had suffered no more human incursions was not because the Fens had become less dangerous – with de Mandeville ensconsed at Ramsey, they had become very dangerous – but because of Maggi's Good Idea.

It had come when Matilda, as usual, was hating the keep. "Might as well have Ely Cathedral balanced on our heads."

Maggi's little nose had twitched. "That old Conqueror couldn't get to Ely, for all he could see it in the distance. Why should bandits get to us?"

"Because, you stupid female, they spot the keep from the Nene, and the Swallen leads out of the Nene straight to us." But she watched Maggi expectantly; the clerk's woman had become her invaluable, humorous, intelligent, responsible second-in-command.

"Right, commander, it does," said Maggi. "But suppose they couldn't find the Swallen?"

Matilda stared then clouted her lieutenant on the back. "Maggi, you're not the fool you look," which was the highest accolade one Fen English could give another.

They took Dungesey's largest barge and jammed it cross-ways between Crease Bank and the Driftway at the entrance of the Swallen. Then, using Kakkr and every woman and child, they half-filled it with peat and poured in water until it settled nearly to the gunwales, the prow and stern wedging more firmly into the slope of the banks. After that they planted it with willow, elder and blackthorn.

Right away the trees had camouflaged the entrance, and now that weeds had also sprouted of their own accord the Nene flowed past an apparently continuous bank.

The approach to Dungesey was now by land or the tortuous, tunnelled streams which led to the back entrance at Wulfholes. The approach by land was almost impossible; drainage had suffered for lack of a male workforce and marsh was going back to quagmire and meadows to marsh. The back-door route by water could only be found by great luck or previous knowledge.

There were disadvantages; blocking the Swallen cut off their most navigable route to the rest of the Fens. But, since de Mandeville, there was no trade anyway. The blockade shut out friends as well as enemies, but most friends knew their way to the back door and Kakkr was watching out for those who didn't. Every day the women expected their men to return and every day Matilda expected a message from Normandy via Cradge, but as yet neither had come.

Matilda killed another mole, reburied the trap, looked again at the keep and moved on. She came to the Stun which marked the boundary between her property and Ramsey's. It was the only piece of stone for miles and piles of littered shells around it showed that blackbirds and thrushes came from far and wide to crack open snails on it.

Matilda took another cautious look round, bent, heaved the stone up and with effort staggered two short paces with it before being forced to let it drop. She did this every time she passed it, leaving square, yellow depressions in the grass behind her. By the time such things mattered – if they ever did – Dungesey would have gained several yards of land at the expense of Ramsey.

She remained doubled, panting, then creaked upright. She must be careful of her back.

Memories of the mercenary transfixed her.

She had made her confession. Ely, with commendable concern for the Fen souls which were without pastors since Ramsey was inoperative, had sent out peripatetic priests to take Easter communion on the islands and hear the sins of their inhabitants. One had arrived at Dungesey.

Alone with the priest after the other women had made confession, "though God knows," Matilda thought fondly, "when they find time to sin," she had asked forgiveness for killing one man and having carnal knowledge of another.

The priest had been indulgent over Fitz Payn, violent death having become commonplace, "for you were in great peril and thou mayest kill in order to stop a soul falling into worse sin", but her night with the mercenary shocked him. "This foulness, and with an excommunicate?"

"I didn't ask if he was excommunicated or not," said Matilda wearily.

"But a carnal sin. Do you renounce the flesh? Are you penitent?"

She'd opened her mouth to say she was, but into her fingers came the memory of the skin over the corrugated muscle on the mercenary's back. "It didn't seem foulness." If what she had experienced with her husbands was licit and the night with the mercenary sin, then something was wrong somewhere.

At last she said she was penitent just to be rid of the man. Her penance had been to live on bread and water for a year (which she had no intention of keeping) and to build a church one day (which she had). But the memory of a sin which didn't seem like sin stayed with her.

In the summer fenland now Matilda looked at her hand and sighed. It was dirty and its nails were black and torn. A swallowtail with its wings hardly dry landed on her fingers, turning them into a plinth for an enamel of yellow, red, blue and black. Too fancy for a mole-catcher. She shook it off and went back to work.

She continued along Monks' Bank which, though not her property, protected the north side of her Washes and was in worse repair than ever. As she turned to come back a flag ran up the keep. She dived into the milk parsley, brushing away the flies so that she could listen. A dragonfly zoomed by, iridescent and noisy. The scent of the umbellifers was so strong it was almost noise. Carefully she parted the heads, trying to make out the flag's colour. Her eyes watered in the sunlight but at last she saw that it was blue, one of her old petticoats dyed with woad, signifying that the danger was water-borne. It was a single flag, which meant the Nene. Two would have meant the Fleam near the peat-digging.

She dashed across the bank to hide under a willow and watch the water. The signalling system wasn't flexible enough to tell her whether the threat was coming upstream or down, but she could swear nothing had passed her. Traffic had come to a standstill since de Mandeville.

The Nene had chosen today to be clear. A shaft of sun from between the willow branches pierced a pool below her and she could see a long, speckled trout resting in its warmth and puffs of sediment as a powter moved along the sludge of the river bottom.

She heard the unmistakable clunk and splash of a rower missing his stroke. The swear-words following were in English and though the voice was familiar she couldn't place it. The prow of a rowing boat drifted into her view. Its oarsman was bent over, doing something to his right knee – or where his knee would have been if he'd had a right leg, which he hadn't. Matilda got a glimpse of a raw, puckered stump end.

She would follow his progress downriver and, if he spotted the blockage across the Swallen, shoot him. The rower lifted his head.

Matilda swung herself down the bank. "Pampi."

The man looked in her direction. "Art'noon, gal." It was the common greeting to a fenwoman: he didn't recognise her.

"Pampi, it's me." She couldn't have believed she'd be so glad to see him, to have an able-bodied man back to help her – but Pampi wasn't able-bodied any more.

"Commander?" He sculled to the bank. "You got any water?" She gave him what was left in her bottle and tied the boat's painter to a branch.

"All right?" he asked.

She told him Wilberta was well and Dungesey still functioning. "What about you?"

There was a long silence. "Stunta won't be back," he told her. Nor would Toki nor Wyrm, all three killed in a battle early in the year far away in the west at a place called Wilton. Stephen's army had been surprised by the Earl of Gloucester's. A sword cut had severed Pampi's leg. What had saved him initially, he reckoned, had been the intense cold. "Froze the bugger, see." Since he was obviously dying nobody had bothered to take him prisoner. Later, when the camp women had discovered him obstinately refusing to die, they had taken him to the local barber who had sewn up and cauterised his stump.

"Don't know why," Pampi said with gloom. "No more use than squit now."

The instinct which brought the eels back to their home rivers from the ocean had drawn him, hobbling on a crutch, from one side of England to the other; a journey so dreadful that he rebuffed Matilda's questions until she grew angry at his self-pity. She rebuked him in good Fen English, the only English she could speak. "You duzzy ole vool, an you only got one leg you'll onyways be useful to I."

He grunted with amusement. "You've changed."

"Everything's changed."

She got into the boat, which he'd stolen by night at Aldreth. He'd wedged a box against the stern so that his stump had purchase as he rowed, but the friction had rubbed its scabs off. When he reached for the oars she pushed him out of the way and took them herself; rowing was another skill she'd acquired.

They went past the barge blockade without Pampi noticing it, which pleased her, though a few yards further on he said: "In't we come too far?" She sculled back and showed him Maggi's idea. He couldn't grasp the need for it. "What'll the barges do now, then?"

"There aren't any barges."

She enlightened him as she feathered down the tunnels to Snailstream. When they grounded she made him sit in the boat while she ran to the hall for salves and a bandage for his stump, but he wouldn't let her touch it. "I'm all right."

"Looks it," she shouted back. The base of the stump oozed blood and mucus and the holes left by the withered ligaments were not fully healed, but the barber had stitched the collops of skin round it into a neat, buffering edge. If he could survive the original amputation he could survive this.

When he'd hauled himself out of the boat – he refused help – she got back in to go and tell the women. It would be pleasing to give Wilberta, who knew everything, the surprise of her life. Less pleasing would be having to tell Maggi and Badda and Milly, Wyrm's wife, that their men were dead. She particularly dreaded telling Maggi. Once she had thought commoners too insensitive for true grief: she knew better now. Maggi's heart was loving and vulnerable and it beat for Stunta – though what she had seen in that military-mad old fool Matilda failed to understand.

The look-outs had done their job: from a distance the peat-diggings looked deserted. The peat bricks were in a long honeycombed wall through which sun and air could dry them. The ground from which they had been removed was a chessboard of black and green squares. Digging peat was a back-breaking business and the women had been at it for a week, but there could be no rest; tomorrow they would all have to harvest the barley in West Field, which was ripe, while the weather held.

The sedge rustled as if with mice and spewed forth women and children – the women clumping like trolls on the boards strapped to their feet to stop them ruining the peat. Rush fringes hung from their hat brims against flies and gnats.

"What's doing, commander?" Under the fringe Maggi's small face was distorted by heat, dirt, bites and anxiety. These women had suffered enough, she didn't want them to suffer more.

She took in a deep breath. She was their lord: it was her duty to tell them.

In August Pampi rowed to Cradge to see if there was a message. He returned with three sprigs of broom: next trip Turold would be carrying three passengers for the Postern. He was working exclusively for Fitzempress now and making regular crossings between Gravelines and the Wash.

As the islanders were still using the hall as their dormitory for safety reasons, Matilda had the keep made ready for guests. "First time the bloody thing's been useful."

Three weeks later Wifil, on look-out, spotted a boat upriver on the Nene. He recognised the web-fingered boy from Cradge but not the three shabby monks with him. As the boat slid into the tunnel of Snailstream hidden crossbows levelled at it – it was not unknown for de Mandeville men to disguise themselves as monks. But a voice called out the password, "Plantagenet." The crossbows lowered.

The youngest, shabbiest monk was Walter, ex-Abbot of Ramsey. Matilda was overjoyed. "Where have you been, my lord?" There had been no news of him since Brother Daniel had been made abbot by Stephen.

"Rome." He had aged and shook with residual malaria from the marshes around Rome which were even more ague-ridden than the Fens. "I was persuaded I had done wrong in relinquishing my post as abbot."

He ate and drank a little and let Epona dose him with St. Gregory's cordial. "The Holy Father has ordered that Daniel be deposed and that I be reinstated as abbot. In his mercy he has overlooked my fault in giving away my responsibility."

"He's been deposed already," said Matilda. "De Mandeville."

"Ah yes, I've heard of de Mandeville." To people whose world had been turned upside down by the man he seemed to speak the name lightly.

Gabbling, Matilda gave him a précis of de Mandeville atrocities, augmented by interruptions from Badda and Milly. "He's sending out men to steal the harvests," Matilda told him. "If it isn't handed over he burns the island." She couldn't sleep at night for fear it would happen to Dungesey.

"It shall all be set right," he kept saying. He didn't understand, not until he'd been to Ramsey himself to seek admittance, and been refused. There he saw for himself the gibbets on the lawn by the gates, the whores and the soldiers who camped in front and the devastated island.

He was brought back to Matilda, weeping. "Did you see?" he kept saying. "There was blood on the walls. Ramsey is bleeding."

234

In Matilda's chamber when they were alone he recovered. "Now tell me about de Mandeville."

She went through it again, but this time started further back, in the time before she, too, had grown up. ". . . and when Adeliza died it was almost worse than anything had been. But the mercenary was . . . was good to me and made me sane before he went away." She poured more wine, nervous at how much she'd told him. She became brisk. "And that's how the Postern came about, and why I'm still here."

The abbot reached for his cup. She was on the last half-barrel; there would be no more. Moths came in through the window with the scents of a fenland summer night, singed their wings on the rushlight and rolled on the table, flapping.

"What's it like to be in love?"

"Well, I don't know." Matilda was surprised and cross.

"It seems you do. Plato said that each man and woman was the half of a perfect whole, spending a lifetime to find the other half."

"Who's Plato?"

"And you have found yours in this mercenary."

"Nonsense. I am a Norman lady. God wouldn't do that to me."

"Is there a God?"

"Eh?" This wasn't embarrassing; it was frightening.

The ex-abbot shifted so that their faces were close. "There's a toad in the Fens," he said carefully, "which mews and clicks in summertime. Fenmen call it 'the Squeaker'. I've dissected it. And it mews and clicks because parasite maggots are eating away its eyes and blocking its breathing while it still lives."

"Yes?"

"It worried me, that toad – even in my innocence I would wonder about a God who created a chain of life in which one thing eats another. Today, at Ramsey, I saw it clearly. There is no God. We are animals grown haphazard to some natural law to prey on one another."

He fell on the floor and began to sob again.

"Oh, for goodness sake," said Matilda huffily. She yanked

235

him up and popped him back on his stool. "Don't you men understand anything? Of course there's a God." She wiped his nose on a cloth. "Blow."

He blew. "How do you know?"

How could she put it? Because His Mother showed me how to hide my son and helped me through the worst experience of my life? Because I glimpsed Him in a damned crossbowman with a bad back? Because I can't help it? She must be objective; he needed facts. "Have you ever tasted a blackberry on the last day of September?"

"I suppose so."

"And it's sweet. But have you ever tasted one on the first day of October? It's sour. Awful. The Devil gets into black-berries on the last night of September. It's always true. And if there's a Devil there must be a God." Everybody knew that.

The ex-abbot stared out on to years of labour and debt and discomfort and shame. "They were right with their rules and administration all along, weren't they?"

"I expect so."

As she watched him go through the courtyard she remembered a girl who'd fancied a spiritual romance with that man.

At the beginning of a blistering September de Mandeville laid siege to Burwell, one of Stephen's castles in the southern Fens. It had been sited by Willem of Ghent and built by Fenchel, the engineer, and proved a difficult nut to crack.

Butterflies accompanied the warlord as he rode round his siege lines to the meadow opposite the north gate of the castle where his soldiers had been picking cranberries in the marsh. De Mandeville stopped and stared across at the castle which defied him with the same look with which he regarded a blue fenland sky or a man dying under torture. He had shown no emotion since the Pope had excommunicated him.

"All quiet, my lord," said his sergeant, wiping his mouth. De Mandeville took off his helmet and exposed his glistening bald head. He was in full mail and smelled of hot metal. They remembered afterwards the question he asked: "What meadow is this?"

236

"Ramsey Lea, my lord; it belongs to Ramsey."

"To me," he said.

The arrow came from the castle three hundred yards away, wavering in the heat. It was nearly spent by the time it stuck into his forehead; he was pulling it out even as he fell from his horse.

They carried him away from the suffocating fens to his manor at Mildenhall where his son helped to carry him into the hall. "Eggs," said the voice of de Mandeville. "Eggs. Eggs."

"He keeps asking for eggs," said the sergeant worriedly.

"Eggs," said de Mandeville.

". . . communication," said his son. "Excommunication. Fetch the Abbot of Ramsey. Tell him he's got his manor back but, oh Jesus, bring him quick."

While he gathered his dispersed monks around him and dictated his letters asking for support, the abbot had made his home with Hugh Bigod, Earl of Norfolk who, to everyone's surprise, had remained loyal to the Empress.

He arrived at Mildenhall on September 15 and de Mandeville's son threw himself at his feet. "Lift the Fiat, my lord. Save my father's soul."

They had made a bed for de Mandeville on the great table, but it would soon be a catafalque. The mount of green skin round the wound on his forehead lifted his eyebrows and stretched his lids so that he stared upwards in horror. "Eggs," he whimpered. "Eggs. Eggs."

"You see he is truly penitent, my lord," said the son. "Lift the excommunication."

"I'm so sorry," said Abbot Walter, "but I can't. Nobody who has laid violent hands on a cleric can be absolved by anyone except the Pope and in the Pope's own presence." He was putting on weight.

"But here is Ramsey." The boy shoved rolled membranes that dangled seals into Walter's hands. "All the charters, the tenancies."

"Eggs, eggs," begged de Mandeville.

Through the open door came the smell of pines and a blackbird's song, but high in the black rafters of the hall the

Devil was hovering to look down into the dying eyes that stared into his own.

De Mandeville's wife rushed to a chest and tried to pull it towards the abbot. It didn't move. She tried pushing. "We are empowered to offer you this chest, lord, full of gold for the poor."

"They will be glad of it, but I cannot save your husband."

The warlord on the table tried to lift his hand to cover the eyes which would not close. His wife pulled at Walter's sleeve. "Just say the words, then, lord, even if they will not save him. Just let his death be peaceful before he faces damnation. I know he's been wicked but our Lord was merciful to sinners – let him die in peace."

The abbot picked her hand off his robe. "It would be breaking the rules, my dear. We're in this mess because I broke them. I will stay and I will pray for him, but rules are rules."

Ordure dripped down the Devil's goatish haunches: they could smell it. They knew the Devil chuckled because the man on the table chuckled in helpless imitation. The abbot prayed steadily, but Satan came closer, his giantism making the hall pulse, reducing and constricting its occupants so that they crouched. The warlord tried to crawl off the table to get away from his diabolic creditor. They saw him attempt to close his popping eyes and clutch at his chest to ward off the talons from his soul, but in the end they heard it torn out of his body in a great suck of air.

The corpse could not receive Christian burial, of course, so it was sealed in a chest and lodged for a while in a cherry tree at Walton Abbey, but the monks' dreams became disturbed by the screams of de Mandeville's soul as it hopped and sizzled on Hell's andiron and the coffin was transferred to an unblessed cave under the Temple in London where it lay for the rest of that reign and most of the next until all Ramsey's tenants had been restored and huge sums paid to the abbey in compensation and the Pope lifted the excommunication.

The de Mandeville revolt was over. His men went back to wherever they had come from, taking women, harvests and valuables with them, leaving waste behind.

Abbot Walter and a handful of monks returned to the deserted abbey to find it stripped and fouled with rubbish, its fields untilled and in the kitchens no food at all, not even, said Ramsey's chronicler, "so much utensils as would suffice for the cooking of cabbages for a single meal".

There was hardly time to draw breath before the Fens faced their next enemy.

14

As if to make up for the summer, late autumn and winter were the wettest in years. Besides their own rain the Fens were deluged with the water from thirteen counties. It purled into rivers and neglected lodes until only the islands and highest embankments stood above its comfortless surface and water birds swam between willow branches in which land birds perched and wondered where to go next. All grazing was drowned and islanders shared their houses with cattle and went abroad in boats and shook their fists at the uplands where the water came from.

Dungesey fetched its harvest store from the hiding-places and Pampi and Matilda quarrelled about the best place to keep it out of the wet.

"Not the keep, you fool," Matilda shouted. "It's damp. It'll get the mildew. It'll be safe enough here in the under-croft."

"What if that floods?" demanded Pampi. "That be damp enough for you?"

It was late and the island women were settling down for the night. The shutters on the north side of the hall kept unlatching and banging, letting in the driving rain. When they were shut again the wind moaned at the cracks. The children were fretful, babies cried and smoke from the fire gusted in the draught. "Not the keep," said Matilda. "It'd be too much work getting it up there." She still had a horror of the keep. "And raiders could find it there."

"Pity the poor buggers who come raiding in this lot," he grumbled. There were times when she loathed Pampi, the male who challenged her authority.

"You're my vassal. You can't tell me what to do."

"I can do that's sense," he yelled back.

Down the bays of the hall the rush screens which partitioned off the sleeping quarters were going up. Quarrels between Pampi and Matilda were too frequent and too short-lived to be of interest but Maggi, as always, was at her elbow. "Better do it, commander. He's not the fool he looks. And the wind's in the north-west."

She calmed Matilda who took a deep breath and tried to forget how tired she was, how damp and how constantly hemmed in by people and noise. Another shutter flew open and banged in time to the pounding in her head. She could taste salt on the wind.

"Is it another Flood?" She was suddenly nervous.

Kakkr, who was telling stories to his grandson by the fire, droned: "It's the Mother coming back. There's a full moon and she comes with it every seventh year. She comes back to her children every seventh year with the full moon."

She was sick of this life, sick of their stupid faces. "Do as you like. I'm going to bed. Build another bloody Ark for all I care."

The next morning the wind up in the Orkneys gusted at 125 miles an hour and coincided with a high tide, piling up accumulated water which became a rogue tide complying with no rules, no cycle, being a law to itself. It crashed against north-east Scotland, deflected and began to travel south, building up steadily as it moved down the coast until the North Sea became elevated. People struggling to keep upright in the wind on the cliffs watched swells the height of cathedrals sail past them.

On Dungesey the islanders began the job of moving the harvest to the keep. The wind nudged them off balance like a playful monster, catching the bales, whipping the string off a barley sack so that grain came out as if blown from a pea-shooter. The women's hair streamed ahead of their faces like the haulms of rushes. The roof of Badda's hut blew off and bowled in giant leaps across the green to crash into the yew trees.

Sulking in her chamber Matilda watched them work and

241

stagger. Pampi was hobbling up on the ash peg-leg Kakkr had carved for him and which Wilberta had padded to the contours of his stump. "He'll make it bleed again," she thought, "serve him right." There were still the peat bricks to take up, and the tinder and the ale and water casks. "Jesus and Mary, we could fix up Fenchel's old hoist. If you want a job done properly you've always got to do it yourself." She secured her cloak around her and went to see to it.

They worked until long after it was dark. Pampi wanted to continue and bring up the animals but Matilda said they were all too exhausted and, since this was manifestly true, he gave in.

The rogue tide moved majestically south. The wind sucked at it from the funnel of the Wash, aggravated by the traction of smaller winds over the vast stretches of shallow water, and the tide paused as if at an unexpected invitation. It accepted and turned.

A roaring which rose above the wind was the only warning before the people of the coast and silt fens were overwhelmed and the sky was taken over by the North Sea.

Five of the huts at Cradge were knocked off their stilts and their occupants drowned or battered to death. Furniture, humans and livestock were tugged along in the undertow to pile up in a mound in the lowest marshes and be found days later. Poultry drowned in their pens. The hermit Wilfram, at Upwell, was rescued by a boat floating in through the door of his hut, the only miracle of the night.

Matilda woke with reluctance and self-pity at persistent knocking. She crawled to the west window and looked out. For a moment she was back in time – the green and the courtyard glimmered as if with snow. Then she saw it was water. The knocking was the boats Pampi had stored against the steps, now floating and hitting the wall.

The flood had broken down the door of the hall's undercroft; she could hear it slopping about beneath her floor. "The animals." She ran out of the chamber, shouting.

The water was over waist-high so they used boats. Maggi, Epona and Matilda rowed to the byre. Epona and Matilda, the two tallest, got out and struggled to unbar the door

242

and shove it inwards. The plough-horses had long ago been replaced by cheaper oxen which now stood with their necks upstretched, lowing. One calf was swimming but another had drowned and his head bobbed against his mother's back. Sedge litter formed a scum on the water's surface. The two women ducked under, came up and ducked again to find the headropes and undo them. The panicking animals swam out through the door, automatically making for the high ground of the keep.

That night Matilda discovered many things; that pigs are natural and humorous swimmers, that sheep drown with the weight of their own saturated wool, that the fenlanders made jokes in a crisis, that she could work till she dropped and then get up and work again.

A roof, not one of Dungesey's, floated past with a dog balanced on one side and a pheasant on the other, both of them too wet and miserable to play predator and victim.

At long last they'd saved everything that could be saved and Matilda sank down in the dark keep in a jumbled mess of peat bricks, cooking pots, wet animals and humans. Her clothes squelched and hung heavy on her shoulders. She was cold. Maggi handed round some soggy bread.

Pampi came last, barely able to move, but carrying a squealing piglet by an ear and a leg. "Good thing we got the ale and rain-barrels up," he said, "because for all we're drowning in the bugger, there'll be no water for drinking in the well." Salt sea had pushed back fresh water and contaminated every well. "Stock won't be able to drink." All that trouble and they would lose them from thirst, anyway.

No stock, ruined embankments. The God who ill-wished her and everything she cared about had won. She could do no more. "It doesn't matter."

Kakkr was still on his feet looking out of the doorway at the flecked, moonlit water. "I said she'd come back."

In Kakkr's coffin-shaped head rested the island's memory and the people revived as he gave them hope. They fed him his lines. "Kakkr's so old he remembers Hereward the Wake," teased Badda on cue.

"I liked his dad the best," said Kakkr promptly. "But I've seen her come and go. I said she'd come back."

"She could stay away for me." Maggi was deathly tired.

"You don't say that," said Kakkr. "She'll leave wealth behind when she go. I remember." In spring the tidal silt would have so firmed and enriched the already-rich peat they'd be able to get crop after crop out of it.

Matilda's face sagged in defeat as she closed her eyes. She didn't know how they kept going, or why. She heard Pampi's leg tap the ground beside her and the grunt as he lowered himself. He dug her in the ribs. "You ever thought what the name Dungesey means?"

Who cared any more? She rolled her head against the peat bricks and kept her eyes shut. The fenwomen were suddenly alert, hushing their children. Outside the waves flopped against the motte's base and the stranded, lopsided cattle mooed with fright.

"Dynja," said Kakkr. "Isle of the Dynja. Old word. Older nor I can remember. Anglish."

She felt Pampi lean over her and opened her eyes to look into his face which was circled with black lines of unabsorbed peat that the water had washed against it. Seeing he'd got her attention, he sat back. "Dynja do mean the 'Place of the Women'. This is the island of the women's place."

"I see."

"More nor that," he went on, "it means the place that belongs to the women. Certain times it gets a woman as lord. When there's trouble." She could tell from the silence and the way they weren't looking at her that this was important to them all.

"Yes?"

"There was a woman lord when we had all that old squit with the Conqueror," interjected Kakkr. "She comes and goes, like the Mother."

"What it is," said Pampi, and whatever it was made him more truculent than ever. "There's trouble when the woman lord comes. We knew there was going to be bad times when Sigward seised us of you."

So that was it. She was the crow of disaster. She was Eve

who had brought sin into the world. "There would be no ice in any place; there would be no windy weather, there would be no grief, there would be no terror, but for me." She looked round at the soaking, shivering children, at Maggi trying to strike flint to the tinder with hands too cold to function. Tears came out of her eyes and made streaks down the black of her face. "I'm sorry," she said, "I'm sorry for being a woman and bringing trouble on you all."

Pampi considered. "That's one way of looking on it, I suppose."

"Is there another way?"

He shifted. "We've always reckoned as she was sent to see us through it."

It was a gift, all they had. They shifted and grumbled so that they wouldn't hear her sob.

They came through it, though the cattle died and the women had to harness themselves to the plough and the harrow before they could sow. When Maggi dropped from exhaustion, Matilda took her place and hauled with the rest.

But the rivers and the sky teemed with the food supply Sigward had once promised her. The barge blockade hid their front door from invaders. And in late spring the crops came up out of the earth as if they were being pushed. They had survived.

That spring Matilda sailed with Turold for Normandy and the Plantagenet court at Rouen, where Edmund was.

By coincidence, on the day she arrived Fitzempress sailed to England with his mercenaries in a miniature invasion force to harry Stephen from the south and take some of the royal army's attention away from his mother and her hard-pressed allies.

Neither his mother nor his uncle, the Earl of Gloucester, had asked for his help while his father, Geoffrey of Anjou, had actually forbidden him to give it, but the boy sailed anyway.

To Matilda's relief Fitzempress had left Edmund behind in

245

Normandy as being too young still, but Edmund was inconsolable. "He's only a bit older than me. He should have taken me. I've as much right to go as those rotten mercenaries. More."

"Are they rotten?"

"They're not bad as mercenaries," admitted Edmund, "and their captain has always been good to me. Fitzempress thinks the world of him, although he's quite old, but it's always dishonourable to fight for money."

Matilda nodded. "Who is this captain?" She knew, but there was an adolescent thrill in hearing him given independent life.

"Willem of Ghent. But you know him, don't you? He brought a message from you when he arrived. And Fitzempress says he rescued you from . . . well."

Part of the reason for her visit to Normandy was to give Edmund her authorised version of the time with Fitz Payn and after. She had sent him messages through Turold, but she wanted to tell him herself. He was aware that the Empress' treaty with Fitz Payn had involved his mother in a supposed marriage. The rumours must have hurt and embarrassed him. She gave him a bloodless description of her disparagement, first by Stephen and then the Empress, "but the marriage was never legal because I did not consent."

He listened carefully, being not only her son, but her lord. She had to account to him. She added: "Nor was it consummated." The mercenary, Willem of Ghent, she said, had come to her aid and escorted her to the safety of Dungesey.

Edmund nodded: "What happened to Fitz Payn? He's disappeared."

She crossed her fingers in the fold of her gown. "I don't know." Somebody must have found the corpse, but there were lots of unidentified bodies lying around England.

"He's probably dead," said Edmund. "These scum are always killing each other." He got up to walk around the chamber. He was getting tall and his voice beginning to break. Like all the young knights and squires at Rouen he aped Fitzempress by dressing casually in hunting leathers but whereas Fitzempress looked always untidy, Edmund was helplessly neat. "We will get the Pope to recognise it as a non-marriage in case the man turns up again and claims our lands."

He took her hands. "All that suffering is over and you shall live in comfort, as befits you." He would grow into a pompous man. "Shall you go back to Risle? Or stay at court? Or you could retire into a convent, like Fontevrault." He said the last wistfully. He would like her to be one of the rich, well-born pensioners who lived with nuns, mixing social life with contemplation and good works. It would tidy her up, restore her to the respectability she had lost.

It would also put her beyond danger of remarriage and leave Edmund to administer her estates free of stepfathers.

She was twenty-seven years old and her son wished her to decline into untroublesome old age. And he could command it. This child was the next master in a chain of masters — father, husband and now son. Legally she was his chattel. Thinking of him as her child to be safeguarded she had set up another male autocrat to rule her.

She took a deep breath to subdue her panic. She must be cunning. "My lord, I stay in England for your sake. By operating Fitzempress' Postern for him I pile on him a debt which he must remember when he is king. He will be king, I think."

Edmund had no doubt of it. "But it is not seemly that my mother should skulk in a marsh with a lot of peasants."

"Don't you see, my son?" Matilda looked deliberately crafty. "Already the Abbot of Ramsey has used the Postern and become our ally. When the day comes he will say to Fitzempress: 'This lady and her son risked much for you in the bad time, reward them now in the good time.' When the war is over we shall have many such allies."

She could see he was impressed. The more friends at court, the better.

"And when this is over I shall stay quietly on my thirds, never marrying, building a church on Dungesey perhaps. I shan't trouble you."

"Very well, mother. But oh," suddenly he was a small boy again, "you're having all that fun doing your bit for the war,

247

and Fitzempress is having all his fun, and I'm stuck here out of it all."

Fun, thought Matilda.

"Never mind," said Edmund, "Fitzempress has promised I can be knighted in a year or so when he is. He wants King David of Scotland to do the knighting, so perhaps we shall use the Postern when we sneak into England for the ceremony." He sighed with pleasure. "Then he'll have to let me fight in all his battles."

Matilda sighed with less pleasure. "That'll be nice."

Now in accord, mother and son enjoyed themselves and went hunting together in the forest around the hills of Rouen which contained the best hunting in the world.

But the visit was not a success. Time had pushed Matilda away from her old life and companions. Father Alors had become involved in local church politics. Jodi was dead, killed in a tavern brawl. Berte was in charge of Edmund's house by the Seine, holding it with the unofficial right of the old nurse. Edmund tolerated her with exasperated affection, but spent as much time as possible at the castle. She was thrilled to see Matilda, exclaimed over the state of her digger's hands and spent the rest of the time talking about Edmund and Rouen.

Matilda went to visit Adeliza's family. She had already sent them word the girl was dead, saying that she had died of marsh fever. She was prepared to spend time elaborating on Adeliza's loyalty and purity, but Adeliza's brother showed little interest. He hadn't seen his sister in years and her death relieved him of the burden of finding her a marriage and a dowry. To herself Matilda swore that Adeliza should have a splendid memorial in her church when she built it.

But it was at court that Matilda felt most alienated. Fashions had changed for one thing. (They were doing delightful things with their hair and Matilda at once used some of her accumulated rent from Risle on a milliner who created her a small, round box of a hat to which was attached a crespin and a barbette.) The average age had gone down, putting her among the older women. The venal stodginess of the Norman court she remembered had been replaced with

Plantagenet style. There was sophistication, enjoyment and, above all, learning. Philosophers, writers and poets took as important a place as barons. There were Arabs teaching mathematics and algebra. Newness, adventure was everything.

The heroine of the court ladies was Eleanor of Aquitaine, the young and reputedly naughty wife of Louis of France, who had insisted on going with him on Crusade, dressed as an Amazon.

"What's an Amazon?" a bewildered Matilda asked of her former lady-in-waiting, Ghislaine, and Ghislaine who, much to her own disgust, was also regarded as the older generation, said: "I think it's a sort of dancing girl. That would suit Eleanor."

The source of all this modernity was the duke himself. Geoffrey had been away on a hunting trip when Matilda had arrived, but returned about a fortnight later to take the head of the table at the feast for St. Joseph's day. Matilda's mouth fell open when she saw him. Slowly she shut it. "Do you mean to tell me," she muttered to Ghislaine, "that the Empress has been wasting all these years fighting a war when she could have been home with *that*?"

"Lovely, isn't he?" muttered back Ghislaine. "And every time he looks at one, one is reminded of what one's got it for." It was crude, but true. Geoffrey le Bel, and he wasn't nicknamed "Handsome" for nothing, had the warming knack of looking at every woman, young or old, as if she held interesting possibilities.

"What's more," said Ghislaine, "one has it on good authority that on a visit to Paris he and Eleanor of Aquitaine not only found what they'd got it for, but used it."

"Really?" Goodness, how she'd missed gossip all these years. She enjoyed herself while Ghislaine made up for them.

Matilda bided her time until the conversation came round naturally to mercenaries, then found herself saying, casually: "I suppose they are as promiscuous as ever?"

"Not with us," said Ghislaine, shocked. "They make do with the sluts of the town. The duke and Fitzempress may fawn on their mercenaries, but any lady of quality who

liaised with one would be beyond the pale. She would have
to be put away."

"Tactful as ever."

"Of course," Ghislaine remembered, "that doesn't apply
to *you*. Everyone knows how shamefully you were treated
and it wasn't your fault."

Everyone did know it, that was the trouble. She was the
Lady with the Past, the one who'd been sold to a mercenary.
She was peculiar, set apart, and although she held her head
up she knew that to the end of her days rumour would taint
her. "Matilda of Risle?" they would ask, "wasn't she the one
who . . . ?"

"Well," she thought, "it's all very interesting but soon I
must go home." Once she had owned a score of homes: now
there was only one.

She found the Rouennais countryside peculiarly unsatis-
fying – hilly, primrosed, forested but somehow just pretty.
She remembered Pampi remarking about his long trek across
England: "They bloody hills kept getting in the way." These
Normandy hills got between her and God. Only the flat,
clean lines of the Fens and their sky had significance for her
now.

It was Berte who put her mind at rest. "Do you remember
that nice lad, Willem of Ghent? Of course you do, of course
you do, I forget. He comes and visits me a lot when he's
here."

"Does he?"

"A lot. We talk about the old days in them marshes, and
he tells me about that Fenchel – he's working for the
Plantagenets now." Berte giggled. "He likes hearing about
you, and wants to know how you're getting on. But of
course I can't tell him much because I don't know."

"Will you tell him," said Matilda, "that I remember him.
Just that."

It was a relief that they had not met. Some things were
better left as they were. But she was glad he came and
listened to Berte. "I'll be gone by the time he gets back."

The problem was: would he get back at all? The news
of Fitzempress' expedition was not good. It had landed at

Wareham, swept through Wiltshire and very nearly captured Cricklade and Purton before Stephen, realising what a very small force it was, counter-attacked and drove it back to the coast. The mercenaries with Fitzempress had been hired on credit and now, cheated of victory and therefore loot, they began to demand their pay.

Letters, imploring monetary help, arrived at Rouen and at the Empress' court, but neither responded. The boy had got himself into this mess against their wishes: let him get himself out of it. It would teach him not to be impulsive.

Matilda did not think of the expeditionary force as "he" but as "they". Fitzempress might be treated well if he was captured, but would his captain of mercenaries?

She knew it was time to go on the day she bumped into Waleran of Meulan in the hall.

He greeted Matilda with charm, asked after her health and enquired where she was living. She did not enlighten him. Although Waleran had gone over to the Plantagenets while his twin, the Earl of Leicester, stayed on Stephen's side, she did not trust him.

That very night she made her goodbyes. "Going back to England?" asked Ghislaine. "What for? Where will you go?" If Ghislaine, who absorbed gossip like a sponge, did not know of the Postern arrangement with the Plantagenets, then the secret was well kept.

Geoffrey of Anjou made a private occasion of his farewell to her. He kissed her hand as she curtsied. Near to, he was more breathtaking than ever. "Our son has told us of your courage in the service you perform for him."

"Yes, well . . ." Matilda forced herself to concentrate. "It won't be much of a service if he's captured, my lord."

The Plantagenet was even beautiful when he laughed. "Henry? He won't be. He'll think of something. You'll see. He always thinks of something."

Encircled on three sides in the encampment at Wareham, with the sea as his only escape route, Henry Fitzempress had thrown a temper so violent he'd rolled on the floor biting rushes and then come out of it. Now he sat on the hearth of the unlit fire, trembling, spitting out stalks and looking sidelong at his captain of mercenaries. "It's still treachery."

Willem of Ghent sighed. "You broke the contract. Loot or pay. They haven't had either. I warned you. We shouldn't have come in the first place."

"Why did you, then?"

"Keep you out of trouble. Besides, I thought your lady mother'd pay up."

Fitzempress wagged a rush at him. "That's where we made our first mistake. So did I. You'd have thought the appeal I sent her would have melted even her flinty old bowels. It was touching, wasn't it?"

"Tears to the eyes."

"But she didn't and she won't." He stood up and fetched a well-worn book out of his jacket. "Let's see what Vegetius says about mutiny."

"You go ahead and have a nice read," said his captain bitterly. The boy was in real trouble. It wasn't that he was in danger; Willem knew, as the Empress and Geoffrey Plantagenet knew, that he could get him away, smuggle him down to the boats and back to Normandy. But this nice little force Willem had gathered for him would melt away to go and find another war where it could get paid. It would leave Fitzempress a loser, discrediting him in the eyes of the English. Not good for his future prospects.

" 'In the event of mutiny,' " read Fitzempress, " 'it will be advisable after the manner of the ancients, to punish the ringleaders in order that, though few suffer, all may be terrified.' " He looked up. "I think he means decimation. Do you think those lads outside would stand still while we shot one in ten?"

"No." Willem stopped worrying. The boy was play-acting: he had an idea.

"Nor do I." He put the book away. "So much for Vegetius. Now then, who haven't we asked for money? We've asked the mater and the pater and Uncle Robert of Gloucester . . ."

"There's Uncle David of Scotland, but he's a bloody long way away."

252

"You know the trouble with you, Willem?" Fitzempress turned a cartwheel. "You're a good captain. And for a mercenary, you're a good man. But you think in ruts. You haven't got" – he flung out his arms – "breadth. Expand your mercenary mind. We've asked mummies and daddies and uncles, but we haven't asked our greatest ally."

"Who's that?"

Fitzempress pointed through the tent to the north and the besieging royal army. "Stephen. You must remember Stephen, captain. Chap who's holding England for me just now." He began striding up and down. "That's what we'll do. We'll drop him a note. Something like: 'Dear Cousin Stephen, please send me a hundred marks and I'll go away.' He'll do it just to be rid of me. Want to bet he doesn't?"

The revelation of genius evokes reflex homage in those privileged to witness it. Before he could stop himself, Willem's hand had grasped the hem of Fitzempress' cloak and pressed it to his forehead. "You clever little sod," he said involuntarily.

"I know." Fitzempress smirked. "I frighten myself sometimes."

Stephen paid up and his fourteen-year-old cousin sailed back to Normandy with his mercenary force intact.

Perhaps by paying, Stephen wanted to demonstrate his shrewdness in getting rid of a nuisance without bloodshed. Perhaps he wanted admiration for his chivalry. Perhaps, as his chronicler, the Bishop of Bath, wrote: "he was moved so that by good well bestowed upon his enemy he might heap coals of repentance and reformation upon his mind."

But there's no justice. A people who had found no reason to smile at national events in years grinned at this one. The amusement spread through castle halls, into solars, down to servants' undercrofts, into inns, into cells and out into the fields so that all England laughed.

The Normans, even Stephen's Normans, wiped their eyes and said: "He's a chip off the old block." And the block they meant was Henry the First of England, and the chip was not Stephen, but Henry's grandson, Fitzempress.

And the English wiped their eyes and said: "The cheeky young bugger."

And even the Bishop of Bath in his eulogy of Stephen made a slip, or perhaps it wasn't a slip, and referred to Henry Fitzempress as "the lawful heir" to England, which for the first time put into words what a lot of people were beginning to think.

15

1147–1149

In the October, Robert, Earl of Gloucester, died, tired out by his long war on behalf of his sister.

With the death of her brother much of the fight went out of Empress Matilda and in the first weeks of 1148 she set sail for Normandy and did not return.

The news filtered into the Fens and to Matilda, who received it without interest. "The war's going on just the same, isn't it?" It mattered much more to her that Maggi had just died.

As, one by one, Dungesey's men escaped from the war and came back, Maggi had pined. Her own man would never come back. Lumps developed in her breast and, though Matilda risked a journey to Ely to take her to the cathedral for a cure by St. Etheldreda's bones, it was no good. At the end there wasn't enough cordial to stop her pain.

On the day of her lieutenant's burial, Matilda sat in her hall staring at nothing, and Pampi came up to stand beside her and dropped a small hairless-bellied puppy into her lap. She didn't touch it: "It's not Fen."

"That's not," said Pampi. "Wrong sex. But he'll be a good dog. I call him Wine and Water."

Matilda picked the puppy up and wiped her eyes on its ears. "That's a ridiculous name for a dog."

"Good un, I reckon. That's all he do."

Three sprigs of broom came by Turold and a month later, for one short night, Dungesey contained everything in the world Matilda loved.

255

Fitzempress was talking as he leaped out of the boat. "The other candidates for knighting went on, but I had to use my Postern, didn't I?" He gestured back into the boat. "That monk there is a candidate called Edmund, a son of your acquaintance, and the other one is my captain of mercenaries because he thinks I'll drop dead if he doesn't watch me."

That night Dungesey's kitchens excelled themselves. "Is this a floater?" Fitzempress crammed a dumpling into his mouth. Down the table Epona was fascinating Turold, and the captain of mercenaries was almost hidden by his cross-bow apprentices while Edmund, to Pampi's delight, had sat himself between him and Wilberta.

Matilda knew she was happy rather than felt it. She had not thought anything could disconcert her again, but the emotions and embarrassments caused by having her future king, her son and the mercenary she'd once slept with under one roof, flustered her. She'd greeted the mercenary with no less and no more politeness than was due to a guest, and since then had not looked at him.

Fitzempress was enough to fluster anyone. Since his arrival he'd been all over the island, climbing the motte, examining the foxes' ears on the village's thatch, bursting into Wealyham, wading Nightlairs, prowling Hogwood, insisting on meeting every living soul and asking them questions about fenland economy, farming and warfare and listening to replies – he seemed to understand English even though he didn't speak it – and generally driving her mad by ignoring all the plans she'd made for his reception. The islanders approved of him.

"What did that man call me?" He pointed a dumpling-laden knife at Pampi.

"A slodger. He thinks it's a compliment."

"Isn't it?" He loved everybody; he loved Stephen for making this knighting into a dangerous adventure. He could have cured Maggi.

"But I'll look after Edmund," he assured her, "and my captain of mercenaries will look after me." He seemed aware that Matilda and the mercenary had not looked at each other

256

since the meal began. "You remember Willem of Ghent, don't you, madam? We understood he was of use to you once?"

Yes, Matilda said, she remembered the mercenary. She could have sworn she said it with no change of expression, but the young Plantagenet picked up something from the air. He gave out a long "Ah Haaa". The look on the boy's round face belonged to one who has made a move at chess which has greater possibilities than at first thought. He watched the mercenary, then Edmund, then her. He put his arms behind his head: "He served you, madam, did he?"

"Yes," snapped Matilda.

The boy nodded and raised his voice. "Edmund, Willem of Ghent served your mother well. How will you reward him?" And the little sod put his tongue into his cheek.

Edmund looked up from his plate, still chewing. "What? Well, my lord, he can have whatever he wants, within reason, of course."

Her son, Matilda was glad to see, had a careful soul. She wondered what the penalty was for giving a prince of the blood a clout round the ear. She said, "The man has been useful to you too, my lord. I am sure he will not be forgotten when you are king."

"When I'm king," said Fitzempress, "he won't be, but in the meantime what have you got that he'd fancy?" With an accuracy which left Matilda gasping, he ran through her entire list of estates. "All escheated of course, except for the fenland. Now didn't Robert of Dunwich get killed at Lincoln and leave no heir? And didn't he hold Stuntney of you?"

Stuntney was an unexploited, run-to-seed manor in the silt fens.

"Yes."

"There you are, then."

Edmund said: "May he have it, mother? It's in your gift, and we have reason to be grateful."

"If he wants it."

"Oh, he'll want it all right," said Fitzempress. "Let's hope

257

it's all he wants. Well, he can't take seisin yet, but we can witness the gift."

Matilda watched her feast disintegrate as the guests were brought to the top table for witnesses and a search begun for parchment, ink and pen. Fitzempress, the only person present who could write, began scratching out the deed. "What's the rent?"

"I don't know."

"Yes, you do, mother," said her son, the fool, "it's a goose-feather mattress every Lady Day."

Fitzempress stood up, walked over to a hall pillar as if to examine its carving, slammed his fist against it, and turned, his face expressionless, to resume writing.

At last the hubbub quietened and two calloused hands were placed within her own, and the mercenary was kneeling before her, looking to see how she was taking it. He too, she saw, was amused. "God blast all men," she thought. She wanted to ask: "How's your back?" but felt the question might be misconstrued by the dirty-minded young Plantagenet.

His Flemish voice spoke the fealty: "I am your man, lady, body and soul to serve you my life long . . ." and she was in a flutter in case everybody heard the truth in it. She wanted to release his hands, she didn't want to let them go. Her neck felt hot. She wished the whole boiling lot of them had never come.

The rest of the evening was torture with Fitzempress trying embarrassing and elaborate ploys to create a situation where Matilda and the mercenary could be alone. To her relief Edmund didn't understand any of them, and stayed stolidly by his mother's side.

The breeze the next morning was joking; it kicked and scattered clouds off to the west, flapping the leaves of the willows white side up and generally making the Fens laugh. No countryside laughed like the Fens; rushes, reeds and water responded to breeze like a baby to tickling.

Matilda stood at the entrance to the hall and her men lined up to say goodbye. "Edmund," said Fitzempress, "I must have dropped my knife somewhere, be a good chap . . ."

Edmund turned obediently and the prince hissed: "Quick. You've got a minute."

The mercenary used all of it kissing Matilda and she so far forgot herself as to kiss him back. Edmund returned to bid his flushed mother goodbye and join the captain of the mercenaries at the foot of the steps. The Plantagenet grinned at her: "I'm a wonderful young man, aren't I?"

"Any more wonderful, my lord, and I'll kick your shins." She could hear him still laughing as they went down the Causeway and out of sight.

She heard the sound in her head for the rest of that year, every time news of his exploits came to her.

The knighting was a success, especially as Ranulf Moustaches turned up to make alliance with David of Scotland and give his allegiance to the Plantagenets.

Afterwards Fitzempress and his band zig-zagged south through England, making for the small army which awaited him in the West Country. Stephen sent a force to waylay him. He knew his true and lethal enemy now. If his own son, Eustace, was to succeed him Henry Fitzempress must be eliminated.

The Plantagenet eluded Stephen so the king alerted Eustace, who was now in charge of the royal army in the south.

Eustace had grown into a forceful young man, intent on kingship. Unlike his father, he didn't give a damn for a chivalrous image. He belonged to the scorched earth school of warfare. Churches, houses, crops were fired as he moved in Fitzempress' wake until large stretches of the West Country were dead ground.

Fitzempress returned to Normandy to gather a bigger army. Again his retreat was not defeat. His fighting had shown leadership and caught the English imagination. In Normandy they welcomed him like a hero. He was sixteen but his father now made him Duke of Normandy, handing the duchy over as if he himself had merely been its guardian.

Stephen's opponent was no longer a woman but a grandson, a worthy grandson, of Henry the First. And one who had the backing of the Pope. If the magnates were ever to

259

administer their estates on both sides of the Channel in peace, their only hope lay with the young Plantagenet.

The war went on, but it was a waiting war. Everybody in England was waiting for Fitzempress to come back and claim it.

16

1150–1154

Somebody was killing the great as well as the lowly. God, or a human assassin, was wanting a speedy peace. For the people who now dropped dead were among the war's proponents.

The Earl of Gloucester was dead. Now Prince Henry of Scotland died, followed a year later by the Empress' uncle, David of Scotland.

Brien Fitz Count of Wallingford died, impoverished.

Stephen's best ally, his wife Matilda, died – even her enemies grieved.

Ranulf Moustaches died, it was believed from poisoning.

Baldwin de Redvers, who'd started the insurrection when he seized Exeter, died. So did the Earls of Hereford and Warwick.

All these people would have stood in the way of a negotiated peace if they had lived. One by one they were being eliminated, leaving more malleable successors who might be persuaded to compromise.

Public opinion, already hysterical, decided there was a peace-loving assassin on the loose. William Fitz Herbert, whose election as Archbishop of York had lost Stephen the support of the Pope, died from drinking a poisoned chalice at mass. Terrified nobles began employing food-tasters.

Some answered the call of Bernard of Clairvaux for a Second Crusade. Waleran of Meulan took the cross temporarily and went to the Holy Land. Lesser men who had struggled to keep the administration of the country going through the war tired of it and went to capture Lisbon from the Saracens.

At home grew a consensus, that Stephen should rule for his lifetime but that, on his death, the throne should go to Fitzempress.

One person didn't see it that way: Eustace, Stephen's son.

Every month Matilda and the Abbot of Ramsey met at the Stun where Driftway became Monks' Bank to exchange news and to discuss Postern business since they were both now involved in passing agents through it.

Every month Matilda expected to see in the stout, dull man something of the abbot she had once known; each time she was disappointed. She was only glad that he did not seem to notice that the Stun had moved to his detriment.

The marshes were noisy with the courtship calls of snipe and ruff.

"I'm planting hemp this year," said Matilda. "It should fetch a good price if building starts again. Any news?"

"Fitzempress is married. Eleanor of Aquitaine, God forgive him. No sooner is she divorced from Louis of France than our young prince has whipped to Poitiers and married her himself."

"Dear Lord, he'll have an empire." Eleanor's land was all south-west France.

Abbot Walter said: "And a wife of dubious morals eleven years older than he is. To say nothing of her former husband who is furious at the alliance and has invaded Normandy once more because of it."

Matilda sighed. "So Fitzempress won't be coming back yet."

Pampi, propped against an osier truncheon, was weaving the special trap for the two-inch elvers which would soon be wriggling up the lodes, shaping it to the flow of water and the way of eels.

"No," said the abbot. He thought: "I have married a wife and therefore I cannot come."

Matilda thought: "Lucky old Eleanor."

In 1152 Stephen summoned Archbishop Theobald and the other bishops to London to demand that they anoint his son, Eustace, as king and successor. They refused. Stephen imprisoned the bishops but Theobald's supporters managed to get him away. Stephen's men watched the ports in order to capture him, but the archbishop left England by a secret route.

"More lampreys, my lord archbishop?" asked Matilda.

"I am tempted, but refuse, my lady. We must remember the fate of our late and excellent King Henry. 'No,' I told Stephen, 'the Pope has forbidden the anointing of Prince Eustace on the grounds that you obtained the throne by perjury.'" The old man had more animation now than in his whole life.

"But when will it end? When will Fitzempress come?"

1152 ended with wicked weather on land and at sea, and everybody knew Fitzempress would not be arriving that year. But he did. He was always able to persuade seamen to risk their lives and his, and always he made safe landfall. But the army he brought wasn't as large as it should have been; he'd had to leave Normandy protected against France. It included a large number of mercenaries . . .

The pennant they lowered to half-mast on the flagpole of Wallingford Castle was so heavy with rain it hung straight down like a stick and resisted the wind's efforts to wave it.

Rain they would have given their eye-teeth for in East Anglia, where crops were withering in the fields for lack of it, was unjustly lashing the Thames basin where there were no crops because there'd been no peasants left alive to plant them.

The wicket in the door of the bridgehouse creaked open – lack of use had nearly rusted it shut – and a herald stepped out on to the bridge, his trumpet displayed, but downwards, to keep out the wet.

Below and on either side raindrops hit the river so hard they formed depressions and bounced up again, as if the Thames was boiling. They thundered on to the bridge planking.

By the time he had reached the other side and stood before the gatehouse of Stephen's Crowmarsh outworks, the herald was soaked, and his cloak dragged behind him, like a little boy's nightshirt.

He blew a call, then shouted: "A truce. The Lady of Wallingford is dead. A truce for the passing of her cortège."

In the ugly, utilitarian bailey of the outworks Eustace bellowed: "It's a trick." Though the hood of his cloak and his hair were plastered to his head he seemed impervious to the rain. He was already mounted as if he could not wait for the battle to start. The other lords stood around the side of the bailey sheltering under its eaves, using their horses as shields. Water-spouts jetted streams out and down on to the cobbles.

Ypres raised his voice: "How can it be a trick? We've known the poor lady over there was dying."

Robert, Earl of Leicester, nodded to Stephen's herald on the bailey allure. "Allow the truce."

"I say it's a trick." Eustace's shouting made his stallion circle and the others stamp in the puddles. "Fitzempress has been trying to draw us away from here all year. He wants the river crossing."

"So?"

"So I say it's a trick." He rode to the portcullis passage and leaned down to peer across the bridge. "Look. Look, the gate's opening. Now's our chance. We can attack."

Sheltering in the passage, his father looked slowly up at him: "Prince Eustace, we must show chivalry."

The prince's voice echoed through the tunnel. "Chivalry, my arse."

Across the bridge the candles of the monks who were to accompany the bier to Westminster dispelled something of the bridgehouse's gloom, but even the incense of their censors couldn't overcome its smell of fungus and urine. As Fitzempress strode in to pay his last respects he brought with him wet, fresh air. His sopping cloak had dragged open, across the chest of his tunic were the three leopards which had been his father's device. His carroty hair was dark with rain.

He knelt briefly: "God save and reward you, lady." But the Prior of Wallingford's Holy Trinity wanted more reward for the lady's – and his – sufferings than that. He drew back the bier cloth and opened the coffin so that the prince could gaze on the mortal remains of the woman who had held Wallingford for him through three sieges. Another monk lowered the candle to throw light on the wizened little face which peered out of the shroud like a monkey's.

"She's old." Fitzempress was startled. "Are you sure this is her? How old was she?"

The prior shrugged. "Thirty-five, perhaps."

The coffin closed, the cortège moved out on to the bridge and Maud of Wallingford was allowed to leave her castle now that she was dead.

Fitzempress had his helmet on before they had reached the other side of the bridge. "And now let's get on with the battle."

A quarter of a mile north where the river curved two armies stood in the meadows facing each other across the Thames. Mud squeezed over their boots and the men had formed tortoises covered by sacking to keep out the wet. Rain hit the sullen backs of Stephen's men and the sullen fronts of Fitzempress' men as if it hated them equally. The magnates' banners of both sides hung in anonymous rags. Both armies were hungry, but there was nothing to eat.

The battle speeches had been made ineffective by the noise of the rain but now the trumpets, shawms and drums cut through it. Each army undulated as its soldiers threw off the sacks and stood to attention.

Out of a total of four thousand men – Stephen's army was slightly the larger – only two had vitality, Eustace and Fitzempress. They rode to the front, forced their horses down the banks, turned back, shouting, cajoling, persuading, boasting, and finally swearing.

A small band formed obediently behind each but after that initial move forward they did not stir.

"A Plantagenet," howled Fitzempress. "On to victory."

"Stephen, Stephen," roared Eustace. "England."

The armies stood still in the rain and the river boiled between them.

On the Crowmarsh side men like de Warenne and de Ferrers had wet on their faces that was not only rain. They had served Stephen since his coronation, but they did not move.

On the Wallingford side tears dripped out of John the Marshal's only good eye; not to fight when the trumpets sounded and this young Plantagenet called was like asking him not to breathe. But he did not move.

From his position by the king, Robert, Earl of Leicester, stared straight ahead and by projection into the eyes of his twin brother Waleran of Meulan on the Plantagenet bank. Neither moved.

Their knights and men endured the rain, watched their lords and did not move.

Fitzempress' captain of mercenaries rode up to his employer and took the bridle of his horse. He leaned over and wiped froth from Fitzempress' mouth. "Not now. Dear Jesus, don't throw one now." He led the boy and the horse away to a clump of beeches where carts had been parked under shelter. He helped Fitzempress dismount and held his head while he vomited. Edmund followed and took up station to keep everyone else away.

Fitzempress' face was so rigid he had difficulty in enunciating. "They're s-standing s-still enough to decimate now–now."

The mercenary shook his head. "It's over. They've come to the end."

"I'm j-just beginning. They'll see."

"Go and meet Stephen on the bridge. He's ready to talk now. You'll inherit."

Fitzempress wiped a raindrop off the end of his nose and looked up. The whites of his eyes were capillaried with red. "Has this been arranged? It's been arranged, you bastard, hasn't it?"

"Eustace won't be in on the negotiations. They're keeping him away."

"Who's betrayed us?" Suddenly the "us" was Stephen and

him. "The Beaumonts? You? Why didn't the mercenaries advance? Whose money did you take this time, you fucking traitor?"

"Think, will you? It's happened. They've all had enough. The archbishop and Henry of Blois have been working for it. De Luci's organised the talk with Stephen. He's king till he dies. You inherit."

"De Luci's a Stephen man."

"He's an England man." Willem of Ghent took off his helmet and threw it on the ground. He grabbed the boy's hair and shook him. "Do you want to fight all your life? Do you want a bankrupt bloody country?" He twisted his hand so that the boy's head faced the river. "It's over. You're better than that."

He let go because Fitzempress' eyes had fixed on the wet, immobile ranks; he was coming out of it. The mercenary retrieved his helmet, walked over to a cart and pulled at its canvas so that a pool of water lying on top poured into his helmet. He sobbed, stopped himself and took the water back to Fitzempress. "Wash your face, for Christ's sake."

The Plantagenet said: "It would have been nice to win the war."

"Win the country instead."

Edmund brought up the horses and helped his prince to remount. When he was up Fitzempress leaned over and poked his captain of mercenaries in the chest. He smiled. "One thing, it'll do you out of a job."

On the other bank Eustace's tantrum ended when he noticed that his father was missing. "Where's the king? Treachery." He rowelled the sides of his horse so that it screamed and reared, but two distinguished and heavy men, Robert the Earl of Leicester and William of Ypres, leaped for its bridle and pulled it back.

"Jacopo," shouted Ypres. A ring of levelled crossbows formed round Eustace's household knights. A voice with a Calabrian accent said: "It is upsetting to shoot members of one's own side. Consider my feelings, dear gentlemen, and don't move."

267

So Eustace's knights stood and watched a struggle between their prince and his father's two main barons. At one point Eustace drew his sword but was disarmed and thrown to the ground where Ypres sat on his head and the Earl of Leicester on his legs until his hands could be bound and he was turned over, unrecognisable from mud. The Earl of Leicester wiped his face: "Listen to me, my lord. You have vast estates by hereditary right, you can enjoy them and be the greatest man in the country after the king – whoever that may be."

Eustace wriggled his head round to look at the bridge where two figures, one tall and slim, one medium-sized and square, faced each other in conversation. He screamed.

"I wish you'd listen," said the Earl of Leicester plaintively. "Opt for the attainable, not the impossible. We are but men."

Ypres raised his rump and lowered it, knocking Eustace's breath out of him. "Listen," he said.

"You see," said the Earl of Leicester, "among my estates is a manor called Pegg, near Malmesbury, which produces the finest medlars in Christendom. I am fond of medlars."

"Pisspot," roared Eustace, "treacherous, shithead nancy-boy."

"After the siege of Malmesbury," the earl went on, watching Ypres stuff a corner of his cloak into Eustace's mouth, "there was no soul left alive at Pegg. Not steward, women, freemen, not serfs. Nobody." He smiled down into Eustace's eyes. He was still handsome but the skin of his neck and chin had begun to droop. "Do you understand?"

A gurgle came from Eustace's throat: "War."

The Earl of Leicester tut-tutted. "You miss the point, my dear. There won't be tithes from Pegg for some years, or from thousands of other manors. Nor medlars. And I am *fond* of medlars."

He glanced to the bridge where negotiations were being completed in mutually respectful bows. Even at this distance the naked, tortoise head of de Luci was recognisable.

They let Eustace up and he ran to meet his father. In the rain Stephen was as point-device as ever, though something had been washed out of him.

"What have you done, father? What have they made you give away?"

"Nothing, my son. I have given nothing away."

"Then we can attack. The battle can start?"

Stephen looked at the sky as if it all depended on the weather. "Not today, dear boy." He smiled at his son. "We could go and attack Hugh Bigod if you liked."

Weightily, the two armies began to disperse. Boots sucked out of the mud and were emptied of water. Cloaks were squeezed and carts repacked. Greetings and vulgar exchanges on the weather began to be shouted back and forth between the two sides of the river.

A muddy figure and its household knights rode like a raincloud of their own towards the east. "Eustace won't give up, you know," said Ypres, watching it go.

"I know," said the Earl of Leicester, "somebody's going to have to kill that boy."

Eustace and his knights rode out of the wet west into the blistering August of the east. Zig-zagging, they set fire to everything they passed; fields, villages, hayricks and trees exploded as if the air round Eustace was combustible. They were joined by other madmen. Those who saw them said the soul of de Mandeville had found a new body.

People began trying to kill Eustace. They bobbed out of bushes and shot at him with catapults. Women flapped their laundry at his horse. When arrows whizzed past Eustace's nose as he went through the glades of Royston Forest, the captured culprits sulked and said they'd taken him for a stag. Branches cracked above his head, trees fell in front of him and behind him boulders rolled down slopes.

When he sacked and burned Cambridge, a Cambridge only just rebuilt after being sacked and burned by de Mandeville, arrows jumped at him like grasshoppers from the reeds of the Cam and Granta.

But Eustace stayed alive, though three horses died under him. With each escape from death he knew he was protected by God for some special purpose.

When he reached Pampisford he set fire to the fenland.

Below its grasses lay peat which had become fibrous through three dry years.

It is a property of peat that, though it is slow-burning, it is sure-burning. Once it is in the right condition and catches alight it is consumed leaving slight, fine ash, and the only way to stop it burning is to take it apart fibre by fibre. Fire in dry peatland can smoulder for years, scorching the boots of those who tread it and turning great stretches into wasteland.

In August of 1153, the fire which shrivelled the upper layer of grass and sedge also caught hold of the peat below. It sent up a glow which could be seen as far north as the island of Dungesey.

Taking her last look at Dungesey from the steps of her hall, Matilda did not see the same island that had presented itself to her first view twenty years before.

It was high summer now and had been winter then; it was impoverished now in animals and people where then it had been rich. "But we should be able to buy sheep next year," thought Matilda, "and get rid of those damned goats."

She spoke over her shoulder: "Don't let Shudda get away with anything. I have commuted half her rent, but the rest must be paid on time."

"All right, commander."

Between the untidy, lower branches of the yew trees Badda and Wilberta were sitting and spinning, the long-drawn up-ending sound of their vowels as they talked mixed with the call of wood pigeons. They were getting old.

"And I have commuted all of Pampi's rents and services, but he's not to know that until I've gone."

"All right, commander."

"Abbot Walter will see that my lord Edmund honours my will's dispositions. He is also making arrangements to have you taught French."

"Have I got to, commander?"

She whipped round. "How can you be a proper steward if you don't speak French? How can you teach the islanders?" Wifil had grown as big as Stunta, but he had Maggi's brains;

270

Matilda had spent more time and trouble on him teaching him manners and estate management than she had been able to spend on her own son. He would make a fine steward. She was vastly proud of him. She said: "You're a great gowk."

"All right, commander."

Even on this day the thick Saxon walls kept out the heat. Light coming through the reed curtain over the door cast striped shadows which bridged over the table and the piles of tallies and keys upon it. She began picking up the keys and slipping them on a big iron hoop. "Kitchen aumbry, hall aumbry, weapon chest, clothes chest, undercroft . . ." When she'd finished she handed the ring to Wifil. "Look after it."

"I ought to come along of you, commander."

"What have we been talking about? Of course you can't come."

She left the hall quickly and, followed by Wine, went to the gates. She paused. So many things left undone. Fenchel's lodge was still standing, useless, at the foot of the keep. She couldn't think why she hadn't pulled it down years ago. Now Milly was complaining that her daughter was doing naughty things in it with Badda's son.

Badda and Wilberta emerged from under the yew and came to stand on either side of her, both carried their baskets and wore their stoutest boots. "There's no need to jostle me," she snapped at them, "you're not coming."

"That we are," said Wilberta. Matilda spat with irritation. Why did the English never realise that she knew best? She changed her tack and tried reason. "How can I leave the island to a lot of men? It wasn't men who saved the island from de Mandeville, was it? Wifil will need you."

They went off grumbling and without saying goodbye. Wine pushed his nose against the back of her knees; he had none of Fen's dignity but he was a good dog. "You're not coming, either," she told him.

She turned left, skirted the manor wall, crossed Upper Green and stooped to pass under the branches of Perecourt. The pears weren't ripe yet. She went down the slope to Wealyham. As usual the huts were untidy. The only living things in the place were a goat tethered to the grass and

Epona, who was sitting on a tussock of sedge, sucking a reed and staring at the goat.

Matilda joined her and the goat regarded them back out of its wicked yellow eyes. It was a billy, ancient and thin; it looked crossly unwell, but the fact that it was alive at all worried her.

"Are you sure you got the proportions right?"

The Wealy woman shrugged. The grey in her hair merely looked like bleaching of the red-gold, her skin was still freckled honey; only her hands showed wrinkles and, like Matilda's, were ungainly with rheumatism. She was still as promiscuous in her soporific way as she'd always been and now she had proved herself an inefficient poisoner. "A fine doctress you turned out to be," Matilda told her.

Epona nodded: "Not used to killing, I reckon."

In an effort to find an instant poison they had been lacing the goat's hay with toxic substances for two days; agrimony, opium, hemp, deadly and woody nightshades, laurel berries, yew berries, iron rust, henbane and dried foxglove; powdered toad in turn had gone down the goat's throat and resulted only in the dreadful-smelling, interestingly coloured droppings which had emerged from its other end.

"You want to kill it, you'll have to slit its throat," said Epona.

"Who'd eat it?"

Their failure continued to munch. "What the hell can the assassin be using?" asked Matilda. "He's killing people off like flies." She stirred herself. "We'll just have to do with what we've got." In their experiments they had put into a phial the most colourless, scentless poisons. "Get ready."

Matilda walked back along the fenline, past the yellowing carr of Wulfholes to Snailstream. She found Pampi on the other bank, testing the ground with his peg-leg. He had been down to the south-west on his duck punt.

"That Eustace is still at Bury St. Edmunds," he told her. "It's like de Mandeville and Ramsey all over again, wouldn't like to take on that old St. Edmund myself."

Ever since Edmund had died howling Christianity at the Danes in the ninth century, he had shown himself a terrible protector of his own; those who attacked his lands rarely lasted long. But to Matilda the Edmund under attack was not the saint but a small boy. The terror of the days when her son had been a vulnerable child had come back to her.

"It can't go on into a second generation," she said. "It must be stopped."

"Fire's still advancing," said Pampi. "Got to Sutton now. They won't be growing nothing for many a long year." Usually Pampi felt the fiercest rivalry for Suttoners. "Dungesey's milk is thicker nor Sutton cream," he would say, but today he grieved for them. He looked up. "We taking the row boat?"

She braced herself. "Epona and I are taking it. You're not coming."

"Bloody am."

God blast the English. "Look, if the fire keeps coming we're going to have to cut the Nene bank and flood the turbaries. Will you leave that to Wifil?"

He sulked. "He wouldn't know where."

"Precisely. So you stay."

She would take with her Epona and an army of dead, a champion, a steward, a merchant who'd never returned to his place of business, violated girls, women grown old before their time, and a dog with blood at its throat.

For most of the Nene's length they encountered boats piled with furniture coming the other way as refugees escaped the fire. "Don't go that way, my gals. Devil's loose down south."

Ely was outlined against a glow so vast it looked as if the sun was setting in the south. Dots of people formed strings around the base of the island to beat out the flames in the grass.

They turned into the Great Ouse and then up into the Lark. It was quieter here. "There's your bittern," said Epona, pointing at the bank. Matilda looked. "If I see a bittern, everything will turn out all right," she thought. But her night-blind eyes could spot nothing but rushes. "If I *don't* see a bittern everything will turn out all right."

273

They rowed out of fens into heathland. They could smell pines and broom and only faintly the smitch of scorching. Mildenhall, where de Mandeville had died, was either asleep or dead itself.

The calluses on the palms of their hands stripped off and they left blood on the oars, but they kept on and eventually passed without challenge under the East Gate bridge of St. Edmund's.

There was nobody about, but the abbey was barred and shut and the portcullis of the water-gate on their left was in place. The walls of the abbey shut out the moon and they rowed in total blackness along the Lark until they were out into flat meadow, where they disembarked, hid the boat then ran back to the shadow of the abbey's outer wall.

The abbey itself formed the biggest part of Bury St. Edmund's; the rest of the town was perched on the side of a hill facing it and between the two ran a street which served the abbey's frontage.

Nobody was around, but a cock crowed and was answered. The east was beginning to lighten and the air held the expectation of movement.

Epona's and Matilda's hands met for a moment, then Matilda moved along the street, keeping close to the abbey wall, past the massive gates, past the square height of St. James's Tower which rose on guard at the western end. The fish-basket she carried bobbed on her back and its lid tapped as she ran. She stopped to fumble behind her neck to fasten it, and looked towards the town.

It was deserted and doors swung open showing empty interiors. She studied the roofscape and chose a house with a second storey which had a window from which she could overlook the abbey gates. She raced over the road and through the door.

A rough table and some stools had been broken and scattered. The cooking pot was gone, either taken by the occupants when they fled or stolen by Eustace's men – cooking pots were valuable.

She climbed the ladder upstairs and emerged into a room which contained nothing at all; some of the plaster had come

274

off the walls to show the lathes underneath. She went to the window and pushed open the shutters.

Below her was a cluttered complex of vegetable gardens, empty hutches and hen coops, wells, outhouses and the roofs of next door. She was within easy bowshot of the abbey gates; she might even have time to get away. Her view was obstructed by some flowers in clay pots which stood on the window-sill beam. She had lived so long among fenlanders she'd forgotten that there were commoners who liked flowers for decoration. The family of this house had been poor, but the woman of it had cultivated for her delight roses, geraniums – and marigolds.

Matilda smiled: "I knew you'd be here."

She got herself organised, took bread, duck and a flask of ale out of her basket and finally her crossbow and a sheaf of quarrels. She had some difficulty in finding the right position; the window was small and if she stood up she couldn't see to aim and if she knelt her head was below the sill. At last she arranged her basket so that she could sit on it and aim diagonally.

In the St. James's Tower, John of Topsham was yawning and peering through the north arrow slit which gave the guard-room some of its light and air, and thought he saw a movement in the window down the street. He watched for a while but the window stayed still.

John of Topsham was a lazy man; he'd joined Eustace's army because the discipline was slack and the loot was good, but he was nervous about being on the vengeful St. Edmund's territory. Perhaps he'd check that window later. He turned round to strip the covers off his fellow-soldiers and their women. "Ups-a-daisy, you sluts, my beauties. Time for a soldier's breakfast."

The abbey gates opened after sunrise and in minutes the street was full of people not only coming out but going in as if they'd sprouted from thin air. Even insurrection couldn't come between merchants, beggars, prostitutes and their trade.

There were enough camp women around and more arriving every minute for Epona to move among them

275

unchallenged. Matilda caught a glimpse of her going in through the gates followed by the Magdalene in her tall hat.

Soon the sun was heating the room. Matilda drank a few mouthfuls of ale and poured some of it on the marigolds.

After a while Epona came out again and lazily put up her hand to shade her eyes while she looked westwards down the street. Eustace was not in the abbey but was expected any moment.

Matilda took her time choosing a quarrel and fitting it into the stock groove. Remembering her training, she didn't put it on the floor but rested it on the window-sill.

John of Topsham stopped chewing his breakfast and went to find his captain.

From the west end of the street came hounds, the blowing of horns, several dead boar tied by their trotters to poles and carried by soldiers, then mounted horsemen. They were out of Matilda's sight until they got opposite the tower.

Men and animals formed a mêlée in front of the abbey; so many of the horses were decorated with gold that she couldn't identify Eustace. She began to panic. One of the young men was vomiting – presumably drunk – and getting a lot of attention, but she couldn't decide whether that was because he was the prince or because he was sick.

"Which one is it? Which one do I kill? Mother, tell me."

If there was an answer she couldn't hear it for the hubbub in the street. "You're here." Matilda was crying. "I know you're here. Tell me, for Christ's sake. Which one do I shoot?"

Sobbing, she turned to look around the room but it was empty except for two soldiers advancing on her.

They took her to the St. James's guard-room and questioned her, hitting her across the face when she didn't answer, but not as if they expected answers, not even viciously, merely as if it were procedure they'd gone through many times before.

Matilda hardly felt or heard them. They advanced and retreated like fish, soundless and ineffective in a void from which Christ and His Mother had withdrawn, taking with

276

them motivation and purpose and leaving creatures which ate each other in a meaningless food chain. They were all partners in a free dance without order and without end. She was crushed by weightlessness; the point to life was that there was no point.

Dimensions no longer existed to give her balance and she was giddy when they stood her up. John of Topsham's captain got fed up with her. "She's as mad as the rest. Put her with the other assassins. We'll wait and see if we get any more today and hang the lot of them together. More effective that way and Eustace needs cheering up."

She was marched out of St. James's Tower and up the path towards the great abbey church, left behind St. James's little church, through the Great Hall and into the cloisters where Eustace's prisoners, their hands tied behind their backs, were looped together by a long rope that encircled their necks and the garth pillars.

Some were failed Eustace-assassins, but not all. There was an innkeeper from Newmarket who had refused accommodation to some of Eustace's knights, a hedgerow priest who had preached against him at Sawston, two small boys who were hostages for their father who had gone over to Fitzempress, a herald from Henry of Blois – still attempting reconciliation – a wagoner who'd obstructed Eustace's progress, a woman from Thetford who'd shouted out an anti-Eustace vision she had been vouchsafed as he passed, and a Jew who had been picked up on Peddar's Way simply because he was a Jew.

They took Matilda to the end of the line, lashed her hands and put her against the pillar beyond the Jew, untying the long end of rope dangling from his neck and looping it around hers to secure it to her pillar.

They walked away up the line, promising the human washing that it would be hung up higher after Lord Eustace had eaten.

A voice with a Flemish accent spoke from out of sight on the other side of the Jew. "What I like about imprisonment," it said, "is the class of company you keep."

Earth and grass rushed up to push against Matilda's feet,

God's air was expelled towards her with a whoosh of harp strings. She felt the sun on her face and leaned back against the stone behind her with the comfort of a feather pillow. "What have you done this time?"

"Nothing have I done," said the Jew earnestly, "I swear. I was just walking this track . . ."

"I took a shot at Eustace," said Willem of Ghent. "I missed."

"Why did you miss?" moaned the Jew, "why did you miss?"

"A woman on your mind?" asked Matilda.

"Another gaolbird. And you?"

"Same thing."

The white stone pillars that ran along the low garth wall of the cloister walk opposite her were in perfect symmetry, swelling out like a bulb from their base and narrowing into carved capitals at the roof. The garth itself was patterned with herb-beds where bees crawled in and out of rosemary and lavender flowers and butterflies landed on marigolds.

They couldn't see each other because any strain on the neck loop tightened it. Matilda managed to turn her head and smile down at the Jew so beautifully that he almost smiled back. "Lovely day."

The Jew humoured her. "Later on it may rain a little," he said, "but now it's lovely."

Farther along the hedgerow priest recommenced the sermon which had annoyed Eustace and past him one of the little hostages began to cry. From the abbey church the bell rang for Nones – not all the monks had been expelled, a few had been allowed to remain to try and control St. Edmund, who had been heard spinning in his tomb.

Opposite Matilda a door stood open into the refectory and she could see some of the activity going on inside where an enormous table was being got ready for a feast. Camp women moved around it laying out huge rounds of bread as platters in each guest's place. Epona caught the light as always, but the woman in the prostitute's hat was not the Magdalene. "Put the stuff in his food," willed Matilda. "Put it in and get away from here."

Eustace's chamberlain, a tall man, strode along the cloister walk leading a file of soldiers carrying casks. The abbey's cellarer ran distractedly alongside him: "Not the best wine, I beg. The abbot . . ." He caught sight of the women in the refectory and shuddered: "Not females, my lord, St. Edmund . . ." Pelion piled on Ossa as he glimpsed the prisoners. His mouth fell open and he grabbed the chamberlain's arm. "What are they doing there?"

The chamberlain glanced round and shook off the restraining hand: "They're going to hang, I believe." The cellarer screamed. "Not there, my lord. It's holy ground, can't they hang somewhere else?"

Of course, he was distracted with his troubles and a little later recovered himself and took some water to the woman prisoner who'd had the vision and who was complaining of thirst. The sun was directly overhead now and blazing down straight on to the prisoners' heads. As he held the cup to her mouth, the cellarer said plaintively: "Heaven protect you, my daughter. But you shouldn't be here, you know."

The woman stared him in the eye: "I want to pee and all," she said.

"Almighty God." The cellarer ran to the chamberlain.

It was perhaps due to his urging that an hour or so into the afternoon the prisoners were unbound to allow them to go to the reredorter and relieve themselves and, perhaps thanks again to the cellarer, the women and two children were taken separately from the men, although two soldiers stood at the north and south walls to watch that they didn't escape.

The lavatory was long and narrow, as wonderful in its way as the rest of the abbey. It was in stone and cool; light from the lancet windows fell on a board of polished oak which ran two feet above the ground on one side in which were a dozen round holes. Below them, in a deep runnel and adding to the cool freshness of the place, was a stream; the Lark, having fed the abbey's stew pond, provided its water, turned its grinding and fulling mills, now took away its sewage. The opposite wall held a long stone trough into which a pipe fed more water.

The visionary was a woman of spirit. As Matilda and the

others stood around helplessly she bellowed at the soldiers: "Turn your backs, you bastards," and was obeyed. She seated herself in comfort over a hole and admired the plumbing: "Do themselves well, these monks."

Matilda comforted the two little boys. "Don't cry. We're in the hands of God and His Mother and I promise you, I *promise* you, everything will be well." She meant it. Her only sadness was for them and her only worry was that Epona would be caught.

They were allowed to drink from the trough and lave their heads before being taken back. This time they were strung along the refectory side of the cloister opposite the men, so that Matilda and the mercenary could see each other.

"He's thinner," she thought, "and older." Then she thought: "I must look a sight," and then she didn't care. "What is it about him? What is it in that thin, low-bred man with a rope around his neck from which he will soon be swinging, that I, with a rope around mine from which I too will be swinging, thank God?"

The Plato person had been right. God had made an unfortunate social error and put the other half of herself in the body of a mercenary crossbowman. "And me with queens in my ancestry." It didn't matter. There was surprisingly little that did.

By the side of the mercenary the Jew was seeking distraction from his anxiety and discussing St. Edmund. "If you ask me he's taking this matter too lightly. Jehovah would have struck down the prince by now. How did he die?"

"What?" Willem was looking at Matilda.

"Your St. Edmund. Did they burn him? Perhaps there's not so much left of him to be angry."

"Shot him with arrows, I think."

"Like your St. Sebastian?"

"St. Sebastian didn't die from arrows. A woman healed his arrow wounds so they battered him to death instead."

The Jew could see he wasn't commanding attention and he was a romantic. "*Dijn vrouw?*" He had languages. "Your woman?"

"Yes." He still didn't know if she was beautiful and it still wasn't important.

"Do you love her?"

"Yes." If they ever got out of this he wouldn't let her out of his sight again.

By late afternoon the feasting began; the prisoners could hear uproarious noises coming through the refectory door. Every so often groups of soldiers and knights with their arms around girls would lurch out into the cloisters to be amusing at the prisoners' expense. Over a soldier's shoulder Epona nodded at Matilda. The poison had been delivered. "Now go," said Matilda clearly to nobody in particular. Epona and her soldier wandered back inside.

Now that she was on this side of the cloister she could see through the opposite walk and through the open door which led into the abbey church. Deep inside something glimmered and hovered. The dying sun from the choir windows caught the silver of St. Edmund's tomb but left its black marble plinth in darkness so that the thing seemed to levitate. She was right in its path, she a poisoner. She began to be afraid. "I didn't want to, I didn't want to kill anybody but it had to be stopped." She glanced to the hall end of the cloister where the boy hostages were looped together. She had been forced to make a choice between slaughter. It had been Eustace or them and hundreds like them. St. Edmund, the protector of his own, glimmered back at her. "You should have left it to me and God."

The feast was ending; the cloisters became full of men, some of them urinating. She could tell now which one was Eustace from the gold band round his head and the way his entourage attended to him. He was the one who had been vomiting that morning and if he hadn't been drunk then he was now. He began a staggering progress round the three sides of the cloister which held his prisoners, leaning heavily on the shoulder of his chamberlain with one hand and flapping the other vaguely at the bound figures. As he passed Matilda she saw that his eyes were not viewing people but obstructions. "Shouldn't have done it," he told them reproachfully, "shouldn't have done it."

281

His face was flushed and twisted as if in pain, but it wasn't a bad face, just young; were it sober it would be stronger than his father's.

He went back to the empty end of the cloister and was helped over the wall so that he stood framed between two pillars with his hands on the coping. His mouth opened and closed as if he wanted to make a speech, but he gave up. "String 'em up," he said.

Soldiers began cutting the rope between the prisoners, knotting each section into a noose and flinging the other end up over the corbels on the roof. Candles had been lit in the darkening church and flickered on St. Edmund's tomb. Some monks began a chant which was less of a psalm than an incantation.

At the other end one of the little hostages had wriggled away and was being chased along the cloister walk. He was caught and brought back.

They were going to begin at Matilda's end and the Jew's, and work their way up the sides to the hall end. She had made a choice of slaughter and even if she had chosen right, even if she should have made a choice at all, it had been for nothing; it was going to go on and on without end. Two soldiers advanced on her, she could smell the boiled leather of their coats. She felt the harshness of the rope on her neck as they slipped the knot down. But this was ridiculous. This wasn't her death at all. Matilda de Risle should die honoured and graceful among her grandchildren. She couldn't be expected to die this vulgar, somebody-else's way.

The mercenary was fighting the soldiers despite his tied hands, flinging his body in an effort to get to her.

"It hurts," said a voice and the soldiers who were beginning to pull on Matilda's rope let it go. "Where does it hurt, my lord?"

Eustace was swaying between the pillars with one hand clutching his stomach and the other gripping the wall coping. "It hurts."

In the church the chanting rose higher and so did the tomb. One of Matilda's soldiers saw it and screamed. "St. Edmund."

Eustace was on his knees now and as all his men turned towards him he slipped out of sight altogether behind the wall, but his hand still clawed the coping. It was beringed but it had the short, grubby nails of a boy, of her son.

"He's been poisoned," she said to the soldier who had been going to hang her. "Give him salt and mustard-water." The soldier paid the madwoman no attention but over the other side the Jew said: "He's been poisoned? And she'd give him an emetic?"

They could hear the chanting and the irregular breathing from behind the wall. "It hurts." The hand scraped its nails on the stone as it slid out of sight. Knights leaped over the wall to get to their prince. She heard scuffling and groaning as they lifted him, then heavy running feet.

She caught a glimpse of his face. The boy was dying. She had seen too much death not to know it.

The tomb of St. Edmund levitated itself higher as they carried Prince Eustace to it to beg its mercy. The last Matilda saw of him was a boy's hand trailing out of a press of bodies.

She looked across at Willem: "I poisoned him." The mercenary struggled to get to her but the rope had been tied to the corbel above him and he was strangling himself. "Vengeance is mine," called out the prisoner priest. One of the soldiers crossed himself. The rest stood around help-lessly.

The cellarer came out of the church and Eustace's chamberlain ran beside him, pleading. "Well," the cellarer was saying, "you can release these people for a start and recall my lord abbot and restore what you have stolen, but I can't promise anything. He looks exceedingly ill to me and as I've said, St. Edmund is a terrible protector of his own . . ." His voice trailed away as he disappeared into the Great Hall and the chamberlain, following him, glanced over his shoulder. "Let them go."

The ropes were ripped down and the prisoners, some with nooses still round their necks, were shoved and jostled out into the empty street. A captain came behind with an armful of cloaks and baggage and threw it after them for its owners to sort out. "Sorry," he said, and ran in.

The Jew stared after him, sighed and spat. "Don't mention it," he said, and went off west towards the sunset.

Willem picked Matilda up and rocked her. "Shsh. It's over." She buried her face against his neck. "I poisoned him, oh, I poisoned him." He could feel her shaking. He carried her over to the abbey wall and sat her down so that she was propped against it. "It's over."

Gradually the shaking stopped but she stared ahead of her into a future that she had poisoned as surely as she had poisoned Eustace. All her life a boy's grubby hand would claw at her. And in any case she could not live Matilda de Risle's life any more. It had been taken away from her years ago and the somebody else that she had become had lost touch with it for ever.

What did she have in common with the well-bred ladies of Fitzempress' court, now that she had won it for them? What could she talk to them about? Drainage? Disparagement? Assassination? "I'm afraid my hands are too crippled for embroidery nowadays, but you should see my poisoning." All her contemporaries were dead or lived on an island in a marsh. She had lost.

A bell began tolling for the death of a prince.

The street was getting dark and bats were flicking across the sky. Epona came towards them and Willem handed Matilda over. "Look after her a minute. I'll find her a cloak, and I've got to get my crossbow before we go home."

Matilda looked up at him. "We didn't win, did we?"

He saw how old and ill she was. "No." Desperately he tried to think of something that would comfort her, and caught sight of the two small hostages waiting, bewildered, for someone to tell them what to do. "I think they did."

He left her to go and search among the baggage littering the street.

Epona sat down beside Matilda. "I put it in the beans," she said, "but I don't think he had any. Didn't seem peckish." She watched the mercenary as he searched, stooping awkwardly, and said: "His back's still poorly. I'm sorry for him."

Matilda sat up. "If anybody's going to be sorry for him," she said, "it's me."

After all, there was still this somebody else's life to live and there was plenty to do. She had a church of thanks to build. There were ducks to shoot and eels to catch and a bittern yet to see. And the mercenary would need help in setting up his manor.

And if it was the last thing she did, if it killed her, she would teach the English to speak French.

Epilogue

Eustace died, it is thought, of appendicitis. His father, Stephen, died a year later, probably of the same thing.

Stephen spent the year left to him in a long, triumphal procession of his broken country. As one of his chroniclers said rather bitterly of him: "He was a man who cared for the appearance of things."

·Christina of Markyate did not achieve a place in the calendar of saints.

Nobody knows what happened to Brother Daniel.

Even after Stephen's death Fitzempress did not sail for England immediately. He knew there was no rush. Sure enough, England waited peaceably for the reign which was to see the beginning of the jury system and the Common Law.